Jacob
the
Trumpeter

Also by Robert Barclay

Non-fiction

The Art of the Trumpet-maker
The Preservation and Use of Historic Musical Instruments
Making a Natural Trumpet

Fiction

Triple Take: A Museum Story
Death at the Podium
Ask Me About My Bombshells

Cover art and design, and maps in the text by the author
Photo in the Prologue courtesy of Michael Münkwitz

Jacob
the
Trumpeter

Robert Barclay

LOOSE CANNON PRESS

Library and Archives Canada Cataloguing in Publication

Barclay, R. L. (Robert L.), author
Jacob the Trumpeter / Robert Barclay.
Revised second edition.
Originally published: London, Olympia Publishers, 2018.
ISBN 978-1-988657-13-4 (softcover)

I. Title.
PS8603.A7244J33 2018   C813'.6   C2018-906514-1

Published by
Loose Cannon Press

www.loosecannonpress.com

Dedication

To Jacob Hintze, no matter where your mortal remains may now lie, know that:

> The God of all grace, who hath called us unto his eternal glory by Christ Jesus, after that ye have suffered a while, make you perfect, stablish, strengthen, settle you
>
> *Der Gott aber aller Gnade, der uns berufen hat zu seiner ewigen Herrlichkeit in Christo Jesu, der wird euch, die ihr eine kleine Zeit leidet, vollbereiten, stärken, kräftigen, gründen*

1 Peter/*Petrus*, 5:10

Acknowledgments

Without my friends and colleagues Richard Seraphinoff and Michael Münkwitz this book would not exist; Michael because he discovered Jacob Hintze's trumpet in the first place, and Rick because he was in the process of writing his own historical novel, thus providing me with valuable impetus, stimulation and critique. And when it came to certain aspects of trumpet playing and brass literature, Rick was there with advice and guidance. Henry Howie helped me with details of Daniel Speer's career, and David Yearsley was similarly helpful during my examination of the travels of Johann Jakob Froberger. David Edwards and Mandy Gomer advised on various aspects of horsemanship, while Graham Nicholson and Major K.R.T (Terry) Seeley were very valuable in rescuing me from the mire of equestrian ballet. Lester L. Field, Jr. and Courtney Kneupper assisted with tricky Latin. Trevor Herbert, Edward Tarr and Friedemann Immer provided insight into early trumpet methods, and Sabine Klaus helped me with the historical context of Nürnberg trumpet-making. Patrick Burrows gave me a wise review of the entire work in its first draft. My sons, Ian and David, have valuable insights into historical writings, so their reading of sections and the discussions that followed were most rewarding. I salute my copy editor Katherine Williams for highly professional and meticulous work. My wife Janet read my work and provided cues to human interactions, and clear directives as to what sections of verbosity and detail should be deleted, and which others should be clarified. The limits of her elasticity and tolerance have yet to be discovered, let alone tested. I apologise to any others who I may have forgotten to acknowledge. All errors of fact are mine, although if I were unwilling to accept this responsibility, I might say that Jacob Hintze's memory must be faulty.

Robert Barclay
Ottawa, 2018

Introduction

As described in the Prologue of this book, my colleague and friend Michael Münkwitz did, indeed, find Jacob Hintze's trumpet hanging up in a church in the small village of Belitz in eastern Germany. The church records and the wording of the votive plaque commissioned by Hintze's widow were almost all the information we had of his life story. We knew he was an innkeeper, we knew that he and his wife, Elisabeth Bauchen, were from patrician familes, and that they had children. We learned that Jacob had been killed in a duel with one Joachim Wadegahte, son of Heinrich. Jacob Hintze had been a staff trumpeter and had been granted the living of the inn on the post road by the Duke of Mecklenburg-Schwerin. That was all, and so it might have remained had I not come into possession of a small wooden trunk filled to the brim with papers. I am not at liberty to reveal the source of these papers, nor can I vouch for their authenticity... or even their actual existence, quite frankly. In fact, I may have just dreamt the whole thing. All I can say is, the story I tell here *ought* to be true. Sorting through these perhaps mythical papers, transcribing from the hand-written script of the original (if it exists), and then translating has been a labour of several years. I have tried wherever possible to keep the voice of the original and to do as little editing as possible. It is not my role to present this as anything but Jacob Hintze's story. My only interference is to set the scene in the Prologue and to close the story in the Epilogue.

I decided to leave all place names in their original form, and like-wise the few of Hintze's phrases in other European languages. There are also terms in German that I have decided not to translate. I have provided a glossary. The dates are in the Julian calendar, which was in use in Hintze's time in the Protestant north, and so are ten days earlier than those in our modern calendar. I have provided endnotes to give readers further information on major characters and incidents. Among the papers was a list of quotations, mostly from the Bible and Lutheran scholars, with numbers beside them. I am sure these were intended as epigraphs, so I have rendered them as such, except for those on the Prologue and Epilogue, which I extracted from the text on the votive panel on which the trumpet was hung. I have left them all in the original language and have provided translations. To make Hintze's travels clearer, I have provided very simple maps.

For the purposes of Jacob Hintze's story, this map shows only the very basic political divisions. Boundaries changed over the course of his life, and after the Peace of Westphalia the divisions became excessively confusing. Large sections are seen on contemporary maps as mosaics of tiny, interlocking principalities. Hintze himself would have been hard put to name even a few of them

Prologue

Der Feind verfolget meine Seele und zerschlägt mein Leben zu Boden
For the enemy hath persecuted my soul; he hath smitten my life
down to the ground

Psalmen Davids/Psalm 143:3

The trumpet-maker placed the little folding stepstool below the votive panel hanging on the whitewashed church wall. It was on the south side of the altar, fairly high up. Sunshine entered from the clerestory above but slanted away, so the panel was in relative gloom. He climbed up gingerly; the stool wobbled and settled, he placed his fingertips briefly against the wall to steady himself, and now he was at eye level.

The Lutheran church in Belitz is a small and ancient building made of red brick, a common building material in that eastern part of Germany, bordered by the Baltic Sea. The church sits in a soft green acre, surrounded by the memory stones of burghers and common folk long gone, and shaded by fine trees, their trunks green-washed by moss on their windward sides. The cobbles of the lane leading to the church hark back to the time of the Democratic Republic; hellish to drive on, costly to maintain, but cheap to install. Quite good enough for the country farmers of the time, the simple people who had seen few cars, and had never dreamed of owning one.

Even in summer the interior of the church was cool, although the sensation on the skin could as much have arisen from the silent peace of the place than from the mere temperature of the air. The atmosphere of the nave was scented with time; a distance compounded of dust and wood, decay and incense, and the cloying aura of long-burnt beeswax and tallow. Not a famous place; not a vast cathedral with riches adorning its walls, or with vaults filled with treasures from devotion, time and long use. A small, rural church in a small, rural backwater, noticed only because it was on the old coach road, one stage shy of Rostock. An obligatory stopping place for people with more important destinations and meetings and deals on their minds.

Years ago, a visiting musician had told the trumpet-maker of an instrument hanging up on the wall. It was probably a military instrument from the First World War, he had reasoned; there were many of those on the market. But here he was at eye level looking directly at a votive panel dated 1677, dedicated to a trumpeter killed in a duel, one Jacob Hintze. And there was his trumpet, still hanging up on one side of the panel. On the other there used to be a sword, the pastor told him, but that had long since vanished. You'd steal a sword, but a trumpet…?

As his brain told him what his eyes saw, comprehension squeezed the trumpet-maker's heart. He nearly fell off the stepstool. Seventeenth century! No question. And here was an inscription, just where you would expect to find it on a trumpet made in the Imperial City of Nürnberg in the days of the Holy Roman Empire. Around the decorative garland on the bell he read:

MACHT WOLFF BIRCKHOLTZ IN NÜRNBERG 1650

Wolfgang Birckholtz he knew of: a famed maker of the period, one of the closeknit cadre of instrument-makers who produced the lion's share of the fine brass musical and military instruments of Europe.

But who in the world was Jacob Hintze?

Jacob Hintze's trumpet hanging beside Elisabeth Bauchen's votive plaque

Chapter One

In which my oldest son shoves a quill into my hand and as good as
dips it in the ink for me

Sprich wahr, und beschäme den Teufel
Tell the truth and shame the devil
Anonyme Sprichwort/Anonymous Saying

"How are you feeling father?"

My eldest, Michael, was visiting from Wolfenbüttel; he's a violinist
there with the court ensemble. He sat me down at a table in the *Neuer
Krug*, the post inn we own in Neu Heinde near Belitz, and looked me
in the eyes.

"Fine. Just fine."

"Are you sure? Come on, now."

"Never better. Why do you ask?" I tried to lay on the old sincerity
but he could see right through me. Always could. He knew. I'd never
told him how my father had died, or his father before him—hadn't
told any of them—but he sensed that not everything about me was
well.

"Be honest with me, papa."

The place was silent; middle of the day with no lingering travellers.
The silence stretched. Ticks of the bracket clock, creak of a board upstairs,
whinny of a horse out in the back.

"I have a little pain now and again…"

"I know you do. I can see it."

Silence again while he appraised me. I could see his mind working
in his face; I could watch thoughts passing and a decision arriving with
the slight nod of confirmation, long before he opened his mouth.

"Remember when we rode to Wolfenbüttel for my audition?" I
nodded. God, that was years ago. He was fourteen then, and now he
was… what… twenty-three. "Every day on that journey you would tell
me the most amazing stories. Remember?"

"Oh, rubbish all of it. Lies. Keeping you amused over long stretches
of track, that's all."

"Oh, right! Just like those yarns you tell around the tables in here
of an evening. Rubbish as well, eh?"

"Well, what of it?" I answered defensively. I had a hint of what he
was driving at, but I wasn't sure I liked where he was going. "No harm
in sharing a few memories with fellow travellers."

"Memories? Not lies then?"

"Memories, damn you!"

He sighed. "Listen: you have a wonderful story locked up in you, papa."

"Oh, come on! I'm nothing special."

"What? Fighting in the war, sailing in ships, marching over ice, carrying secrets?"

Now he had me worried. I suppose over the years since I had retired from the Duke's service I must have spilt a lot of yarns, kind of loose-lipped, but there are other things that should never be told. Or so I thought then.

"Am I really any more interesting than any other soldier who's served his time? Survived as long as I have? Nothing makes me special."

"Horseshit! A man who has spoken with princes, bandied words with kings. And if even half of it's true, you owe it to us to tell it."

"But I do tell it, in my own way."

"*Write it down!* Write it down so we can all read it."

"*Write?* No, no. I'm not a bookish sort of man."

"Rubbish! The house is full of books…"

"…mostly your mother's…"

"…and you read and write all the time. You know it."

"Even so, I don't have the time for such nonsense." He was edging me into a corner, getting me on the defensive. No swordsman likes that. "Anyway, it's far too busy around here."

"I've already raised the idea with mama and the kids. They're all for it."

"Oh, have you now? You cheeky bastard!" I got all prepared to dig my toes in, blast his impudence. Ganging up on me, were they? I folded my arms over my chest. "So, now I won't."

"Oh? It is all lies and rubbish then? Just as you said. Everyone will know it's all invention. I wouldn't be surprised if they stopped listening to you…"

What a corner to be squeezed into, the clever little bugger. I sat there for a while realizing this weasel had me beaten. I was a bit angry at first—I hate to be beaten—but then I thought, why not? 'Tell the truth and shame the devil', as the saying goes.

"I'll think about it," was all I said to him. Damned if I'd surrender that quickly.

"Think quickly, Papa. You're not as healthy as you…" I started to rise out of my chair. "No, stop! No protests. Don't fool yourself, because you can't fool me. Sit down, *please*. Write it now, or it won't get written."

"I've *told you* I'll think about it. Now piss off!"

"I have to return to Wolfenbüttel in three days. Why don't I see what you've done before I leave?"

"I said *piss off!*"

He was right, of course. So, here we go. I may be an innkeeper now, but I will always be a trumpeter. My name is Jacob Hintze. Sure, you see an innkeeper, but what about these fine cavalry whiskers and the goatee? A little grey now, I'll admit, but my blue eyes are as sharp as ever. And I've still got a cavalry swagger about me, damn you. A trumpeter is not just a common soldier, and this host of yours is not a common innkeeper, as I will soon tell you. Sure, I was brought up on a farm and learned a lot about the ways of crops and cattle, but I was from a patrician family with our own coat of arms. You had to be well-born or you'd never get an education and work all your life in a duke's service, as I did. So, don't judge me by what you see now. It's not what I like to do, truth to tell, but I'm too damned old and beaten up to do much else and, frankly, I'm not long for this world. Michael was right, blast him; when you're under a sentence of death, as I am, it makes you want to tell your story, and I just hope I can get it done before it's too late.

Me and my wife Elisabeth have kept the *Neuer Krug* for the past seventeen years, with the help of two of our sons and both daughters. The other two boys are out in the world, Michael in Wolfenbüttel and Jürgen far east somewhere. The *Neuer Krug* was willed to me in 1658 for good service in the old Duke's army; that's Adolf Friedrich, Duke of Mecklenburg-Schwerin, may God bless his memory.[1] So, our family runs the inn, giving beds to you people going on your high and mighty ways to grand places, watering your horses, serving you a not-bad ale.

There's more to our living than just running the inn, though. Once the Peace of Westphalia was signed in 1648 the House of Thurn und Taxis established the postal service in Mecklenburg, although the bickering over routes and jurisdiction would sicken you.[2] Still, that was when places like ours became regular stopping spots. Once you've got a reliable service for the mail, you're going to need changes of horses, beds, meals, all the facilities. We don't hurt for a *Thaler* or two, that's certain. So I serve you, I beat the bugs out of your bed sheets, I keep the fire going, and I send you on your way, so maybe you won't think too badly of me, if you think of me at all.

But I'll always be a trumpeter. That was my profession for a good portion of my fifty-two years. Fifty-two isn't a bad age to get to, when you think of the total shit storm of the Thirty Years War, especially if you were right in the middle of it as I was, and watching your comrades being blown to blood foam and gristle in front of your eyes. I've peed myself like a baby a few times, filled my hose on occasion, and galloped away screaming. I can bet you've never had some fellow's guts shot in your face like a bowl of tripes, nor still have a scar above your right eye from the piece of his ribcage that came with it. Or broken your arm so badly the bone was sticking out, all white and frightening, until the sawbones shoved it back in, slapped on the wood splints, and bound it up with linen.

Feldtrompeter, that's what I was during the war; a field trumpeter. It was my duty to pass battle orders from the officers to the cavalry by trumpet signals; no easy job for two reasons. Firstly, you ever try playing *anything* while on horseback in the middle of a battle? Your mount shying under you, the blasts of harquebuses, the yelling and screaming, horses neighing and everybody wound up like clock weights. Of course you haven't. That for a start; then add the whole range of signals you had to know by heart: orders to saddle-up, trot forward, wheel, charge… and, yes, withdraw as well. Can you imagine for an eye-blink what would happen if you messed it up? That's why a field trumpeter isn't just anybody; it's critical that he's intelligent, educated, cool under pressure and capable of both taking orders and relaying them. Not just by signals either; there are written notes and then there's the spoken word. Messages have to go at the gallop between divisions, and quite often once they've read the written note they'll turn and you ask for 'the word'. Your *Feldtrompeter* is privy to the highest level of planning and strategy; he stands in the tent when the higher-ups are discussing their operations, so he follows the ebb and flow of battle and war. What's written in haste on the notes you shove into your scrip is the shorthand for the discussions that have gone back and forth.

But all that is not even the half of what some trumpeters do, as I will tell in due course.

So, if you hobnob with the high and mighty, you had better be one of them. Either you're noble born or you carry your humble roots very well. Still, I wonder: If they had known just how 'noble born' I really wasn't, maybe they wouldn't have been quite so friendly. My father was a patrician, and that may mean a lot in some societies, but in the German lands of my day, the title could be quite… flexible. He owned the land we farmed, a decent enough house and all the home comforts, but still we were close to the earth as it were. Not above getting our hands dirty if we had to, especially those times of year when farming takes on a new frantic tempo. Water under the bridge when you think of what happened to the farm, the house, the family, the livelihood…

But I'm getting ahead of myself.

Thirty Years War; that's what it's come to be called.[3] I've heard it called the Eighty Years War and that's more realistic. It was eighty years since Spain and France and the German-speaking countries first started having at each other over the stupidity of the body of Jesus Christ. Well, it wasn't really a fight over Christ's body at all, was it? Of course not! Whether some conjuring trick over a bit of stale bread and a sip of cheap rotgut signifies anything at all, is not the point. The point is that greedy, brutal bastards in positions of power will take any cause and dirty it to their advantage. Sure, it began with the great schism between the Holy Roman Church and the fire that Martin Luther lit in Wittenburg, but it was soon taken over by the dynasts: Habsburgs, Bourbons, Dutch, Swedes, English, all the little German states, the whole of God-damned Christianity tearing at each other's throats. I shouldn't criticize, though; I was in it from my teens, played my part in it all, and profited mightily from it.

The Treaty of Westphalia was supposed to end it all. I was at the Battle of Jankau a couple of years before that, and by then everybody had had enough; just too impoverished and exhausted to continue if the truth be known. But kings and emperors and bishops signing parchments cannot make hatreds evaporate just like that. People will carry on hating other people until the end of the world. So, with all the horror and violence that's happened to me since I signed up to fight with Swedes and Scots and God knows what other mercenary garbage against the Emperor and his Holy Roman God-damned church, it's probably been better than the pigs and cows and bloodshed that would have been my whole, and quite short, life on what used to be our farm.

Well, enough of that. You'll hear more before my story's done.

I was born in April of 1624. My family lived in a fine house in the Duchy of Mecklenburg, not far from Belitz. It was larger than most with the exception of the places owned by the really rich and influential, but like them we had glass windows, which cost a great deal but were so much better than stretched cow skin or wooden shutters. There was a necessary cupboard indoors as well, something you didn't find in many farmhouses. Even though built on the old-fashioned style, the house was roomy, and had a first floor.[4] We didn't have to share it with the livestock like our tenants did. We kept cows and pigs, so there was a lot of butchery and dairy to take to market. And we had horses, which we mostly rented out to the postal service. Thurn and Taxis didn't operate in the north in those days, of course, but our own less efficient service took up the slack. Changing horses was a good source of extra income, and for me it was an early introduction to riding, and the care and upkeep of horseflesh. I was around horses a lot whilst growing up, and it stood me in good stead later.

Although Güstrow was closer, our favoured market town was

Rostock on the Warne, a little way inland from the Ostsee. It's the bigger town and the wares are better and more varied. Being a patrician and landowner, my father had a lot of business in Rostock. The men he met were mostly in the trades—wool, grain, general merchandise and so on—and most had a hand in shipping, because Rostock was a Hanseatic Port, even though the League, as such, had fallen to bits through greed and selfishness. The Sound Dues that the Danish had imposed on any ship passing through the Øresund—the best and most direct way into the Ostsee from the west—were an extra cost burden, and especially irksome to the Swedes. But there was still some pride in saying Hansa Rostock if someone asked where you were from.

There was a lot father had to deal with, what with loans, payments for produce, the setting of tariffs and the never-ending debate over the detested 'soldier tax', where the occupying Swedish forces imposed payments from their 'hosts'. All the town men were continually fearful that the fighting would swing their way again, and that the fragile kind of peace that held in the towns, at least, would be thrown into the fire. It had happened some years back when that Papist bastard von Wallenstein kicked out the princes of Mecklenburg-Güstrow and Mecklenburg-Schwerin because they had sided with Denmark, and then confiscated Wismar. Their father had divided Mecklenburg between them some years back.

Von Wallenstein's hold only lasted a few years; there was the fiasco of a raid on Stralsund and the pathetic incompetence of the Spanish fleet in the Ostsee to be praised for that. The Swedes soon saw to it that Protestant rule was returned to the region; Swedish rule, in essence. The Swedes were all-powerful. If anything like that happened again you might as well kiss goodbye to any of the agricultural and mercantile agreements the aldermen might make. And they all knew a mighty girth strap was tightening around the leaner and leaner flanks of the northern German lands, and what little stability we had was in the past, and the days of what little was left were numbered.

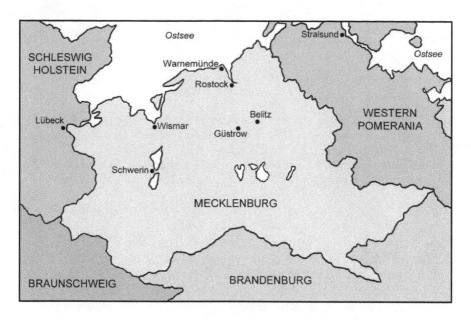

Jacob Hintze's Mecklenburg

Chapter Two

In which my oldest son checks on progress and then leaves
me to get on with it

*Da ich ein Kind war, da redete ich wie ein Kind und war klug wie ein Kind
und hatte kindische Anschläge; da ich aber ein Mann ward, tat ich ab, was
kindisch war*
When I was a child, I spoke as a child, I understood as a child, I
thought as a child: but when I became a man, I put away childish
things

Korinther/Corinthians 13:11

"Oh yes, this is good." Michael sat down opposite my desk in the office of the inn, and read quickly through what I had written so far. "Lot of historical detail. Political stuff. Could get boring."

"You need to know what was going on. It's not just about me!"

"But politics…"

"It's what I saw. I won't vouch for the accuracy of any it, but if you want me to tell you my story, you'll have to see it the way I saw it."

"Exactly. Just writing down the truth for the family."

"Truth? If you want truth you'd better get a scholar. I only know what I saw and heard as a lowly servant to the high and mighty. Truth!"

"Well, the truth as you saw it, naturally. Nobody else is going to read it, are they?"

"Hope not. Give me shit for getting stuff all wrong…" I was a bit defensive, having never written much of anything like this before, even though I'd had the schooling and could do it in several languages if I had to. "Do you want me to write this or not? Damned if I'll throw what I've already written into the fire."

"Yes, yes, of course. It's just that I'm keen for you to cut to the chase."

"Well, I will. From here on it'll be all about me. That make you happy?"

"Papa, just reading what you have written so far makes me happy. You know that." He paused and then smiled. "So, are you going to write about the bone now?"

"Oh, you and that stinking bone! Of course I will."

"Good. And now I'm saddled and packed and ready to leave for Wolfenbüttel."

"God speed my son," I said as I put the papers back in their folder and walked him to the door. "Come home again soon."

The whole family was out there in the yard, waiting to hug him and wave him goodbye. We saw him into the distance, and then I went in again, sat down, picked up the quill and dipped it.

One memorable time, where I suppose my story really starts, papa took my older sister Annamaria and me in the donkey cart to the Rostock market. This was a huge expedition because it was a ride of three days in the cart, stopping to sleep at places on the way, and staying a night with papa's friend and business manager Herr Schleef. It must have been autumn because the apples were fresh and crunchy. We weren't off to sell produce—that was the job of our manager—but to accompany papa on his regular business in town. I was ten years old then, dressed in my best hose and jerkin, and carrying a little overnight bag. Little Clara was still too small for such expeditions, although you could see how envious she was as we left, clinging to mama's side with such a scowl on her face. It was a huge treat for us to go with papa on his business at the town hall, the *Rathaus*, with merchants, city councilors and so on. He was a big wheel in city and regional politics, even if he only farmed for his living. And he wasn't above working the farm if he had to; as I said, he was right there helping piglets into the world in the middle of the night, butchering their parents when their time came, or mucking out the horses. He could have sat back and let our tenant labourers do it all, but it just wasn't in his nature to sit on his hands.

Papa was big man with a huge beard shot through with grey, sharp steel eyes, but with a gentle mouth that belied them. He was strongly muscled; you had to be if you worked the land, and a lifetime of labour soon made you that way. You can be wide in the shoulder and tall, and still not have presence, though, but people took notice of him. He was one of those men who fill a space, who demand attention, and whose utterances, opinions and judgements are heeded. Even so, he was fair and kindly, and I have not come across many human beings who can combine authoritativeness with benign humanity. I simply loved him because he was my papa, and his absence after all these years still leaves a hole I'll never fill.

The day we arrived in Rostock papa was really alive and full of purpose, but not too busy to think of us. Bringing me and Annamaria into town really was an exceptional treat, especially the bit where he left me in the charge of my sister while he went off to the *Rathaus* for a few hours. He dropped us in the *Hauptmarkt* where the market was in full swing, gave Annamaria a little leather purse with a few coins in it, squeezed her hand, and patted me on the shoulder as we climbed down from the wagon. It's a huge square with the *Rathaus* on the east side and the massive redbrick *Marienkirche* over on the northwest corner. The whole stone-paved area was filled with stalls and wagons; people from all over Mecklenburg came to the city to sell their wares, make deals, buy produce to take home, and do a lot of plain ordinary gambling, whoring and drinking. There were entertainers of all kinds: musicians (sort of), jugglers, fortune tellers and acrobats, and even one enterprising fellow with a table of mushrooms made of painted clay. For a few *Pfennig* the city folk could bring the mushrooms they'd found and he would tell them if they were edible. People like us from out in the countryside had a laugh at that. We know all the plants inside out; it's only these soft city folk who might think they were likely to die if they didn't part with a few coins.

The place was a bedlam of noise and stink, the cobbles underfoot slippery with dung mingled with last night's rain, and leavened with straw sweepings and waste. The aroma of cooking food and exotic spices blended with the more human and animal smells, until your nose was beguiled. And overall was the din of traders shouting their wares, yelling laughter, the roar of the crowd around a spontaneous fistfight, and the blatting and thumping of music on crude instruments of every sort. This great sensory wave overwhelmed me as soon as I stepped from the wagon, and I was absolutely in heaven.

All this in the eyes of a little boy, fresh off the farm. But in truth, there was a sick, frantic quality to it that a kid like me couldn't perceive. Month by month, year by year, it was all being whittled away. There was less food, fewer goods, and a dearth of travellers as the war gripped tighter and tighter. Everyone was spilling their seeds in a frenetic dance of death before it was all taken away. It was madness; it was feverish jollity, celebration in the face of tragedy, want and extinction. It was ignorant little people caught up in the mighty jaws of history doing what ignorant little people do.

To my eyes it was all glorious.

Annamaria, God rest her little soul where it belongs in Heaven, was only thirteen but papa believed that was quite old enough to keep an eye on a ten-year-old, even a little miscreant like me. I was a little hellion, I'll be the first to admit, and already you could see that father was wondering what the hell he was going to do with me when I got older. Labour on the farm, sure, but he knew even then that I would be the most rebellious one of all the brothers. Stolid Hans, unimaginative Jürgen and Michael the smart one, they would buckle down and keep the land prosperous, but that simply wasn't going to be good enough for the youngest. And papa sensed it even then.

"C'mon, let's go steal apples," I yelled as soon as papa's back was hidden by the closing *Rathaus* door.

Annamaria made a grab for my sleeve but her fingers slipped off, and I was away to a nearby stall. I darted in, grabbed an apple—I had done this before, and was well practiced—and was well gone before the old crone in charge could even yell. You'd expect there'd be a huge hue and cry, with enraged merchants chasing the little bugger, dodging in and out of stalls, bowling folk over, knocking down merchandise, all the usual images. None of it. Annamaria's purse yielded a *Pfennig* or two, the old crone was mollified, and I ate half the apple. All serene, and me unrequited through mayhem forestalled. That's mostly what the little purse was for; taking the steam out of me.

"Thanks for buying us an apple," Annamaria smiled, all false innocence as she crunched her share. "Even if your method of purchase is a little unorthodox."

You have no idea how frustrated I was! And just as she smiled, the corners of her chewing mouth mocking me, a little juice trickling from her lip, my life took a turn. I can see her dear face in my mind's eye right now as the main crossroads of my life came hurtling toward me.

I heard the sound of a trumpet.

I had never heard a trumpet before, but I knew this was what it must be. Those clear ringing notes; notes that called me in a way I really can't describe. I had always liked to sing, and joined in many of the ditties we all sang around the fire in the evening, or during our work in the fields and byres. *Mit lust tret Ich an deisen Tanz...*[5] Christmas was especially rich for me, because we would attend the service in Belitz where the choir sang those fine works of our Lutheran composers: plain music for plain folk to belt out, stripped of all that Catholic elaboration. (This is hindsight; at that time I simply enjoyed the lovely simple harmonies and the swelling grandness of it all.)

That sound captivated me that day. Most of the folk not guarding stalls or making deals drifted over to the north side of the square where the notes had come from. There was a troop of soldiers gathered around this pompous, important looking geezer who was reading some sort of proclamation. There stood the trumpeter in gorgeous regalia, his instrument bell down at his hip, elbow out, poised to raise it to his lips again. I had no idea what the proclamation was all about, but the sight of that trumpeter swinging his instrument crisply up to his mouth and playing those notes again, mesmerized me. They're really just the sounds you get when you make a farting noise into a tube, those notes, when you think about it, but I couldn't get them out of my head. They fell together, each in its place, in such a logical, precise way that even my ignorant ten-year-old mind could imagine an... order... a pattern that was bigger than me, something that was

13

outside myself. You hear of people being struck by Christ and turning their lives around, as we are told Saul was on the road to Damascus. Well, you can laugh all you want, but unless it's happened to you, keep your opinions to yourself.

I had heard the sound of the trumpet.

I don't remember the rest of those few days away, except in little snippets, until we got home and I resolved to recapture those notes if I could. But how? What is there on a farm that a kid can blow into? This was where I got a bit lucky. Around the back of the *Schlachthof*, where all our butchering was done, was a pile of bones, the remnants of the animals we had turned into food for ourselves, and trade goods for the market. A thighbone from a cow had a nice hole down the middle, and once I'd got Jürgen to cut the ends off with a saw, I had a pipe. I swore him to silence, but I was sure he wouldn't talk. The silent type was our Jürgen; not the keenest cleaver in the *Schlachthof*, but the warmest and most loving of my brothers. The hole down the middle of the bone was too big for my small lips and I nearly cried when I couldn't make much of a sound. Then I hit on the idea of making the hole smaller at one end. I got Jürgen to drill a hole in a rounded piece of shoulder blade. I smoothed the edges of the hole as best I could by scraping with a knife, and then he helped me fix it in place with some pine gum. Not bad for two farm boys!

The first notes I made were magic—only because *I* had made them—but they were nothing like what I'd heard that day in Rostock. It was wretched, it wasn't music, but it was all mine. I longed and pined for those notes, lodged in my head but nowhere else. Still, I worked away at that first 'trumpet' of mine, tightening my lips and raising the notes until I could get three and sometimes four. What was I thinking, a ten-year-old making raspberries into a smelly old bone? And it did stink, that rotten piece of cow! And I was so shy of this stupid thing that obsessed me that I used to hide away in the bushes along the line of our property, practicing as much as I could. I hid away, I think, because I felt I'd be laughed at. But one day I forgot to hide away first, and blew a few notes in the farmyard on my way to the bushes. The old man heard me while he was bleeding a sow, and came out of the byre with his bloody knife dripping in his hand.

"Go on. More. Do it again."

Chapter Three

In which I take a liking to the trumpet

Du wirst dich nähren deine Hände Arbeit; wohl dir du hast es gut
For thou shalt eat the labour of thine hands: happy shalt thou be,
and it shall be well with thee
Psalmen Davids/Psalm 128:2

Father was impressed. I don't think there was a musical note in him, but I suppose he recognized a skill when he heard it. Before you knew it, he was taking me with him to Rostock the next time he had a meeting. He had some wares to take to the city so we hitched up the wagon. Otherwise we would have ridden, which I always preferred, not just because it was a day quicker.

We entered the familiar foyer of the town hall and ascended to the office of the *Stadtpfeifer*, to whom I was quickly introduced. *Stadtpfeifer* means town piper, but in larger towns like ours the title had a much broader function. He was the official who oversaw and organized all the city's music on official occasions. This might include the parades in the church calendar, weddings and baptisms of notable folk, feasts and banquets, and playing cantatas and other sacred music with the church choir and organist. He also supervised musical training and education of apprentices. Our *Stadtpfeifer* was not himself a piper; he played the viola da gamba and the shawm in ensembles, but was also proficient on many other common instruments.

He was a strange old gent; thin, upright and courtly, with sparse grey hair grown long, and a mannered way of getting about. I was reminded of one of those long-legged spiders that live in the beams of our hayloft. He met us in a passageway, and ushered us into a wood-panelled room with cupboards and shelves, more books than I could ever have imagined, with sheets of music all over a wooden desk and some on the chairs and floor as well. I had seen music sheets in our church, so I knew what they were, even if the lines and symbols meant nothing.

I was mortified as papa showed off his little prodigy carrying his laughable bone. I was required to blow my notes, although I just wanted to melt into the floor or wake up from the nightmare. But the man inclined his head wisely and did something so extraordinary, so magical, so desirable, that tears ran down my face. He opened a chest and brought out a trumpet!

"Play this," he said with a smile. "See what comes out."

It was a beautiful thing that trumpet, although it was nothing special. One long flat loop of brass tubing—a bit battered even then, I recall—a bell with some writing on it, a real mouthpiece, and a red cord binding it all together. To me, it was an arrival, a place I had longed to be. Oh, I cannot tell you how glorious that moment was! All the notes—the ones I had heard in the market square, the ones that were held only in mind, the ones that refused to come out of my old bone—were there! And there were more. Clean, crisp, bright.

"Now sing," he ordered me. "Sing those notes you blew."

I sang them as best I could, but there was one that hurt me because it wasn't right. I could see in his face that he knew it, and I felt failure storming me. I knew my cheeks flushed and I wished again that I could melt away or awaken. He only smiled.

"Ah, that's the seventh note. It's a strange thing that the seven heavenly spheres are matched by the seven metals in such pure harmony, yet the seventh note of this scale so upsets our sense of order."

"But that's the sixth one." I played them again from bottom to top, feeling bolder in his kind company.

"Ah, not quite," he replied. "You see, there is a note one octave lower than you can play on this instrument. It is the note we call the fundamental, and it is impossible to sound."

"So, this bad note is the seventh? I see. But, can I not play it properly?" I asked.

"It's hard to do so, and strains nature. But now sing it as you think it should be."

I sang the seventh note so that it didn't hurt my sense of order, and he smiled.

"You see. We don't use it on the trumpet. You will find there are more as you rise up the scale, but these we can wrestle away from their nature and make something of them. This one we leave to God to explain, if it be His will."

"Tell me, sir," I asked, "why are all these notes so strangely placed? The low notes are so far apart, yet the upper ones become closer."

"It's a matter of disposition of harmonics; the music of the spheres."

He could see from my face that he might as well be speaking Greek. "Now," he steepled those fingers again, "there was once an ancient Greek philosopher named Pythagoras..."—he *was* speaking Greek!—"...who showed how musical notes are arranged. You divide the note in half then in thirds, then in quarters, so the intervals become smaller and smaller. Octave, fifth, octave, third, and so on."

"As I push upwards, I find finer and finer distinctions, then?" I wanted to know more about these intervals but I was feeling over-whelmed, so I asked no more questions.

Well, the *Stadtpfeifer* knew then that I'd got the music in me... and your world changes.

Of course, I'm giving my old papa a bit more credit than maybe he was due by making out he was so concerned with my getting along in the world. Really keen to push his little prodigy forward, eh? Truth is, Hans, the oldest of us brothers, could run the farm—he was most like father—Michael could keep its books, as he had been given a few years' education at the *Gymnasium*, and Jürgen could be the main manpower.[6] Annamaria and Clara would get married off and do the scut work in somebody else's kitchen, and I would have a life of nothing except pig manure. I was a hungry mouth to feed, and one fewer was a blessing to papa. That was the problem with having a big family. It was unusual in those years, what with the war, and the plagues and fevers and all the other ailments that came from God knew where. Pestilence, war, famine, death; the Four Horsemen were busy in those days, especially among the young. It was some cause for celebration when a baby got to be a year old. Now you could call it by name, make the baptism at birth mean something, treat it as if it might even become a person.

So, while our family's whole estate was large and could support us and the labourers we employed, at least for now, you could see limits to the number of mouths that it could feed. And I think even then, my father saw another problem in the wind: he had a secure place among the high and mighty of our little corner of Mecklenburg, and he had got there through his huge personality. Did he, I wonder, question whether any of his sons could step into his boots? Not Jürgen, the lovingest of my brothers. Hans the oldest was the logical choice, but he didn't have that... presence that papa had. And Michael, although the intellectual, would be least able to carry himself among men of his station. The fact is, father had got to where he was by pure ballsiness, a characteristic that seemed to have slipped the generations. The offspring didn't have it, and he knew that the men around them would sense that. Also, division of the land on the old man's death, and the duties and responsibilities, would probably be beset with legal issues and squabbles. Little me was just one more complication in a looming change of order.

A larger change of order we saw all around us. The war was tearing our land to pieces, and although I didn't know it then, it was only a matter of time before farming became untenable.

—

What do you do with a musical ten-year-old if you're a patrician farmer with mouths to feed and in the middle of a destructive war? My singing showed the way forward, especially when the *Stadtpfifer* decided there and then to introduce my father and me to the organist of the *Marien-kirche*. We crossed the square and entered the hush of that massive redbrick building with its paintings and sculptures, the organ and the wonderful astronomical clock. I was always in awe of the place, but now I felt small, insignificant and quite frightened as the door boomed shut behind me. The organist was soon found, and we were ushered into his office. Why, I wondered in a strange abstraction, did these musical old men always scatter their papers willy-nilly? While papa stood by, I think a little bewildered by all the interest in me that he had precipitated, the two of them gave me all sorts of musical exercises. It became clear that I had an innate musical awareness and a potential for successful training. It is strange now to think back on it. I had always liked to sing, and even from a very young age I recall being surprised at how badly it was often done, but this new and grander exposure to music was like a heavy curtain being flung back upon a glorious coloured window.

We returned to the *Stadtpfifer's* office in the town hall, and there my small dreams and expectations began their long tumble. He seated us in his office, steepling his fingers below his chin. It was as if he didn't know quite what to say, and there was a short silence.

My father opened the conversation. "Clearly, Jacob has talent. Is there a place for him among the musicians of Rostock?"

"Yes, but no," the *Stadtpfifer* replied with a sigh. "Yes, with years of training he could play amongst us, but no, not as a trumpeter."

"Why not? Why not as a trumpeter?" I broke in, turning bright red as I realized my rudeness in interrupting my elders.

"Because we may not play it."

"May not *play* the trumpet?" my father asked. "You mean, you are not permitted?"

"Exactly. As you know, the trumpet is the prime symbol of dukes and princes and kings. And it is most jealously guarded by them. In all places across the German lands, there are strict laws about who may and who may not play the trumpet. Trumpeters are soldiers whose job it is to lead troops into battle, and to entertain their leaders on all courtly occasions. They are bound into a *Kameradschaft*—something like our guilds—and their privileges are jealously guarded. Our Duke, Adolf Friedrich, prosecutes his laws with some energy. Such is his zeal, he has even included *pauken*, the pair of round copper kettledrums that accompany their playing, in his strictures."

"So, what about the trumpet Jacob just played upon today?"

"I should not have it, and it is only by one of those little quirks that it came into my possession. We would be advised to forget that you saw it here, and I might regret that I brought it out." He sighed and spread his hands wide. "My excitement at young Jacob's talent outmaneuvered my probity. I hope I don't live to regret it."

"So, there are no trumpets among the town musicians?" my father repeated.

"We are allowed trombones, but God help you if you even make it *sound* like a trumpet!"

"You're joking!" Papa barked.

"Not at all. I heard of one fellow who was beaten by a group of trumpeters because he mocked their calls on his trombone. You have only to hold the slide shut and play in the high register, after all."

Even as a ten-year-old this sounded absurd to me, but I had had no exposure to the ways of the bigger world. All this talk of illegal trumpets had thrown me into a funk.

"They aim their blows for the teeth…"[7]

A long silence ensued while my father and I took this in.

"We are forbidden by law," the *Stadtpfifer* continued, "to include trumpets among our instruments. If we need trumpets for any occasion, we must approach the *Kameradschaft* to provide us with players. And they are a proud, arrogant bunch, let me tell you."

"So, if I were to be trumpeter, what then?" I interrupted again. "Where would I go?"

"Your father would petition the *Kameradschaft* for apprenticeship and they would consider your application. You would become a soldier; certainly a cavalryman. But you are far too young yet." And in an aside to my father, which was clearly within my hearing, "And it is not without some cost."

"So, what is to be done now?" my down-to-earth farmer father demanded.

"Wait. As I said, he is too young to consider in any profession. His talent is raw and must develop with time." He turned his kindly face to me. "You must be patient Jacob, and perhaps in a few years something will appear."

This wasn't good enough for me, and I felt my heart shrivel in my chest. Years to the young are measured in centuries; I wanted it now. To give the *Stadtpfifer* his due, recognizing my potential on the trumpet he could have aimed me at the lowly occupation of trombonist in the town band, and in time I could have been trained to that craft, and surely to many other musical instruments. Except that I had now seen and heard the pomp and glory—heeded the martial call if you like— and second best would be nothing to me. I am sure, even at that young age, I would have refused any offer in that direction. As I told you, I was a headstrong little fellow even then, and I had very fixed ideas about where I was going.

Clearly, the *Stadtpfifer* had seen this higher destiny, but it had put him in an awkward position. He and the organist had praised my musical talent to the skies, and now the practical reality of what to do with me presented itself. But I had to thank him for his altruism, even though the path he launched me on precipitated me into Hell and then out the other side.

But that comes much later.

The aside to my father about the costs of an apprenticeship was more pointed than I realized. Although I didn't know it then, the true state of affairs on the farm and throughout the whole region was verging on desperate. The war was tearing the land to pieces in a vicious whirlpool of spending, wastage, debt and impoverishment. Farms, towns and livelihoods were swept away by armies that tracked back and forth over the countryside laying waste to everything. A company of savage hungry militiamen could impoverish whole communities, plunging them into a spiral they would never get out of. And the tracts of wasteland the armies left behind caused ripples of horror, poverty and disease to spread across country. Papa and my brothers had not found it hard to conceal the shrinking revenue, the tumbling prices and the withering prospects from their little farm boy, but the days of plenty were far gone. To send me away for an apprenticeship? Now, today, it was impossible; in three or four years when I was ready, even more out of the question. My father simply didn't have the means.

We stayed with Herr Schleef in Rostock that night, and returned to the farm at the close of a long, tiring and highly emotional visit. Since we had set out from home, I had passed from humiliation to elation, through ecstasy to fear, and now I was back in resignation to the normal grind of the farm. Mama greeted us at the door, and it was clear she had been waiting with impatience for our return.

"What news from Herr Pinklemann?" she asked directly, for that was the *Stadtpfeifer's* name. "Does Jacob have a talent?"

"Does indeed," replied my father shortly. "But more of this later. It's bed for him now!"

I wasn't stupid. All through our long return journey, and on the last day as the sunset came on and the moon rose between the stands of trees before us, I knew that papa's ruminative silence meant bad news. Had there been any plans for me in his mind, it would have been in his nature to wear them on the outside. I would have known by gesture and expression, if not by word. What he kept silent within himself as we creaked along home was nothing good for me. And so it turned out. It was over the next few days that I began to learn of the coming hardship, and the impossibility of my dreams. From the moment I had heard that trumpet in the marketplace, and had seen those fabulous uniforms, I had dreamt such grandiose and wondrous dreams! And when I had actually placed my lips upon a mouthpiece just that morning, and had sounded those heavenly notes, I had felt my fantasies to be within touch. To have touched the very hem of Heaven, and to have had it whipped away, was bitter indeed.

I couldn't bring myself to blow those horrible coarse notes on that stinking piece of bone. I went out into the field not long after our adventure in Rostock and flung my bone trumpet as far away as I could, tears of rage and grief streaming down my face. I went into a depressive funk, which must have hurt my parents even more than their failure to fulfill my dreams. So, I continued my chores around the farm—largely concerning upkeep and maintenance of swine—and slowly came around to a real world where all I was doing now, would be all I would ever do.

Chapter Four

In which the trumpet becomes my life's path

Lobet ihn mit dem Schall der Trompete...
Praise Him with the sound of the trumpet...
Psalmen Davids/Psalm 150

I must have been much on Herr Pinklemann's mind because a few weeks later a horse came along the main road from Rostock, turned in and trotted up to the house. The *Stadtpfeifer* swung himself down from his saddle and came to the door, where mama had come to greet the unexpected visitor. He had a long canvas bag slung over his shoulder, and seeing me as he entered the house, he smiled broadly.

"Jacob, I have been thinking of you," he said. "And I have brought you something."

I reached forward, but he held the bag away with a smile playing on his face. "But first you must make me a promise. Will you do that?"

I was quite mystified, but I nodded.

"You must look after this... this thing I have in this bag. You must treat it as a treasure. You must never let it out of your sight. And it must be a secret. Will you do that?"

My father and two of my brothers had by now come into the room, and they all watched this unfolding scene with amusement.

I nodded again, not having words to deal with my thoughts. I knew what he had in that bag, but I didn't want to admit to myself that I knew. It was battle between anticipation and disappointment, with the outcome on a knife edge. Then he opened the drawstring of the bag and drew out... the trumpet! The one I had played upon! He passed it to me and I stood there in front of him, overwhelmed. I don't know how long I might have stood in dumb wonder, trumpet in limp hand, if my father had not spoken.

"Go on. More. Do it again."

I raised the trumpet to my lips and cried again, this time in joy, as I found all the notes just as I remembered they were. I was ten years old; how can I explain the ecstasy and joy that overflows the heart at that age?

The old *Stadtpfeifer* beamed, first at me and then at my parents and brothers, and finally it seemed to the entire world as the notes sang out. I eventually found my voice to thank him and promised I would treasure the trumpet for as long as I lived. Oh, the promises of youth.

In the weeks and months that followed I would take 'my' trumpet to bed with me so that it was always at my side, and play it whenever the chores of the day allowed. I read and memorized the engraved inscription around the bell garland:

MACHT CONRAD DROSCHEL IN NÜRNBERG 1617

I would try to imagine where this Nürnberg place might be, and what journey the trumpet had taken to come to me.[8] It was a well-used thing, battered and dented as these utensils become with long use, and it was probably in need of more loving care than I knew how to give it. But I played it and played it, and played it more.

To hear me describe this, you would think that I had a God-given talent, dropped upon me from above; that I could pick up an instrument and play like those carved angels decorating the organ case in the *Marienkirche*. Even I knew this wasn't so. Although my family couldn't perceive it, Herr Pinklemann was well aware of how raw my talent actually was, and how much work it would take to gain any kind of proficiency. His support and encouragement were entirely founded, not on what he perceived now, but on what he predicted to himself that I would become. But his largesse in lending me the trumpet initially contained elements of guilt; both he and the *Marienkirche* organist had recognized and praised my talent, and only then discovered that due to our family's situation, it could never be fostered, never fulfilled. These were bad times for any kind of ambition, and my little life was only a tiny stone in the shattered and gutted political edifice that was the entire German world.

Lending me the instrument assuaged guilt, certainly, and it was not actually as difficult to accomplish as one might imagine. As he confided later to my father when they were alone together over a glass of wine, this trumpet hadn't had much use; it was an old-fashioned cast-off from the *Kameradschaft* that had come to him by a circuitous route. He could quite happily see it in my hands where it would be played and appreciated, and also have it out of his own possession in case it were noticed by some officious functionary. In truth, he told us, the trumpeters of Mecklenburg-Schwerin were forbidden to play upon instruments made in Nürnberg, the capital city of the enemy. As if the material of the instrument, he had remarked, were in some way polluted by its origin. It must have been nice to have the luxury to be so choosy.

All this Herr Pinkleman told my father at the time. It was only much later, under very sad circumstances, that a great and far more important truth emerged.

So, over the next four years a relationship of a strange sort grew between my family and Herr Pinklemann. He would visit us for what he described as purely social reasons—and in fact he and Papa were developing a solid friendship—but his ulterior motive was to watch over my development. I thought then, that Herr Pinklemann could have got himself into a great deal of trouble if this clandestine activity had been discovered. Why he continued with it was a mystery to me then, but I understood that if it were found out, he would be prosecuted by the *Kameradschaft* and undoubtedly lose his position with the City. I supposed he had started on this course as a way of making amends for raising my and my family's expectations too high, and I thought perhaps it continued because he couldn't bear to see a raw talent such as mine go unfostered. For now, I believed he had put himself and his livelihood in danger for me, and I swore to thank him every day as long as I lived.

One day near the beginning of this strange arrangement, this shadow tutor of mine came by with a sheaf of loose pages for me to look at. Looking at it was all I could do, because they were written in an incomprehensible language. Father had taught his four sons to read and write in our own tongue—and he had favoured Michael with more than the rest—but that was as far as any education went. Herr Pinklemann gained my undying respect... no, I will be honest here, my love, when he left the pages with me, trusting that I would keep them well.

"Here are trumpet calls from the Danish court in Köbenhavn, written many years ago," he told me as his finger traced the lines and marks. "I will show you what these marks mean, and how you can read them."[9]

There were about twenty pieces and he had chosen examples well because they were simple to execute, and were most instructive of tempo and rhythm. These ink marks upon lines meant nothing to me at that point, but under his careful tuition I was able to follow them and sound the calls. Though I didn't know it then, he was assessing my ability to learn and to memorize.

"Not much in the trumpet sounds for cavalry," he remarked, "has changed much since these signals were written down." This was a prescient statement.

And so began a period of intense, long-distance tuition which, in retrospect and with due credit to an old man who might have been losing his faculties, was an act of pure selflessness. I had never met my grandfather, but I felt he must have been very much like Herr Pinklemann, and I think the old man came in time to take that place. On one memorable day, my shadow tutor brought me a handwritten sheet of music; to borrow, not to keep.

"Now, this paper," he said, laying it on the table in front of me as he brought the candle closer, "is but one page of a description of our art by an Italian. It was copied some years ago. You will guard this with your life, Jacob. It is even more valuable than your trumpet."

"Here," he said, turning the paper to me, "let's look over the notes together. It is a *Sonata per un clarino solo*. You will work upon it."

Over the following months I worked hard on that piece and had it memorized. I became so fond of it that when Herr Pinklemann told me he had to take it back, I took quill and ink, and with a wooden straightedge I ruled out the staff and laboriously copied the music, even though I knew it by heart. He was most impressed when he saw that I had copied the writing as well as the music. Even knowing it by heart, I kept that blotted and much-used piece of paper, lost it and found it again. But that's a tale that will keep until later.

Learning that piece was a tough assignment, and I often went back to the Danish trumpet calls as easier and less demanding exercises. My facility with those calls, and with the harder Italian sonata, would have remained a useless and pointless talent, initiated by that turning point in life when pure happenstance took control. A little boy in the market on one particular day at one particular time. I'm not one to debate the nature of freewill or destiny—I leave that to the scholars and clerics—but I do wonder what would have happened if things had fallen another way; if I had not been given the means by a pure coincidence of time and place, to move up and out.

There was hideous disruption and horror in the autumn of 1636. Only a ride of a few days south of us, two armies had met in a fearful battle at Wittstock, and as was usual after all these engagements, ripples of disorder spread far and wide.[10] I was only twelve years old at that time, but I remember the look on the faces of papa and my brothers when we heard, faint on a wind from the south, a rumble of what I thought was thunder.

At the dinner table perhaps a week later, they spoke openly of the battle; how the Imperials and their Saxon allies, who were fighting for control of all the north German states, had met an army of Swedes and Scots; how the Imperials and the Saxons had been routed and driven south. News of this kind was always filtering in to us from afar, brought by refugees from the conflicts, displaced landsmen, broken soldiers, families with nothing but the ragged clothes they wore.

This was the normal situation throughout my life. I had never known peace, and would not have been able to define it, if asked. Neither had my brothers, while for our parents it was a lost dream of their youth. Conflicts were continuous, made bearable only by distance. We simply carried on because that's what people of the land do. Twelve-year-olds cannot see any larger picture, but this vignette I do remember because it was so close, so immediate.

I absorbed my family's fear and made it mine.

Chapter Five

In which I answer a call and am terrorized by a duke

Und Könige sollen deine Pfleger und ihre Fürstinnen deine Ammen sein
And kings shall be thy nursing fathers, and their queens thy nursing
mothers

Jesaja/Isaiah 49:23

It was a little after my fourteenth birthday, so it must have been late in the spring of the year 1638, when I played a few notes on 'my' Droschel trumpet while at the front of the house. It had been increasingly difficult to find time to practice. There was too much work for everybody, yields from the fields were reduced, and there was less feed for the animals. Pestilence had been visited upon the land, Famine was an ever-approaching phantom, all around us this senseless War raged on, and quite a number of our labourers had been 'recruited' to join the army, to find their fortunes but encounter only Death. Those Four Horsemen as foretold in *Revelation* were present among us.

In the years since I first blew on that whittled piece of bone I had grown and developed, showing the fullness of my father's physique. I was lucky in my breeding to have the power of Jürgen and the brains of Michael. The dissatisfaction and boredom I owed to no one. And playing was the only joy left to me, in a dull and never-ending round of toil. I had taken to playing outdoors in short sessions grabbed in between my chores, not realizing how careless this was. I used to put the trumpet in a small grain bin behind the house at the beginning of day. I had been doing this for a long time, heedless of the main Rostock-Schwerin road passing right by our door. One day, in a moment late one afternoon between the chores of my pigs and the digging of a much-needed drainage ditch, I stole a few moments. I took the trumpet out of the bin and sounded a number of the Danish cavalry commands that I now knew intricately.

The notes sang out, as pure as that first time when I had been so smitten. Had I not been at the side of the house fetching the instrument at that moment, I would have heard the approaching hoofbeats of a consider-able troop of cavalry. As it was, I emerged, played my pieces, and only then heard the sharp skidding of hooves, the scattering of gravel and the commands of the leader as they reined up and turned my way. Ten or twelve of them, in the Duke's service, trotting up our lane. They wore soft, wide-brimmed hats and steel breastplates, and carried their helmets on lanyards at their sides. Each had a pistol in a holster beside the saddle, and a sword hung in a scabbard from the belt.

"Go on. More. Do it again." The *Hauptmann*—or so I thought he must be—sat four-square in his saddle and looked down, his eyes passing from me to the trumpet and back again. He was a tall, square man, this captain, with hard eyes and a cruel mouth. I shrank inwardly from fear.

"Play, I told you. Play."

I played a single cavalry piece, only a few bars, badly and in extreme nervousness. My legs felt weak and I could hardly control my breathing. He waited, staring at me in expectation, so I played a few more shaky notes. Not impressive, but he had heard better only a short time before.

"Where d'ye get the trumpet?"

I had a strong feeling that it would be unwise to tell the truth. The image of Herr Pinklemann rose up in my mind, and I knew that the things he had told me would lead to exposure and a great deal of trouble. It was only as this sweaty, hard faced military man stared down at me, that I fully realized how foolish my old *Stadtpfeifer* friend had been.

"In… in the family, sir. Don't know…" I lied in a cold sweat, unable to concoct a convincing story.

"Horseshit! Lemme see." He held out his hand imperiously, and I knew to refuse would be dangerous. These were clearly troopers of Adolf Friedrich of Mecklenburg-Schwerin—they carried the familiar device of the quartered shield with two bulls, the dragon and the hand with a ring—so in essence they were our protectors, even in land that was nominally within Güstrow's territory, but this meant absolutely nothing in those times. Our lands were 'protected' by Swedish troops, along with their Scottish mercenaries and other assorted scum. They were supposedly driving out the Imperial Habsburg forces, but helping themselves to anything that happened to be in their way in the process. We were fearful of anybody in uniform.

I handed the trumpet up to him, and I thought from the way he took it, that he knew nothing of instruments. He had only to look at the inscription on the garland to discover its Nürnberg origin, surely. He glanced over the trumpet contemptuously, sniffing at its admitted less-than-perfect condition, and tossed it carelessly back to me. I caught it in the middle by its cord binding.

"Your horses?" he asked, cocking his head over a shoulder, indicating our nags in the yard.

I nodded.

"You ride?"

I nodded again.

"You have a rare talent there boy. Wasted on a farm. What's your name?"

"Jacob, sir. Jacob."

"Well, listen here Jacob Sir Jacob," he replied. "You be careful blowing that thing around here." He had a cryptic look in his eye, and there was shade of... almost humour about his mouth. What I had perceived at first to be the *Hauptmann's* cruel nature appeared now to be a thin plaster over something much more complex. "Never know who might hear it."

With that they swivelled around with a clink and creak and jingle, trotted back to the road, and sped west into the setting sun. I was really torn by this encounter; I feared these men because of their power over me, and wished I hadn't been so careless, but a small part of my mind revelled in the thought that a dozen cavalrymen had turned off their road just to hear me play.

Papa emerged from behind the house and asked me what this was all about. He had heard the racket, but had come out too late to see what was going on. When I explained, he gave me a strange look, which mystified me. It seemed almost to mirror my own mind, half fearful, half proud. He grunted and went back to whatever he had been doing. Increasingly he, and Mama too, were more distracted and less engaged, as if withdrawing into themselves. They worked hard in those years, too hard, and it was sapping them of the old vitality I remembered as a child. My brothers, too, were more and more introspective. Jürgen, of all of them, seemed to be pulling away; less capable than the others of understanding what was happening all around us. I tried often to bring him back to me. I would tell him of little things that had happened, of strange dreams I had had, or try to engage him in news of the bigger world that came our way, but nothing penetrated the brooding shell. We were all spinning down into sadness.

The summons arrived four days later.

I was at my chores behind the house when I heard the horse approach. It was a post messenger, not unusual as we offered changes of horse. However, I had been living every hour of the last few days in horrid anticipation of just such a visit. He dismounted, came towards me and demanded to see the master of the house. I went to call my father from the near field, trembling in fear that my stupidity in playing outdoors had brought some sort of trouble. Why else would a messenger be sent here?

Father came around the house, wiping his hands on his jerkin, stopped and stared dumbfounded at this liveried vision standing beside his horse.

"What business do you have here?"

29

In answer, the post messenger drew a letter out of his scrip. He thrust it into my father's hands, mounted his horse and was gone, a small cloud of dust and a clopping of hooves the only evidence that this vision from another world might ever have existed. The letter was sealed with red wax, impressed with the same device I had seen on the cavalrymen. Father broke the seal, opened the letter and read it out:

> Duke Adolf Friedrich of Mecklenburg-Schwerin, by the grace of God, commands the attendance upon him of one Jacob Hintze on May the seventeenth at midday. The same Jacob Hintze is enjoined and warned that should he fail to attend, and further should he fail to bring with him the trumpet he had been playing, he will suffer the full penalties assigned under the law.

"And it's signed by him with a great flourish." Papa was perplexed, a worried frown drawing his face down. "What in God's name... Is this a summons for good or evil? What have you brought down upon us, my boy?"

We had a serious family meeting that evening. Two things will give some idea of the seriousness of the occasion: my mother and sisters were invited to sit with us, and father brought out a flask of wine. Outside of the holy days of the seasons, I had never seen such a thing.

"To refuse the summons would be madness. He must go," said Michael.

"Of course he must go!" replied Papa crossly. "D'you think I'm going to hawk in the face of the Duke? Of course he must go! The point is, why is he wanted?"

"Because they have heard his wonderful music," said Jürgen, "and they wish him to play for them."

"No, no! It is not so simple," replied my father. "He should not be playing the trumpet in the first place according to the law. He has been engaging in illegal activity, and if I were not so taken up with all..."

"Against the law? Why?" asked Michael.

"Only the trumpeters of the *Kameradschaft* are permitted to do what innocent, stupid Herr Pinklemann has been encouraging and fostering in Jacob. And now... Ha! The piper must be paid."

"Why?" demanded Hans. "Why has Herr Pinklemann done this?"

"Because he has lost control of his faculties!" Father shouted. "Oh, why didn't I see this?" He paused and rubbed his hands wearily across his face. "Well, I have been inattentive and now..."

There was a long silence as papa placed his face in his hands and sighed.

"So there may be serious consequences?" Hans broke the silence.

"Yes. Yes, there might well be. You can't just give some country yokel a trumpet to tootle on…"

I was stung. "Hey! I'm not…" but father waved me down.

"Even if you were God's gift to music, I could never afford to post the bond that would be needed to secure you an apprenticeship."

I had not heard this actually expressed before, although I knew it to be true. The bond was a huge sum of money; without a patron, swineherds like me didn't aspire to such heights.

"There are two possible reasons for this summons," my father continued. "Yes, Jürgen, it may be they like his playing. It may be that his talent will outweigh his sins, and that he will find favour with them. If so, they release him and he is forbidden to pursue this trumpeting business, and all is well. If not, it's a world of trouble."

"So, three days hence he must present himself at the court." Hans spoke up for the first time. "Would you like me to go with him?"

"I think I would rather go myself, but thank you. As a patrician and landholder, I might be able to present his case and gain some favour for him. It's worth a try. Otherwise…"

I resented them disposing of my life amongst themselves in this way; I was not a mere roach in the grain. Nevertheless, plans were made to get two horses ready for the morning. It was a long ride to Schwerin, some fifty or so miles to the west, and would take the full time before the appointment.[11]

This would be a hazardous journey. With the land ravaged by marching armies, either fighting each other or gorging themselves on their 'hosts', you could never be certain to travel unmolested. Mother and my brothers knew this, and father knew they would be living in fear until we returned.

All through that long ride my father nervously coached me, schooling me on my deportment and behaviour. What to say, when not to speak, how to stand and conduct myself. He was worried, of course, that our house would be brought into disrepute. Several times in that ride we crossed the tracks of troops who had scoured the land and left ruin and waste. This devastation bewildered me at the time, and it was only later I was to witness at firsthand how warfare reduced innocent lives to rubble. I realized then how protected I had been at home, and it came upon me that I was now venturing into a frightful and menacing world. We were not apprehended by anyone but beggars, although our constant vigilance became exhausting.

I had never been so far from home, or in such a magnificent place as Schwerin. Rostock is a fine city, built upon the wealth of merchants and shipping, but Schwerin was built on a grander scale upon the wealth of the Ducal Court. The castle of the Duke sat upon an island in an arm of a large shallow lake called the Schweriner Innensee, connected to the town by a causeway. It was not as magnificent as the rest of the city; an ugly pile of bastions and defensive works with large, half-finished sections where, we were told, some Dutch architect had started building before the money ran out and he was sent packing.[12]

After we had cleaned most of the road off our clothes in the small inn we had found just two hours before, my father and I crossed the causeway, entered a decorative gate and presented the parchment summons to a watchman. I carried the Droschel trumpet across my shoulder in the bag that it had come in, fearful of this talisman of my wrongdoing. We were led along corridors and up sweeping stairs by a uniformed flunky of some kind, and I couldn't help but notice that the general condition of the walls and floors was unkempt, bordering upon shabby. The continual warfare was having its effect even here. Up another flight of stairs we went before arriving at huge double wooden doors flanked by guards. One of the guards stepped aside and opened one of the doors, but before we could enter the other guard placed his hand upon my father's chest. "Just the boy. You wait here," and he indicated a wooden bench. Papa drew in a breath to protest but bit it back, sitting down slowly in pure anguish as all his plans for my defence crumbled like ashes. His anguish was nothing to the fear that was turning my bowels into a thrilling, unstable liquid.

My first impression upon entering was of the Duke himself, like a lodestone that attracted all eyes in the room. Duke Adolf Friedrich of Mecklenburg-Schwerin was seated upon an ornate chair, raised on a dais a foot or so above the level of the surrounding floor. The light from high windows on three sides was behind him. He stared directly at me from his height on the chair while an equerry of some kind motioned me forward. As I approached him his features became clearer; a high forehead, narrow-set eyes and a dominant, bulbous nose. A small wisp of a moustache brushed his upper lip, over a down-turned mouth which, to my eyes, was not in its most genial con-figuration. The Duke watched me closely in silence as I approached slowly across the tiled floor, never once shifting his gaze. I stopped a few yards from him at what might have looked like a respectful distance, although it was driven more by my reluctance to approach closer. He motioned me forward until I was right below him.

It was only then I became aware of others in the room. Aside from the liveried individual who had shown me in, there were two resplendent and well-armed guards either side of the Duke, some petitioners and the hangers-on who always infest the presence of power wielders, and another individual who I should not have been surprised to see. There stood the *Hauptmann* with his close-cropped grey hair and steel eyes, neatly trimmed moustache and beard, arms folded across his chest, and still sporting that sardonic twist of his mouth.

The Duke drew in his breath and fixed me with his eyes. "The trumpet is the symbol of power," he rasped. "My trumpeters are my authority and my symbol." He was around fifty years old when I first met him that day in Schwerin, and his voice betrayed years of command, good living, and hardship as well. Suddenly, the voice soared to a roar. "*They. Are. Me.* Who mocks my trumpeters mocks *me!* Who flaunts my laws flaunts *me! Is that clear?*"

I could not move, could not respond in any way. I felt like that pillar of salt we were taught about in the Bible.

"When some *person* has the temerity to mock my trumpeters and my laws, *he mocks me!*" he roared. His voice crashed around the room, bouncing into a horrid stillness. No one moved.

My terror was now absolute. Awful visions of punishment poured into my head. Sweat sprang out all over me, my heart and lungs were squeezed in my chest, and I was instantly as cold as the grave. In the memory of all the horrors and terrors and fears of a long life as a soldier in battle, this experience comes back to me first. I stood there in that huge and overarching silence for what seemed like an age before the Duke spoke again in a tone that sounded almost resigned.

"So, *Hoftrompeter* Breitkopf," said the Duke to my *Hauptmann*, "this is the little miscreant, is it?"

"Yes, sir. That's the one."

Hoftrompeter! The highest rank of player! Not just for the military, but for the court as well! And I had thought he was just a captain of cavalry; he had no trumpet with him when I saw him, and I had thought he was less than curious over mine. What game was this?

"Kindly repeat the circumstances of your encounter." The voice was now laconic, almost bored, a startling contrast to the shouting rampage a few heartbeats before.

"We were returning in haste from Rostock when we heard trumpet calls where no trumpeter ought to have been. We encountered Hintze here."

"And his presence here is important why?"

"I think you should here him play, sir."

The Duke turned wearily to me. "All right. Play your damned trumpet."

I couldn't. Riveted with fear, rooted to the floor, it was as much as I could do to take the instrument out of its bag and hold it up to my lips. Nothing came out; no sound emerged from my paralyzed face.

"Go on, boy!" he urged. "Where's your manhood?"

I took several deep breaths, calming myself as best I could, and raised the instrument again. Relax, I told myself, relax. To my immense relief, calmness did descend on me. I don't know what devil possessed me then, but I played the very trumpet call that had caused the squad of horsemen to rein up that day. The *Hoftrompeter* smiled ironically at the first notes, nodding his grizzled head.

"Go on. More. Do it again," urged the Duke.

I played the Italian piece I had memorized. It was mostly in the high register, but swooping down to dance and flirt around that ugly seventh. My confidence soared and I played much better. Again, the ironic half smile from the enigmatic *Hoftrompeter*.

"Well, *Hoftrompeter* Breitkopf?" the Duke asked with a raised eyebrow. "Well?"

"First one's Magnus Thomsen, sir. From the Danish book. We don't play it that way anymore. That's what we heard, few days ago."

"And the other?" The Duke's voice was level, smooth and threatening.

"Bendinelli. Newer stuff. Difficult."

"Well played?"

"Not well played." The *Hoftrompeter* locked his eyes with mine. He had power over me, and he was enjoying the power he knew he wielded; a farmyard cat with a thieving rat. "Not well played, sir." He paused. "*Damned* well played."

"So!" The Duke clapped his hands, a signal for a collective release of breath and a stirring among the figures scattered through the room. Even the two guards appeared to relax as tension melted away. "We have established that the boy can play, have we not?"

"Yes, your Grace. He is indeed a trumpeter."

"How old are you boy?" The Duke leaned forward a little in his chair, squinting slightly at me.

"Just fourteen, sir."

"Just fourteen? My *Hoftrompeter* tells me that yours is an extraordinary talent, and that I would be well advised to retain your services. What do you say to that?"

"I would... I..." This was a cannonade. I was in such a state of disbelief I could not speak, think or act coherently.

"And such is my *Hoftrompeter's* judgement," continued the Duke, with what I thought was a caustic undertone, "I am prepared to waive the bond of one hundred *Thaler* that is the normal requirement. Do you wish for a place in my household, Jacob Hintze?"

I found my voice. This was glorious. It was all of those dreams rolled into one and bowling, golden, into my arms. I stammered some sort of reply—I cannot remember what I said because my ecstasy overwhelmed me—and the Duke smiled.

"But before we proceed much further along these pleasant lines," Duke Adolf Friedrich continued smoothly, "there are certain things we need to know."

Did a cloud really cross the sky outside those tall windows? Did the room really take on a chill? There was certainly a new and ominous silence. I felt thumbscrews on my soul.

"Who taught you to play the trumpet?"

The image of that kindly old *Stadtpfeifer* rose in my mind, and I knew that if I revealed the identity of my tutor I would doom him to punishment and dismissal. I could not bring myself to do it. Behind my rigidly held expressionless face I cursed and raged at his stupidity.

"I... I taught myself, sir." This was no lie, as Herr Pinklemann was a viola da gamba and reed player, although he had taught me all I knew of musical theory. The Duke's expression shouted disbelief.

"And where did you acquire this trumpet of yours?" he asked icily.

Again, the image of the kindly old man rose in my inner eye. No, I could not tell him. The lie that I had told the *Hoftrompeter* about it being a family possession would be ridiculed. This was tearing me to pieces.

"I cannot say."

"Cannot? Or *will not!*" he thundered. "Do you dare to thwart me, boy?"

I stood mute for several heartbeats. "I cannot say," I repeated in a small voice.

"Where did you get that *trumpet!?*" he demanded.

I was silent.

His voice slid from forte to piano, and dived steeply down in pitch. "Do you not understand," he enunciated clearly and slowly, "that we are offering you a place in this house which will take you forever away from filthy drudgery? Hmm? Or are swine of more importance to you than a long life of fine music in our service?"

He leaned forward in his chair so that his spine was almost horizontal, his bulbous nose nearly level with mine. "What do you say?"

I could only repeat what I had said before: "I cannot say."

The face turned purple, he flung himself upright, and yelled, "Then, by God, you'll leave my presence. You dare to defy your duke? Get out, get out! Throw him out!"

One of the guards seized me by the elbow and began to haul me away from the Presence, but a voice intervened.

"Your Grace, may I say a word?" It was the *Hoftrompeter.*

"No, you may not! Who are you to defy me when it was you who

35

wasted my time with this toad? Does your rank give you that right?"

"If I might..." Breitkopf's mild voice seemed to penetrate the Duke's anger in a way I would not have thought possible. A still, small voice of what would turn out to be reason and salvation.

"What? What? Say your piece, damn you."

"It seems to me, sir, that what is seen as intransigence might indeed be probity."

"Speak in plain words, you fool."

"The lad is clearly protecting a guilty party, but that is not at issue. The issue is that he is prepared to forgo any future glory he might be granted here in your lordship's court rather than... ah... tell on a friend."

"So? So?"

"I think—and it is, I quickly state, only my humble opinion—that such fortitude in the face of dismissal, disgrace and punishment is a mark of steadfastness, honour and courage. The lad, your Grace, is not for sale."

Adolf Friedrich, Duke of Mecklenburg-Schwerin, sat upright in his chair, looked this inconsequential farm boy right in the eye, and furrowed his brow. Even in my stool-softening terror I could see the thoughts moving behind his eyes. He nodded extremely slowly, coming gradually to his conclusion.

"You have balls, boy. You have balls. But never forget that better men than you have died screaming at the stake for such balls."

I fell into my father's arms outside the big double doors, shaking, shuddering and weeping. It was quite some time before papa could be persuaded that all was well, and the poor man must have been in a stew of agony until he could extract coherent words from me. At the Duke's command we were taken to the refectory and given a meal of meat stew, bread and apples, although my appetite was away somewhere else. I did do fine service to the ale, though. Papa was in heaven, more effusive than I had seen him this past year. It was if all the cares of the farm had been lifted from him for this brief time, and he was delighted in the fortunes of his youngest son.

We had only just emptied our ale pots when *Hoftrompeter* Breitkopf appeared and sat across the board from us. I was stricken with fear again, but the ironic turn of the lip was now a full smile and so I was somewhat reassured.

"Your son will likely do well in our service," he told my father, "but you must know that he has a long and hard road." He turned to me. "Playing the trumpet is all well and good, my boy, but it's only the beginning and it's but a small part. We have to shape you up and make a soldier out of you first."

"He's a good, hard-working lad, and he'll do you proud," my father effused. He was continuing a tendency to answer for me, but I was still somewhat tongue-tied with awe anyway.

"Tell you something. Yes, he can play the trumpet. The stuff we play in the field, most likely lads can be taught that. But he can write, and he knows his way around horseflesh, and those are assets. Bye and bye we'll find out what he's like with a sword and a pistol. Good day to you."

He got up from the bench and turned to leave, and then something occurred to him and he turned back. "Another thing. Give the trumpet back to whoever gave it to you. Nürnberg stuff. Not to the Duke's liking. There'll be money aplenty for a new one. We don't buy foreign."

And he was gone.

Much administration work needed to be taken care of before my apprenticeship would formally begin, so we were instructed to return home, collect all the necessary proofs, titles, deeds and certificates, and await a summons. That was a fine and uplifting ride filled with jollity and good spirit, even though we had to be watchful constantly, and again crossed those hideous tracts of wasteland.

It was on the road back home that I believe my father first started to see me as a grown man.

Chapter Six

In which I begin my training and education

Zu einem Feldtrompeter bin ich erwählt, beim Hauptmann halte ich mich auf,
und warte auf ihn, bei Nacht und Tag…
I am a field trumpeter by calling, and I will stand beside my master,
and do his bidding by night and by day…

Jost Amman

Parting from my family was miserable beyond belief. Yes, I was excited at the prospect of a world opening up before me, but it was still tearing grief to leave my comfortable life behind. Michael, Jürgen and Hans bade me farewell early in the day before they went about their duties, Michael giving me a bang on the back and telling me that school was just fine, keep your chin up.

I parted from mother and my sisters at the door of the house, clinging to Mama last of all and being pulled reluctantly from her embrace by my father, who was keen to have us mount our horses and get moving. Now that my destiny was taken care of, I felt that Papa was in haste to get me on my way, and have this little problem behind him. But perhaps I am being unjust. Mother, indeed, was reluctant to see me go. The tears were in her eyes and the trembles were on her lip, but she held together well for the benefit of her two daughters. They were all smiles and waves, and showed none of Mama's anguish.

I swung up onto my horse, my pitiful little bag of necessities slung over my shoulder, and set off. I twisted backwards often in my saddle with an increasingly stiffening neck as I watched the house and our land dwindling bouncingly behind me. I carried little as I had been told that everything I needed would be provided. 'My' trumpet remained behind, to be returned to Herr Pinklemann with heartfelt thanks. Supplying me with all I needed would not be out of beneficence, of course, but with the intention of enforcing uniformity. I was to find that the first thing I would have to set aside would be individuality. So I had some few clothes for the road, some little food items care of my mother, and the mouthpiece from the Droschel that suited my chops and could not be parted with. Every trumpeter becomes familiar with a mouthpiece, and thereafter his 'chops' demand that familiarity. I was sure Herr Pinklemann would forgive this small 'theft'.

The ride to Schwerin was uneventful, aside from several hours of drenching rain on the second day, which turned the roads into a quagmire and covered us from head to foot in the rich soil of the Schweriner Seelandschaft. Father was obliged to pay extra at our inn that night in view of the mess that had to be sponged and hosed off us and our horses. The next day we would need to be as clean and presentable as possible.

Father was there for the paperwork, and as soon as we arrived at the castle we were sat down on hard chairs at a trestle by some sort of administrative notary with quill and ink and seal. He would have looked well in any ill-lit and dusty counting house; a thin, beaky old rail with every possible feature of his anatomy downturned.

"Your son is to be apprenticed to Hartmund Breitkopf," the notary informed my father, as usual assuming me to be a chattel to be discussed as if I were elsewhere. "*Hoftrompeter* Breitkopf will be here shortly," he continued fussily, "but until he arrives there is much to be seen to."

This was another shock to my system. Breitkopf? Hartmund? I suppose it was logical; he had 'discovered' me, had vouchsafed for me to the Duke, and must have some sense that I would be worthy of his training. But I had assumed I would be assigned to an underling. Knowing he would be my master filled me with more anxiety than assurance, perhaps because I had no idea of what was going on behind those eyes.

The key issue in accepting me in the first place was the assurance of my worthy birth. It was essential that a trumpeter be of good ancestry. As I said at the beginning, we were a patrician family, land-holders with a coat of arms, but even so we were close to the ground, as it were.

"It is extremely important that proofs of the boy's birth and ancestry be furnished," the notary told my father, holding out a manicured hand for the documents he was just drawing out of his scrip. "I understand you are farmers." Not posed as a question, but certainly as a veiled criticism.

The paperwork father had brought included deeds and title documents and, of key importance, my birth certificate duly notarized. All these were handed over, scrutinized at length, sniffed over and laid aside. It was touch and go that we would be sent packing at one point when father refused to give up my birth certificate. He hadn't realized that this document would be retained by my master, and only given back at the end of my training.

"I understand the bond of one hundred *Thaler* will be waived," the notary remarked, not without another pointed sniff. He seemed to 'understand' a great deal. "This is, I need not tell you, an extraordinary privilege."

"No, you need not indeed tell me. Or anybody else," my father remarked. "I *understand* that Duke Adolf Friedrich himself authorized it."

The acid was not lost on the creaky cleric. I would not say his face coloured—there wasn't enough blood in him for that—but I think it made an effort. Finally, the last piece of paper was inked and sanded, father applied his seal across his signature, and I was sold. At that moment *Hoftrompeter* Breitkopf stepped through the door.

"Yes, the bond is indeed waived," he remarked. "But I value the applicant none the less, and I would advise you to agree." He eyed the completed papers. "I will go through the apprenticeship agreement with him in detail and furnish you with the signed copy in due course. I see the rest is done, so you may leave."

The cleric scuttled out of the room with his papers, leaving one large document on the trestle, and Breitkopf took his place. His appearance and demeanour made me and my father look quite ordinary. He was dressed in a leather jerkin with a diagonal bandolier across the chest, a shirt with slashed sleeves, a doublet in the Duke's livery, and woolen hose almost hidden by high floppy riding boots. I wouldn't have expected him to be wearing his sword indoors, but he had it in its sheath at his side, clattering as he swung onto the chair. I think he must have included the sword because this would be a formal occasion. He had much about my father in him; he filled a room, demanding attention with his presence.

"All right, young fellah," he started without preamble, "you're mine for two years. This document..." lifting the remaining paper "...contains the rules and regulations by which you will be bound to me. We will go over this presently. You, sir," to my father, "have fulfilled your part of the business, and now it is up to the lad and me to conclude our arrangements and apply our signatures."

This was clearly the signal for Papa to now relinquish me and pass me over to my new master. Poor father. He had reveled in my being selected, delighted at my fortune—and I'm sure was a little relieved to see me taken care of—but when it came time to part he was woeful. He rose to embrace me, first shaking me by the shoulders at arm's length, then throwing his arms about me. His eyes were moist as, with a backward glance of parting, he left the room.

My new master eyed me from head to foot, sizing up what he had let himself in for. I sat mute, not knowing what I should say, or if I should speak at all. I was in awe of him, but more in awe of the huge future that hung in front of me like a dense barrier of fog.

"You are completely lost," he remarked, "you have no idea what's going to happen, and you think I'm an ogre. Right? Wrong?"

"I… I'm pleased to… to be here," I began, getting my voice back. "But I don't know…" I ran down again.

"Let's set you straight." He rubbed his hands. "While you train to be a field trumpeter I will be your master. You will answer to me, or to those I designate in my stead, and to no one else. You will be on call to me, any time of the day and night, and you will do exactly as I tell you. Understood?"

I nodded.

"As *Hoftrompeter* I am not in charge of your military duties; your cavalry duties. For those you will report to your squadron commander, Helmut Weitz, who you will also obey unswervingly and at all times."

He picked up the document again. "These rules and regulations are similar to the *Ordnung* with which all trumpeters must comply. That document you will sign in two years, at the end of your bondage to me, assuming, of course, my satisfaction in every particular." He fixed me with his eye and I nodded again, meekly. "We will go over these present rules and regulations quickly now, but I will expect you to know them inside out and backwards."

Over the next half hour every single thing an apprentice could and could not do was spelled out by my master. I was to be supplied with room and board, clothing, and even an allowance for candles and small beer. Rules for my deportment, behaviour, and type of dress on all occasions were laid down. There was a strict curfew. I would adhere to a rigid schedule of hours of study, work and service. In those hours not taken up by my master's tuition or his demands, I would be required to serve the court in whatever capacity was deemed necessary. I would be paid some small sum of coin on a weekly basis to buy whatever minor goods or services had not been provided, but not before these items were vetted and approved. I was intrigued with the sections regarding breaking curfew, the consumption of strong liquors and carousing with loose women. Having never tasted either of the latter, but with the fourteen-year-old's lust for discovery, I wondered how I might find a way to rectify the deficiency.[13]

"You will be given a room in a nearby house," the *Hoftrompeter* told me, "and share your eating arrangements with three others who are here as apprentices. I will provide you, in writing, with a weekly schedule, which you will adhere to at all times. Questions?"

I had many but my mind was whirling. One thing that did concern me was the loss of the Droschel trumpet; I had lived with it, slept with it, and over four years I had come to know its every nuance intimately. I felt its absence in my heart. "Will I be given a trumpet?" I enquired meekly.

He looked at me sternly, but with a slight easing of the lines around his mouth. "You know what it's like to be without one, eh? Well, we'll be getting you sorted out and straightened up, so there won't be any time for music just yet. Got your mouthpiece?"

"Yes. I couldn't leave without it. It's..."

"Good. Knew you'd be sensible. Keep your lip in shape by buzzing on it." By this he meant playing notes on the mouthpiece without the trumpet attached. It was a miserable excuse for music, but that wasn't the point. And in the absence of even a mouthpiece, a trumpeter would still exercise his lips in this way. "I know it's tough, but that's what you're here for in the end, so it'll all get sorted out. Report at the front gate, first hour tomorrow morning. Dismissed!"

I crossed the bridge from the *Schlossinsel* and entered the town, looking for the address of my accommodation that I had hastily written down on leaving. I found the place in a narrow lane off the Ritterstrasse, and knocked on the door.

"You'd be Hintze," said the round, middle-aged woman who opened the door, looking me up and down as I squeezed past her in the narrow entryway. "I'm Frau Walther. There's no Herr Walther. He's with God in Heaven, and I hope he's giving Him an easier time than he ever gave me. I was told you were coming. Your room's on the third floor. I haven't got to the stove yet, so supper won't be for an hour. Go on up. What are you waiting for? It's the only room at the top, can't miss it."

I climbed to the top of the house and pushed the stiff door open. I set my sad little bundle down, sat myself on a three-legged stool near the tiny window, and surveyed the room. It was under the eaves, a triangular space where one could only stand upright in the centre. On the walls there was some water-stained plaster clinging to the diagonal wood laths, but not very much. A rope-woven wood frame with straw paillasse and coarse blanket constituted the bed. The only other item of furniture was a wooden box of the sort you see herrings packed in, acting as a stand for a facecloth, a ewer and a basin. Cracks in the floorboards let light in from the room below, and a muffled sound of voices rose.

I rested my elbows on my knees, put my hands in my face, and cried long and hard.

I really didn't feel like eating, even though I had had nothing since the morning and the sun was now just over the rooftops across the street. On the other hand, there was nothing in that room to occupy me except my own thoughts, so an hour or so later with little else to do, I wiped my face as best I could and went down to the lower floors, following the scent of bread and meat. The further down the stairs I went the more my stomach told me this was a wise decision. I entered the kitchen space where Frau Walther was officiating over a trestle set with bowls and spoons. Three youths of about my age were already seated, tucking into an aromatic stew and chewing on slabs of bread. There was a pot of ale beside each place.

The lad nearest to me stopped his munching, swallowed quickly and greeted me. "What's this? The new boy. I'm Berthold Steiner; Bert. Take a seat." He waved a hand around the table. "This is Heinrich, and here is Joachim."

Heinrich nodded and smiled, mouth working on a crust. Both he and Berthold were friendly and welcoming enough, although I could see from the quality of their clothing, and their cursory comparison with mine, that they considered me a shabby-looking fellow. Pointless to explain to them that, because I had only just arrived, I was not yet fitted out with suitable attire. All three were dressed in what I discovered to be the issue clothing for apprentices: grey wool for the shirt and hose, black drawers of linen, and a doublet with plain wooden buttons, also black. Low black boots completed the outfit. It was clear that off duty we would be plain and unremarkable.

Joachim rose slowly from his seat, looked me up and down from head to foot, taking his time doing it, and bowed mockingly.

"It is a great pleasure indeed to welcome you amongst us."

Spoken by another man it would have been a welcome, but there was a sneer in his tone and a twist to his mouth that made it clear what he thought of me. His eyes were pale, dead and frightening in a way I couldn't fathom. He was finely dressed, more so than the other two, because it seemed that his cloth was of a better quality and a finer cut. He carried himself extremely well; an inch or so taller than me, perhaps a year older, and clearly fit and agile. His dark hair was grown long, cut and shaped meticulously, and he sported the makings of a small moustache and beard. There was in him a grace of movement and a confidence that many could study, but few could emulate. This Joachim thought very well of himself, and assumed others did too.

I took my place at the table, accepting with thanks the bowl of stew and slab of bread that Frau Walther passed to me. I now realized I was quite hungry and started on my food with great enthusiasm, sipping occasionally at my ale. As I ate, Joachim, across the board from me, eyed me with distaste, watching as I spooned the stew and dipped the bread. It was acutely uncomfortable to be watched so closely as one ate, and I felt that every small slip of the spoon or drip of the gravy was remarked, noted and criticized.

"Where're you from?" asked Berthold. "What's your apprentice-ship in? I'm studying to be a violinist in the Duke's court." I couldn't help but like this open-faced lad with his straw hair in disarray and his wide, welcoming smile.

I chewed and swallowed quickly. "Er... Near Belitz, not far from Rostock. We farm... own land there."

Joachim's sneer widened. "Farm boy, eh? Standards are slipping."

The other two looked down into their dinners and remained silent. They appeared to be cowed by him, perhaps afraid to assert themselves in case his favour turned away from them. To my first impression they seemed to be the perfect bully's foils; nice enough people but easily led, afraid to make choices.

"So what are you here for?" he continued. "Kitchen duty?"

"I'm apprenticed to be a trumpeter."

"Trumpeter! Some chance! You have to be a gentleman to even think about that." He stood up and pushed his stool back. "You'll never do."

I forbore telling him that I had been scouted by the *Hoftrompeter* and expressly invited by the Duke, and that my bond had been waived at his command. Let the bastard think what he wanted. He left the room with not a backward glance. This was my first encounter with Joachim Wadegahte. I disliked him from that point, I will admit, but I did not make an enemy of him; it was he who made an enemy of me.

The other two stayed at the board, relaxing visibly as we continued the quizzing and the backwards and forwards. Heinrich told me he was from Wismar, had been apprenticed to the court pastry chef, and that he had already got a taste of what was to come, which involved sweeping, cleaning, carrying and emptying, and nary a hint of pastry. Berthold was already an accomplished violinist and had studied with Johann Schop, which surprised me a little as the instrument was not yet as popular here as it would become.[14] He told me that the violin was an Italian fashion that the French had latched onto, and that it was slowly becoming appreciated in the German lands. I was also surprised when he told me he spoke English quite well, a language I would meet all too soon.

Joachim, they told me, was apparently training to be a cavalry officer, and considered living amongst us apprentices to be an indecency of a quite temporary nature. Heinrich observed that he would make an excellent cavalry officer as his stupidity and pride were exactly the qualifications required. We all roared. These two were excellent company, so my loneliness and homesickness were at least set back, if not banished.

Soon it came time to return to my room for the night. I was by now quite anxious to empty my bladder, but horribly self-conscious over asking about the amenities. I felt that if I asked my new friends, I would be branded for life as some country yokel—exactly the seed that

Joachim had so cleverly planted—so I held my peace and wondered what ever I would do. I really did feel like a coarse country bumpkin, and I did indeed wonder if I would ever be able to measure up. I had to thank Frau Walther for her perception in taking me aside as I put my foot on the first stair.

"Just leave your night soil in the pot you'll find in the wooden box. The girl will see to it after you leave tomorrow morning. There's water in the jug for your washing, and I've left you a cloth."

Chapter Seven

In which I encounter Italian, French, English and women, but nary
a trumpet

*Und sie wurden alle erfüllt mit dem heiligen Geiste, und begannen zu reden in
fremden Sprachen, wie der Geist ihnen gab auszusprechen*
And they were all filled with the Holy Ghost, and began to speak
with other tongues, as the Spirit gave them utterance
Apostelgeschichte/Acts of the Apostles 2:4

I have never had trouble waking with the sun. No matter how tired
you might be, the routine of the farm conditioned you to rising early.
I came down the stairs from my room the next day before any of the
other lodgers, but even so Giselle, Frau Walther's skivvy, was there
before me. I thought of what she would be doing in my room after I
had left, and got all hot and flustered at the idea. Breakfast was a slice
of bread and an apple with a mug of small beer, taken in the downstairs
kitchen, then I was on my way across the bridge to report for duty.
The funk and tears of the night before had evaporated and I felt confident, although still very apprehensive. I reported at the front gate as
commanded and was met by some sort of court functionary. I was
surprised that my master was not there to receive me, and asked if I
was to be taken to him.

"*Hoftrompeter* Breitkopf," he replied shortly, "is far too busy to
concern himself with you. You are to be taken first to the wardrobe."

I was sure he was eyeing my clothes with disdain, but over the
course of the morning I observed that he was quite even minded; he
eyed everything with disdain.

I followed meekly along, feeling humiliated and once again awfully
young and small. The wardrobe was a long room fitted with shelves
along either side on which was a wide array of clothing of various
kinds. I had noticed that all members of the Duke's court wore his
livery, and even off duty the dress code was strictly enforced. Hence
the apprentice garb I had seen on my housemates last night. A tailor—
I assume that's what he was, although he wielded no shears or measure
anywhere near me—sized me up and brought a set of clothes from a
shelf. There was a woolen shirt and hose to match, black drawers with
ties at the leg, and a plain black doublet.

"Come. In here. Try 'em for size," he said leading me to a curtained
alcove. "Don't know why I still bother 'cos I never make a mistake."

Sure enough, when I emerged and modeled the clothing it passed muster. He then took another set off the same shelf and handed them to me. One to wear, the other to wash. I was pleased with the feel of the underdrawers; they were easy on my skin unlike those I had come with, which were particularly uncomfortable when riding. The cloth of the rest, though not of the finest quality, was worlds better than my homespun, so I was mightily pleased with myself. I wished for a looking glass—one of those things made by some art with mercury and silver—but these were rare. I had seen one once as a child in the *Rathaus* in Rostock, and remembered my fascination at seeing this 'me' yet 'not me' so clearly. From another shelf the tailor handed me a cape, a woolen cap and a pair of coarse raspy gloves. These, with a pair of black boots, completed the outfit.

Next, I thought, would be the livery I would wear when on duty, but here came a huge surprise. There was none. I stood like an idiot with my old clothes bundled in my arms while the tailor eyed me with impatience.

"On your way! On your way! I'm busy man."

"But what about…"

The flunky who had brought me here seized my elbow and led me down the passage. "The purser is next. We have to see him about your stipend."

"There are no other clothes?" I asked in a quivering voice.

"Of course not! You'll wear apprentice garb until there is some service in the Court that requires livery. And, depending upon your usefulness, that may or may not be any time soon."

We entered another room, this one occupied by a large desk behind which sat a fat, smooth-faced man with ink-stained fingers. My escort waited outside the door. The purser, which was what I assumed he must be, looked up from his document, smiled and waved me to a stool.

"Hintze? Here's your coin for this week," he said, handing me a pen. "Mark there. Oh, you can write your name. That's good."

He passed me a small leather pouch with a few copper coins in it. "You'll not want for much because you can get your candles, your beer and whatever else is set aside for you in the stockroom. They keep a tab. This money is for stuff we don't supply, but whatever you buy, you'll need your master's permission."

"I think my needs are fairly modest," I replied meekly.

"Better be!" he roared with laughter. "Can't have you going into town and buying quinny at your young age. Besides, need to save your *Pfennig* for weeks to get enough for that!"

This jovial fellow came around from behind his desk, slapped me mightily on the back, and ushered me back into the charge of my escort. The final stop on my tour of the bowels of the castle was at yet another office where I was given a sheet of paper ruled in squares. Set out down the side were the twelve hours of the day—from the first at sunrise, when I was required to report, to the last at sunset—and across the top were the days of the week. The hours were sounded by a bell mounted in a clock in a tower of the *Schloss*, the hours being a little longer as it was now late spring. Many of the squares on my sheet were already filled with miniscule writing, beginning with the first and second hours of the day, which told me what I already knew because here I was. The third hour of this day, which I guessed would be sounding soon, had 'kitchen' written in it. Was I to be fed already?

"Now," said my disdainful flunky, "off to the kitchen and report there. Down there and turn left. Go on!"

No, I was not to be fed. I was given a wooden bucket and a coarse brush, and was down on my hands and knees scrubbing trodden-in food filth and greasy spills from the floor for the larger part of the remaining hours. No more tears, no more weeping and anguish; all of that was replaced with a burning anger that I kept within me only by a monumental effort of will. I raged at the injustice of it. I had been hoodwinked, taken for a fool. Kitchen duty! Exactly what Joachim had predicted my fate would be. Where was the trumpet, where was the fine livery, the horse and sword that I had dreamed of as I made my way here? I went back to my room that night in a foul temper, hating both the world and myself. I didn't weep, but I skinned my knuckles punching the wall, and hurt my toe booting the shitpot box.

This menial and soul-destroying work continued for the week. By the last hour of the day I would be aching and sore from the endless scrubbing. I would go back to the rooming house angry and filthy, and like as not I would encounter Joachim Wadegahte at our meal and receive more sneering insults. He smelt the kitchen on me, and could not resist repeating his view that this was my fittest calling. I ate and drank quickly and fled to my miserable bare room. I hardly looked at my trumpet mouthpiece for two reasons: firstly, when I got up to my room at the end of the day I was just too damned exhausted and dispirited; and secondly, on the one occasion I did try to buzz, Joachim made me the butt of dirty jokes about the noise in front of the entire household.

I was within an inch of running back home, and it was probably only desperate bodily tiredness and no idea of the road that prevented me.

It was only on the last day of my weekly schedule, in the first hour, that the name Breitkopf was inked in. I couldn't wait to see him. I arrived early and was kept standing at the gatehouse until the hour struck. There he was, striding towards me with that wry twist to his mouth that I found so hard to read. I was fawningly keen on one level to speak with him, but I was determined to maintain as cool a head as possible. I hated to show him any weakness.

"I've neglected you a bit," he began, which cheered me hardly at all, "but new pairs of hands have to be broken in. Come with me."

We went up a few flights of stairs and entered what was obviously the trumpeters' dedicated domain. The Duke's trumpeters stored their instruments in this room, and this was where they met to practice and rehearse. The *Kameradschaft* kept themselves distinct from all the other instrumentalists, who had their own music room for storage, practice and rehearsal elsewhere. Trumpets, banners and other regalia on racks lined the walls, wooden shelves contained music, books and ledgers, and two pairs of massive copper kettledrums on tripods occupied one end of the room. I looked longingly at the instruments, but I received a slow shake of the head.

He ushered me into a small office, more a cubicle off the main room, and clearly his personal space. He shut the flimsy door behind me and we sat on wooden chairs across a table from each other. He produced another sheet of paper, ruled in squares like the last one. I had resolved in my mind a few things I wanted to say, but when I was sitting in the presence of my master the words failed me. A few days ago I would have complained petulantly, whined at my lot, and begged him to give me what I wanted, but by now I knew this would hardly do any good. He knew what was best for me and I was his to use as he saw fit.

"How were the first four days of your apprenticeship?" he asked with a slight smile, challenging me, I thought, to speak my mind as I had first intended. But I had come a long way in those four days of scrubbing floors, passing through anger to resignation, and then to the realization that I was being tested.

"I am at your service sir, and through you Duke Adolf Friedrich, in any capacity in which you see fit to employ me."

His smile spread slowly outwards from the quirk in his mouth to the rest of his face, and then he threw his head back with a barking laugh.

"You're my boy! You would be amazed at the number of starry-eyed apprentices who go running back home to mother. We can't have weaklings, so we weed 'em out. I knew you had balls the way you stood up to the Duke, but we have to run you all through the form."

This was exactly what I had expected and so, with what he said and the way he had said it, I became cheered and bit more optimistic.

He addressed himself to the sheet of paper he had brought with him. "Now, from here on we get a bit more serious." A thought distracted him. "Have you been buzzing on your mouthpiece?"

"Not as much as I should," I confessed because I knew I ought to be putting in an hour or so each day, but it had been impossible without withering scorn back at the rooming house.

"Well, it's all the trumpet you'll get for a while. We can't have you losing your lip, so you'll have to do better."

"Yes, sir. I will try."

"No!" Suddenly his mood had turned. "You're *not* going to just *try*. I want an hour per day from you. That's an order. Is that clear?"

"Yes, sir," I said again, feeling the colour rise in my face.

"You are an asset of the court. The Duke's property." He relaxed a little and smiled again. "We don't want his property damaged through neglect, do we?"

"No, sir."

"Now, as you are aware," Breitkopf took on a lecturing tone, "a trumpeter is not just someone who blows notes. What else is he, eh? Tell me all the things a trumpeter must be."

"He... he must be able to ride a horse. He must be able to fire a pistol. He must be a swordsman..." I ran down.

"Yes, yes, yes to all those things. He is the most versatile of soldiers. This we know. But what is more important than all of these together?"

I couldn't think of another attribute. I had seen my *Hoftrompeter* and the squad of cavalry ride up to the house that day—so long ago now, it seemed—and I could not imagine another thing they would want or need. I sat nonplussed until he spoke up.

"Education," he replied slowly, spelling out the syllables on his fingers. "Education. The trumpeter takes messages, he communicates, he acts as a go-between. A herald moves unscathed between bitter enemies. He is trusted for his intelligence, his probity, his integrity. D'ye see?"

"Yes, sir. He must be at a higher level than many other soldiers."

He nodded vigorously. "He must be at a higher level than many other soldiers!"

I had a curious thought, almost a premonition. "Every trumpeter, sir?"

"No, not every trumpeter. Most trumpeters do nothing more than play the trumpet. They remain *Feldtrompeter*, field trumpeters, and that is their calling and their career." He paused, eyed me speculatively, perhaps thinking to add something further, then, coming back to the paper in his hand, continued briskly. "Now, look at next week's work."

I scanned the rows and columns quickly and saw many references to 'tuition' scattered across the week. There were still, I was sorry to see, some tasks that appeared menial in nature.

"Here, first two hours of the day on Monday, we have you sitting with a scholar who will bring me up to date on your education. You have your father to thank; you wouldn't be here if he hadn't made sure you could read and write, but I need to know how well."

"Yes, sir. My brother was sent to the *Gymnasium* for two years, but it was costly…"

"Aye, well, there's no *Gymnasium* suited to us soldiers. You don't need number, geometry or cosmology where you're going, and music you'll get with me. And you won't get any damned Latin either. No reading Seneca and Ovid, although Julius Caesar and Suetonius might be useful. No, what you need is working languages. Go further down the sheet."

I scanned further down the week and was almost frightened to see French, Italian and English in three of the little boxes. I had had no idea this would be demanded of me. All my dreams centred upon this mythical me, dressed in fabulous livery and seated on a fine horse, waving a bright sword while heroically blowing the call to charge. My aspirations withered a little.

"You will be required," Breitkopf continued, "to sing in the ducal choir for Sunday services, and any other occasions during the week. And, of course, you will attend divine service every week. Here…" he indicated a time slot "…is your vocal assessment. What's the state of your voice?"

"I… I have… it's completely changed now. Sir." He waved me down.

"You can obviously sing in tune, and you read music. The *Kapell-meister* will see to the rest. And here," he continued, pointing at the close of the week, "we have some physical assessment. We're checking on your brain work and your pipes, but we'll need to know how the body works as well. You look fit enough."

"The work on the farm…" I began, then retreated in acute embarrassment at my humble home life and the lowly status it implied.

"Yes, alright," he waved his hand dismissively, "we both know where you came from. But we also know your background, your family's patrician status, your worth. You wouldn't be here if you didn't fit. You fit, that's all there is to it."

He picked up an ivory letter opener from his desk. "Now, your teeth. Open. Let me look."

He used the letter opener to root around in my mouth, pressing my tongue back and spreading my lips quite painfully.

"Not bad. Could be better. These teeth are your life's blood; lose them and you lose everything. Make some *Kieselghur* and a little water into a paste and rub every day with a cloth on your finger. Not just the front, right down to the back. And use a wood stick to work over your gums. What fruit do you like?"

"Apples, sir, when I can get them."

"Good. Need something with a good crunch. If you can't get apples eat a raw carrot or a turnip. See the victualer if you can't get 'em at your lodging. They're included in your allowance."

He paused, assessing me. "Come back here at the sixth hour. You'll be meeting the trumpeters. Dismissed."

I went down to my hated chores in the nether regions.

When I returned to the trumpeters' domain just before the sixth hour I found a crowded, noisy space filled with a dozen men preparing as if for battle. Trumpets had been taken off their dowels, music stands were laid out, and a pair of copper kettledrums on tripods had been dragged into the centre of the room. Their battle was to be with the music on their stands and there was a cacophony of discordant sound as each ran through his gamut; the lowest of the *Flattergrob* and *Grob* to the highest in the *Clarino* register. In massed trumpet music the parts are divided according to the register the players use. *Flattergrob*, a designation I found amusingly appropriate, was the lowest part, *Grob* was next, *Faul* and *Principal* were nearer the middle, and there were two high parts for *Clarino I* and *II*. Together, these parts crossed the better part of two octaves, and found their way into a third right at the top. Trumpeters were assigned to these parts and were rarely permitted to play outside them without explicit direction.

Hoftrompeter Breitkopf spotted me lingering at the door and waved me in.

"Gentlemen! *Quiet! Quiet!* This is my apprentice, Jacob Hintze."

To a man the whole trumpet corps turned and stared at me. It was disconcerting to be examined like a specimen, and I felt again the same unease that Joachim Wadegahte's stare gave me. I was being examined, assessed, and found wanting. I felt angry at being judged by this superior bunch, but I kept it to myself. They were not dressed in their fine livery, thank God, but even so the contrast between their 'stand-down clothes' and my apprentice's apparel was stark enough. But humility is what they expected and required, and humility is what I would give them. Cursory examination over, they turned to their work.

"Now, the new piece," Breitkopf addressed himself to the group, who all turned their attention on him, mercifully taking it away from me. "Friedemann, Albrecht, you take the top parts, the rest of you as

52

you were."

The piece they played was in four parts, three instruments to a part, except for the highest part, the *Clarino II*, where the designated two played while Breitkopf listened with crossed arms. I noticed that most players had no music stands; they apparently played by ear. I had never heard kettledrums being used before and was astonished at the resonance and volume of their thunder.

My God, this trumpet corps was good! Their volume, their intonation and their cohesion filled that room to glorious overflowing with a great brass wall of sound. You must remember that this was the first time I had heard any trumpet being played since that time so long ago in the market in Rostock. I was overwhelmed with the experience, but more with the knowledge that I could be one of them. Yes, they were good, although you wouldn't have known it from the detailed and pointed criticism they received. They played the piece, only about sixteen bars in length, at least five times, each time with, I supposed, improvements, although I was no judge at that time.

At the end of the hour my master dismissed the corps and came over to me, wedged tight into a corner of the room and making myself as unobtrusive as possible.

"Like the idea of being one of 'em?" he asked. My expression told him everything. "Well, work hard, study hard, do exactly as you're told, and we'll see. Off with you!"

I did extremely well at the physical assessment. I was shown to a large chamber, half storeroom, half exercise floor, where the arms and armour were kept and used. A bandy-legged *Feldwebel* with enormous biceps, wide shoulders and a small head ran me through a set of exercises with weights, then had me running as hard as I could around the perimeter of the space. Once he was satisfied with this, he led me to a square on the floor marked with white lines.

"Catch!" he yelled and hurled a wooden stave about five feet long at me. He held one himself at about forty-five degrees to his body. "Come on! Find your way through!"

I thrashed away mightily with the stave—I had played this game with my brothers, so I knew how good I was—always on the offensive, while he kept to the defensive, and I never came anywhere near him. Finally, with me panting and gasping and his chest hardly moving, he slapped me on the back and said I would do.

That was all the physical assessment I was given at the time, although throughout my schedule there were sessions in various martial disciplines. A trumpeter was also a cavalryman, a fully armed and armoured warrior. The martial was therefore spliced into book-learning in a seamless round of activity that occupied six days of the week, the Sabbath being set aside for worship, study and contemplation. And as an apprentice I was also a chorister.

I liked Herr Johann Vierdanck the *Kapellmeister* from first acquaintance, a tall, initially forbidding, man with a long, intolerant nose and piercing eyes.[15] His first words belied his appearance as he welcomed me into his studio, a small chamber next to the choristers' dressing room, and sat me down on a stool.

"As you know, all apprentices are obliged to sing in the chapel choir if they are able. *Hoftrompeter* Breitkopf has told me," and here a huge smile transformed his face, "that aside from being able to play the trumpet, you might also have some musical talent."

I was clearly in the presence of a standing joke so I smiled as well. I had been nervous about this meeting ever since I had seen it on my schedule, but from this point I began to feel more and more welcome.

"Do you sing? Have you sung?" A steely eye pierced me.

"Yes, sir, in my church." The sort of singing we did in Belitz was of the most basic kind, but I had sung since I was a child and had reproduced the trumpet tones when Herr Pinklemann had asked me.

"Then let us hear what we have. Come with me." We passed through a door into a large room filled with musical instruments on racks and tables, and dominated by a two-manual harpsichord. He sat himself down at the keyboard and sounded middle C. "Sing this note."

I sang a long 'Aah', feeling highly self-conscious. He pursed his lips and nodded his approval.

"Now the octave, starting at C." I sang again. "Hmm. Crisp and clean, fine tenor, but not a great deal of body. You sing up in your head." He swung round and slapped me on the stomach. "It needs to come from here, but we'll draw it out of you in time."

He stepped away from the keyboard and pulled a folio from a shelf. He placed it on wooden lectern that he dragged forward. "You read music, I take it? Hmm?" I nodded. "From here. Not the words; just the notes, sounding 'Aah'."

As soon as I saw it I was delighted. It was a lovely melody I knew well and had sung often: *Nun lob, mein Seel, den Herren* by Johann Gramman. However, I had only sung the first few bars before he waved me to a halt.

"Ah, you naughty boy!" he cried, waving a finger in my face. "You know this piece. I can tell. Have to find you a piece you *don't* know. Test your sight reading, eh?" He opened up a drawer, brought out a folder, and riffled through some more sheets. "Hah! Know this? Be honest now."

This piece was hand-written, not printed. I looked over the music and assured him that it was unfamiliar.

"Not surprised," he remarked. "Very new. Just written it. Now again…"

And so I sang the notes again, this time right to the end of the page.

"You'll do very well," he said rubbing his hands together. "That's all for today. I can tell Hartmund that he has chosen wisely. Off you go."

Try to imagine the typical scholar; an ancient file in a black gown, long white hair falling to rounded shoulders, rheumy eyes peering from behind spectacles, a little spittle at the corner of a toothless mouth. That's how I visualized one Herr Doktor Martius who was to test my education. I entered his study and found myself in a book-lined space dominated by a large globe of the world and a desk covered to over-flowing with papers. The only person in the room was a short haired, slim young man writing at the desk.

"I… I was looking for Herr Doktor Martius," I stammered.

"Then you have found him. You would be Jacob Hintze?"

I stood, open-mouthed. I was making a habit of finding myself in situations where words failed me.

"Of course, you were expecting some creaking, grey-bearded eminence," he said, smiling. "But don't worry, I come by my credentials honestly. I have been a student in Louvain, Montpellier and Oxford, have studied astronomy with none other than Marin Mersenne, and have corresponded with Hevelius."

I knew none of these places or the people either, so if this was intended to impress it fell flat. I continued to stand in the door and look blankly in his direction.

"Come on in. Where's your tongue?" He beckoned me in and waved at a stool.

I found my voice. "Yes, sir, I apologize. I had thought you'd be an older man."

"Perhaps I am. Perhaps I wear well. Who knows? So," he rubbed his hands together, "*Hoftrompeter* Breitkopf has told me he wants you assessed; see what sort of education you've had and what measures need to be taken to repair the damage. Read this!"

He shoved a piece of paper across the desk. It was a section taken from the rules of our craft, and was hardly challenging. "If it happens that a trumpeter behaves dishonorably," I read, "towards a widow or an honest man's daughter and makes her pregnant, and still marries her, but she is confined and gives birth too soon afterwards, then this man, apart and aside from the punishment which he incurs from the duly appointed authorities…"

"Very good, very good," he interrupted. "You read precisely and well. Have to find something more challenging." He scrabbled among his papers. "Ah, yes. Try this."

'This' was a page of a letter written in a crabbed and almost indecipherable hand, clearly in our language but not in the way we spoke it here. "That the spheres… pass in circular… fashion about the sun… is not truly shown…? Er, shown by… mathematical…"

"Good enough, good enough," he cried. "You have managed to read the hand of one of the worst of my many correspondents. You can thank God it's not in Latin."

He seized a quill and a sheet of paper from the desk, passed them to me and said, "Copy out the piece you read before, the rules, in as fair a hand as you can muster."

He sat back in his chair with his hands behind his head, elbows out to the side, while I dipped into the inkwell and wrote as carefully as I could. I worked for some time—far beyond the pregnancy and the punishment, and almost to the marrying of a person of ill repute—wondering how much longer he would keep me at it. Finally, he called a halt and stretched out his hand for my work.

"Hmm. Nice hand. Should send you to Danzig. Tutor Hevelius."

So began my schooling in languages. An hour or two per day, sometimes less if I was called away for some mindless labour elsewhere. I would read aloud, memorize and study with Herr Doktor Martius, and then I would take paper, pens and ink home with me. I made good use of my ration of candles, especially when the days started to draw in. I found that I had a facility for languages, picking up the subtleties of everyday speech with ease, at least in Italian and French. It would have been quicker were I ten years younger, but still I was pleased with my progress, and so was my tutor. We started with French and Italian, and once I had a solid grounding there we moved to English. I could see the logic of it when English was clearly a bastard amalgam of romance languages and my own tongue, but it was harder to catch the idioms and usages. In spite of what my master had told me, Herr Doktor Martius did drill some Latin into me; not enough to converse or write, but sufficient for me to make out fairly simple texts, and to appear to know more than I actually did.

"What do you know of ciphers?" Herr Martius asked me one day. The answer was, of course, absolutely nothing.

"Here." He hauled out an old book and passed it to me. "This is a copy of *Steganographia* by Johannes Trithemius. One of my true treasures."

I opened the book at random and saw that not only was it in what looked like Latin, it also contained charts, lists and tables that made it even more mysterious, if that was possible. I looked blank, which made him smile.

"You will need at some time," he said, taking the book back, "to write messages that may not easily be read by others. This book is only useful to me as a thing of great power and beauty. Trithemius was among the first to describe the art of making one's writing obscure. In fact, this work was so obscure that the Holy Roman Church placed it on the *Index Librorum Prohibitorum*. They thought it was a book of magic, and still hold to that view even long after they were informed otherwise."

"So, I don't need to read this?" I asked hopefully.

"Good God, no! But a brief introduction to the concepts described in *La cifra del. Sig. Giovan Battista Bellaso* would not go amiss."

"And what are those concepts, Herr Doktor?" I enquired with a sinking in my heart.

From a drawer he pulled out a piece of paper on which was printed a chart of the alphabet, repeated over and over again, shifting each row of letters sideways as they went down. "This is a *tabula recta*, and by adding a key, which only you and your addressee know, you can make your writing into reversible gibberish."

"But why would I have to do that?" I was supposed to be learning to play the trumpet, surely. What use would I have for writing rubbish?

"You will learn its usefulness to you in the fullness of time. For now, it is enough that you master these few simple skills. Now, let's write a message together..."

Creating cyphers was yet another topic that had to be drilled into me, and hard work it was. The cyphers I mastered were fairly simple, but with head-thumping mathematics an enemy could unravel them. They would suffice, I was told, for whatever occasion I might find.

The summer passed this way, the days lengthened into autumn, and still I was reading, studying and exercising, working at menial tasks as well, and wondering when I would ever get back to playing the trumpet. It was some time in the late summer of that year that a wondrous discovery came my way. There's nobody raised on a farm doesn't know the ins and outs of swiving, but knowledge of swine and cattle doesn't prepare you for being in the waggoneer's seat, so to speak. It was a warm morning, and I don't remember why I didn't have to report for duty that day. I was lazing in my bed, half asleep in luxury and dreaming lusty thoughts, when the door opened and in came Giselle the slop maid, bucket in hand. Now, she wasn't what you would think; just because she was a cleaner, emptier of pots, general dog'sbody about the house didn't mean she didn't have some charms. I guess she was in her mid-twenties at that time. She was an orphan who Frau Walther had taken in a few years past, probably, knowing her, out of the goodness of her heart. An orphaned young girl in a big town can go downhill damned fast, so the place she had in our establishment wasn't to be scoffed at. Food, board, a little spending money. She had checked me out a couple of times over the last few months. You know, you're passing the door and she catches your eye, or you're eating your dinner, and when she puts the bread down, she presses a springy tit momentarily against your shoulder. Nothing that a third party would remark, but signals none the less.

So, there I was lying on my back, suddenly discovered, and in a state that young men of my age are often in when they wake up in the morning. The evidence provided by the bedcovers was unmistakable. She paused in the door. Our eyes met, and we made a static portrait as the light shone in through the window and the sounds of the morning drifted in from outside. She stirred first, slowly closing the door with her hip, putting the bucket down and coming over to the bed.

She knew what she was about, so I simply let her take the reins, knowing wench that she clearly was. She pulled the cover down and quick as a flash jumped on top of me, shift pulled up over her hips, legs splayed to either side. She slipped herself home and it was just a few thrusts of her hips before the roaring, pulsing explosion came. It compared with taking yourself in hand in the same way a wisp of straw compares to a haystack. She hammered away long after I had finished beating my tattoo, and then she rolled off to my side, grabbed my hand and forced it down to her. Sawing her slippery place up and down against my hand and wrist soon taught me what she wanted, so I began to knead her until she arched, reared up with muffled squeals, and collapsed panting beside me. Shock, awe, ecstasy and a good leavening of terror were what I was feeling.

"Too quick..." she panted.

"Too quick?" I was lost in a haze of disbelief. Only the sun streaming in and the raw smell of her convinced me this wasn't a dream.

"'Course it was!" She was regaining her breath. "You've got to learn how to slow down, give a girl a better time."

An image from the farmyard came unbidden into my mind. You didn't see the livestock taking their time over it, I thought, so here was something new to think about.

"But why?" I was grasping at reason, my body still tingling with waves of pleasure. "I mean, why did you... we... you just do that?"

"Do it? Because I like it, you fool! What d'you think? Fucking's the only enjoyment I'll ever get in this life, so I take it whenever I can get it."

"Isn't there... I mean... a risk?"

"What, of being caught at it? Not a chance. Frau Walther's half deaf anyway, and she probably knows what's what. I think she even knew about Herr Walther. 'S probably what killed him."

"No, I meant..."

"Oh, that. You mind your own business and I'll mind mine!"

"I didn't mean... I just..." I was lost at sea in a sexual tempest, and I couldn't spy land.

"'S long as some wise crone can find me savin, laurel, madder... Anyway, I've got to go," she said, pushing herself up on her elbows. "Take it for what it was, all right? I'm just a shit cleaning wench with a taste for cocks. I enjoy servicing you young gentlemen, or I wouldn't do it."

"*All* of us young gentlemen?"

"'Course. I'm not choosy." Giselle slipped off the bed, got to her feet and picked up the bucket. "But a nice young hard one like yours, all primed and ready to go. Well!"

I shut my eyes, thinking of this enjoyment parceled out, and trying to image either Heinrich or Berthold doing what had just been done to me. Waldegahte, yes. He would do it, but the other two? I wasn't sure, and I was damned if I would ask.

As if in answer to my thoughts, she said, "But not Wadegahte. I wouldn't have him inside me for anything. Not that bastard!"

"Why are you telling me all this?" This latest was definitely more information than I really needed. "I could get you into really serious trouble."

She eyed me then with a curious expression. "I don't think you would. I'll tell you something. I don't know what it is about you. They're gentlemen maybe, but you're not like them. I trust you."

"Even when it's telling on one of my fellows?"

"Yes, even then. Anyway, he wouldn't dream of touching me. Every time he looks at me it's like I just came out from under a stone. He wouldn't put the toe of his fine boot in my piece. Besides, he's got a fancy romp of his own in town."

"He *has?*"

"Oh, yes. Keeps her in ribbons and perfumes and whatnot, and screws the arse off her."

This was unbelievable. The swine had all kinds of money, and I was pretty sure his father had bought him out of a few misdemeanours, but to keep a woman in secret?

"But what about the curfew?"

"Oh, come on sweet Jacob!" she said with her hand on the door latch. "You've been here long enough to know there's ways round that. D'you think Ma Walther watches the door all night?"

"But there's the Town Watch."

"Sure, load of senile old tosspots who can hardly keep their eyes open. Most of the young men are gone for soldiers."

With that she left the room, closing the door behind her. I lay there as the two halves of my existence came slowly together and melded: the part where all was as it had been before when I was just a boy, and the other part where my entire universe had changed when I became a man.

Strangely enough, I was afflicted with the fear of being caught and punished, the fear of Giselle having an 'accident', and the guilt and embarrassment of being found out, but never a thought of sin. It never crossed my mind that together we had committed the sin of Adam and Eve. Perhaps this is as it should be?

Of course, I was madly in love with Giselle from that point onwards and imagined ludicrous scenarios as only an adolescent boy can. I imagined myself as a fine trumpeter with a position in court, my wife on my arm and our prospects absurdly rosy. I can only imagine now the horror of my father; for even a fourth son to contemplate a liaison with a serving wench! And the shunning by colleagues, of course. But the horny inner fantasies of youth never see the light of day. The boy grows up but keeps his secrets.

She never came to me again. I am almost certain that my clumsy behaviour and guilty demeanour whenever she was present in the kitchen were noted with some amusement by Heinrich and Berthold, although we shared nothing of our suspected and imagined common and carnal knowledge.

Chapter Eight

In which I fire a gun, begin swordsmanship and learn the handling
of a cavalry horse

*Orandum est ut sit mens sana in corpore sano. Fortem posce animum mortis
terrore carentem*
You should pray for a healthy mind in a healthy body. Ask for a
stout heart that has no fear of death
Juvenal (Decimus Iunius Iuvenalis)

In lockstep with the cultivation of my mind was the cultivation of
my body. The books were interspersed with hard physical labour.
Guns, swords and horses all would need to be mastered before the
cavalry trumpeter could emerge.

There were six or seven of us awaiting initiation in firearms. We
were ordered to meet in the range, an interior courtyard where target
practice was held. All the others were destined to be infantry, God help
them; yokels from farms, tavern loafers, all disposable manpower to
be transformed into soldiers to fight in the increasingly pointless war
against the ungodly Catholics. The Duke was now sending troops
enlisted by levy throughout the duchy—the Swedes drove hard bar-
gains for the protection of all the northern states—but had not yet
committed the core of his elite fighting men, among whom I would
soon be numbered.

The *Feldwebel* in charge of firearms was a short, stocky man with a
paunch, a round bullet head and quite the reddest face I had ever seen.
He was an active, quick-talking man, and when he handled his various
weapons his small, neat hands were skillful and deft. On a trestle beside
him were a number of lethal and mysterious-looking weapons, two
small casks and several powder horns. Most of the harquebuses, the
long weapons used by foot soldiers, were equipped with matchlocks
where a smouldering cord would be dipped into the gunpowder in the
priming pan. You couldn't use a thing like that on horseback, so
wherever cavalry had firearms the more advanced wheellock would be
used.

"Now then!" he yelled. "Who's cavalry here?"

I raised my hand and glanced around. I was the only mounted
soldier in the group and they all eyed me as if I was a freak. In our
units cavalrymen were cuirassiers, which meant that we carried a
wheellock pistol and broadsword and were armoured with a cuirass, or

breast plate. We had no mounted harquebusiers, probably for reasons of economy. Arms manufacturing in the north was nowhere near as advanced as in the south, so supplies of guns were limited. You could smell envy of Nürnberg at every turn, although it was brushed off by extolling our superiority with edged weapons and pikes.

"Just the one cavalryman? Well, you all need to know this, so pay attention. What I say about the pistol applies to the harquebus as well, which is what you foot soldiers will deal with later."

He picked up a pistol and waved it at us. "The wheellock pistol. A huge advance on the matchlock. You," he pointed straight at me. "Why?"

"Because... because you couldn't have a burning match while you're riding?"

"While you're riding, *sir!* Yes, mighty inconvenient. For you. Might burn holes in your gorgeous uniform. So here's the wheel." He flipped a hinged piece back and deftly slid a cover open. "Now, this piece I've just pulled back is the dogleg. It's got a clamp here that holds the pyrite. You!" He pointed at one inattentive oaf who was more interested in the toes of his boots. "What's pyrite?"

"Um, er... A *Seeräuber?*

"Pyrite, not pirate, you stupid bastard! Anyone else?"

I put my hand up. "Sir, it's a stone that strikes sparks. We... er, the servants use it for starting the kitchen fire."

"Good. Sparks are just what you need when there's gunpowder around, hmm?"

The *Feldwebel* picked up one of the small wooden casks from the trestle, tipped it over and spilled out a small portion of black grains into his hand. "Fine powder for small arms. Rule: the bigger the grains, the bigger the gun. This is the finest you can get. Pistol powder." He opened the second cask and showed us the coarser grains for the harquebus.

This was my first exposure to gunpowder and I looked at these little handfuls in fascination. Its chief component, nitre, is derived from urine, which is collected in a pit then purified to bring out the crystals. I began to see the magic of gunpowder, because all four of the natural elements of the world cleaved to it. It began with earth—indeed, we are all clay formed by God—and then it had passed through us to become water. When lit, the nitre would pass through fire, and its smoke would disappear in air.

There followed a long explanation of the loading and firing, with practical exercises for all of us before we were actually allowed to fire the thing. Each of us was overseen by the *Feldwebel* with great vigilance, and coached if we had forgotten any stage in the loading, which most of us had. My shot went far wide of the target, and the shock right up my arm to the shoulder was a surprise. The smell of the powder smoke was delicious! Nobody had a misfire, the so-called flash in the pan, but it was only because we were rigorously overseen and took five times longer than necessary. We were allowed just one shot each. It was only later I discovered that gunpowder was in very short supply at the time, and that in many engagements the shortage quickly rendered the fire-arms useless, unless you clubbed your enemy over the head with them, that is.

Once we had all taken our shot, the instructor addressed me directly again. "So there you are, unhorsed in battle, lying in the mud with your pistol in your hand while this Catholic son of a whore has his sword at your throat. You point your gun at him. You pull the release." He paused dramatically, holding his arm out at full length with his finger crooked, sweeping his eyes around the whole group, all of whom were by this time most attentive. "You pull the release," he repeated, "and..." The tension mounted. "Then... *click!* Nothing. Suddenly, you're dead. Why?"

The reason was that you could not possibly perform the loading procedure while on attack, so the gun had to be preloaded in the rear before advancing. With the loaded weapon in the holster beside the saddle, and the cavalryman galloping into attack, the powder could be shaken out of the pan, or the wadding could become dislodged so the ball and charge became loose. And, of course, keeping your powder dry was essential. Later in our training we would practice the *caracole*, and then all this would come into focus.

At the end of a long day I became convinced that if my life depend-ed upon a wheellock pistol I would be in deep trouble. I was told, years later, that our weapons were notoriously unreliable, but the man who told me this was from Nürnberg where everything mechanical is superior, so he probably had an axe to grind.

I may not have taken to the pistol, but I did love gunpowder and everything about it. And one day it would serve me in horror, and its smell would live with me thereafter.

Although I had little faith in the gun, the sword was a different story, but it took me a long time to get the full mastery of it. The sword became my weapon of choice, and my skill with it would later save my life several times over. I think if I am to be remembered at all, it will be first by my trumpet, and then by my sword. We used an exercise room off the armoury for swordsmanship and again the group com-prised mostly men and boys enlisted from all corners of the duchy... with the exception of my good friend and lodging companion Joachim

Wadegahte. He was destined to become a fine cavalry officer, of course, so swordsmanship for him would be *sine qua non*, as we Latinists would put it.

It was a bit humiliating to be issued with wooden swords by the instructor, but you could see the sense of it. We each donned a leather cuirass attached around the back with straps and buckles, and slipped leather bracers over our forearms. Until we learned to defend our-selves, the safest course was boffering, which is the use of soft or dull weapons. We were instructed to aim for the torso, counting each touch of the cuirass as a point.

But there is a great deal to be learned about swordplay before you even start to swing a blade. We had to practice and memorize a range of stances and moves with such names as *Vom Tag*, which was the starting position, to others called *Ochs* and *Pflug*, and lots more besides. There were subtleties in the strokes you used, but also in the moves you showed to your opponent. You would show a limited number of the range of possible moves, thus setting the pattern of your opponent's evaluation in his mind, then you would break out with something new to take him off guard. You can use *Alber* a few times, for example. This is the Fool's Guard, as it's called, where your point is in front of you and down; hardly a guard at all. Do this enough times to fool your opponent, but not too many, before taking the advantage away. Fundamentally, you are either on the attack or the defence, attacking with your stroke or defending against your opponent's, with the goal of breaking the rhythm of stroke and parry. And it is essential never to stand still; if you could not out-fence your opponent, you could keep him moving, thus wearing him down and waiting for a mistake.

It took great physical effort to keep up the continual dancing, from the toes to the balls of the feet, swivelling the ankles, bending the knees and sliding the hips. I congratulated myself on being much fitter than most, and with my buzzing practice was a lot better in the wind, so even though I was younger and smaller in stature I didn't lose too many contests. But the constant sparring took a tremendous toll on the wrist and forearm. I would return to my lodging with my whole hand and arm hot and aching, and all this with just a wooden blade. Eventually the sustained practice gave strength and suppleness, so when it came to metal weapons I knew I would be ready. I also tried switching from right hand to left—a huge advantage in a swordsman, and a great surprise tactic—but although I practiced long and hard I could never master the sinister. Our mother had always told us the left hand was the mark of Satan, so perhaps it was better so. Besides, there would be no use for this skill while on horseback, where all your tools are in the command of your right hand.

Wadegahte trained with us. He was a difficult opponent. His dislike of me lent strength to his attack and he used his superior height most effectively. In a real sword fight the easiest way to deal with a taller opponent is to go low, but you just don't do that in boffering, tempting though it may be. I've been in sword fights where I've taken a tall man quite out of the picture with a mighty boot in Adam's arsenal. (Mind you, that technique was nearly the death of me, as I will relate later on.) Much as I would have relished applying the boot, it might not have gone down well. So, in most of our bouts he counted more contacts than me, and went around crowing about it.

It was only much later, when I was obliged to defend myself in battle, that I discovered much of the courtly behaviour we were taught on the exercise floor went out with the slops. You did whatever you could to overcome someone who was intent on murdering you. Close contact, dirty moves, shoving, kicking, tripping, anything at all. There is no such thing as decorum when your life is on the line. This isn't some fancy dance with blades on a polished wooden floor; it's war.

The Duke's household cavalry consisted of a single squadron of two hundred and fifty horsemen. This was all the fighting men our Swedish 'liberators' allowed. The price to the Mecklenburg dukes of being freed from Wallenstein's rule was heavy. Swedish soldiers were garrisoned in all major towns, 'for the protection of the populace', and a so-called soldier tax was exacted for their upkeep. This was pure extortion because the punishment for failure to pay was harsh. And this in a time when yields from the farms were as low as they had ever been and the towns were crowded with refugees from the wasted countryside. Our little enclave in Schwerin with its dedicated cavalry, trumpet corps and fine deportment was an artificial island, a looking-glass to the *Schloss* in its lake, maintained out of the Duke's purse under sufferance from our Swedish 'guests'.

The household cavalry was commanded by Helmut Weitz, although at this stage in my training I saw almost nothing of him. He appeared fleetingly on horseback, an austere presence, ramrod straight, with fine curling moustaches and hair falling around his shoulders in the current style. He was always impeccably turned out and both expected and demanded that his high standards be reflected in the deportment and dress of the men under his command.

Horsemanship was an essential part of the trumpeter's training if he was to be more than just a jobbing player at court. It was a pity, I thought, that at this stage I still wasn't actually playing the damned thing. There was a great sand-floored exercise yard on one side of the

Schloss, and that's where I reported several times a week all through the summer. I would not be assigned a horse for myself until the successful end of my apprenticeship, but I did manage to persuade the stable-master to make sure I had the same mount for every session. He was a knowledgeable horseman, naturally, and when he found we spoke the same language, all was good. Because of his rank, I knew to approach him with deference, but it always pays to make friends of such people because the investment usually pays off. This thought came back to me some weeks later when I noticed my dear friend Joachim, with a face like thunder, seated upon the most unlikely of nags. He had clearly not endeared himself to the stablemaster and was being paid in his own coin. Nevertheless, his privileged officer position enabled him to avoid training with rest of us yokels.

Only when our instructor, *Rittmeister* Kulikovski, was fully satisfied with our progress would we ride with the seasoned men. Until then we were a ragbag group with varying levels of expertise. No matter what anyone may tell you, the horse is not an extremely intelligent animal. But if you had ridden horses for as long as I have, you would know that there is a special kind of communication between mount and rider, and it's all done with little bodily signals. So it wasn't long before my assigned horse knew me and what to expect of me, and from then on it was easy going.

At the beginning, though, it was different. As I had ridden horses since I was very small, I naturally thought I knew everything about it, but there were two rude awakenings when I went to put my foot to stirrup prior to swinging up into the saddle. There were no stirrups! We were obliged to practice without them for several sessions, all the better to school our poise. This wasn't as bad for me as it was for the other gentlemen who had probably never had to do this before. Me, I would leap on a horse bareback all the time; no groom around to saddle it up for me, and why bother if you're just going two fields away? The second rude awakening was the control of the horse with the snaffle and bridle. I had ridden all my life with two hands on the reins, but a cavalryman needs his right hand free for access to his toolkit. So both reins were held with the left hand, one above the other, signaling to the horse through turns of the wrist. There were also subtle signals through the knees and the rider's position on the saddle.

Schooling of horses for war is a brutal business. Conditions on the battlefield are like nothing a horse will experience anywhere else, and cavalry mounts have to be prepared for the worst. Already as year-lings they need to have been exposed to loud noises, terrible smells, and fire and smoke. The rotting carcasses of animals long dead are dragged into the practice ring, and bales of hay are set alight. Highly skilled riders then trot the horses between these stinking and blazing obstacles while blank-shotted guns are fired. By a process of elimination, the mounts that can be schooled to withstand these conditions are set aside for further training. Those that fail on repeated exposure become draft animals or are sold away for whatever purpose.

On that first day, I and the dozen or so other cavalrymen reporting with me, were instructed to take our horses at a walk under the beady eyes of *Rittmeister* Kulikovski, who was of the most acerbic kind. He was a Silesian, and although he had been in Schwerin for years his accent was heavy.

"You!" he screamed as soon as we had begun. "Ja, you wid de grey shirt!" All the rest were in livery; I stood out as the only apprentice among them. "You're sitting in de sattle like a sack of pig sheet! Straighten you back!"

I sat as upright as I could, as we were instructed to accelerate to a sitting trot, although it felt unnatural. I had always rolled with the horse, relishing its swinging motion under me. Now I needed to concentrate on poise, keep my neck straight, eyes ahead, and feel my legs accommodate to the motion.

"Upright! Upright! Imageen my sabre up your arze." And he pulled it ringing out of his scabbard and waved it at me. "You keep you back ramrod straight, you hear? One slump of you back and you can think of dis thing stirring you giblets!" All the others sniggered at this, but I felt a wave of anger. Christ, I thought, I've been on horseback since you lot were hawking up your mother's milk.

After a few weeks I could do anything asked of me on horseback.

Except play the trumpet.

Unlike all the others in the training ring, I was the only trumpeter in the group, and the other fellows hated that. We trumpeters were always treated badly by other court staff. At first I thought it was something about me, but later I came to realize that anyone in the *Kameradschaft* got the treatment. And quite honestly, we brought it on ourselves, us *Kameradschaft* members; we were a stuck-up, arrogant bunch of arsewipes when you think about it.

Hoftrompeter Breitkopf proved to be the only one who could coach and instruct me on the precarious business of playing the trumpet while riding, but this would have to wait until the *Rittmeister* considered my horsemanship up to scratch. I knew damned well how good my riding was, and I knew that if I were judged right now he would find no fault, but curtailing my training would be the last thing he would do. Nor would Breitkopf override him because the esprit of the cavalry was far more important than pushing for a trumpeter's privileges. I was in it until the end with the rest of them.

I could handle a gun, I could swing a sword, I could ride a horse, but my right arm ached for the reassuring heft of a trumpet.

Chapter Nine

In which I receive an urgent summons, make a quick journey home
and encounter mortality

*Des Bleibens ist ein Kleine seit, voller Mühseligkeit, und wers bedenkt ist
immer im Streit*
Life is short and filled with misery, and whoever thinks on this is
filled with woe

Johann Leon

Letters were delivered by the post to the main gate of the *Schloss* and
the keeper there would place those for the higher up folk in slots with
their names on paper labels. We lowest of the low would have to sort
through a pile tossed into a wicker basket on the floor. My father wrote
fairly frequently over the first few months of my apprenticeship,
passing along general news of the family and the farm. He always included love and wishes from mama, my sisters and my brothers. I
would reply by return post if I could, describing the goings-on in
Schwerin and the high points of my experience, but omitting the low
points when things had not met my expectations; when I was so home-
sick I would weep in my bed. His letters meant the world to me, so it
was with a little nagging worry that I noted their frequency dropping a
little.

A letter arrived in late September with my father's usual seal, but
when I popped it open I was surprised to see just a few lines from
Michael:

Dearest Jacob, father is unwell and asks for you to come to him.
Are you able to get time off to visit? It must be soon.
Your brother Michael

I sat down heavily on the bench in the gatehouse foyer while the
square of sunshine through the portal, the darkness of the interior, and
the hubbub of the world receded and dilated. A fist of income-
prehension squeezed my chest as the world pulsated. It was some time
before I even knew where I was.

"It must be soon."

The gatekeeper came out from behind his counter and looked
down at me in concern.

"Are you all right, son?" His hand on my shoulder brought me
back to the world.

"Yes, yes. Thank you."

"Bad news?" I know he was sympathetic—he had always been a kindly old buffer to us apprentices and servants—but at this moment I wanted none of his attention. I stood up, folded the letter, ran quickly upstairs to my master's office and knocked on his door.

"Come in." He looked up from his work. "Oh, no, you're not with me today. Check your schedule... Ah, what's wrong? Sit."

I held the letter towards him, unable to speak, and sat down quickly on a stool. He scanned the words speedily and frowned. "Clearly a very urgent summons." He put into words what I had not yet been able to admit to myself. "I think we'd better find a way... Hmm..."

The upshot was that by the next day my master had granted me leave for four days and had even assigned me a horse from the court stables, for which I was immensely grateful. I could not stay away any longer, he told me, for fear of upsetting my apprenticeship schedule and jeopardizing my career. I would have liked to argue my case—I feared what he had voiced, that the summons was urgent because death was approaching—but he was adamant on that issue, although I didn't think badly of him because of it.

I had little to take with me; some food that a sympathetic Frau Walther had given me, a few papers I considered important, a little loose money and not much else. Having had almost no sleep, and what I did have haunted by dreams, I set off on a rainy, overcast morning and headed east. I really did try to spare the horse, but I knew I was setting a damaging pace. It was a horrible journey and it seemed as if the elements had ganged up on me to make my road even more miserable. I reined up at the house late in the evening, soaking wet and muddy, and ran straight in. They had heard me ride up, but they were mighty surprised to see this young, self-assured-looking fellow swing down from the saddle. I felt far from self-assured as I ran into my mother's arms while my sisters clung to me. Not yet six months and so much had changed. Was it my imagination or had mama shrunk in size and stature, and had her hair been as grey as this? And Annamaria was taller, I was sure, and more womanly. Michael and Hans came forward to shake my hands and pull me into a hug, and it was only then that I missed Jürgen. I assumed he was still out in the fields. Father was my main concern.

"Where is he?"

Mama led me upstairs while the others hung back. My father was in bed with his eyes closed, covered with a thick blanket even though the room was over-warm. If I thought my mother had diminished, the sight of my father was shocking. That great big hale, hearty man with the huge presence and full voice was a shrunken shell. I could not believe what I was seeing. He opened his eyes and a smile found its way to his face. He lifted his hand and beckoned me over. I sat carefully on the side of the bed, afraid to jar or shake him, whereupon he took my hand and gave it a gentle squeeze.

"Knew he'd let you come," he whispered. "That Breitkopf... knew he was a good man."

I looked into his eyes, my lip trembling, not knowing what to say. That big grown fellow who had ridden his horse these thirty miles was reduced to a little child.

"What's wrong?" I eventually managed to say. "What's wrong?"

He pointed weakly to his side but it seemed he couldn't speak. Mama spoke for him.

"It's a growth. In his side, just below the ribs. The physician, Herr Löwe from Rostock, is doing what he can. He's given him a tincture of poppy for the pain, and he's tried to sweal it away with hot poultices of herbs and *Kieselghur*, but nothing seems to work."

A little of father's energy seemed to return. "My father, and his father before him... Same thing. Seems to pass... down the generations... So... glad you came."

I sat there dumbly not knowing what to say. I wanted to cry, to yell in anger, to stamp in rage, to break something, but none of those things came out. Just this miserable nodding child holding a cold blue hand. Soon he fell into a sort of sleep and began to snore, labouring for each ragged breath. We quietly left the room and returned downstairs.

I stood with them in the kitchen with no words between us. Poor Clara was in tears, sitting on the bench with Annamaria's arms around her and mama on the other side, while Hans and Michael stood almost as if in indecision.

"How long does he have?" I asked, knowing the answer would be unbearable.

"Herr Doktor Löwe says it may be a week," my mother replied, "or perhaps sooner."

"We have called upon the pastor," said Hans, "and he is ready to come at a moment's notice to apply unction and give absolution."

We made a numb tableau while the wind pushed the shutters, the rain pattered and the candle flames swung this way and that.

"Where's Jürgen?" I asked into the silence.

"He's left," said Michael. "Gone to join the army, fight with the Swedes against the stinking Papists."

There were armies of mercenaries, I had heard, marching under the Swedish banner, rampaging to the south of us.

"They took him?"

"No. Didn't need to. He enlisted."

"Enlisted! Why, in God's name? Why?"

There was a silence in which all eyes went to Hans, tacitly acknowledging him spokesman for the family. "Same reason you did, Jacob. Call it a higher cause, if you like."

"But I'm apprenticed to be a trumpeter. Surely, that's a completely different thing."

"Not in his eyes. Not in ours. You're both soldiers. And you're both in harm's way."

"But there's a place for him here! Here on the farm."

Their expressions said otherwise.

Hans sighed mightily, shaking his head slowly from side to side. "There's nothing for him here. The farm's practically in ruins, almost all our labourers have been enlisted—stolen, more like—so what is there? What is there for any of us?" he asked into a silence.

I was lost. I didn't know what to do or say. Papa going, the farm going, the lovingest of my brothers fighting God knew where. I stood there, in that familiar kitchen with the familiar faces around me, and felt myself adrift. My whole world was turning upside down, or even perhaps inside out. This house, this home was where my soul returned; here, in this solid, reliable place that ought never to change. The court at Schwerin and my little garret were temporary places away; they had none of the firm reliability of my birthplace and my heart's foundation. But now home in all its comfort and welcome and permanence was whipped out from under me.

I sat heavily on the nearest stool. "But... I thought all was going well here. I thought..." I didn't know what I thought anymore.

"We all concealed the truth from you young ones," said Hans. "Father thought it wisest. I don't know if it was so wise in the end."

"So, what now?" A hopeless question, asked of a hopeless boy.

"We carry on, of course!" Michael spoke up. "We've had this land for generations, and we'll have it for generations more. This stupid war *must* end soon. Better times will come. They must come!"

Hans shook his head slowly. "We can just hope you are right. I'm sorry, Jacob, that I sounded so hopeless, but..."

"But we go on!" Mama interrupted. "Michael is right. There is no other way." She rose from the bench, came over and wrapped her arms tightly around me. "Go with our blessing, my dear Jacob. Go and fight and win. Think of Jürgen, and go and fight and win."

My father died in October of 1638, just five days after my return to Schwerin. When the letter from Michael arrived, telling me the sad but inevitable news, I recall an unreality, a disbelief, which only slowly came around to acceptance. This episode in my life is not clear. Maybe I have willfully forgotten a great deal of it, or perhaps even now I really don't wish to recall it. Either way, it adds precious little to my story. I see the funeral now through a thick mist. Once I had returned again to Schwerin the situation at home became an unreal phantasm. I could push it away for a time, but it would come back and catch me with a clutch of the heart. I couldn't reconcile my present life, so filled with hard work, complexity and new experience, with the old world that was so forlorn and bereft.

Soon that old world would be swept away…

Chapter Ten

In which I finally blow a trumpet, learn more of the trumpeter's craft, and play at court

Una debole Opera, quantunque a me faticosa, nella quale tratto l'arte della Tromba da i suoi rimi principi, fino a quella perfezzione estrema, che fino a'tempi nostri è venuta
[This is] a little work, though quite laborious for me, in which I discuss the art of trumpet playing from its rudiments to that extreme perfection that has been reached in our times
Girolamo Fantini

Home life on the farm and court life in Schwerin became distinct in a way they never had been before. With the death of my father I think I shifted my paternal allegiance to *Hoftrompeter* Hartmund Breitkopf, not by any means as a father figure, but rather as the adult male who ordered my life. Letters still came from Michael, although with nowhere near the frequency they had in papa's day, and slowly I felt I was growing out and away. This is not to say my heart wasn't torn frequently by thoughts of my family's predicament, but in some way they were encased and preserved in another place. I had seen beads of amber found along the coast of the Ostsee with insects frozen in their depths since the Flood, and I somehow came to see my other life in a similar way. It was really only in my bed at night that these thoughts came, because during the days and months that followed I was kept enormously busy and highly stimulated.

Especially when I was finally permitted to play a trumpet.

I had gone quickly from my lodgings to the *Schloss* on the wonderful day when I blew a trumpet for the first time in the Duke's service. I remember it well because the weather had turned cool and I had put my cape across my shoulders, which I hadn't done since the spring. My schedule of the week showed a session with my master on Monday morning. I entered the trumpeters' domain, crossed to his cubicle and knocked on the flimsy door.

"Enter!" My master was sprawled behind his overflowing desk. I stood to attention while he eyed me up and down in a speculative way that was a little disturbing. I felt like a specimen.

"Tell me, Hintze, why are you here?"

"Here…?" I was at a loss; I wondered if he meant here in this office, here at the court of the Duke in Schwerin, or even here breathing the air of God's creation.

"Why are you here, apprenticed to me for two years, half a year almost gone already?"

"Because... because I want to be a trumpeter."

"So that's it? In a year and a half from now you'll be a trumpeter in the court of Duke Adolf Friedrich of Mecklenburg-Schwerin, all dressed in fine courtly clothes and blowing away with the rest of them? Is that your ambition?"

"It's what I have dreamed about for years," I ventured, and then feeling a little nettled I added, "Not a bad ambition for the fourth son of a small landholder. Sir." I couldn't bear to say farmer.

He sighed in exasperation, picked up a sheaf of music notes and shoved them across the desk to me. "Look at this six-part piece. The parts are actually written out, instead of just the single *Principal* line." This perplexed me at the time, and I was only to find out what he meant later. "Typical stuff. Good workman-like piece by Nicolaus Hasse. New man, young organist from Rostock.[16] The bottom parts, *Grob* and *Flattergrob*, you don't even read the music. If I gave you a great big mouthpiece you could play them right now; you have the chops. Not yet fifteen years old and, damn it, you could play along by ear. Wouldn't even need the music. Right?"

I looked over the familiar low Gs and Cs. "Yes, I think I probably could."

"Yup. No probably about it. You'd just thump away at two or three notes for your entire working life. That's it; life's over at fifteen." He flung his hands wide in a gesture of dismissal.

"And perhaps go to war?" I really couldn't get what he was driving at.

"Ah, yes, charging around the battlefield, playing your calls—by ear, I should point out—all heroic and splendid. You could do that right now, as well."

I nodded, really not sure what words he expected me to say.

"Jacob Hintze," he sighed, slapping the papers, "this is the stuff you'd be expected to play at court. Damn it man, you could play it top to bottom in your sleep! Is it enough for you?"

"I would be satisfied..."

"Well, I wouldn't be!" he yelled suddenly. "I wouldn't be! You see, I don't take on just anybody as my apprentice. True, there are some members of the *Kameradschaft* who take on apprentices with, let's say, a limited capacity. Yes, we can box their ears until they do as they're told. We always need *Feldtrompeter* for the battlefield, but I happen to aim higher. And you would be very wise to agree with me."

"Higher where...?" I was mystified.

"Higher where, *sir!* Sit!" he commanded me. He turned from his desk and pulled some folios and books off the shelves behind him. "It's time to expand your education. Look at this." The music folio he laid out and swivelled around for me was a choral piece, *Jubilate Deo*. "This is Michael Praetorius, published, what?... less than twenty years ago. See here," he flipped to the introductory page, "where he specifies that the trumpets and kettledrums are to play elsewhere in the church."[17]

"Not with the choir, of course," I ventured. "We... I mean the players of the *Kameradschaft...*" I stuttered at my presumption, "...are quite separate."

"Exactly. Not with the choir. Explicit. The music stops, we play, the music starts again. This is the traditional separation of roles. Now look at this."

The next music folder was *Jubilate in Neomania* written by Heinrich Schütz.[18] "Look here: a trumpet line integrated with strings, cornetto and voice. Published just recently. Herr Vierdanck studied with him, you know. Perhaps he'll write something like this?"

I followed the lines with my eyes. The trumpet part was high and intricate, a great deal of it in the fourth octave, but I was sure I could get my chops around it, although not well. Ah, those tricky odd numbers! But this was a revelation!

Then the *Hoftrompeter* pulled a single sheet of paper out of a folder... and I thought I would faint with fear. It was the very sheet of music that Herr Pinklemann had lent me, and which I had so laboriously copied! How did he get it? Did he know about Pinklemann, then? Impossible.

"Here's Bendinelli." He smiled at my confusion. "You've come across him, of course. This is your piece from *Tutta l'arte della Trombetta*."[19]

"I had... but... Herr Pink..." and then I stopped, heart beating and in a cold sweat, realizing I had put my foot right in it. Miraculously, he waved it off.

"Yes, him. There's a story there, but that's for another time." He picked up a book while I recovered my composure. "Now, here's Fantini, printed this very year. Two Italian trumpeters who have brought the art of trumpet playing to such a high level that church musicians are taking notice. Imagine the future! *Kapellmeisters* bringing the trumpet in among the other musicians, and making it an integral part of their works!"[20]

As my heart pitter-pattered back to normal I wondered, as I had wondered before, about our relationship. He was my master and I was absolutely his servant, and in the military world respect for order and station are vital to smooth working. Yet here was the same master, an austere and unreadable man, quite transformed by his enthusiasm. I saw a human side in the glitter of his eyes and wondered again who he really was when he wasn't with me. Or when he wasn't being a soldier.

"And it's happening right now!" He slapped the books. "Right now! The trumpet is truly the instrument of God, and now we—the trumpeters!—can celebrate His majesty in the music of His holy church."

"Both Italians…" I mused.

"Yes. And Catholics, of course. Our musicians, painters, architects all look south. Catholic, Lutheran, it's all the same to us. But it takes time for innovation to cross the Alps."

"Alps?" I asked, again feeling like a bumpkin. "I have heard of the Alps. But where are they?"

He looked quizzically at me. "You really are raw clay, aren't you? The Alps are a vast range of snow-covered mountains that divide the north from the south. Over those mountains comes creative expression, but it comes slowly."

I looked over the Schütz piece again. "I would love to play this…"

"And you will, or stuff like it. With the talent you have, and the time I'll spend on you, you will. You'll become a good trumpeter, but you *can* become a musician."

"I am flattered, sir, that you consider me worthy…"

"Horseshit!" he interrupted. "Why did you think I took you on?"

He saw pride growing in my raised chin and faraway look as I contemplated the future.

"And don't get any fancy ideas above your station. You remember who you are, or I'll have you back on your hands and knees scrubbing shit off the kitchen floor."

He dismissed me with a wave, but just as I was leaving he stopped me. "Look. Report here at the tenth hour today. We'll put a trumpet on your face."

I went through the rest of that day in a daze, waiting for the late afternoon bell—there were chores of all kinds, some lessons, I don't remember what—before reporting as instructed. My master led me over to the racks of instruments in the outer room and lifted a trumpet off its vertical wooden dowel.

"This'll be your instrument, so make sure to ink your initials just here…" he indicated the projecting end of the wood block, bound with blue cord between the mouthpipe and bell, "…and guard it carefully. It's the property of the Duke, as are you, so it must be kept at all times spotless and in good repair. To judge by the state of the instrument you came with, you know precious little about care and attention. That will be rectified."

It was a curious instrument to my eyes, unusually wide in the bell and considerably heavier than the Droschel, which was the only trumpet I had ever known. I took my mouthpiece out of my scrip unbidden and buzzed on it for a short while to get my embouchure in shape. With the *Hoftrompeter* eyeing me with that half smile of his, I plugged the mouthpiece in and played joyously. It was bad, it was horrible, it was out of tune, but it was glorious beyond description. I played scales and a few familiar pieces, trying to get the measure of the instrument. It was early yet to begin getting at all familiar with this trumpet, but its strangeness persisted. After a little longer Breitkopf waved me down.

"Different, eh? But you tell me."

"I can't reconcile the upper and lower registers, sir. It's either flat in the low G, C and E, or sharp above the C on the staff."

"Right. No trumpet part crosses between the two, so whether you're playing low parts or high parts, you tune accordingly. A trumpet in tune across the whole gamut is a rarity, as is the player who can correct for it."

"But, sir," I replied, "the old Droschel I had was pretty good…"

"That's as maybe," he cut in with some sharpness, "but this is what we use here! Play some more."

It was a loud, bullish sort of instrument, perfect for the battlefield and for fanfares in court, but it lacked a certain refinement and subtlety. Engraved around the narrow bell garland was:

JAN SANDER IN HANNOVER 1623

So this was clearly the northern style preferred here. But perhaps my memory is playing me tricks; perhaps I was not nearly as sophisticated as I am making myself out to be. After all, I was only fifteen years old at the time, and hardly experienced. Nevertheless, although I got used to that trumpet, and others like it that I took with me to the battlefield, I could never be truly comfortable.

It was clear from the *Hoftrompeter's* snappiness that my likes or dislikes in instruments had touched a nerve. I remembered his words about the Droschel on the day my father had delivered me into his care, so it was obvious that metalwork made by southern Catholics was clearly not to his fancy.

After a number of joyful scales and improvisations he stopped me again.

"Well, your tonguing, what there is of it, is all to hell. We've got

our work cut out there for sure. I won't even talk about your trills…"
He sighed.

"I haven't had the opportunity…"

"Don't worry! You'll get it," he said. "Now, as to your tuning; you
have a wonderful ear… no, stop bobbing and thank-you-sir-ing, God
damn it… but you need to refine your lip to complement your ear.
Listen."

He took his own instrument off the peg, popped his mouthpiece
in, and without the hint of a warm-up played the lower notes G, C, E
and G, and then played the ones above the B-flat, C, D, E, F and G in
tune with the lower ones. You have to hear it done to know how
impressive this is.

I played far past the allotted hour with my master's eyes and ears
upon me the whole time, and with many stops for correction and
demonstration. It was like release from a dungeon or having fetters
struck from my soul. It also taught me how much I still needed to
learn, but instead of finding this daunting, I reveled in the delight I
would encounter on the road ahead. I was then given a stern exercise
in care and preservation, which included emptying out the accumulated water from my breath by tipping the trumpet down by the bell
and then down by the mouthpiece receiver. I was issued with a cleaning
cloth, spare cords and wire, and a little bag of rottenstone powder, a
mild polish, traces of which had to be removed scrupulously upon pain
of censure.

"Now, before you leave for your lodging," said Breitkopf, "bear
this in mind: the best way to teach your lip is to play with another
instrumentalist. I'll see what I can do, but the court musicians here are
not all that friendly to such ideas. Not hostile; just a little cool. Off you
go!"

I hove back to Frau Walther's in a joyous mood, which continued
through the evening as Berthold and Heinrich and I consumed more
beer than was good for us, and roared with laughter about God knew
what.

It was a day or so later that I approached Berthold with my idea. If
the best way to practice my tuning would be to play with another instrument, it occurred to me that Berthold and his violin would be ideal for
this, and he might even appreciate the practice himself. I got permission—somewhat reluctantly given—to take my trumpet back to the
lodging house. When I explained to my master what I was trying to do
he took me aside for some much-needed musical advice. He led me to
a cupboard in the trumpet room.

"Here, take these." He handed me two coils of brass tubing, their
ends tapered to fit the trumpet and the mouthpiece. "The length of

your trumpet dictates the key you play in, of course. This one's a pigtail," he told me, holding up the smaller one. "It lowers your instrument to C. And this longer one gives you B-flat. You could go lower but it quickly gets precarious."

I plugged the C crook into my trumpet, inserted the mouthpiece and played the notes of that scale. I did the same thing with the B-flat. It was strange how the simple insertion of pieces of tubing could so alter the character and feel of the instrument.

"Now, with these you've got three keys you can play in. But if you can't find anything in either of those three, your fiddle player will need to transpose." He reached up to a bookshelf, brought down an old folio and blew off some dust. He opened the pages and spread them out on the table. "Some *Bicinia* from Andreas Bevernage, sixteen-twelve. You won't find many copies of this around. Here we are; look at this line here." His finger traced the top line of a duet and I followed it with my eye. "See, it's all good at the top, but down here you won't get that A. Could play a G but it might get ugly. You could always leave it out."

I traced the line of music, running through it in my head, and thought, yes, I think I could handle this. My musical understanding was expanding rapidly, perhaps too rapidly.

"Try it right now," he told me. "Crook in C."

I read the line once again, inserted the pigtail crook, put the trumpet to my lips and played the first four bars. It was bad but I could see how this might be possible. My master smiled, apparently not too dismayed at the mess I was making.

"Now this." He opened up another folio. "This piece is in F major, so with your trumpet pitched in D you could play the top part if you play a fifth up. You start on C instead of F at the bottom of the staff, d'ye see?" I nodded, trying to follow his thinking and not doing a great job of it. "Then your friend would have to play down two steps and start on a D instead of F. Right?"

Breitkopf noted my puzzled face. "Too much too soon. Of course. Try the first one, get a feel for it and work up. Report back to me in a week."

I saluted him and turned for the door, but as I was about to leave he did one of his characteristic afterthoughts and called me back.

"Your friend; is the violin his?"

"Well, he carries it everywhere with him, sir, so I suppose it is."

"Tell him not to talk about this, especially to the *Kapellmeister*."

"Why not, sir?" This didn't accord at all with my view of Herr Vierdanck. "If I may ask?"

"We're very old fashioned here. There's friction between us and the chapel. It's best not to do things that might make... certain people... entrench their positions even deeper. Also, the court musicians will give your friend shit if they find out, regardless of whether their boss knows or not. So, just between yourselves, right?"

I was confused. "I... I'm sorry to ask, sir, but Herr Vierdanck was very welcoming when assessing my singing for the chapel choir."

"Of course! It's trumpets and the *Kameradschaft* where he draws the line. If you can sing he'll recruit you from the latrines. Dismissed!"

It is hard to describe what it's like to play music with another person. I had sung in church since an early age, but playing an instrument with another musician was a level of togetherness much greater than that. I wondered what the reaction in the rest of the house might be to the disturbance, but I need not have worried. What began as impromptu practice sessions at the top of the house in Berthold's room or mine, made a segue into entertainment. Frau Walther invited us downstairs where she, other lodgers and even Giselle, would sit around in the kitchen, listen to us, and applaud mightily. Berthold and I did wonder whatever our rooming house audience made of all this fancy music, but their appreciation was certainly genuine.

My master located even more music, mostly Italian, and I got a sense that he was happy I had taken this private initiative. It relieved him of the political issue of trumpets versus the other instruments, and the potential result of too much fraternizing. As I look back on it now, I realize how lucky I was to be so well positioned at such a turning point in our craft.

There was an essentially practical side to playing the trumpet in the cavalry, and my master was very careful to see that I didn't get too involved in 'art music'. I was apprenticed as a soldier and cavalryman, and this was the basis of my training; I would be a field trumpeter first and foremost, and that must be my role as long as the war lasted. Breitkopf has spotted my musical talent, and while he encouraged it in what amounted to my 'spare time'—if an apprentice ever had such a commodity—this was kept clearly outside of 'work'. I had been playing military music since I first picked up a trumpet, and that is what we concentrated on. Those pieces that Herr Pinklemann had laboriously copied out from the 'Danish book' were some of many, but I had not heard of Magnus Thomsen or Heinrich Lübeck at that time. They had written copious work sheets years ago for the trumpet corps at the court of Christian IV in Köbenhavn, and I found the compilation we used at the court in Schwerin was quite similar in scope.

When my master had said, regarding the piece by Nicolaus Hasse, that the parts had been written out instead of just the *Principal* line, I had been confused. Now it became clear; all those pieces I had played from Herr Pinklemann's transcripts were actually just the *Principal* parts of full ensemble pieces. All we had in our workbook was the middle line; all the rest were improvised. Why bother writing all the parts out when it was unnecessary, and when the players likely couldn't read music anyway? For the lower parts improvisation was comparatively easy. As my master had said, right now I could just thump away at two or three notes for my entire working life. The *Clarino* would be a whole order of magnitude harder.

Then there was our meat and potatoes, the cavalry calls. There were dozens of these and they all had to be confined to memory. I spent hours over the workbook playing *Buttasella, Walk, Trab, Kanter, Galopp, Links abbiegen, Rechts abbiegen, Halt* and many more, over and over again. It was soul destroying from a musical standpoint, but absolutely critical in the military context. Show me any musician in any court ensemble in the world whose colleagues face death if he plays a wrong note!

It wasn't too long before my weekly schedule showed slots for practice on horseback. My master had set aside one-on-one sessions where we would meet in the ring and he would ride alongside me, shouting instructions or insults as my behaviour warranted. It is a strange cavalry custom that while on horseback, instructors and colleagues alike can be as abusive as they wish, while the target must school himself to ignore the larger part of it yet heed the advice. So I began to play those calls that I had drummed into my head, and some of which had been with me since the age of ten, but now from the saddle.

It looked so easy...

Well, it was easy to hold the mouthpiece to my lips at the walk, especially when I learned the art of keeping my body upright and allowing my legs and pressure in the stirrups to maintain my poise. Those exercises without stirrups I had done earlier really paid off now. But it surprised me that at the trot, playing the instrument was almost impossible, while at the canter it actually became easier again. The trot is a very jerky, up-and-down sort of pace where your upper thighs are working and the saddle is coming up to meet your bum. You can push down on the stirrups, then allow the saddle to come up and meet you, but it's hard to keep the motion even enough to be sure the mouthpiece will stay where you want it. Besides, we never used the trot in cavalry drills and formations because it looked so sloppy. But you could sound a signal on the trot if you had to by standing up in the stirrups and letting your knees and thighs smooth out the ride, though it wasn't easy.

At the canter, playing calls is altogether smoother and although your legs do a lot of hard work, it's less trouble to keep your body level enough to play. Playing the trumpet at the gallop will always be impossible. Nothing good will ever come of it, and some dangerous misinterpretations of signals could result. The general rule, it seemed, was that when a signal was to be sounded, the rider would rein up if possible, make the call, and then proceed as before. I eventually discovered that in battle conditions the rule book was so much waste paper.

One added complication, which never occurred to me until I was actually on horseback with my trumpet, was the banner carrying the device of the dukes of Mecklenburg-Schwerin. It was attached to rings on the bows of the instrument and was a heavy damned thing, thickly embroidered onto a woven backing, and banging about in the slightest breeze. Yet another skill to be wrestled down and mastered.

Much later on, during the Duke's horse ballets—which, like everything French, became more and more popular after the Peace—we would be required to play while on the move. It seemed that the better composers were aware of our difficulties and would score for pieces to be played either at the walk or the canter. In my later life I have gained a great respect for such composers as the Austrian Johann Heinrich Schmeltzer, who clearly had our capabilities in mind. Even so, no matter how well rehearsed we were, the musical result was never as satisfying, not that it mattered much because the entire spectacle, including the firing of guns, brought the music into a subservient role.

Near the close of the year there was one of those days that have stayed in my mind forever. I reported as usual to *Hoftrompeter* Breitkopf. He was standing behind his desk, always an ominous sign, and his face was creased in stern lines.

"We have a serious problem, Hintze," he began. At once I began to worry that in some way this almost mythical existence of mine was in jeopardy, and that it would all come to an abrupt end. He had this almost cruel way of playing with my state of mind. I had noticed it first when he had told the Duke "Not good" at my audition, then stretched the tension out before finally reporting "Damned good." It obviously amused him to do this, but it played hell with my heart.

"There has been a sudden illness among the trumpeters," he said, still ominous. "Three down with a flux and a fever. Two of them, Hermann and Jiri, play the lowest parts. And tomorrow evening we have to play a new piece in six parts before the Duke and his honoured guests from Hamburg and Lübeck."

I wondered why he was telling me this, unless he was warning me against contamination, except that I had not been anywhere near any of them. But then I thought... music in *six* parts? My mystification began to dissipate with a slight rise in his lips. The bastard was playing with me! The face broke into a smile and a light suddenly shone on me.

"Yes, any other piece in the repertoire and we could manage short-staffed, but not this one. Can't play the lowest part on one instrument. Report to the wardrobe to borrow livery and be here at the third hour tomorrow."

"Yes, sir!" I cried. "Yes, sir!"

"All right, all right," he waved, and as I turned to leave. "And don't forget your bloody mouthpiece!"

It was huge pleasure to visit again that long room fitted with shelves along either side, and to meet again the same tailor as he disdainfully selected for me a suit of livery. Once again I removed my clothes, but this time donned such finery as I could only have imagined: a loose-sleeved white shirt with tight cuffs, a doublet embroidered with the Duke's device, drawers of fine blue wool, hose to match, and high soft boots. I could only imagine how fine I must look, and how pleased papa would be when I told... A stab of anguish passed through me; this was not the first time I had been caught this way. Curiously, though, these lapses gave me some solace because I felt that in some way he must still be present. Why otherwise would my heart do this?

"Now, remember," the tailor wagged a finger at me, "as soon as you're done you bring this stuff back. It's not yours for a long time yet. Remember, you're not even a field trumpeter, and even when you get there, that's all you'll be as long as the war lasts."

When I appeared in the trumpet room at the time ordered, all dressed in my borrowed finery and trumpet in hand, I was greeted with raucous laughter from the throats of a dozen men. All were dressed in their stand-down clothes, as I had seen them when they rehearsed; I was the only one dressed for court! Scarlet with shame I sidled in at the door. An extremely tall gentleman, one of the *Clarino* players who I had identified before as either Friedemann or Albrecht, came forward still smiling, banged me on the back, and drew me forward by my arm.

"Don't you mind this lot, my son," he laughed. "Working for a bastard like Hartmund Breitkopf, they need all the laughs they can get. Stand over here."

The rest of the crew laughed louder, then my master waved them to silence and we got down to business. I was assigned to the lowest, easiest part of the piece, needing only two notes, the G and the C, but unlike the other man playing that part I was allowed a sheet of music to follow. One repetition and I knew the written music would be unnecessary. My master was right; I could play this stuff in my sleep, although I knew it would be a colossal error to let anyone know that. Massed trumpet music has the advantage that talent can be under-played in a wall of sound, so I passed unnoticed. I cannot describe how wonderful it was to be practicing with the *Kameradschaft*, and my inexperience, my inappropriate clothing, my youth, my lowly status became nothing.

Then, to march in the company of eleven other trumpeters into the great hall, which I had last seen on that day so long ago when I was grilled by the Duke, was utterly fantastical. To play before the Duke and his court and guests was beyond any dreams. I remember being so nervous before our entry that my bowels almost betrayed me. I had clenched my arse cheeks as tightly as I could, imagining the humiliation of a catastrophic explosion in the middle of the music. Oh, my borrow-ed livery! However, as soon as we assembled and prepared to play, all indisposition melted away and I played as if possessed. Indeed, I was possessed; I was in a place that existed only in my most fantastic dreams.

You always crash to earth. That is the lot of people made of clay. As I took off my finery in the changing room of the trumpeters' domain I realized that I had been offered just a small window into the life I coveted, but a year and more of hard work would be needed before I could even think of being there again.

Chapter Eleven

In which there is an incident with a pot of ale and I am obliged to disappear

Wein ist ein Spötter, und starkes Getränk ein Zänker, und wer wird die Irre geführt, indem es nicht klug ist
Wine is a mocker, strong drink is raging: and whosoever is deceived thereby is not wise
Sprueche/Proverbs 20:10

It was in the spring of 1639 and I had been apprenticed for nearly a year. I was now playing the trumpet extremely well and still glowed at the honour of donning the Duke's livery on that one occasion, playing with the members of the *Kameradschaft* at court. In my bed at night, I would play over that wonderful experience, hearing every note of the ensemble and seeing again every colour in those sounds and sights behind the eyes in the moments before sleep. It didn't matter that I had been one of a dozen and playing the lowest notes of the gamut. I had been there!

In addition to my increasing skill on the instrument, I was learning the whole multifaceted craft of being a successful military man in a ducal court. My swordsmanship was still at the wooden blades stage, but I was developing quick reflexes and good positional play. While I wasn't as strong as some of the trainees, and a good year or two younger than most, I could hold my own with confidence. Horsemanship I had taken to as second nature, of course, and there was little I needed to be taught, but some things I had been obliged to unlearn. I had found the work with pistols less satisfying; they were ugly, clumsy things and I imagined that the chances of defending myself with one were pretty slim.

A year into my apprenticeship I was conversing well with Herr Doktor Martius in Italian and French, but rather struggling with English. This was, I think, because the good Doktor was not as fluent in that tongue as in the Romance languages, but I knew that were I to sit and talk with an Englishman I would soon pick up the nuances that make that language such a trial for us foreigners. In my precious time off I would go to the market on the special days when tradesmen come from far and wide, and try to engage them in conversation. This was not a completely successful strategy as visitors to our area of the world included Danes, Swedes, Pomeranians and Finns, and I was reluctant to burden my poor head with too many more foreign tongues. I longed to find an Englishman, but even though they were both our allies and our religious brethren, not many came to Schwerin. I often thought how much better it would have been to be in a port city like Rostock or Wismar. Had I known, it wouldn't be long before the English tongue was thrust in my face.

During this busy time of my life I often felt the unreality of all the experience that was pouring into me. It was an unreality on a personal level, true, but it was reflected in a much larger unreality. All my descriptions of the wonders of the court of Adolf Friedrich, Duke of Mecklenburg-Schwerin, and my small but wonderful part in it, paint a false picture of the true state of the duchy. The *Schloss* and its surroundings were, in truth, an artificial and protected island in a sea of terror, destruction and wastage. It was the same with most of the larger cities, especially those where a court resided. Around them the war raged on, while they pulled their petticoats up around themselves, withdrawing more and more from the reality outside their walls. The festivity, the opulence, the luxury were all enjoyed with a frantic, feverish gaiety. Eventually, as in the case of Brandenburg, warfare overtakes them, and they fall. Berlin had been what Schwerin was now, and I am sure that many in our population knew they were on borrowed time and were spending their happiness while they could. The Catholic incursions to the south in Saxony could not go unanswered, so it was inevitable that Mecklenburg-Schwerin would become even more embroiled. We would be sending more than just foot soldiers.

Life at the boarding house would have been pleasant if it was just the companionship of Berthold and Heinrich, but there was Joachim to contend with. Mercifully, he seemed to spend a great deal of time elsewhere and only graced us with his presence at odd intervals during mealtimes. When he did appear, I was the target of whatever criticisms he could bring to bear, and it saddened me that my two friends didn't come to my defence with more energy. I don't know what power he held over them, but just being at the table altered everyone seated there. On those occasions I would eat as quickly as possible and scuttle back upstairs to study. He accosted me one day when I was already in a foul mood. It had been a tough day; I had suffered the humiliating chore of mucking out the stables all afternoon, so I had stopped off at an inn nearby to drink to my woes. I had a little more beer than I was accustomed to—far too much if the truth be known—but if anything it just made things seem worse. I entered the lodging and took my place at the table, and there he was, already halfway through his stew. Frau Walther passed me a bowl, and then handed me a large beaker of ale. Once again, I was condemned to eat my entire meal quickly to escape Joachim's overbearing presence.

"What's that?" he announced to the table at large, sniffing loudly. "What do you say fellows? What's that smell?" They looked down into their bowls. He sniffed again. "I know what it is! It's pig shit, that's what it is. Isn't that so, farm boy?"

It takes a lot to push me, but the beer was doing the driving. I lashed out. It was a waste of good ale, but there was both horror at what I had done, and great satisfaction as well, in seeing his shock as the whole pint pot shot stingingly into his face. He leapt up coughing and spluttering, dashing the foam out of his eyes, and I think he would have come at me with his fists if the other two lads hadn't, quite uncharacteristically, seized his arms and held him back.

"You'll pay for this!" he raged. "By Christ I'll make you pay for this!"

"Hey, hey, hey!" shrieked Frau Walther, turning from the stove with a wooden spoon in her hand. "Get out! Get out! Both of you. We'll have no horseplay in this establishment! Out!"

Bert and Heinrich released Joachim and he stormed out of the room. Once he was out of their sight the boys clapped me on the back, all smiles, and tried to shake my hands. I shrugged them off, closer to tears than I would let on, and went up to my room. Not much studying got done that night as, with head spinning, I worried over the repercussions. His father was influential in court circles, and I didn't doubt the coward would go crying to papa.

It wasn't long before the summons came. A meeting with my master was not on the schedule for the following day, but a flunky came to me in the stable where I was cleaning saddlery, and told me to report. The *Hoftrompeter* was standing behind his desk, rather than sprawled as usual, his rigid stance a harbinger of trouble.

"What the hell's all this with a pot of ale?" he demanded as soon as I came through the door. "Remember the Rules?" he barked. "Recite the relevant section to me *right now!*"

One of my first tasks had been to hammer the *Ordnung* into my memory. "An apprentice will not behave in an unseemly manner to his fellow apprentices, he will not engage in roughhousing or bring his station or the station of his calling into disrepute by any..."

"Yes, yes! Of course you know the bloody rules! And there are specifications for punishment laid out there as well, are there not?"

"Yes, sir."

"Then what in the bowels of Christ were you thinking? Have you no idea how influential at court the Wadegahte name is?"

He was as angry as I had ever seen him, and I should have been quaking in fear, but I felt a stiffening and a pride that was quite new to me. I was damned if I would make excuses for myself or apologize.

"With all due respect sir, he deserved every drop of it. He has repeatedly provoked me and now he knows there are limits to what I will tolerate. But I will accept punishment for my behaviour as you see fit."

"Of course you'll accept whatever punishment I dish out, God damn you! But don't you dare even *think* of doing anything like that again!"

"But, sir…"

"Shut up before I change my mind about you!" He glowered at me for an uncomfortable, squirming period, then his expression changed to one almost of resignation. "And now we're in a hell of a mess."

"Sir?" The 'we' filled my heart with an unaccountable optimism.

"Your punishment, as far as Heinrich Wadegahte is concerned, is to send you packing back home. Done! Finished!"

My heart withered in my chest and I felt a wave of weakness and unreality. The optimism of a few heartbeats before dissolved. I gripped the back of a chair, and he saw the fear pass over my face. He shook his head slowly from side to side.

"Not so fast. I haven't apprenticed you as a trumpeter just to piss it all away over a pot of ale. Once you've achieved status in the *Kamerad-schaft*—and by Christ you had better or I'll kill you!—you'll see that we hang together."

I felt a huge welling of renewed optimism. It was a level of security about my position and place that I hadn't yet known. This man was still an enigma, and for all my dealings with him, I just couldn't read him. But here was a sign that I was valued. "Well, sir, if…"

He waved me down. "I have to show that you're being punished." He paused for a moment, frowning. "I can back Wadegahte Senior off on the banishment; it's my call, not his. But I think you're going to have to disappear."

"Disappear?"

"Until the dust settles. If you're not in Wadegahte's sight you won't be in his thoughts. You're gone from your lodging, you're dealt with."

"Disappear?" I repeated.

He nodded.

Chapter Twelve

In which I learn a secret and take a sea voyage

Da sahen sie die Werke des Herrn, und seine Wunder im tiefen Meere
These see the works of the Lord, and His wonders in the deep
Psalmen Davids/Psalm 107

I believe the scheme for my disappearance, and my master's complicity in it, marked the point where I considered myself in, not out. He had said, "Once you achieve status in the *Kameradschaft*," and that 'once' had filled me with a glow. There was still the problem of what he meant by my disappearance, of course.

"Yes. Disappear," said *Hoftrompeter* Breitkopf eyeing me speculatively. He took a long, deep breath, blew it out slowly through pursed lips, and seemed to come to a decision. "I think we need to bring you up to the next level."

The next level? Why, I kept thinking, am I always struggling to understand? Why is it that I always feel so ignorant, so out of touch? There are only so many times you can say "Sir?" with that upward inflection before you're treated as the village idiot.

"Sir?"

"Tell me. Why the education? Why the English lessons, and the French and Italian, why the writing and the composition? Why the learning of cyphers?"

"Because they are all part of the duties of the trumpeter."

"Exactly! Because they are all part of the duties of the trumpeter." He stepped out from behind the desk, turned briefly towards the window, then spun on his heel to face me. "Let me offer you a hypothetical scenario." He pointed a finger directly at my face. "You are a duke. You want support in warfare from a foreign prince. Your communication is extremely sensitive and secret. How would you communicate?"

"I would send a messenger, sir." I could see where this was going and a tingling excitement welled up in me.

"Right. Not exactly the job for those Papist postal bastards Thurn und Taxis, wouldn't you say? Not going to stick the message in the post, are we?"

"But a trumpeter is trained as a messenger," I offered, "and he is well able to defend himself."

"Himself be damned! To defend the message he carries, you mean.

And to adopt disguise and pass unobtrusively. And to be trusted above all others. And to write so others may not read. You have read, and I hope by now memorized, the *Vorrechte*, the Privileges, so you will know what a unique position we occupy. And those privileges were hard won. Yes, the trumpet is the symbol of imperial authority, yet that is but the half of it. We have those privileges because our masters recognize in us a valuable commodity. We do not simply carry a message from one place to another. We cannot be back and forth across mountains and oceans and the tracts of our enemies just so as to ask our master's wishes or to clarify certain obscure points. We must be intimately familiar with those wishes and those obscure points so as to be in a position to negotiate. There is *quid pro quo*, and we must be able to negotiate *in loco dominum*. As messengers we *are* our masters."

There had been periods during my apprenticeship when my master was absent. Sometimes I would not see him for weeks on end. I would ask where he was in as offhand a way as I could, but nobody knew, or at least they weren't telling me. My dawning comprehension must have been visible on my face.

"Of course you know all about Cesare Bendinelli, do you not?" he asked, throwing me completely sideways, a trait of his that I was beginning to get used to.

"Bendinelli? I... yes... the piece from... er... *Tutta l'arte...*?" Where was this going?

"No, you do not know all about Cesare Bendinelli. You don't know the half of it. Interesting character Bendinelli. Guess where he was at the age of twenty."

"Sir, I have no idea. Somewhere in Italy perhaps? Across those Alps?"

He pointed a finger directly down at his desk. "Right here in this city, playing trombone for Johann the Seventh, Duke of Mecklenburg-Schwerin."

"Trombone?"

"Trombone, trumpet. Not the distinction then that there is now. *Trombone, trombetta*; Italian practice."

"Here in Schwerin?"

"Yes. And why? Why here?"

He didn't expect answers and I offered none. Sir? would have been as much as I could muster, so keeping my mouth shut was the wise option.

"He wasn't just some young Italian with a wanderlust. Even at that young age he was very likely a trusted courier, but we will never know the true circumstances. It's not the sort of activity that gets recorded."

"You mean he was carrying messages?" Being caught up in excitement, I was quite forgetting deference. "Er... sir."

"Likely so. That and more. That's what we do." He smiled. "When we're not playing the trumpet for the court and the army, of course. But later in life as court trumpeter, in Wien and then in München, Bendinelli acted openly as emissary, diplomat and statesman. For which he is now well known. He'd paid his dues."

I was still mystified as to what this had to do with me. I had come into this office fully expecting him to tear my head off and shit down my neck, and here he was talking about this Bendinelli! "Where does my, um, punishment come in, if I may ask? Sir?"

"I have messages to take to England. Not openly as an emissary to our Duke; covertly. You will come with me. We will be father and son, merchants in leather goods."

My mind reeled. I couldn't grasp what had happened to me in the scant time since I had closed the door. England? Across the sea? And in disguise! I wasn't ready for this; it was all too sudden, too impossible.

"Please," I appealed to him, "could I have some time to think? I don't know what's going on..."

The harsh, military side of *Hoftrompeter* Hartmund Breitkopf came out again. "No, you do not have that luxury. Either you do as I tell you, or you make the Wadegahtes happy by creeping off home and going back to mucking out the pigs."

A great wave of nostalgia and anguish flooded over me as I thought of the farm, the family and my lost past comfort. I think, as he watched my face, he misread my expressions as one of cowardice.

"Your choice. To be made *now!*"

"But, is there danger?"

"Good Christ! You're in the bloody army! Of course there's danger."

"I don't have a choice really, do I sir?"

His face softened and he smiled gently, almost wistfully. "No, you don't, because there's no chance you'll run away, is there? Not the ballsy little bastard who stood up to the Duke. But yes, of course there's danger." He paused in thought. "It's ten, eleven years ago since Thilemann Hoffmann met his end, may God rest his soul."[21]

"Who was he? Sir."

"Court trumpeter for the Elector of Brandenburg in Berlin. Murdered while on a diplomatic mission. It never came out officially of course, but he was carrying papers related to the Treaty of Königsberg, signed the year before and already worthless. The Elector Georg Wilhelm was vacillating between the Swedes and the Catholics and a lot of poor bastards were caught in the middle."

"My father spoke of the devastation." I had overheard a conversation he had had with my brothers when I should have been asleep. I remembered recurrent nightmares where my father's voice echoed with: "It's going to come here. It's going to come here." Then I would think I had woken and while the echoes of his voice faded this huge disembodied face would loom over me and the mouth would open and it would be filled with rottenness and corruption...

"Brandenburg was devastated. The Höhenzollerns are only now recovering. At least half the population slain, towns obliterated from the map, churches desecrated, farms ruined. And the foul pestilences from the rot and wastage infected us all. God, there was a south wind out of Silesia one week, and we had the stink in our noses of Berlin burning."

It was coming here. I knew it was. And I knew it was only a matter of time before we would become embroiled. A matter of time before I would see war and death.

"Right!" He clapped his hands together. "We have to prepare."

That evening after supper I spoke quietly to Frau Walther, explaining that I had to go away, I was not sure for how long, but asking if she could keep my things safe in my room. I assured her that the rental of the room would continue to be paid, as would my board. This had been agreed between me and my master in order to secure her help, and I could see the counting of change behind her eyes as she calculated all the food and beer she would not have to serve. I swore her to secrecy, asking her to say, only if questioned directly, that I was away she knew not for how long, and she had no idea if I would ever be back. This done, I slept in my room for the last time, had my breakfast as normal, and parted with the smallest pack of necessities I could manage. Frau Walther tried to press a bag of food into my hand, as she had that awful day when I had returned home, but I took her quietly aside and asked her not to because this gesture was out of the ordinary and might make the other fellows suspicious. A huge wink was my reward.

Hoftrompeter Breitkopf met me at the stables where two horses were saddled and ready to ride. These were not fine cavalry horses by any means, and we would exchange them as we went. He carried a stiff leather bag on a strap over his shoulder.

"We will ride directly to Hamburg," he told me as we swung up into our saddles. "I am Herr David Lausmann, a trader in leather goods, and you are my son Hans." He slapped the leather bag with the palm of his hand. "Samples of our wares. You will pound this information into your head as we ride, because the slightest slip could betray us. Me. Betray me

93

and my messages."

I wondered as we rode why he would take the risk of trusting me to play such a critical part. Wouldn't it have been better to leave me behind, arrange for some sort of disappearance, and not have the extra worry? No, he assured me, my presence was perfect; it provided an excellent camouflage, because whoever would think of a courier doing this very thing? Even so, he warned me to speak to no strangers whatever the circumstances, except when he was present. I did wonder if this might be overly cautious, but I said nothing.

"You'll find, Hans," my 'father' observed at one point, "that our accommodations will not be of the highest quality. We are travelling as traders of modest means."

We approached the Hanseatic Port of Hamburg late on the third day and found a very modest lodging indeed. It may have been spring according to the calendar, but this last day of our ride had been beset with cold winds from the east and passing spatters of rain. We ate a modest supper and quickly found our way upstairs to an equally modest room. Tomorrow we would take ship for England, so we needed all the rest we could get. It was strange for me to be rooming with my master; we shared a room, we shared washing and other more intimate facilities, and we laid our paillasses side by side on the floor. It was the destruction of an order that had come to be second nature to me. How could he be my master, aloof and distant as he ought to be, yet still share this closeness with me? I was acutely uncomfortable.

Just before he pinched the candle out, he put my mind somewhat at rest. "Yes, you're wondering at the upset of order. I can feel it in you. Let me just say that when you're on the battlefield—and by God you will be before too long—this will feel like a stroll hand-in-hand with a pretty maiden. Goodnight."

And the room went dark.

We made our way on foot to the Hamburg docks, searching for a ship leaving for London in the next day or two. This proved to be a difficult task; the Habsburgs had lost their overland route between Spain and their territories in Flanders when France entered the war in 1635. All commerce between the two was now by sea, and it was rumoured that a mighty armada was being assembled to supply Cardinal-Infante Ferdinand, commander of the Spanish army in Flanders. Not many sea captains were willing to sail too far beyond the coast, even though our route across the North Sea was nowhere near the reputed enemy shipping lanes. Breitkopf had not allowed for this, underestimating seamen's conservatism and willingness to absorb rumours. Finally, we located a modest ship, agreed an exorbitant price with the captain, and brought our meagre belongings aboard. The negotiations had taken a great deal of time, all of it spent over beer in a dockside tavern, and I considered it highly likely that no deal could possibly have been made without copious lubrication. I watched from the sidelines, admiring my master's sleight-of-hand in filling tankards unevenly but subtly, so that one party always consumed more than the other.

The hauk was the little cargo ship favoured by the Hanse, a round bellied craft with two masts used mostly for trading between the cities of the League from the Low Countries to Scandinavia. They generally didn't sail much beyond eyeshot of land anyway, although they did cross the sea to England when the weather was fair and there were no Spaniards around. It's a wonderful thing, beer.

My master and I were shown to our 'cabin' down a short ladder by our ancient mariner. It was a squalid little cubbyhole with one side sloping, two hammocks strung from ropes, and a tiny port. The wooden cover of the port had been unbattened and laid aside on the deck, so only a little square of light lit this hideous space. I threw my meagre belongings down wondering what the devil I was in for.

"Should suit you, gentlemen," he rasped, and hawked inexpertly through the open port. The trailing edge of his gob, swinging like bar shot, caught the frame and dangled there in the breeze.

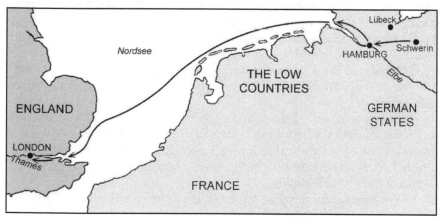

Jacob Hintze's mission to England with Hartmund Breitkopf. Judging by his description, the sea leg of the voyage was not as direct as shown here

We sailed down the Elbe on the ebb of the tide, watching from the deck as the banks at either side receded. The ocean opened before us, and what a sight for eyes that had never seen such a thing! There was this straight line where the sea met the sky, but off to the side the water appeared to fall downwards and away, yet when I looked there, it too was level. It is only when you are on the sea that the curvature of the earth, which you were taught in your lessons, really comes home to you. I had visited Rostock often enough with my father, but had never seen where the sea opens out at Warnemünde.

The shoreline diminished behind us until the whole world was grey seas under, with our cork of a hauk bobbing in its centre; a little wooden cockle sitting in a watery void. It filled me with fear of the unknown and a horror of drowning, but this was soon overtaken by something much worse.

Anyone who tells you that setting sail across the ocean is romantic and exciting has never done it. We had hardly cleared the estuary of the Elbe when our hopeless little bumboat began a rocking, swirling, rolling motion that threw you every which way, and had you wondering which way was up. It was a creaking, swaying, thudding nightmare, with a stink coming up from the bilges that would poison a hand of oxen. Vomiting in our cabin looked like a certainty, but my master had other ideas.

"Get up on deck! Now!"

I heaved myself up, crashing against the door jamb then reeling across to thump against the companionway. Once up on deck I swung hand over hand to the rail and fed the fishes, gulls and whatever other creature wanted them, all the meals I had eaten in days. I thought it would never stop, and only when I was a spent, retched-out shell, did I slump to the deck and wish I were dead.

"Stand up. Look at the horizon." Breitkopf was there beside me. "If you stay up on deck and keep your eyes where sea and sky meet you'll be fine."

"Thank you, sir," I muttered greenly, feeling at least stabilized if not ready to dance a hornpipe. I did not 'feel fine'. He insisted I eat a few crusts of bread and drink a mug of small beer. Even though I was utterly hollowed out, and would normally be hungry, it took an effort to choke the victuals down.

"You need something to retch on. If you're empty you'll tear yourself to pieces."

But it did get better following his advice, with the bonus that being up on deck it was convenient to hurl the bread and beer overboard when it was their time to abandon me.

"Drink it down, it'll do you good," he told me over and over, alternating this with, "bring it up, it'll do you good."

He kept me fed and watered and staring at the sea for the rest of that appalling day, even when the grey skies we had seen since Hamburg turned into slinging, stinging rain that came at me sideways and soaked me through.

As the sky darkened into evening I made an attempt to go below, but I had hardly got down the ladder before the waves of nausea began and the most recent loan of bread and beer began to be called in with interest. Up I went again, staring through the murk where I thought the horizon ought to be, and finding a modicum of stability. It was clear there was nothing for it but to sit up on deck all night, wrapped in a damp cloak, shivering in misery, and wishing to Christ I was back at home mucking out the pigs and that all this was a horrible nightmare. Any number of times I had to get out of the way as sailors shoved past, seeing to the banging, flapping, creaking rigging, setting the sails as we came about on a new tack.

I must have slept.

Chapter Thirteen

In which I enjoy the pleasures of London

Behold now this vast city; a city of refuge, the mansion-house of
liberty, encompassed and surrounded by His protection
John Milton

The hauk bobbed and dipped and rolled all through the night and
into the next day, and the day following that, while the rain came in
again, blown at us out of the east. It was a huge relief to spy land off
our port quarter, and a hideous landfall it was. England greeted us with
fogbanks, levels of sucking grey mud, the reek of saltmarsh and the
crying of seabirds. On either side of the ship, Essex and Kent presented
low, water-washed expanses of a type of dour and depressing landscape
I hope never to see again. There's a place on the south bank of the
Thames estuary that they call Foulness, and once you pass there you
know why. Approaching London from the sea, as the low banks close
in on you from either side, the capital city opens its legs to your ship
like a toothless old whore.

We docked at a place called Gravesend (the English have such
horrible but appropriate names for places) and, God help me, as soon
as I stepped down the gangplank and set my feet on land I was sick
and reeling. The land tipped up to receive me, then threw me sideways
until I was as nauseated as I had been shipboard. I nearly began spewing all over again. The stomach settled as we took a day-long coach
journey to London, some distance to the west, but as soon as the air
of London met my nostrils my food began to rise again. I knew
Rostock and Schwerin well, and I had passed through Hamburg
briefly, but London was the largest city I had stopped in. It was also
by far the filthiest. The streets were tight and narrow, the upper storeys
of the houses jutting over and blocking the light, and the entire walking
and riding surface was a slippery sea of horse dung, garbage, slops and
human excrement. The dirt of our towns goes unremarked—that's
what towns are like—but this was exceptional. Even on a short walk
between houses boots accumulated a layer of filth that needed scraping
off before entering a door. The smell was indescribable. My first
assessment of London was simple: somebody should set fire to the
whole lot and start again from the bare ground. But, you know, withal
there was something magical and beguiling about this bustling, busy
place. You couldn't help but be drawn into it all. And the more I saw

of it as we walked its streets, the mightier and more magnificent it became.

We lodged in a small tavern called the *Sprig of Rosemary* in a place called Islington, and not a bad place once you were inside.[22] They gave us a fine room with chairs and a sideboard, and bedframes for the paillasses. I searched for fleas and found none, a comparative rarity. The weather had turned extremely cold, with a sharp wind from the estuary, but our landlord kept a roaring fire in the common room. After a meal, at which I discovered how hungry I was, we spent the first evening engaging in conversation with other lodgers, drinking a few beakers of ale, and declining tobacco. My master had advised me against trying to smoke sot-weed before this, as he claimed it did no good for a trumpeter's wind, but the air was so filled with it that I smoked it whether I wished to or not.

I could see that *Hoftrompeter...* Herr Lausmann, was as tense as a wheellock spring, but I could also see that he needed time to settle in to his mission. One aspect of all this strangeness did delight me; I was among Englishmen so I could listen to their talk and pick up the rhythms of it. A large part of learning a language well lies in catching the tempo, and I had a natural ear for that. I'm not saying I learned a great deal, but I picked up more in one evening than in a dozen lessons with Herr Doktor Martius. The conversation ranged over many topics, although it was clear that the political state of the nation was on everyone's mind. The war between Catholic and Protestant seemed to have no boundaries and the *Sprig of Rosemary* was filled with folk who had wonderfully loose tongues.

My master's business the next morning was in an area called Shadwell, in amongst docks, warehouses and very low establishments. While having me with him to provide camouflage, I wondered if my presence was a distraction he would prefer to do without. He had noticed my roving eye the night before as I watched the harlots hawking their wares in the streets around Islington.

"There's poison in their loins," he had warned me. "One night with such a Venus will condemn you to a lifetime with Mercury.[23] Do not be tempted!"

He need not have cautioned me; one whiff of their stench, one glance at the ruins of their teeth and their fallen breasts was sufficient.

"I have several liaisons," he informed me after our breakfast, "and you must wait on me."

"Can I not come with you, sir... father?"

"No, you may not. Stay close to the inn, do not wander too far, and answer no questions of anybody. Is that clear?"

I spent that day—slightly disobediently—in and out of the narrow, crowded streets of Islington, listening to the chatter, which I picked up more and more, and generally absorbing the atmosphere of the place. First impressions are never reliable; I soon found the bustle and noise and activity of the capital city very much to my liking. I discovered that conversation with the traders and hawkers came more easily, and the young hoydens selling fruit, pies, oysters and eels seemed, in particular, beguiled by my accent and my bearing. I enjoyed bartering with them over their prices and meeting their eyes and smiles. Even with all this, though, I kept an eye out for any suspicious characters, and made sure to volunteer no information about myself. Withal, I was a silly boy playing at spies; none of it was more than a game to me. I came back to our lodging at the end of the day very pleased with myself.

On his return to the *Sprig of Rosemary* in the early evening, my master's mood appeared considerably lightened. After we sat in the common room over veal pies, oysters and an apple, he ordered a jug of wine to be brought up to our room. When the serving wench left, pulling the door closed behind her, he flung a log into the grate and turned to me.

"I have neglected you, Hans." He took two glasses from the sideboard and poured. "Here, drink up. Let's sit quietly and let the wine smooth our minds before we sleep."

I tasted wine for only the second or third time in my life. I didn't know what to make of this stuff. Beer and ale were refreshing to the thirst, which this was not, but it satisfied in a different way. I had some more, and the excitement of the day, wound up in me, began to slacken. I dared ask him the question that had been on my mind since he had left me that morning.

"Um, sir… father… can you tell me anything about what we're doing here?"

"No! I may not. I am a mere courier. I can tell you nothing more."

"So, Duke Adolf Friedrich…"

"…has nothing to do with the content."

"So, we just pass messages along?"

"Yes. It's *quid pro quo*. On a rare occasion Duke Adolf Friedrich will charge us with conveying open messages to his counterparts, one ruler to another, but much more often our work is covert…"

Suddenly he put his finger to his lips, rose stealthily from his chair and crept to the door. He gently took hold of the rope that passed for a door handle, flung the door wide, seized with both fists the clothing of a man standing there, and hauled him bodily into the room. Flinging him down, he was within an ace kicking him when he held back.

"God damn you, Robert, for a bloody fool!" he yelled. "What in hell are you doing here?"

"Heard you were here. Thought I'd drop in," said the man, climbing to his feet and patting imaginary dust from his clothing.

"How, damn it? How did you hear?"

"We keep our eyes on this place. German leather merchant, hah! Knew it could only be you." He smiled. "Who's the lad?"

"My apprentice, Jacob Hintze."

A tall, open-faced individual with long sandy hair, a pointed beard and clear blue eyes faced me with a quizzical expression. He sported a fine cape over a doublet of some rich fabric and had a small dagger in a sheath at his side. There was a swagger and self-possession to him that could become irksome.

"Bringing 'em in early, are you not?" He held out a hand to me. "Robert Ramsay at your service."

"I am pleased to meet you, sir," I replied in my best English, and was rewarded with raised eyebrows, a firm hand and an appraising nod.

My master shut the door carefully and waved Ramsay to a chair. He tipped wine quickly into another glass and thrust it at him irritably. "If your lot know we're here, who the hell else does?"

"No worry," replied this nonchalant Ramsay character, gulping the wine down. "One of ours told me; server in this place. Useful pair of eyes. And so here I am."

Breitkopf's irritation seemed to subside. "Well, it's good to see you again, you stupid bastard." He looked over at me, motioned me to sit, and went round our glasses again with the jug. "Hintze, I have known this character for a couple of years, and the less you know about what he does the better it will be."

"Oh, come now, Hartmund. I am simply a trumpeter and cavalryman in the King's service. You know that."[24] Here was that habit of understatement and deprecation; I would learn in time that no Englishman I encountered was what he professed to be.

"What I do know is, your presence here means nothing but trouble."

"No, really, just cautioning. I don't know the content of the messages you brought, or for whom, but it's pretty clear to us that Catholics and Protestants on the Continent are playing King against Parliament to their own advantage. There's evil brewing in this nation, and you risk being swept up in it."

"Hintze," said my master. "Let me explain a little of the politics of this strange nation." He received a nod from Ramsay. "King Charles is Anglican and he rules an Anglican nation. Like us, Protestant. However, he is married to a French Catholic, Henrietta Maria, and apparently tolerates her religious nonsense. She, in turn, is surrounded by a troop of Popish beetles who act as her advisors. Advice in religious matters is one thing, but do they overstep their authority and delve into the political?"

"Exactly," rejoined Ramsay quickly. "The good Protestant folk of England are a little bit anxious about a Catholic body slipping herself between the royal sheets."

"Is that why the King is failing to support the Protestant cause against the Holy Roman Emperor?" I asked. "That's what they were saying downstairs last night."

"So your big ears have heard that much?" put in Breitkopf. "I'm impressed with your comprehension of tavern English. Yes, that's what the people think, but it's probably more complex."

"They said he couldn't afford it."

"Yes, in a nutshell!" shouted Ramsay. "The economy of England is in poor condition and the demand by the royal purse is excessive. The Crown is at war with the Scottish Covenanters and must levy taxes to support the army. And the King has ruled these last years without Parliament. To fill his purse he *must* recall Parliament."

"What is Parliament? Sir?"

"A body of representatives chosen from throughout the kingdom, whose wise counsel guides the Crown." Ramsay replied. "But King Charles is appointed by God to rule; he has that divine right, which is governed by the laws of this land and is consecrated by her Church. And he has done so until now without Parliament. But there's a new player who could well tip the balance."

"Cromwell," said Breitkopf.

"You've heard of him? Yes, one Oliver Cromwell, a staunch Puritan, and a formidable force.[25] Likely the King will be obliged to recall Parliament, and when he does, this Cromwell may prove too much for him. This country, Jacob, is on a knife edge, and there are many here who think it will only end badly. And there is no doubt in our minds that Catholic France has sent emissaries to the King, in an attempt to upset an already unstable situation. They tried gunpowder on Charles's father."

"Gunpowder?" I asked. "What do you mean? Who? Er… sir."

"Catholics, under a man named Catesby, laid gunpowder charges beneath the chamber where Parliament sits. It was by pure luck, and a timely informer, that our King Charles was not orphaned at the age of five."

"They'll do anything!"

"Yes." He paused for a mouthful of wine. "But Catholics overseas are less of a worry now than Englishmen here. Breitkopf, I am a king's man through and through, but when I see the way things are going, I am sorely tried."

"You think there will be civil war?"

"I do. And it is of no concern of yours. You have enough troubles of your own."

"Robert, I was charged by my Duke to convey messages. I know not where they originated, and I cannot reveal their content. Let me just say that our little duchy neither makes the wine, nor drinks it. We are a mere conduit, as the funnel is between the barrel and the flask."

"May it stay that way. All I am saying is, take care you are not caught up. I treasure our friendship."

The two shook hands, clasping hand to wrist, wrist to hand, and here I got an inkling of a brotherhood of messengers with wide connections, and for a heady moment I had a vision of my future role in it.

With that we finished the wine, bade goodbye to Robert Ramsay, and retired to our paillasses.

The next day, a Sunday, my master told me to accompany him to the Chapel Royal for holy service at Hampton Court Palace. We would take a skiff upriver from a dock near the London Bridge. All the way from the inn to the dock he was scanning the crowds, peering over his shoulder, occasionally standing still while people passed. He seemed satisfied we weren't followed, while I rather enjoyed all this cloak-and-dagger stuff, imagining I had fallen into an exciting adventure. We boarded a skiff rowed by two well-muscled boatmen who would take us up the Thames to the Palace.

"Can you tell me anything more about Mr. Ramsay?" I asked once we were seated in the stern of the boat.

"Sergeant. Sergeant Ramsay," he replied, eyeing the boatmen and perhaps deciding the creak of the tholes and the swish of the sweeps would not mask even quiet conversation. "A fine trumpeter."

He said no more, so with this I had to be content. We watched the river pass in silence until Hampton Court Palace appeared on our left, a lovely redbrick place set among water meadows. The weather was fair, although not warm, so this interlude up the river underlined by the steady swish of the sweeps had been a balm to the soul.

"Music," my master observed, "is not healthy here. There was the golden age of Byrd and Gibbons and Morley. Droves of 'em left and came to the German lands in the last generation, much good it's done them now. Musicians and musical impetus now come largely from overseas. Last flush under James, moribund under Charles. Crass Scottish yokels. You will find the music very old fashioned. Foreign musicians in plenty, but little or no originality."

"There's music there today?"

"Yes, voices and instruments, but his Majesty will not attend. Too taken up with his Scottish troubles. Royal patronage is the key, and there's precious little of it in these distracted times."

Breitkopf paid our fare, stepped off the skiff and instructed the oarsmen to return for us later in the afternoon. Quite likely they would be back and forth before that because there was a lot of traffic between Hampton Court, the West Minster and the City of London. As soon as we were on the towpath and walking in the direction of the Palace, my master became more open about our recent guest.

"Robert is one of the select trumpeters who accompany the King, although he alone is privy to the King's secrets. His brothers, and his father too, are all trumpeters. Generations of service to the Crown and, as you now know, Robert's duties extend beyond his paid employment. A very serviceable gentleman, something of a rogue, and a heart of pure English oak."

"They, at least, are appreciated by the King?"

"The King needs the pomp, his show. Don't they all? Loud noises, fanfares, entradas, but not a lot of what might be called music."

We crossed the drawbridge to the main gate where Herr Lausmann presented a paper to the sentry. A nod in our direction gave us access to the Base Court, through which we passed to the Clock Court, and so by a series of galleries into the Chapel Royal. This was a gorgeous space, lit by high windows, ornately decorated, and with a hammer beam roof, a thing I had never seen before and marveled at. We found pews to the side, slid ourselves in, and prepared for the service. The choir was already in place, and while we seated ourselves the musicians entered. I was interested to see sackbuts and cornetts in addition to the string players, as I had assumed the former would be used only for court and other secular occasions.

The service was quite glorious, voices predominant and instruments restrained. The winds were used sparingly, only in the sections where the instruments and voices all played together. Yes, it was old-fashioned, but even so, a beautiful celebration of the holy service. We left the Chapel Royal quite unobtrusively and returned to the little wharf where out boat waited. Our return journey down the Thames was fast as we went with the flow, but I was surprised that the fee was the same considering the easy time of it our oarsmen had. We returned to the *Sprig of Rosemary*, ate a leisurely evening meal, and then moved into the common room for a little wine and some more leisurely conversation.

So ended my first visit to far places in the service of my Duke.

—

Our return voyage was the outwardbound journey reversed, but this time my seasickness was not as severe; perhaps only a day's dinners, instead of what had felt like week's, were fed to the fishes. We had accommodations in the same hauk with the same sea captain, and the same unaccountable inability to find his way to port. It seemed to me that my master had wasted a great deal of money on beer during the negotiations prior to our outward journey, as drunkenness seemed to be his normal state. God only knew what cargo he had laded for the return journey, but a rank, fetid, oily smell permeated the entire craft and probably formed a halo around it for all I knew. Flocks of yelling gulls followed us like carrion birds over an army. This contributed nothing to the state of my stomach. I learned as we disembarked that the cargo was sheepskins.

The ride back from Hamburg was uneventful, except for one tract of land we crossed at the end of our first day of riding. Dwellings were burned, farm utensils scattered and overturned, fences torn down, and not a trace of domestic animals. An army had passed this way, taking or destroying everything in its path. It reminded me again of the fragility of all that I held dear.

Chapter Fourteen

In which I enjoy a young lady, acquire a lifelong enemy and lose a good friend

Denn alles, was in der Welt ist: des Fleisches Lust und der Augen Lust und hoffärtiges Leben, ist nicht vom Vater, sondern von der Welt
For all that is in the world, the lust of the flesh, and the lust of the eyes, and the pride of life, is not of the Father, but is of the world
1 Johannes/1 John 2:16

It was almost like coming home, my return to Frau Walther's lodging. At least there was the jocular familiarity of Heinrich and Berthold. But there was also my dear friend Joachim who had unwittingly consolidated my apprenticeship, and given me a tremendous boost of morale and position. Not to mention an adventure beyond my imaginings. As I sat down again at the table and picked up my spoon, I swore that I'd be damned if I'd let the bastard think he'd beaten me.

"Oh, here's our farm boy, back from his punishment," he smirked. "I thought they'd got rid of you for good. Should have!"

I nodded and smiled, continuing a conversation in English with Berthold that the idiot had interrupted. It was such a joy to know that he understood not a word, and that every time I glanced in his direction as I spoke, he thought I was referring to him. His face became increasingly thunderous before he finally took himself off in a huff. Even then, I think, I was plotting his comeuppance. As he sat there in his fine clothes, wearing that supercilious sneer, I had begun to think of that piece of pleasure-fluff he kept in town… and I imagined scenarios.

It was not long before my scenarios began to take on solid form. One day, while returning to the lodging from my duty, who should come towards me but the man himself with his pretty piece of slit on his arm, a flaxen-haired beauty with those blue eyes and high cheek-bones you see in the Danish. He made to pass me, pulling his woman close to his side, but I swung sideways to block their way. She would have to step into the gutter to pass, and that would never do.

"Good evening to you," I cried with a huge smile and a sweep of my feather-plumed hat. "Joachim I know, of course, but I have not yet had the pleasure of an introduction, Fraulein." By this time I had got my little chin beard well started and trimmed, and fine whiskers were curling nicely beside my nose. Oh, I really saw myself as such a dashing young cavalier!

He made to push by, a furious look on his face, but she smiled and held him back. "I'm Ingrid." She looked right in my eye, and by God there was kindling, logs and ready pyrite unless I was very much mistaken. "And you must be Jacob Hintze. Joachim has told me *so* much about you!"

The bastard must have, and none of it good, but to see her smiling face you'd think he'd praised me to the skies.

"Come on, we're late," he snarled and pulled her past me. She brushed close and I felt a hint of pressure from her arm, picked up a sweet aroma, and received the horniest expression over her shoulder that I had ever seen in a woman. What's all this? thinks I.

It must have been about three weeks later, I was in the market one evening buying a little something to eke out Frau Walther's generous but boring fare, when there she was in front of me with a little basket on her arm.

"Ingrid!" I cried. "How nice to see you again."

"Oh, Jacob," she replied, "this is such a coincidence. I have just bought a whole apple loaf and was wondering who *ever* to share it with."

Well, by God, you didn't need an education from the *Gymnasium* to read this particular manuscript.

"It would be a pleasure," I replied with great gallantry, "not only to share the sweetmeat, but to share it in a company which trumped its very sweetness."

Christ, I'd learned a thing or two during my 'banishment'. So off we hove to her apartment, a nice top room in a fine area of Schwerin, and there without much more ado we got at it. I've never had my clothes off so fast, nor had I ever seen all the rigmarole that fine ladies conceal from prying eyes. I thought she'd never get done with all the laces and buttons and whatnot. But finally, there she was all white skin, hard pink nipples and a tuft of flaxen curlies. The sweetmeat we shared on her soft silken bed with the tassels and curtains swinging in time to our bouncing, beat the hell out of the apple loaf, which never did get eaten.

It was an ecstatic coupling, but what brought me into the most crashing, explosive crescendo was the fact that she was *his*. I was whacking into Wadegahte's piece, looking down into her moaning, sweating face; a face that he had stared down into and triumphed over.

Our couplings were usually quite mechanical. We would agree on a day, and I would show up, we'd trot our stuff, and off I would take myself. It was a business arrangement fore and aft, with enormous passion amidships. One evening, though, once she had regained her breath, she started a conversation. Even though I was worried about getting back to my place before the Watch began their patrols, I stayed and talked.

"It's not just about the fucking," she began, as polite young ladies will. "But I need more than I get from him. He gives me all sorts of stuff, money and things, but he's useless."

I could have howled in glee but I held my peace and kept a straight face.

"Useless?" I asked in mock incomprehension.

"In and out like a ferret. It's all about him."

Well, surprise, surprise, I thought. Selfish bastard. Pity though; I thought she meant he couldn't get his troops to stand to attention, but that clearly wasn't the case.

"Glad to oblige a lady," I murmured smugly.

She hoisted herself up onto an elbow, one tit swinging, and looked down at me. "But aren't you apprentices banned from consorting with loose women?" she asked coyly as she ran a finger down my chest. "It's in your rules, you naughty boy."

"Loose? Who says you're loose? You're tight, tight, tight, that's what you are."

She laughed and jumped on for more.

I wondered, not for the first time—or even the tenth—what would happen if her boyfriend ever found out. Half the time I was fearful of the shit storm that would pour down on me, while for the other half I wanted him to know he'd been cuckolded. I wanted to see his face, see him realize that farm boy had been throwing logs on his fire. Quite the dilemma.

In the end it was taken out of my hands.

I reported one day to the exercise room where we practiced swordsmanship and found that Herr Wadegahte had been assigned to the same rotation. We had graduated to steel swords now; not the light, sharp blades of the cavalryman yet, but heavy practice things with deliberately dulled edges. By now we were considered capable enough in defending ourselves, and should our sparring partner land a hard blow a bruise might result, or at worst a cracked bone. We wore the leather cuirass and the padded bracers on our arms, which we had used in boffering with the wood blades, and the target area was still the torso between hips and shoulders. As before, the scoring routine was to keep a gentleman's tally of the number of strikes.

It would have to happen sooner or later that we would meet again in combat, but this was our first encounter with metal blades. Having faced Wadegahte with the wood blade I knew he was a furious fighter, especially when paired against me, so I feared the worst. He swaggered up to the mark on the floor, leering at me and doubtless confident he could best me in a contest of strength. We faced each other at the requisite distance, swords at our sides, and my God there was evil in his eyes. The swordmaster gave the command to start, and then left us to go off and deal with the next pair. We took our combat stance, raising our blades to *Vom Tag*, then slowly circled each other as both our blades came down slowly to *Pflug*, each waiting for the other to strike.

He darted his blade suddenly forward, a thrust I easily parried, and then we were at it in earnest. He was taller and stronger than me, anyway, and I was soon on the defensive, but there was an anger and a purpose in him. I blocked and parried continually, looking for an opening, varying my moves and always avoiding staying in one spot, but I couldn't find a pause in which to go on the offensive. Once you get set into a pattern of defence it's extremely difficult to break the rhythm. Then it came to me as we circled that not one of his strokes was aimed at the torso. Every thrust he made had one single aim; he was going for my mouth. He knew! By Christ, he knew about me and Ingrid!

He was going for my mouth, my lips, my teeth. He was out to ruin me.

Now there was fear mixed with my defence. I could hear it all now: the oh, so sincere apologies, the oily lying bastard weaseling his way out of blame for such a terrible accident, while I spat the blood-clotted white chips of my wrecked career onto the exercise floor. And where the hell was the swordmaster? Would he just ignore this? Of course he would; he had five other contests to oversee, and what was different about this one? And how could I turn my back and refuse to fight? Any career among cavalrymen would be finished by the gossip and rumour that would follow such cowardice. He would see to that. No, I had to face him and take what was coming.

All too soon I began to tire with the continual parrying and blocking of his increasingly aimed blows. He was breathing heavily but I had begun to pant more than he with the exertion. Trumpeters don't lack wind, but this was more than I had ever had to do. Twice I just missed catching the flat of his blade on the side of my jaw as I twitched my head to the side, and I knew it was only a matter of time before one of his swipes would land. How I longed to give him a great roaring boot in the fork.

Round and round the practice floor we went, clash, zing, clash, until I knew I had to find a way to break the rhythm. The thrust, parry, thrust, parry must be broken if I had any chance of stopping him. Just before I ran completely out of energy I found what I needed; the tiniest pause in the rhythm. I caught his eye and yelled, "Ingrid!"

Yes! He hoisted the blade up high and aimed an almighty swing in pure stupid anger. I flung my left arm over my face as his blade thudded into my bracer, swinging my sword down onto his wrist in a following motion. He yelped and I heard the blade clatter to the floor. Relaxing slightly in relief I wasn't ready for the onslaught of fists that followed. Shielding my precious face once again with both forearms, eyes closed tight, I knew it was only a matter of time before he broke through and maimed me.

Suddenly the blows stopped. The swordmaster had him gasping and seething in a struggling bear hug. "All right, all right! This is swordplay, not boxing, you stupid bastard."

Wadegahte glared at me, wrestling and panting, with such hate in those frightening eyes I pray to the good Christ I will never see again in a human face. Then time slowed for me. I stood foursquare in front of that piece of hog shit, and I looked him right in the eye. Slowly and purposefully I pursed my beautifully intact lips, and buzzed 'Withdraw' followed by 'Lower Your Colours'. It was beyond stupid, but equally beyond irresistible.

I knew then that he would lose no opportunity to kill me if he could.

One evening early in 1640, towards the end of my apprenticeship, I sat down at table with Berthold. We had become close with our regular music-making, but this evening that usually sunny face was wiped clean. His bowl was untouched in front of him, and his bread sat half chewed on the table.

"What's up?" I asked. "You've got a face as long as my horse's."

"I'm done," he sighed, and there was moistness in his eyes. "Two months more, that's all there was, and they're sending me home!"

"*Home?* Why?"

"This bloody war! That's why," he wailed. "Musicians fleeing our lands! The great Heinrich Schütz in exile in Denmark, or scuttling around between safe houses. The court ensemble of the Elector ruined. Where's it all going to end?"

"So you're finished?" I couldn't get this terrible news into my head.

"I am. The court and the chapel can no longer afford to pay musicians, let alone apprentices. Two months!" he cried. "That's all I had left."

"But not the *Kapellmeister!* Not Herr Vierdanck!"

"Yes, Herr Vierdanck as well," he replied wearily. "He has been organist at Stralsund for some time anyway, and the rumour is he'll return there for good. Lost to the Swedes."

"What about the choir?" I thought of the high standard that

Vierdanck had achieved and how it would all go to waste.

"Oh, not the choir. The holy service will continue. The choristers aren't paid anyway," he finished bitterly.

I think it was at this point that the war really came right into my face; not the news of death and destruction across the land, not the pestilences that ravaged the face of the earth, not the shortages of everything, not even the whittling away of my family's fortune. No, the anguish on my friend's face did it. That was the point when it really hit this innocent, isolated boy, wrapped in his great dreams. Berthold's misery laid the obvious on what I already knew but avoided.

I placed a hand on his arm. I was saddened and sympathetic, but felt guilty as well because he knew that I enjoyed protected musical status at the court. Violinists were a luxury; cavalry trumpeters were a necessity. He put my thoughts into words.

"It's all very well for you," he said, and then quickly became apologetic. "But I don't begrudge you; please don't think that!"

"I know you don't, Bert. But look at it this way. In the end we're both disposable. The difference is, you'll go on to play music somewhere else, but if I am disposed of all I will get is a funeral."

He smiled weakly at that, clasping my upper arms in his strong fiddle-player's grip. "I'll go to England and try my hand there. My father knew William Brade the violinist when we lived in Hamburg.[26] There's a contact in London. It must be better there than here. I'll do all right…"

I only hoped he would. The opposite had been the case a generation ago; English musicians had been leaving to settle in Germany. I wasn't sure things were much better now from what I had seen when I visited, but I couldn't even hint at my experiences there, of course. He left a few days afterwards, and it was only then I realized what a true friend he had been. There is a certain intimacy that develops between people who play music together, and I imagine that what I felt in my heart must have been like the anguish felt by a broken love.

He left yet another hole in me; another aching place. I wondered sometimes if I was like Job, whom God treated so cruelly, but that is to question the path that He has decreed we are destined to follow. Idle speculation…

"Now we start to get serious!" *Hoftrompeter* Hartmund Breitkopf stood in front of me with his arms crossed. I had reported for my one-hour daily playing session as usual, but I had noticed that the following two hours of the day had been left blank. "Your lip is young. In the last year we have done a great deal of development, but we haven't pushed it yet. Now we begin. Pick up your trumpet."

As I brought the mouthpiece to my lips I saw the steel in his eye and the straightness his back, and I felt a new tension.

"Play *Buttasella*," he barked. This was the order to mount.[27]

I played. "Louder!" he shouted. "Again, again!"

I played. "*Trab! Kanter! Links abbiegen!*" all yelled in quick succession and in no order. No sooner had I played one than he was shouting another. This continued until I was exhausted, until my lips felt like raw meat, until my breathing was coming in gasps.

Finally he called a halt. "This exercise is absolutely critical!"

I caught my breath enough to puff, "Yes... sir..."

"Yes, sir!" he repeated. "You must know each and every one of these calls so well that you can play them in your sleep. You must react to an order to play *instantly*. You must never, *ever* make a mistake. You must play with such clarity that even the most tone-deaf and stupid cavalryman can have no doubt what he must do. The life and death of highly trained soldiers hangs on your lips and your brain. Do I make myself clear?"

"Yes, sir!" I said again, with a bit more breath, and this time, by God, I meant it.

And so began the most intense and exhausting phase of my training. From here on I would eat, drink and sleep with the book of calls. In the beginning my trust of the *Hoftrompeter* wavered; I really felt that this new intensity was going to damage me, and I was on the verge of saying so a few times, but day by day my strength improved to the point where I wouldn't be returning to my lodging with throbbing lips and aching jaws. He knew what he was doing.

"Here's a nice one. Try this." I was just recovering at the end of one of these intense sessions when with a smile my master handed me a hand-written tune. "Give it a toot."

I read through this simple signal a couple of times, handed back the paper, then played it three times over. "So what of it, sir?"

He smiled. "It's called *Zapfenstreich*."

"Striking bungs? What the... Er, sir."

He laughed. "It's just been added to our calls. As soon as the sun touches the horizon we signal that all bungs be replaced in their barrels, so no more drinking."

"And the *Streich?*"

"A line of chalk struck across the bung to prevent tampering. Closing the taps at sunset."

"So, it is an order that there will be no more drinking after nightfall?"

"Orders follow incidence. Mercenaries, pressed men, opportunists, all take advantage. Look: outside of us elite troops, the armies that fight this war are composed of desperate men. Driven off their land, impoverished, dispossessed, willing to put their faces into the mouths of cannon for a few *Pfennig* and all the ale they can drink. Curbing excesses and putting men on the field who can see straight the morning after; that's how the order came about."

"It's a nice piece." I played it again. Of course, you hear it everywhere nowadays, but it was new then.[28]

Chapter Fifteen

In which I am initiated into the *Kameradschaft* and prepare for war

*Ich, Jacob Hintz, schwöre, dass ich die in der Ordnung aufgestellten Ansprüche
einhalten werde…*
I, Jacob Hintz, do swear that I will uphold the standards as laid out
in the *Ordnung…*

Jacob Hintze

"Jacob Hintze, it is nearly two years since I brought you here."

Hoftrompeter Breitkopf was sprawled as usual behind his desk in the trumpet room. "Another month and your papers will be signed. What d'you say?" He waited.

My third spring in Schwerin was approaching, and my mind was running back over those twenty-three dense months, reviewing the triumphs, the heartaches, the pleasures and the pains. In this scant time I had piled on experience until I was nearly overwhelmed. The little boy with a raw talent who had stood on this spot two years ago was gone forever; a young man, sophisticated in the ways of the world, facile in languages, skilled in weapons—a horseman, a musician and a courier—now faced his master. I had been transformed by this enigmatic man, a man I still could neither fathom nor figure, but it was through his faith in me that I stood where I was. Father, mentor, tutor, confessor; nothing fitted. Nothing helped me to locate and understand the essence of him. I owed him everything I now was, and I knew that it was a debt that was impossible for me to repay. I knew, also, that he found his repayment in his product; he had the satisfaction of a composer in the completion of a sonata. He had often referred to me as clay, and it was his hands that had done the moulding. From every indication I received, he was happy with his workmanship.

"Well? Gone all quiet."

I snapped back to the world. "I was thinking, sir, of how far I have come. All the things I have learned." I sensed that it would be unwise to start thanking him; he would do one of those waving-it-off hand gestures, I was sure. Probably tell me it was horseshit.

"And soon you'll be launched…" He was frowning and, I would swear, for the first time since I had known him, unsure of what to say. He looked me over, his head slowly rising and falling; a gentle, slow nod. "Out there on the battlefield…"

"Sir?" My habitual comeback when he was at his most unreadable.

He came to a decision and his entire manner became suddenly brisk. "Jacob Hintze, you are now a valuable property of the duchy, trained, educated, coached and primed. We will soon be called upon to serve his Grace in our struggle against the Holy Roman Empire. It is no longer sufficient to provide our allies with men levied from the fields and towns. We will be drawn in. It is demanded of us. Although our Duke would be the first to deny it, since the Swedish crown liberated the duchies from von Wallenstein, he is a vassal. His is indebted for his throne. Deeply indebted."

"My father spoke of von Wallenstein. He said he was a duplicitous schemer. I remember those words exactly."

"Yes, he supported the Empire against Denmark, for which service he received Mecklenburg as a prize, then the Danes joined with Sweden and booted him out. But his allegiances were always suspect—too damned powerful—so the Emperor had him put to sleep."

"Is that true? The Emperor could just order him assassinated?"

"No, indeed! All he said was 'I want him dead or alive'. Loyal servants did his bidding. Made him very happy while he denied any complicity."

"So now, we owe it to Sweden to go to war?" In my curiosity I was quite forgetting deference. "Sir."

"Sweden, France, and forces from Hesse-Cassel and Brunswick-Lüneberg, are marshalling to push south and they require cavalry, they require seasoned soldiers, they require our best. So this…" He waved his hand, encompassing it seemed the entire world, "…this paradise you have been living in must all come to an end. You will ride."

I will ride. I will become a soldier. I will go to war. It was all still unreal. My mind slipped sideways, away from facing these truths, focusing instead on trivia. "What becomes of music at the court, sir?"

"What there is of it now, in this wrecked mess of a world. The chapel choir remains, of course, although once your apprenticeship is done you'll have no part in it."

This news came as somewhat of a relief to me; while I enjoyed singing in holy service I grudged the time it took from activities I thought more important.

"The trumpet corps continues to play, of course," he continued. "We're undermanned with the loss of Reinhardt." (He had passed away, having never recovered from the flux.) "Those older members who have seen action will remain here, and the younger ones who have not will be deployed. There are just two; you and Martin." Martin played *Principal*, as I did, but he was a most private fellow. I hardly knew him.

The glory of the battlefield, my naïve dreams of heroic service, so distant and fantastic and idealized, suddenly came rushing at me. It was real, it was present, and I was frightened.

"And…" he paused. "Don't get your stupid self blown out of the saddle. You're too valuable to waste."

This parting shot as I left his office hardly assured me at all.

It was a rainy day in April 1640 and I had hurried through the town from my lodging. I crossed the bridge quickly, entered the gatehouse and shook the water off my cape. Wiping the rain from my face and brushing my wet hair down with my hands, I strode up the stairs to the trumpeters' domain. A meeting with my master was entered for the first hour, and even though I arrived early he was already there at his desk. The clerk who had administered my apprenticeship formalities two years ago stood by the window. *Hoftrompeter* Hartmund Breitkopf was dressed in full court regalia, not the usual stand-down clothes in which I usually encountered him. He motioned me to be seated, then pushed forward a pile of papers.

"This paper," he began, picking up the top document from the pile, "is my assessment of you, to be forwarded to the *Kameradschaft* for formal approval."

This was it. I knew it was coming, and now here I was in the moment. This was the day when my apprenticeship would be formally completed.

"The undersigned Jacob Hintz," he read, "has passed all the necessary… blah, blah… comported himself with dignity at all times…" Here he looked up from the sheet and fixed me with his eye. "…has done nothing to bring himself or his station into disrepute…" Again, the look. The clerk perked up his nose quizzically but made no comment. "And has in all things met the standards… blah, blah, blah. You'll have a copy to go through later." He passed me a dipped quill. "Sign right there."

My hand was shaking; you can still see the tremor and the blot to this day. Then it was done. I handed the sheets back and he slashed his signature below mine.

"Next, the *Ordnung*. You know these rules inside out and backwards, but I am obliged by the procedures of our company to ensure that you know them, and that you signify such in writing. Do you swear that knowledge?"

"I do."

"Sign there."

Again I signed, this time with less tremor. Again he countersigned.

"Finally, the oath. Attention!"

I rose from the chair and stood up as straight as I could. My master rose from his desk and came round to stand in front of me. The clerk came forward to flank him.

"Repeat after me: I, Jacob Hintze, do swear..."

"I, Jacob Hintze, do swear..." I repeated in a less-than-steady voice.

"That I will uphold the standards as laid out in the *Ordnung*..."

"That I will uphold the standards as laid out in the *Ordnung*..." Now my voice was firmer.

"And will obey all rules, regulations and orders..."

"And will obey all rules, regulations and orders..."

"As long as I do live." And here his eyes met mine again.

"As long as I do live." I inclined my head slightly, remembering that parting shot of his. "As long as I do live," I repeated in a whisper, almost to myself.

"Sworn in front of *Hoftrompeter* Hartmund Breitkopf, in the presence of Herr Nicholas Schlauklug."

I repeated this piece and we signed a third document. As soon as he laid the quill down he strode forward and grasped me by the hand. His grip suited him; firm, dry and hard. As he squeezed my hand I realized that in our two years together, this was the first time we had touched.

"*Feldtrompeter* Hintze! Report to the wardrobe for issue of livery, and then return here at the seventh hour in full dress. Dismissed!"

So it was done. I floated away to the wardrobe in an unreal haze, and there I was fitted with livery, two changes of stand-down clothes and, wonder of wonders, a wide-brimmed hat and a pair of the longest, softest riding boots I had ever seen. The duchy might be in tight financial straits, but the appearance of her retainers was clearly still a high priority.

I reported back to the trumpeters' domain a little before the seventh hour, all dressed in my finery and feeling as if I was living in my own dream. I pushed the door open and stopped with a jerk. There in front of me, all arrayed in their best livery and fronted by kettle-drums, was the entire trumpet corps of the duchy, instruments poised. A huge wall of sound blasted at me as I stood numb, dumb and awe-struck. It was a thundering fanfare from the Fantini book; as the great chords and harmonies poured over and around me tears came to my eyes.

All this for *me?*

Once the last sustained notes had died my master came forward, gripped me by the upper arm and drew me into the waiting crowd. They shook my hand in turn, giving me words of praise, encouragement and advice. Jiri, Friedemann, Hermann, Martin, Adolf, they were all there for me. Surely, apprentices didn't usually get feted this way?

When the fuss had died down and the trumpeters had gone about their business, Breitkopf sat me down in his office. "There's a place here for you. The fellows all know it. You have an exceptional talent and you will go far in our service."

"I cannot thank you enough..." I began, but as usual he waved me off.

"First time I heard you I knew we were onto a good thing. Couldn't let such talent go to waste. Purely self-serving."

"Well, you may say so, sir," I replied, "but I will be forever grateful."

"Good. Your gratitude is noted. But first, before you make fine music in the service of your Duke, you have your duty to perform."

The cavalry was going to war. We didn't know when, but we knew it was inevitable.

It was my sixteenth birthday. *Feldtrompeter* Hintze's service had begun.

Playing at court with the trumpet corps was unforgettable for me; it had been the single goal in my mind ever since that day at the market in Rostock, and now to be actually doing it carried an air of unreality. I was assigned to *Principal*, which came easily for me, and in no time I was one of the dozen, only marked out from the rest by my youth. None of the others, I am sure, were under twenty-five. You would have expected some jealously, some envy, against a young fellow suddenly assigned a place in a highly proud and stiff-necked corps, but I didn't experience much of that. Or, at least, what jealousy they had was turned into teasing and practical jokes. At one practice session almost the entire corps erupted into laughter when I couldn't get a decent note out of my instrument. I had been a little late and had grabbed the Sander off the peg without checking it. The session had to be stopped while I reached into the bell with a bent wire and retrieved the dead mouse.

One among them didn't roar; old Wilhelm just eyed me with a slight sneer on his face, but when he saw me laughing as well, he quickly masked his expression with a smile.

Over that summer, with the threat of war looming over me like the stormy weather that came from the east, Hartmund Breitkopf was absent more than he was here. Big, kindly Friedemann took over his role, and on one wonderful occasion I was assigned to *Clarino I*. Friedemann must have had great faith in me because we were to play entradas, fanfares and other pieces for Duke Adolf Friedrich and his sister-in-law Eleonore Marie of Mecklenburg-Güstrow. The two were necessary allies but they despised each other. When Adolf Friedrich's brother had died in 1636, his heir was just a boy, so Uncle Adolf Friedrich took control, becoming Regent of Mecklenburg-Güstrow as well. This did not sit well with mother—in fact, she was teeth-gnashing furious—so there was a sort of truce until the boy could come of age. The whole court could see that this was the 'sort of truce' that involves ice, sneers, sharp comments and avoidance of close proximity. They were only social by political necessity. It's hellish to have such a lust for power.

I played well. I could have played better. At the close of our performance, back in our domain, Friedemann praised my playing, but I knew, and I think he knew I knew, that there was better stuff in me. I thanked him for giving me the part and he told me there would be more where that came from, and so I was content.

And still battle loomed.

Letters from home continued, although reading between Michael's lines I could see that all was not well. Visits home were impossible for me; only the emergencies of death and my master's goodwill had allowed me to visit earlier. I wrote more frequently than I received, but I didn't begrudge my brother that. Annamaria was serious about some fellow, and arrangements were being made to arrange a betrothal. I think in our father's day Annamaria's wishes and desires would not have been considered, but these were softer and more giving times in our family.

One melancholy piece of news that summer was that dear old Herr Pinklemann had passed away. I prayed for him the following Sunday, and thought often afterwards of what he had done for me. But I think the debt I owed him was paid in full because Michael told me that he had sat at the old man's bedside in Rostock, and when he relayed my news of playing in the ensemble of the Duke's court, the old man had smiled and whispered some words about his protégé. He was seventy-four.

"It is all unduly and excessively complicated." This was our squadron commander Helmut Weitz trying to explain the involvement of the Baltic States in the warfare against the Empire. "Field Marshal Johan Banér has very kindly scoured the Imperial vermin out of Mecklenburg, Pomerania and elsewhere along the northern coast, and so *quid pro quo* demands that we now assist Sweden in further endeavours." He was putting it quite politically; we were in thrall to Sweden, plain and simple, and Sweden told us what to do. "You have heard of this alliance the Swedes have with the French?"

We had all heard some talk of shifting alliances, of treaties made worthless before the parchment had curled, but it was all too much for the limited understanding of the greater number of our squadron, me included.

"Axel Oxenstierna essentially runs Sweden. He is Regent and acts as advisor to Queen Kristina who, although she loves painting and poetry and art and music, knows nothing and cares even less about policy. Granted Oxenstierna is a very wise councilor. He's also a wily, scheming, unscrupulous bastard. (You didn't hear me say that.) He is receiving millions of *Livres* in French gold in this alliance he has forged with them. Johan Banér is his latest tool, a very capable commander of considerable experience, who will join forces with the French army under the Comte de Guébriant in attacking the Habsburg realms in the south. So, Catholics and Protestants joining forces to fight Catholics. Clear?"

I think our blank faces must have told him all he needed to know.

"Alright," he sighed. "The politics can take care of themselves; the job of us soldiers is to go and kick Ferdinand III in his great dangling Catholic testicles."

That much we understood.

There was an air of excitement about the exercise yard. We worked hard in our cavalry squadron on manoeuvres, knowing as we all did, that these practice sessions would soon be matters of life and death, not evolutions of grace and elegance. Our squadron numbered two hundred and forty men, and this would be the entire force of cavalry that Mecklenburg-Schwerin could contribute to the Swedish-French alliance. We followed the military model laid out by Gustavus Adolphus of Sweden, the greatest military genius of his age. (Even so, he might have accomplished more if he hadn't got his silly head blown off at the first Battle of Breitenfeld in 1632.) In battle, following his model, we would combine tactics with infantrymen armed with harquebuses, dashing out from between the volleys in lightning strikes while the enemy were stunned with gunfire. However, our chief routine of practice at home was the *caracole*, where the front line of an advancing squadron makes a single half turn to the left, discharges the pistol, then continues the turn, returning to the rear rank to reload. Meanwhile, the next rank in line comes forward to make the same manoeuvre, and so on. Only when the enemy was overwhelmed with the gunfire would we draw swords and go in for close work. The ranks in the *caracole* can be ten or twelve deep, and as many as twenty-four or twenty-five wide, so great skill in horsemanship was essential, and continual mind-numbing practice could not be sacrificed.

Two trumpeters were assigned to a squadron, me and Martin. It was strange; we later shared duties, tentage and food, yet we never got even close to each other. Martin was a private man until the last time I saw him. Duplication was necessary, of course; a squadron can lose mounted men in battle, but it dare not lose its sole means of communication. As I had observed to Berthold, I was disposable. However, just because two members of the squadron were trumpeters didn't mean we had no share in combat. We would be expected to fight along with all the others, trumpets slung on bandoliers over our shoulders so our hands were free for pistol and sword. We were issued with field trumpets, again made by Sander and others in the north, but coarser and less refined than the ones we played at court.

One disconcerting side of all this was the presence of Joachim Wadegahte, whose family connections ensured he would be primed for leadership. He was now a *Subalternoffizier*, or subaltern, one of four reporting to our Helmut Weitz. He gave me no overt trouble during training, except to maintain his nasty attitude towards me whenever possible, and always behind Weitz's back. While in training here in Schwerin he was circumspect, confining himself to sneers and snubs, but I didn't trust him to keep his distance once we were in the field. Being in a position of command, he had the potential to put me in harm's way and write it off to the exigencies of warfare. I would have to be on my toes.

The horse I had been assigned almost from the beginning of my apprenticeship was now mine. He hadn't been given a name, so I gave him one. I called him Jürgen because he was solid and reliable, and because I think he loved me. Our mounts were heavy, fifteen hands or so, but not as large as some I had seen in use by harquebusiers on horseback. When I came across the Finnish cavalry I was quite taken by their beautiful mounts—sleek, fast and nimble—but they did seem flighty and skittish, and I wondered how well schooled they could be for battle conditions. Ours were stolid and firm and, I felt, more reliable in a tight place.

A tight place was in the offing.

But it was not until October of 1640 that Weitz martialed us and we finally set out, by which time the flurry of preparation followed by the frustration of inaction had turned us all snarling and nerve-wracked. We were commanded to ride south to meet contingents from Hesse-Cassel under Peter Melander, and Brunswick-Lüneburg commanded by Hans Caspar von Klitzing. Then we would continue south in search of Johan Banér's Swedes, who were supposed to be joining the Comte de Guébriant's French troops. We would all assemble in Erfurt before making a combined assault on the Imperials under General Ottavio Piccolomini.

I was lusting, aching for war.

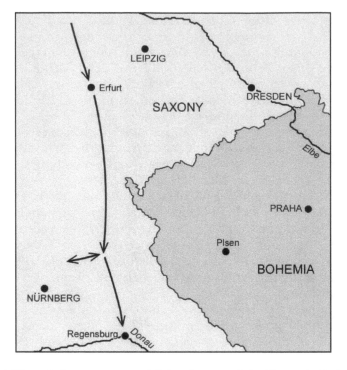

Jacob Hintze's first campaign with Johan Banér and the Comte de Guébriant

Chapter Sixteen

In which I ride to war in my first campaign

Sagte der Teufel: »Ah, wie weise diese Wahnsinnigen sind, mein Spiel zu spielen! Lassen Sie sie weitergehen; Ich werde den Vorteil ernten. Ich freue mich darüber«
The Devil said: "Ah, how wise these madmen are to play my game! Let them go on; I shall reap the benefit. I delight in it"

Martin Luther

A squadron of cavalry can travel fast when needed, but it depends upon how far. Riding all the way to the south of Saxony required more supplies than we would carry ourselves—food and drink, gunpowder and shot, farrier's equipment and a host of other necessities—so we were encumbered and slowed down by the pack horses and their attendants. Not the least of the encumbrance was the holy component. Each unit of the army had its own pastor, who travelled with all the necessary equipment for divine service, and ours was a somewhat casual rider. There was holy service every Sabbath—I measured the days by it—and the same before every engagement, of course. Many men wished to be shriven before entering battle, but I always felt secure in myself that God would receive me with a clear soul should my time come. I trust my Lord that He knows what's in my heart.

Reaching our first rendezvous with Melander and von Klitzing at the right time was another problem, because it was a moving target. Messengers had delivered information on their location some days before we left, but of course that information was out of date before it even reached us. By the time we got ourselves organized to leave they had doubtless marched already, so we would have to chase them. We needed to estimate the speed at which they marched—which would be a great deal slower than us because they were sending infantry—and then calculate where and when we would intercept them.

It was only as I rode across the stricken landscape of Saxony that the true extent of this conflict, and my role in it, came upon me. The loss of my friend Berthold had thrust the privations on me, and I had heard of the horrors of Brandenburg and Wittstock, of course. Then the tracts of wasted land I had ridden over on my way to and from Hamburg had been further testimony. But now, I suppose, riding to war as a soldier, it hit me full in the face. Not just the war, but my short

life in it. As our squadron found its way south I knew for the first time
that this sixteen-year-old had become a man. When my father and I
rode home from Schwerin over two years ago, I had felt that he viewed
me as now grown up; his death hastened me further into maturity.
Then when Giselle had jumped athwart me that sunny morning I felt
within myself that I had become a man. Not so. I only stood on the
threshold of manhood as I rode to war in that bleak, early-November
wind.

I yearned on that long ride finally to be facing the enemy and playing all those battle calls I had so laboriously studied and practiced. My
head was full of them, and the chance to execute them when it really
mattered drove me on. So far, my work, shared with Martin, was
virtually confined to *Buttasella* at the beginning of the day and *Halt*
when we stopped to camp for the night. We had no need for
Zapfenstreich in its true meaning, but we still played it to signal lights
out. Oh, to be on the battlefield!

It is ironic to me now that the campaign I cut my military teeth on
is said to be the most stupid, ill conceived and pointless of the entire
war. We all talked this around and around as we rode, and as we
camped; why would any general in his right mind make forays deep
into enemy territory in winter? Why our Duke would agree to send us
was obvious; the Swedes gave him no choice. But one hint of doubt
could lead to charges of mutiny, and we had all heard of the awful
punishments for that offence already carried out by leaders in the field.
Hitherto, warfare had been a summer pastime for the great ones in
power, so overturning this sensible tradition seemed to us to be court-
ing disaster. Forage for horses would be minimal, and although food
for the troops was supplied according to a fixed schedule, it wouldn't
last long; we would be limited by what little could be looted from the
stores of the hapless peasants along the route. Wet and cold weather
would limit seriously the effectiveness of firearms and, above all else,
it would be a misery for the serving men. Breaking camp in winter and
marching to battle was unheard of, but this is exactly what de
Guébriant did, presumably with the compliance of Banér. Perhaps he
was relying upon surprise—the Imperials under Piccolomini would be
in winter quarters and hardly be prepared to withstand an attack—but
many simply thought it was madness. We rode only because we were
under orders.

The further south we pierced into the heart of Saxony, the later in
the season it became and the colder it got. I had never been so cold.
Yes, I had been out in the fields in midwinter when the wind was all
from Russia and snow drove stinging sideways, but at the end of the
work day there was always a warm fire, furs, rugs, blankets. All my life

there had been warmth. Now our bodies descended into cold and there was no respite. Toes became vague, fingers became stupid, noses and ears were lumps of senseless leather. When we stopped for the night we burnt anything we could find; we set watches around our fires throughout the dark hours, so someone always kept the flames alive. We ranged the area where we picketed, ripping out boards from sheds and barns and fences, splitting them with our swords and feeding them to the flames. But our fire was still just one warm hole in a world of whirling cold.

We came across the fresh and unmistakable track of Melander and von Klitzing not far north of the rendezvous at Erfurt. An army marches across country in a long, thin, destroying swath. These are the tracks I had crossed in my youth, although their true horror only came to me when I was among those who made them. Ten thousand men and horses strung out for miles as they tramp and trot side by side, cover at most ten miles a day. Add to their number the ammunition and weapon wains, bag and baggage, blacksmith and farrier and armourer, and the camp followers: wives and children, cheap tinkers, victualers, priests and whores. As when the smell of wet earth in the air is the harbinger of rain, so their coming is presaged by the stink of sweat, urine and feces borne upon a foul wind long before even the din of their passage is caught by the ear. We knew they were ahead long before our scouts reported sighting them.

Not one in ten of these infantry is a career soldier; they are pressed in the levy, hauled away from their farms, scooped up out of the alleys and whorehouses when too drunk to resist or, worst of all, they are mercenaries in it for the loot, the pillage and the rape. When an army like this stops to bivouac, their thin line of march coalesces and spreads sideways, men spilling in to swell it until it is a bloated circle a mile and more wide of clamour, mud and stink. Then the army forages. Every three days or so those ten thousand men will need sustenance, and sustenance quickly gets to be in short supply. Only elite troops like us, the cavalry and mounted lancers, were well and regularly fed. The foot soldiers look after themselves, and most of them are in it only for what they can take out of it. Allegiance to a cause is a foreign notion to them, or at best a joke. They will range wide, spreading out from the sides of the camp in raiding parties, and they will take. Deer from the forests, cattle from the fields, grain from the barns. Friend or foe alike, they will take. And God help any landholder, priest or alderman who resists their hunger, their thirst or their lust. So, every three days or thirty miles, the thin track on the map of their passing is punctuated by wide, stripped circles of destruction like foul beads on a rosary from Hell.

It was a week after meeting Melander and von Klitzing, and

incorporating ourselves into their combined company, that we arrived at Erfurt. If the stink and chaos I had already seen was bad, this was ten times worse. Between thirty and forty thousand men were now gathered in a vast clot overlapping the landscape. Pissing and shitting close to their tents, drinking water from fouled streams, sharing tainted food, all these things led to sicknesses that ravaged the camp. I reckon more soldiers died from living in the camps and marching with the army than were ever carried off by lead balls, swords and pikes. It says much for military organization that such a rabble could ever be marshalled into a fighting force with a single purpose, let alone be directed to advantage.

Of course, there was the need of an enemy, and that's where Field Marshal Ottavio Piccolomini came into the picture or, to be more precise, stayed out of the picture. Naturally, the Imperial forces knew of our presence and had scouted our location. Piccolomini was no fool; he could see he was badly outnumbered. The year before, he had lifted the siege around Thionville and destroyed the French army, taking only a quarter the losses of his enemy, but there he had twenty thousand men while his enemy fielded scarcely more than half that number. Now the odds were reversed, and he was one to choose his battles wisely. He would avoid engagement with us at all costs, especially in winter. He fled; we chased.

So began an absurd game of cat-and-mouse. Through the end of November and well into December we penetrated further south, skirting Nürnberg well to the east. We never sighted the enemy, and although we often knew their location and direction of march, they were able always to outpace us. We were slow to receive explicit orders from above, and this led to confusion and delay. Most of us believed this was due to the endless squabbling between Banér and de Guébriant. We swore they spent more time arguing over tactics than they did in actual planning. It's my opinion, for what it's worth, that Johan Banér and Jean-Baptiste Budes, Comte de Guébriant share the blame equally for a campaign that was such a disaster. Banér was a known complainer and a heavy drinker; he had had furious rows already with Alexander Leslie over the tactics of the Battle of Wittstock some years before. Leslie had lost many of his best fighting men in order to prevent the rout of Banér's forces, and he was justifiably furious over what he referred to as ineptitude and indecision. On the other hand, it was said of de Guébriant that he was headstrong and impulsive, and never heeded anyone else's advice. Who knows which view to believe? But I do know that between the two of them we had a fine formula for cooperation.

With Banér and de Guébriant continually pulling each other's hair, it was a wonder they had ever agreed to combine forces in the first place. Perhaps it was political; a forced marriage where the bride and groom learn too late they actually detest each other. We all felt that if they had worked with each other, instead of opposing at every turn, we might have had some success, even in winter.

This inept game of cat-and-mouse did have one high point for me. We had camped somewhere north of Regensburg in mid-December, and de Guébriant now felt the need to send a message to the Imperial forces with the usual threats and insults: that he intended to engage, that he would give no quarter, that he would chase the bastard to the gates of Hell and beyond, and so on. Such goading between armies before battles was falling out of fashion, though; communicating gloating triumph or craven capitulation after the event were the more usual messenger's tasks in those days.

The whole army was well supplied with mounted trumpeters from the cavalry divisions, but it turned out there were few who could speak both French and Italian. The result was that, as a trumpeter and linguist—although I was never confident as to how firm my grasp of those other two languages really was—I had been identified by Helmut Weitz and called into de Guébriant's tent. Here was where I really understood and appreciated Hartmund Breitkopf's forceful tuition. His role had been to create two things in me: a versatile and useful messenger, and a fine player of the trumpet. The latter aspiration had been held up at the level of field calls, and would only resume if there was ever peace in this realm—and if I survived until then—but for the former I felt I was ready and able, and up to the task.

Until my head was in the jaws of the vice, that is…

When I arrived at the command tent I heard what seemed to be a furious exchange between two voices, but as I was shown in a sudden and deathly silence fell. The tent was full of toads of all sorts, poring over maps, poised in the act of scribbling notes, or paused in the middle of whispered exchanges. All eyes seemed to be on me. I was led by some sort of camp assistant to a screened corner where Banér stood at one side of a trestle with arms folded, and de Guébriant stood at the other. The trestle was covered with maps, documents and writing paraphernalia. You imagine that the famous figures you hear and read about are larger than life, but here they were—the Swede, a long-nosed fat man with a sneer, and the Frenchman, a slim ramrod in his late thirties with his hair in ringlets and a wry turn to his mouth— caught arguing like that man and his shrew wife in the play. De Guébriant glared at the aide who had shown me in, dismissed him with a wave, and turned to me.

"*On me dit que vous parlez Italien, garçon.*" How well, or how poorly, I spoke Italian was not something I felt happy to reveal. I simply saluted. "Well," he continued in heavily accented German, "if you so much as hint to Piccolomini that you do, I will personally see to it that you are disemboweled! Do you understand?"

No, I did not understand, not in the slightest, but, like my lack of confidence in languages, I was reluctant to reveal this ignorance as well. I remained silent.

"Do you speak *any* languages, God damn you!" shouted Banér. "Or do you communicate in salutes and nods where you come from? Or farts maybe?"

Banér appeared sick to me; he had a dyspeptic look about him, and I am sure he was carrying an ailment he wished to disguise. Just in the short time I was in his presence I could see him making a valiant effort at deportment while pain passed though him. He threw up his hands, strode out of the screened enclosure, and stood with his back to us at the far end of the tent. As he strode between them, the toads stirred and got on with their business.

"Yes, sir. I mean, no… sir," I turned to de Guébriant. "I… I speak French and Italian, and English as well. Sir."

De Guébriant swung his face suddenly close to mine and began spitting rapid-fire questions at me in French: "What is your father's name? What is your mother's name? Where do you live? How far away? Does your sister drink beer?…" and so on, as fast as he could make me answer. He didn't give a damn about who I was; he was testing my comprehension. Just before my mind and tongue began to betray me he stopped, grunted and nodded. Then it was a quick switch into Italian, the same relentless volley with spittle flying, but different questions. Again I answered as quickly as I could, my tongue falling over itself in haste. He stopped as I was stammering my ninth or tenth reply—something to do with my grandfather's bowels—and knowing I couldn't keep it up. He grunted and nodded again.

"*Bon!* You're to deliver a message directly into the hands of *General-Feldwachtmeister* Piccolomini," and here the wry turn to his mouth reached its maximum, as if smiling at some private joke, "and not for one instant will you hint that you understand him when he speaks in his native tongue to his staff. Is that clear?"

Now I saw what was in the offing. He was intending to have this young messenger use his ears to pick up information. All in a great rush, Breitkopf's training was being thrust onto me. I was elated at the trust in me this showed, but terrified at the prospect. I wasn't ready for this; I was too unsure, too conscious of failure, too damned young and inexperienced. I was almost literally shit scared. It was no secret that Banér thought the whole idea stupid, and I wished with all my heart that he had won their argument, because I was sure that's what it was about. Arguing in front of underlings didn't seem to worry them in the slightest. I seriously believe they thought nothing of exchanging sharp words in front of inferiors because we simply were of no account. It was of no more consequence to them than a blacksmith and his wife arguing in front of a rack of tongs and hammers.

Le Comte de Guébriant sat down at the trestle, dipped his quill into the ink and wrote a quick note. He sanded the ink, folded the paper, dripped wax and impressed his seal.

"You are to deliver this into his hand. *His hand!* No other." He thrust the message into my hand. "He will be angry. You will demand a reply." Me? Demand? From an angry general officer? I placed the letter in my scrip and saluted.

"*Capitaine!*" he roared, "*a moi!*" and the aide returned smartly into the screened enclosure. "Show this... boy... directions." And to me, as he dismissed me from his presence, "Use your ears. Do not fail me."

The *capitaine* led me to one of the tables where a hastily scrawled map was laid out. "We believe he is here," he said, showing me a point some distance to the west, and dangerously near Nürnberg. "It is not half a day's ride," he added, looking up at me, "if you are quick."

I was quick. The sooner I got this horrible task out of the way the better, but as I rode I began to swell with self-importance. I saw this heroic figure in his fine livery, trumpet at his back, thundering over the landscape in a do-or-die mission. (My God, young boys are fools!) Then, not far along the way I had another of those ugly setbacks in my mind as I thought of how proud Papa would be... would have been. After about three hours I rode Jürgen up the crest of a hill and saw the Imperial encampment spread out below me. I kicked into a gallop and reined up at the enemy pickets.

It is most disconcerting for the first time in your life to have a loaded pistol pointed directly at your heart. I swung down from the saddle and tethered the horse to a tree. My livery, my trumpet and the letter from my scrip proved credentials enough to give me safe passage to the command tent, but running the gamut between lines of enemy tents and campfires was frightening. Heads turned as I passed, and as soon as my uniform was identified there was an almost palpable enmity. Yes, by the rules of combat the enemy gave messengers free passage, but it was never intended to be easy.

Good God, Piccolomini was fat! I have seen portraits of him where they show a little girth in line with nobility and good living, but the real thing was grotesque. I was shown into his presence and immediately riveted by his little piggy eyes. Even though on campaign, he sat in an elaborate chair, almost a throne, and was dressed in the most flamboyant and impractical style.[29] He was surrounded by officers, assistants and sundry support staff. As with our staff tent, there were folding tables loaded with maps, paperwork and writing instruments.

I had only to open my mouth to commit a terrible mistake, although it had to be explained to me later. "A message *Herr General-Feldwachtmeister*," I said in German, thinking to use his full title. Unbeknownst to me, he detested the title. He felt he merited *Generalissimo* and no less, but the Emperor had deemed otherwise. He refused to be addressed by the German title.

His face coloured and I watched his hands tighten into little fists. There was a long, porky-eyed pause while the entire tent held its collective breath. The colour lessened; the hands untightened.

"Quale messaggio si presume di dare a me?" he rasped.

Thinking quickly, I put on an utterly blank face. He asked me again, and I formed an expression of complete confusion. I even opened and shut my mouth a few times.

"Mio Dio," he said in Italian, turning to the officer beside him, "the morons have sent me one who knows no Italian!"

One of his other officers, a knowing looking old file with a thin, wise face, stared directly at me and said, *"Ma lo fai parlare Italiano, non è vero, maiale?"* This pig put on the best ignorant yokel expression it could muster, praying he didn't see through me. I was terrified my slightest change of expression would betray my thoughts. I think these few moments of monumental restraint and pure play-acting paid huge dividends later in my career, and probably saved my life at the time. He seemed satisfied and nodded slowly. My heart slowed a little.

"Give it me," demanded Piccolomini in broken German, snatching the paper out of my hand.

He tore off the seal and scanned the lines. Again the face coloured and this time the hands crushed the paper, knuckles whitening with the force.

"He is goading me!" he yelled in Italian. "He calls me a coward! Hear this: 'Nördlingen and Thionville were pure luck; you dare not meet your equal!' By God, we'll attack the swine! They are freezing and starving. We will attack."

The same knowing old file stepped forward. "That is exactly what he wants, sire. It is true that his troops are not as fit as ours, but he is well situated and he greatly outnumbers us. He might well prevail." He glanced quickly at me again, but I was ready; not a wooden lack of interest, which would have him smell a rat, but an expression of struggling yet failing utterly to comprehend. A two-edged dramatic sword, but I played it well.

"What then? What then?"

"We do exactly the opposite, sire. We send a message with this pig," indicating me with a cocked thumb, "saying that we will give him battle. He will then waste time and effort entrenching his position…"

"While we are off smartly in the opposite direction!" the fat one finished, God damn his bloated Catholic carcass. "Genius, Antonio! Pure genius!"

When I saw behaviour like this for the first time, I began to appreciate the stupidity of most men in high office. Piccolomini was one of these swine born to power; ruthless, unprincipled and quite incapable of being wrong. But not clever; no subtlety and not a vestige of thought of any subterfuge except his own. I believe he truly followed the Catholic cause in pure bone headed ignorance. He was the type who have been fed the myth of empire in their nurse's milk, and what to most thinking human beings was a rag-tag mess of squabbling self-interest, was to him a mighty power. It was all a great game. But now, as I recall this years later, I do wonder whether I really held these views at the time. I was equally wedded to the Protestant cause through my own upbringing, and it was a mess of equivalent proportions. Perhaps this larger and more cynical picture comes through later experience.

Piccolomini lowered himself down onto a stool at the table and scribbled a letter, with the knowing cove looking over his shoulder.

"Tell that bastard Jean-Baptiste Budes, Comte de Guébriant," he told me in his mangled German, "that we will attack. Now!"

He shoved the letter at me. "Get out of here before I send back only your head."

I needed no further persuasion and I think I made better time on the return journey. The comfortless winter sun was setting behind me as I rode into our encampment.

De Guébriant received me in his tent, and I had the strong impression that he had not moved from there since I had left. I handed him the message and watched him tear it avidly open. "So, he is goaded into battle is he? Hah! But what did he tell you to say?"

"That he will attack as soon as possible, sir." He looked at me quizzically. I actually enjoyed this moment of suspense. I had power over this great man, and he was hanging on my words. I continued in Italian, "But he will actually let you dig in and await him, while he runs away as fast as he can."

"Excellent!" he clapped his hands in glee. "Well done, my boy! Well done! You will be commended for this day's work. I will see to it."

It would be a wonderful story to tell: how my subterfuge and *sang froid* turned the campaign, how our entire fighting force readied itself to march, how we overtook the surprised and unprepared Ottavio Piccolomini, and how the Habsburg forces were routed. The truth of the matter is, the squabbling continued, nothing was decided, and by the time we again marched south it was far too late. We never saw a trace of Piccolomini again. At least, not on that campaign.

My triumphant debut as a messenger turned to ashes.

We continued south with excruciating slowness, eventually meeting the Donau somewhere upstream from Regensburg. By this time the army was ragged, suffering more and more from the cold, and running dangerously short of supplies. One heartening aspect was our excellent supply of powder and shot, as we had used none. We heard through campfire gossip that there was more wrangling, and that harsh words had been exchanged over our approach to Regensburg. Our leaders were apparently arguing over whether to lay siege to the town, as the Diet was in session. De Guébriant thought it would be an important political coup but Banér disagreed. By this time, though, this odd couple had been at loggerheads for so long, they would likely disagree over anything and everything, and be damned to common sense. Rumour had it that Melander and von Klitzing were wondering why, exactly, they were still here.

I think Johan Banér had more sense, and I also think he was much more in tune with the needs of his troops than the Frenchman. The fact is, many of the infantry were now starving. They had ranged as far and wide as possible, stealing whatever they could find, but by the end of our march south there was nothing to be had in the whole stripped land. I saw men tearing the moss off trees and chewing it, stuffing handfuls of leaves in their mouths, anything to assuage the terrible hunger gripping them. Boiled boots were apparently edible, if you forgot the suffering you would bring on in the days following. There was a story going round that at the close of the siege of Breisach a couple of years back, soldiers in the service of the Empire had resorted to eating the bodies of their comrades. I believed it, seeing what was happening around me.

My little troop of cavalry were more fortunate than the foot soldiers... just. We had stocked our saddlebags with old bread and some hard heels of cheese that kept well, and when that ran low I showed them how to make a soup of nettles, scrabbled out from under the snow. Who knew? Those effete town types had no idea of what there was to be found under their very feet. Farm boy showed his resourcefulness then, and even the proud Wadegahte was seen wolfing down a bowl. We survived. At least we never had to eat our horses, as quite a number of cavalry regiments had done, or dine on the draft animals that hauled the artillery and supplies.[30]

Wadegahte never bothered me, never came near me. I think he was utterly dispirited by this whole campaign, his mighty sense of self-importance having been dealt a heavy blow. I hated the pointless stupidity of it myself, of course, as did all our men, but I like to think that my upbringing had given me a much solider base of stoicism. But the privation only brought out the coward in him, and he withdrew into himself.

A siege of Regensburg would be ludicrous with the present state of our troops, but that is exactly what was attempted. In early January we were able to assemble on the north bank of the Donau, and some of our number crossed on the ice to make half-hearted forays. With the river frozen hard it might have been possible for all of us to cross, and then perhaps a full siege could have been undertaken. As it was, the ice began to break up and it turned into a soaking farce. I believe if we had attempted this in summer, fording the Donau higher up and with our forces in much better condition, it might have been a turning point in the subjugation of the Habsburg realms.

Might-have-beens don't belong in my world.

Our two mismatched commanders finally gave up the idea of a seige, and we Mecklenburgers headed north in the company of Melander and von Klitzing. We heard that Banér and de Guébriant had also parted company, and that the Swedes had wandered east through Saxony, laying waste as they went, ending up along the high waters of the River Weser, accomplishing little. Spring came to us as we rode north, but the wasted landscape made a mockery of the flood of new greenery. There are some blank weeks in my memory here. I was assailed with terrible aches and fevers, riding my horse day by day in a vile fog of the mind, descending shivering and sweating into my tent, and rising again the next morning to continue the nightmare. I turned seventeen before we arrived finally, exhausted and spent, back in Schwerin.

Losses to us on this campaign: around forty from freezing, fevers and the bloody flux.

Heroic cavalry signals blown on my trumpet: none.

Chapter Seventeen

In which I return to what I had thought was normal. A fragile
interlude

*Denn wir haben nicht mit Fleisch und Blut zu kämpfen, sondern mit Fürsten
und Gewaltigen, nämlich mit den Herren der Welt, die in der Finsternis dieser
Welt herrschen, mit den bösen Geistern unter dem Himmel*
For we wrestle not against flesh and blood, but against
principalities, against powers, against the rulers of the darkness of
this world, against spiritual wickedness in high places
Epheser/Ephesians 6:12

"So now you've tasted military life in the field." Hartmann Breitkopf
was at ease behind his desk as usual. "Sit. Sit. You're off duty for now."

I had been back nearly a week from the south and had been
spending my time getting myself thoroughly clean, attending to the
terrible condition of my kit, and resuming serious trumpet practice.
The cavalry met for regular drills as if almost six months of their lives
had not been carved away, but our sharpness and esprit would take a
long time to return. I was thankfully back at Frau Walther's—one piece
of stability in a life of change—but this time in a larger room with an
oaken chest, and no longer under the eaves.

I sat, trying to think of something to say that wouldn't sound trivial
or naïve. When my fever had allowed me, I had done much thinking
on those long, tedious days of slow riding north, but had arrived at
nothing I could call resolution or comfort in myself.

"You may have got precious little credit from de Guébriant," he
spoke into my silence, "but Weitz told me about it." So Weitz had at
least noticed me. "Good job! Wearing your eyes out over all those
candles and banging your head against grammar books seems to have
paid off."

"I was terrified, sir," I told him, breaking my silence. "Absolutely
terrified."

He nodded slowly. "I should hope so. Fear is the best tutor of
behaviour. Now tell me: who are you?"

That threw me. I had found readjustment to life at the ducal court
in Schwerin punishing, and I was having difficulty reconciling the
perfumed fantasy of music and polite deportment with the sordid
reality of war. Having been on campaign, I had seen that part of my
military career from the inside, and now the boy trumpeter was
realizing that all his musical aspirations were now playing second fiddle

in a violin solo. Second fiddle to the real reason for employing him. I was a soldier; I had signed on as a soldier, and my life would be soldiering. But I was so torn…

Breitkopf, that too-perceptive bastard, saw all this in my face and my manner. We were close in a way that is uncommon between master and apprentice, or commanding officer and underling as it now was. I often wondered if he had treated all his protégés this way, but it was hardly something that could ever be expressed. And I was still uncomfortable with the conflict between the closeness that our relationship had fostered, and the necessary aloofness that rank required.

"I am trying, sir," I began, "to put all my experiences into some sort of order…"

"I asked you," he said, more insistently this time. "Who are you?"

I came to the resolution that must have been with me all along, awaiting a moment to descend. "I am a soldier, sir."

"Yes, you are a soldier. As long as you are serving our Duke in time of war, you are a soldier."

"Yes, sir. As long as this war continues."

"But you have come back, have you not, with deep misgivings? Bellona, fair goddess of war, has exposed her privy parts to you, and you have gone galloping off in ardour. And after three months of pursuit, she pulled her petticoat tight about her knees, didn't she? You have come back unrequited and dispirited… No, no," he waved my protestation away, "you know it's true. You have come back a man, yes, but you are half the boy you used to be."

"Yes, we all came back with nothing," I admitted. He wanted honesty and I would give it to him. "Nothing accomplished. Futility."

"What do you believe?" Another hard question demanding a hard answer.

"Believe…" I said, playing for a little time while my thoughts settled.

"Deep down. In your soul. What do you believe?"

"I believe," I replied slowly, "that the Holy Roman Emperor must be stopped. That we must have the freedom of our beliefs. I was brought up to believe that Martin Luther had set a new path for Christians. I was brought up to believe that the Catholic Church is corrupt and venal."

"Worth all this devastation? Your beliefs?"

"It's not Christianity, this war. It's power. Jesus Christ would be appalled."

"So, you will fight? Amid all this ruin and devastation and death, if you are called upon again, you will fight?"

"We have to! Sir. I have to. That's the bond I signed." My mind went back over the things I had seen. "There are atrocities on both sides—I have seen them—but we cannot win this war if we fail to meet the enemy under his own terms. Use his own tools; fight the way he fights. The land is ruined but we have to fight on."

My master had forced me to face all this, and it did settle my mind. A sureness of purpose had replaced my doubts and misgivings. I thought then that I saw a way forward, but it was an illusion.

A strange period of my life began now. Our foray into Saxony had been costly, and the result negligible, so Mecklenburg-Schwerin's contribution to the ongoing warfare became slight to nonexistent. A period of what passed for peace descended, but it was a fragile and enclosed thing, while news from all points of the compass was bad. Our region was devastated. Life outside the towns was grinding to a halt amid disease, famine and want. The northern princes, shreds of the earlier Protestant alliance, were continually attempting to seal pacts of non-aggression; Lübeck, Hamburg, Mecklenburg, Pomerania all trying in vain to create stability. Hartmund Breitkopf was rarely present. I knew without ever having to ask that he was about much more important business than blowing notes on a trumpet. I should have felt jealous that he had not considered taking me with him, but I did realize that on that one occasion he had been more or less obliged to, and would not willingly risk himself again.

Music at court was seriously curtailed, although of course the trumpet corps remained intact. This would be among the last of the princely trappings to be abandoned. We played the routine fanfares, entradas and sonatas that courtly protocol demanded, and I am sure the greater majority of the players were perfectly content; a steady job, bread, sausage and beer, stability and order. Not me.

Into this crockpot was thrown headfirst a young man who had been given a taste for war, and who knew that until this realm was at peace, his ambition to play fine music for the delight of the Duke and his court was on hold. I was torn between my young ambition and harsh truth. I prayed for peace; I lusted for war.

Towards the autumn of that year I managed to get a leave pass, so I saddled up good old reliable Jürgen and rode slowly east. I was keen to see the family—letters were a poor substitute—but my old horse had seen a lot and he wanted gentle travel with lots of opportunity to forage. I took my time, sleeping wherever I could in my soldierly way, and on the morning of the third day I came in sight of home. Mama and the girls greeted me; the boys were out in the fields and would only know I was here when they came in at midday, perhaps for a slice of bread, a wrinkled apple and something to drink.

Mama gripped me tightly, too tightly, her head just up to my shoulder, and she had trouble letting me go. Now, I think, she felt the full reality of what her youngest son had become. Just like me, and the girls too, she had thrived on a rosy vision of her young man in his livery, galloping heroically, trumpet to lips. Even when she had told me, just before Papa's death: "Go and fight and win," even then it had not fully sunk in. Only when she learned through my letters to Michael that I had been away to war, did the truth come home; I was in death's way and she clasped me as if to hold the life in my body, as if by the pressure of her arms she could stop time. She wanted to live only in this moment.

As she hugged me, she was also hugging absent Jürgen.

Mama was smaller, older, and her spark was expiring. Clara had grown steadily, filling out in those girlish places, and Annamaria was fully a woman. Michael and Hans had been joined by Annamaria's man Lukas; his farm had fallen finally into ruin, and his parents had gone to live in Rostock with their older son, who was a merchant. Lukas was a spare pair of hands and a willing heart, and they needed him badly. Mama gave me food and drink, and I was conscious that I was eating in fine style at the family's expense. She was treating me while the others would want. While I ate she told me all the news of the neighbourhood, the church and the town. But only, I noticed, the good things. I spoke sparingly of my experiences, confining my talk to the goings on at court, but I knew she saw all this as chaff, while deep in her heart she did not want to know more.

When the boys came in they greeted me uproariously, even Lukas who I had never met before. Those three boys put on a show for me, but no matter how much bounce you put into your actions, how wide you make your smile, or how positive are your words, you can see the truth in the eyes. When my squadron rode into Schwerin, back from the hardships of Saxony, we put on the same show. It may have fooled most folk who were there in the streets to greet us, but we knew. Look into the eyes. The tired eyes.

I didn't stay long; couldn't. And every hour I did stay impressed on me more and more that all this was transient, that it couldn't hold. I don't know if I was granted a premonition then, but as I look back on it now I would swear I *knew*. In my last view of them, they are standing at the gate, just by the drive where the cavalrymen found me all those years ago.

I see them now.

Chapter Eighteen

In which I return to war, get a horrible surprise and see the battle
for Leipzig from an interesting perspective

*Kämpfe den guten Kampf des Glaubens; ergreife das ewige Leben, dazu du
auch berufen bist und bekannt hast ein gutes Bekenntnis vor vielen Zeugen*
Fight the good fight of faith, lay hold on eternal life, whereunto
thou art also called, and hast professed a good profession before
many witnesses

Timotheus/1 Timothy 6:12

Johan Banér died in May, just about the time we had returned from
the south. Judging by what I had seen of him, his hard living and
drinking had probably done him in. He had retreated to Halberstadt
after his campaigning and died there. Following his demise, his forces
joined with von Königsmarck and Wrangel. We heard that his men
had carried his body onto the field at Wolfenbüttel that summer. Well,
they obviously had a higher opinion of him than me, but mine is only
based on slight acquaintance and rumour. Later that year, Axel
Oxenstierna assigned Lennart Torstensson as Field Marshal to lead the
Swedish forces. Anyone who knew anything about him said he was by
far a better commander than Banér. That he was utterly ruthless in his
pursuit and destruction of Imperial holdings is not in question. Now
began a reign of terror, as he marched almost unopposed through
Saxony, Silesia and Moravia. All the principal fortresses on his route
were sacked and destroyed. Glogau, Olomuc, Zittau and more fell and
were rendered impotent and, at the maximum extent of his march, he
didn't fall far short of Wien. I had seen the kind of destruction caused
by an army marching through any territory, friend or foe, and I thank
God we were not involved at that stage. I had told Breitkopf that we
must fight the enemy with his own weapons, but in truth I would have
found it hard to play a part in any of that.

It was on Torstensson's return through Saxony in 1642 that the
demand went out to all Protestant princes to provide more men and
arms. Messages had come to us that the army of the Holy Roman
Empire under the command of Prince-General Ottavio Piccolomini
would be joined by Archduke Leopold Wilhelm of Austria. So, it
seemed, I would encounter Piccolomini again, although not within
spitting distance this time, I prayed. Had I known then how wrong I
was, I wonder what I might have done, but the future is not to be
known, and we cannot question the destiny God has laid out for us.

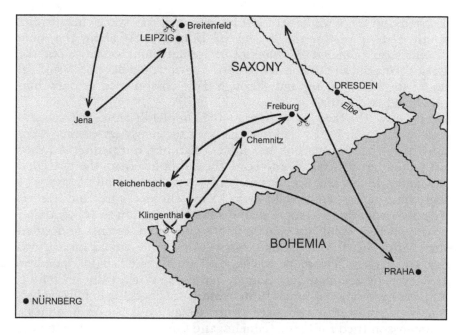

Jacob Hintze's second campaign, with the Swedish army under Lennart Torstensson

Once again, our squadron of two hundred and forty cavalrymen rode south in the autumn with fair Bellona, and Minerva too, urging us on. My trumpet colleague on this occasion was a man named Dieter Walser, who was not of our court. He hailed from somewhere in Brandenburg and had joined us quite recently. I heard that Martin, my earlier colleague, had been reassigned. I left reliable old Jürgen in the court stables; he wouldn't do well on these long forays, but I missed him and hoped he would remember me when I returned. Sometimes I protected that horse and worried about him more than I did my own body.

We would be one of a dozen squadrons of cavalry, ours under the Landgraf von Hessen. Fully half of these squadrons were Swedish, and we were told that the Finnish Hakkapeliitta under General Torsten Stålhandske would also be there. These were lightning-fast cavalry on light horses, who relied on surprise. They cried out *hakkaa päälle* as they attacked, meaning 'chop them down'. We had heard of these fighters and were keen to see them in action.

We met von Hessen in early October somewhere north of Jena, led to him by the clear evidence of his passage. We marched with him in the direction of Leipzig, which was slow going as he also carried foot soldiers and artillery. The plan was to combine forces with

Torstensson who, we heard from messengers, was somewhere to the south east of us, on the border of Bohemia. At about this time Torstensson cornered Piccolomini in mountainous country, but the Italian occupied an unassailable hilltop. Attack would have been suicidal under these conditions, and although Torstensson tried to draw him out, he refused battle.

By now, the Swedish army was suffering badly from sickness and lack of supplies. It was said that many of the newly levied men were unused to scant provisions and forced marches, but neither did they have the merciless rapacity to seize their supplies from the wretched peasantry. If that was so, they certainly weren't the kind of savages I had come across, and would again to my endless regret and misery. The Swedish army was more than decimated, and it was only a matter of time before combat would be impossible. So Torstensson decided that before his forces became too weakened, he would march into Saxony, sack a few more towns, and thus replenish his supplies. However, by this time Piccolomini had come down from his hilltop and was harassing our forces from behind, not engaging in full combat, but weakening the rearguard with forays and surprise attacks. Torstensson tried for Liska, Camentz and Grossenhagn, but each time the enemy was too close, and the attacks and sieges had to be abandoned.

We arrived in late October, drawn for days by the sound of heavy gunfire ahead of us and by a drifting pall of smoke high in the eastern air. Torstensson had begun to lay siege to Leipzig and was bombarding from the east with cannon fire. He might well have been caught this way, with his back to the enemy, but for a fortunate chance. Some enemy combatants had been captured, and under 'questioning' revealed that Piccolomini had force-marched within a day of Leipzig, was now supported by the army of Leopold Wilhelm, and was further reinforced by several Saxon regiments. This was no harassing raid from behind; this was a full-scale assault. We learned later that there were sixty squadrons of cavalry, eleven brigades of infantry, and forty-six cannon. The odds were now heavily tipped in favour of the Empire.

Torstensson should have run away. In fact, that is exactly what he appeared to do. But first he had to convince the enemy to the contrary; that he would stay dug in and fight where he stood. And that was where I got flung into the fire. Again.

I was surprised to be summoned by Landgraf von Hessen around the sixth hour of our second day in Leipzig. I was just one of many signalers, and I was sure he knew nothing of me. As I made my way through our lines I wondered guiltily if it was something I had done, and if so, what. So it was with some anxiety that I reported to his tent.

"Hintze," he began, looking down his nose at me from his considerable height. "We have received a request from the Field Marshal for a messenger who has both experience and fluency in languages. Your commander, Herr Weitz, has recommended you."

I was confused; I couldn't imagine that news of my little exploit in last year's campaign could possibly have reached this high, and it wouldn't have excited any interest anyway. As far as the official record went, it might as well not have happened. So why was I singled out from among scores of trumpeters in dozens of companies? It made no sense at all.

"Yes, sir," I replied in mystification, "I speak French and English…" I didn't want to mention Italian, perhaps because of some awful premonition, but he fixed me with his eye, stared and waited. "…and… Italian."

"Your talent in Italian has been well recommended," he said, nodding. "And you also, I am told, exhibit great poise and cool-headedness under pressure."

Normally you dared not challenge a superior officer, but this was so fantastic, so unlikely, and frankly so frightening that I felt I had to speak. "I am honoured at your lordship's opinion of my slender talent, but I think it has been much exaggerated…"

"I have heard otherwise," he interrupted waspishly. "And you would do well to agree with my assessment."

I flushed and my ears felt as if flames were coming off them. "Yes, sir!"

"Yes, sir, indeed! We have no room in this army for a false modesty that might well be a cloak for cowardice."

I stood rigidly to attention, knowing I was close to the edge of insubordination and that, if it were crossed, it would be irreversible.

"Now," he huffed, "you are to take a message swiftly to the enemy commander and place it in his hands, and no other." I felt the weight of the past bearing on the present. Not Piccolomini, please! Please God, tell me you want me to take a message to Archduke Leopold Wilhelm. I would ride through Hell to take a message to him. "You are to take this," and he handed me a folded and sealed paper, "to Prince-General Piccolomini and return to me with his reply."

My heart sank. I was dead. He would know me; of course he would remember me as soon as I spoke, and he would instantly realize my duplicity. It was a slender hope that I would be unremarked, but it was all I had. Perhaps they would give me as much attention as they would a set of saucepans. But if that other officer of his was present—the knowing-looking old file with the wise eyes—I was finished. My head would be returned, that I was sure of.

"I will tell you the substance of the message," my executioner continued. "He is told that we challenge him to come to battle and that we will await him here. We are tired of his cowardice and expect him to face us. You must also emphasize the imminent arrival of the Comte de Guébriant with Hessian and Weimar reinforcements." In fact, de Guébriant was nowhere near Leipzig, and Piccolomini would obviously know this. He would see right through this fabrication, and assume that Torstensson was using it as a ruse to cover his weakness. He would almost certainly attack. This was Torstensson's clever double bluff, but it was death for me.

I would have no option but to obey my commander's order; to disobey would be mutiny, and I had seen the hanging rags and bones of those who had chosen that route. Death by disobedience or death by obedience. Fine choice.

I slipped the paper into my scrip, saluted and turned about wordlessly. An underling took me by the elbow and led me over to a table where maps were laid out. I nodded dumbly as he showed me the site of the enemy encampment, scarcely half an hour's ride east. I returned hastily to my tent for a few necessities, took a long look at my trumpet for what I thought could well be the last time, and headed for the picket where my horse was tied up. I walked with a great heaviness in my heart. I am not sure if it was regret for all that might have been, fear of imminent death, or fear of the manner in which my death might be brought about. I imagined my mother when the news was brought...

As I was about to mount, who should I see walking towards me but Joachim Wadegahte with two of his perpetual cronies.

"Ah, our valiant messenger," he cried. "Off to face the enemy in his lair!"

He crowed with laughter and the toadies joined in. Suddenly it all came together in my mind: he knew of my mission! He must have contrived this entire thing. He must have heard from Weitz that a messenger who could speak Italian was being sought, and had persuaded him that I was the best candidate. The silver tongued bastard was condemning me to death, and in the most cowardly way.

"Big hero, eh, farm boy?" he whispered to me in an aside as he came alongside. Then loudly to his friends as they went on their way, "By God, I wish I could lay down my life for our holy cause!"

I rode east in the early afternoon, following a rough woodman's path through forest and across heath, my horse's hooves thumping reassuringly on the track. The rhythm of my riding helped put things into a better cast. Surely, Piccolomini would only know of my previous deceit if the plan had worked, but Banér and de Guébriant's constant bickering and delay had prevented that. Only if he suspected that I spoke Italian would he become suspicious, and even then could I not claim to have learnt it since? It seemed to me now, with time to think it all through, that I might just be able to act myself out of trouble. As my head depended on it, it would have to be a dramatic tour de force.

It was not long before the smell of the enemy came to my nose (the wind was from the east) followed soon after by the din. As I spotted the first signs of the encampment, two sentries stood across my path; I reined up in front of them, then seeing who I was from my livery, and guessing at my mission, they stepped aside.

Good God! Piccolomini was even grosser than I remembered him; he overflowed his fancy chair, and the eyes were set even deeper into their folds. The wise old advisor was at his elbow, I was unhappy to notice. The Prince-General tore at the message clumsily with his white, pudgy hands, ripping the paper half down before he got it unfolded. The instant I was shown into the presence I knew he remembered me. He scanned the paper and immediately addressed me in Italian.

"You! They have sent the same moron a second time, have they? What words have you to add to this insulting message?" He whacked the paper with the back of his hand. How could I play this? Incomprehension? Comprehension? I decided to speak haltingly and poorly in Italian.

"Leader says reinforcements… coming. You must face… us."

"Ah, so you speak Italian now, do you?" He fixed me with a stare and then suddenly roared, "Do you take us for idiots? You moron, you pig!" He rose from his chair, dashed the letter onto the ground and stamped on it. He leaned his raging face into mine, yelling insults and showering me with spittle. His breath smelled as if he had just taken a shit out of his mouth. This sudden anger terrified me.

The old advisor stepped forward and addressed me in rapid Italian. "Had we realized then what we now know, that you did not understand Italian at that time, but you do so now, we would not have said what might have been said. And do you comprehend that by transgressing the code of conduct your life is now forfeit?" He knew I understood this complicated construction, the subtle bastard. In my fear I had failed to conceal it. My acting career was clearly coming to an end. All I could do was nod.

"So, he presses us to attack," observed the fat Prince-General, sitting back on his chair and regaining some poise. "Which means the opposite. He is fearful of our might, so he will run away. Is that not his plan, pig?"

I had no idea what the plans were, and I said so. There was no point in asking me anyway because by now I was a liar as soon as I opened my mouth.

He began to rage again. "Guards! Here! Here!" The two likely lads I had passed at the flap of the tent came in smartly. "Take him out! Hang him up!"

And there, far from home in an Imperial military camp outside Leipzig, my life might have ended. Except, the wise old file—may God bless him and keep him for all eternity, I thought, Papist and Italian bastard though he was—stepped forward and said, "Hold a moment. This one might still be useful to us."

"How? How?" asked Piccolomini. "He is nothing. Worthless!"

"We may need a messenger to return to the enemy. Why waste one of ours when we can use this worthless clay?"

"So we keep him with us?"

"We do. We guard him closely, assess the need for a messenger when we meet the enemy, and dispose of him should his services not be required." Here he smiled and rubbed his hands together in a sinister fashion. "And let us exchange his livery for one of ours, so should he come in harm's way, his own people will make an end to him." And then this dirty old file—may Satan roast him and keep him for all eternity, I thought, Papist and Italian bastard—laughed in my face.

So the two likely lads hauled me away, stripped away my livery and flung replacement clothing at me. I kept my scrip, for whatever good it might do me, but the rest of my gear was lost. Once I had dressed, I was forced down to the base of a tree and tied tightly there. By now night was falling, but it wasn't long before I heard trumpet calls, not unlike ours, and realized the army was on the move. I was soon released from my bonds and hurled up onto my own horse. My ankles were tethered together with a rope passing under the horse's belly, and another rope was passed around my neck. As we got underway, an old cavalryman, whose sneer of contempt told me he had better things to do than look after me, seized the rope and fastened it to his saddle. Thus, as surplus baggage in the train of the army of the Holy Roman Emperor, I entered my first battle.

At the beginning of November the forces of Archduke Leopold Wilhelm of Austria and Prince-General Ottavio Piccolomini, greatly outnumbering the combined Protestant forces, advanced on Leipzig with me reluctantly in their number. Seeing that his challenge had stimulated action, Torstensson immediately raised the siege and marched quickly north through the pass at Seehausen, luring the

Imperial forces after him. Even though by morning he occupied the high ground at either side of the pass, he chose not to attack, allowing us instead to proceed even further north into the area of Breitenfeld. The Imperial army was already in a celebratory mood because it was at this wide field eleven years earlier that Gustavus Adolphus had won the first great victory for the Protestants. The tables were now turned, or so the Imperialists thought. Riders on either side of me were chortling about the coming slaughter, praising their generals and anticipating already the post-victory celebrations. My guardian tweaked the rope around my neck repeatedly, and the others guffawed at my nodding and gasping as the coarse stuff bit into my neck. Their optimism was well founded; with Torstensson fielding no more than twenty thousand men, and many of those far from their peak fighting form, it looked like dire results for my side.

And this imbalance, perhaps, caused the Imperial leaders to become incautious.

As dawn approached I saw we had crossed a deep ditch and were now drawn up in a line facing almost north. The 'enemy' faced us in a long line stretching east and west for some distance. As the sky lightened I could make out the banners of Wittenburg, von Hessen and Torsten Stålhanske to the left, and imagined my comrades out there in front of me, not half a mile away. But they might as well have been in far Cathay. In the centre of their line were Wrangel, Liljehok and Mortaigne, and to the right, as the rising sun glanced off their armour I thought I could make out the devices of von Konigsmarck and Robert Douglas. I was somewhere in the middle of the Imperial side, held not far from the command in case my 'services' were required. It was as close to an elaborate murder as makes no odds. The Duke of Gonzaga and the Counts of Bruay and Borneval were to my right, with the Count of Buchhajm to the left, with the artillery under the Count of Soye.

It seemed an eternity of waiting, a hideous and frightening almost-silence, as each side waited for the other to make a move. I sat on my saddle, ankles tethered below, and prayed as I had never prayed before. All along the lines there were muttered prayers and men crossed themselves in that Catholic way, raising their eyes to Heaven. Some had rosary beads that they worked between their fingers.

It began with a shocking thunderclap of artillery, the thuds of the guns beating into your chest, the fountains of smoke and fire shooting forth, and the awful sound of men and beasts being mown down by chain, ball and grape. The Swedish lines were taking a terrible beating, hugely disadvantaged by the smoke, which concealed their enemy and spoiled their aim. Swedish artillery was by far superior, so it was with agony that I watched them cut down while unable to mount answering fire. As if in response to this hamstringing, the entire Swedish line suddenly surged forward and it became a general melee with harque-buses, pikes, swords, lances and the butts of guns when powder was gone. I spotted our *caracole* shooting, wheeling and returning to load, just the way we had been trained, and I had a brief spurt of pride. There were my lads! Then order broke down and I lost sight of any organization. I had no idea how the battle was going, stunned by the terrific noise, blinded and coughing with smoke, and still tethered to my guard. The rope around my neck gave a mighty tug that nearly unseated me, and I saw my guard clutching at his chest in agony and sliding off his mount to the ground. The rope slackened, I dug my heels in, and charged slantwise across the lines, along with many other horsemen, thinking I might escape with them into the flanking woods. I learned later that I was among Colonel Madlon's cavalry, who appeared to be running away.[31]

To my left the struggling lines of the mighty clash of forces heaved and swayed. A desperate trumpet call rang out, the lines parted as if ploughed aside, and a phalanx of Swedish cavalry headed straight for me. I was buffeted against an Imperial rider as, to my horror, the cavalry charge parted to reveal the muzzles of several large field guns. Fire and smoke belched out directly at me, a clap of sound rang my head and squeezed my chest. The cavalryman at my side fountained outwards and upwards as a mighty shock blasted over me. It was as if a mass of wet hides fresh from the tannery vat had been flung at me from the side. A deep, oily thud with a squelching and viscid under-tone. This is the sound a man makes when he bursts. A huge engulfing wave of mess and stink threw me sideways from the saddle, the tether-ing rope tearing at my ankles. My horse crashed down dead, pinning my left leg under him. The man beside me just an eye blink before became a gouting trunk that toppled off its shying horse and fell across me, pinning me into the mud. Covered with one dead horse and half a man, bleeding from a rip in my scalp, and scarcely able to breathe, I realized that, somehow, I was alive and not badly injured.

The battle raged around me, with lines of Protestant pikemen and gunners streaming into the melee. While men screamed and cursed and died, amid the clashing and thumping and fusillades, I cringed and shook and cried. I justify it to myself now: Stay under cover and play dead or enjoy the real thing. Much later, several hours it seemed, the noise died down, the trumpets called retreat, and the sighs and groans of the dying could be heard. I had no idea who had won and who had lost. Carrion birds rustled and chittered as they worked on the eyes and lips of the dead and near dead, and upon the soft edges of open wounds. It was only when a soldier in Swedish livery came close to me, picking among the corpses for signs of Protestant life, with a stretcher party at his rear, that I realized we might be the victors. I tried to ease myself from under horseflesh, guts and mud. He saw me move, saw my livery, and made to go at me with his sword.

"Friend!" I gasped. "Prisoner! Landgraf von Hessen cuirassier regiment." I pointed to the rope, still looped from my upper ankle and passing over the flank of the horse. Thank God he realized the truth or the wise old file's plan would have come to fruition right there. He cut the rope, helped to slide most of the horse and human intestines off me, and led me off the field. It was a walk through Hell. Smashed men and horses were scattered willy-nilly; here a broken skull with the face torn off; there a great smoky cavity where a heart had once beaten; detached arms, heads, legs… a youth my age, drained white, gripping in his hand a small glass perfume vial, token of a sweetheart, carried into battle.

The Protestant forces had carried the day. Against formidable odds the Imperial army had been beaten and dispersed. Perhaps I am unfair to Ottavio Piccolomini who, I was told, led his men by example, making at least six forays among the enemy and only being forced to retreat when the majority of his men were beaten back. He must have been mounted on a massive beast, like the ones we used for hauling drays. Leopold Wilhelm also distinguished himself in the losing cause, leading his men as one of them, and only quitting when the general flight forced him to. These two leaders compared favourably with Lennart Torstensson, who was so crippled with gout that he could only direct from a position of safety. His days of mixing in with the lads were far gone, and he was not yet forty years old. Five thousand Imperial soldiers died that day, and many more were killed in the pursuit that followed. Of the Swedes, Torsten Stålhanske was severely wounded and Liljehok died on the field. Losses to the Protestant side were around two thousand, with an equal number wounded. Among our dead men was the reassigned Martin, the trumpeter who had remained a stranger to me, and who would have no one to recount his fall.

The immediate advantage of victory for the Swedes was the spoil: some hundred wagonloads of baggage, forty-six large and small artillery pieces, fifty ammunition wagons, and many other stores of provender and clothing. Of most interest to Torstensson, I am certain, was an entire wagon of red wine casks. Also captured were ensigns and standards, hugely symbolic of triumph.

Chapter Nineteen

In which we chase the Papists to Klingenthal and I see my own
bones

Nacket bin ich von Mutterleibe kommen. Nacket werde ich wiederum
dahinfahren
Naked came I out of my mother's womb, and naked shall I return
thither

Hiob/Job 1:21

Joachim Wadegahte's face, when he saw me risen from the dead, was
worth Leipzig and all the property the Swedes ransacked from it. I was
walking slowly and tiredly back to our tent area when I came across
him. Shattered, exhausted and wretched as I was, I put on a great big
brave grin just for him. And as soon as I saw his face, I knew his guilt;
it was written all over him in the way it often is with the shalow coward.
I couldn't bring myself to speak.

I had no sooner washed myself roughly in a nearby stream and
reported my return to Commander Weitz, than I was detailed again.
He looked me over with his assessing and rather forbidding manner,
and inclined has head slowly.

"Your gift with Italian is needed once more." He saw my face fall;
I was far too weary in mind and body to conceal my thoughts. "No
need for concern. My use for your skill is confined to our own camp.
You need travel no further."

My immense relief showed, quickly followed by puzzlement. He
sent me to the area where our prisoners—those who were worth
ransoming—were housed in a quickly assembled tent set on muddy
ground. Dejected fighting men, their fight all taken from them, stood
or squatted or sat on roughly shaped logs. There was little sound; just
muttering and some groaning from the injured. A surgeon beckoned
me over to a cot where a thin, pale young man was lying. He was filthy
and feverish, with bound injuries to both his arms.

"Italian. Can't understand him," said the surgeon. "Sounds like
'musician'. He's all yours."

"*Cosa vuole da me?*" I asked him. "What do you want me for?"

"I am a musician," he mumbled. "Leopold Wilhelm… personal
musician… They have to know I'm valuable. Tell them! Tell them!"

It's a horrible truth about great battles involving thousands of men
that only those worth ransoming survive. There is the obvious cull on
the battlefield itself—the sword at my throat only hours ago was

witness to that—but surgical help to those rounded up had to be saved for the most deserving. If judged a nobody, this poor man was doomed.

"What is your name?"

"Verdina. Pietro Verdina. I am… musician…"[32]

"Trumpeter?" I naturally assumed he was cavalry, because no other music of any kind would be heard anywhere near the field of battle.

"No, no. Violin, lute…"

"Why are you taken in battle?" What monstrosity was this?

"My prince requires… his entertainments at all times."

Well, this was fantastic. None of our commanders would have dreamed of taking a fiddle player to the front lines. The only entertainment any of them indulged in was a keg of wine and a large mug. Not even a camp whore.

"I will tell them you are a person of standing, and that your prince values you." What else could I do? And the gratitude on his face was reward aplenty.

"*Grazie. Dio ti benedica.*"

I think that of all the strange things I encountered in my career, this is high on the list. What kind of effete, thoughtless, self-indulgent prick would expose people like him to harm? I know we trumpeters were considered disposable, but we were trained to fight and we expected to have to do it. But a lute player? What a callous bastard Leopold Wilhelm must be, I thought. Well, Habsburg, Catholic, what do you expect?

I would love to report that my warfaring was done with for the time being, but that was hardly the case. Around fifteen hundred Imperial infantry and some cavalry had escaped to the south, and so a substantial portion of our forces was dispatched to chase them down and finish what had begun at Breitenfeld. We followed them quickly, deep into southern Saxony, cornering them eventually around the middle of November in Klingenthal on the mountainous borders of Bohemia. We came upon some of them hiding in the forests of the Aschberg, the mountain overlooking Klingenthal to the south, while others had occupied the woods around the town and the buildings themselves. Twenty four hundred of us under Count Magnar Svendssen made an easy job of occupying the town, but thereafter it became a slow and tedious business. The Aschberg and the forests up to its summit provided excellent cover for the few harquebuses and cannon that had been spirited away from Breitenfeld, and for a while during the afternoon we were held up, with no progress and some loss of life. It probably would have been possible to withdraw to the lower ground and starve them out, but Svendssen clearly wanted to finish the business, so the order was given to storm.

My company occupied an open and slightly elevated field midway between the beginning of the forest and the town. Cavalry was virtually useless among the trees, but we were well stationed to spot breakouts into clear country and to ride them down when needed. The forces under Svendssen's command were below us and to the east, and were screened from easy vision by a rise in the ground and a long stand of dense bushes and timber.

"Trumpet! Here! Quickly," called my commander, passing a hastily written note to me. "They are to be prevented from breaking out down there." He pointed to where a large force of infantry armed with pikes, swords and firearms was pouring out of the cover of the trees, unseen by our men below them. "Quickly now!"

I stuffed the note into my scrip, kicked my horse into a gallop and rode like hell in their direction. I had spotted a defile to my left where the hill fell away, and I reasoned that if I got into there I would be concealed, at least for maybe half a mile, before coming out again onto the open grassland. I galloped down, hunched over the saddle to keep my head low, although it made little difference. Halfway along, the defile took a slight turn and there in front of me were five or six harquebusiers lugging their great weapons and prop sticks towards me. Enemy! I knew how cumbersome those stupid things were, so I headed my horse straight at them in an attempt to ride them down. They scattered right and left, one of them dropping his gun in haste. In retrospect, I think they had been detailed to cover this defile and were in a better state of readiness than I had thought. One at least had his slow match burning, and he must have swivelled his weapon around and loosed off a shot. I heard the roar, and knowing how hopeless those things were against fast moving targets, I was totally shocked and surprised when my horse leapt and shied under me as the ball embedded itself. He went down whinnying and thrashing and I was thrown from the saddle into a clump of gorse.

There are times when I know my Saviour is watching over me. Two of the more courageous harquebusiers had drawn their swords and were running towards me, when I spotted a riderless horse not fifty yards away. If it had been lowered down from Heaven on a rope I could not have been more amazed. Babbling some sort of silly prayer, I dashed in my soaking drawers towards the horse, seized the bridle and attempted to mount. My left arm was a useless stick that obeyed no command of mine, but I was able to scramble up, pulling on the bridle with my right hand, and then I was off and away with the enemy cursing behind me. I galloped across the plain where the defile opened out, reined up at Magnar Svendssen's tent and delivered the message, fumbling it into the hand of an elderly aide.

"They're breaking out... other side of those bushes..." Orders rang out, riders mounted and a flanking manoeuvre was quickly underway.

"Easy lad." The aide was looking directly at that useless left arm of mine and frowning. "Get yourself down. Gently now..."

I looked where he looked. My shirt was ripped wide open and a huge white splinter of bone jutted out of a mess of blood and muscle on my upper arm. Then the golden aura that had surrounded me since I had fallen melted away, and a searing, roaring pain made me topple from the saddle. He must have caught me and helped me down, but I remember none of that.

The Lord Jesus Christ and Satan were wrestling for possession of my immortal soul. Our Good Lord held me clasped tightly in His arms, while Satan tore at my sinister arm, wrenching me down into Hell and damnation. I don't know how long this tug-of-war for my soul went on as pain of an intensity beyond imagining coursed through me.

I awoke in a tent. I was lying on my back with the arm immobilized in wrappings. I rolled my head and scanned the tent. It was a charnel house, a shambles of horror where groaning, screaming, sobbing men were having wounds attended to, or succumbing to their injuries in agony or blessed resignation. There was a stink of vomit and gore, piss and shit. The greater part of my mind believed that Satan had won the battle, and that I was in Hell and beyond even Christ's harrowing. A numbness of soul lay over my senses.

A surgeon in a blood-soaked apron saw my head move and noted my open eyes. He came over.

"Clean break," he smiled. "Lucky little bastard, aren't you?"

I couldn't speak. I was only just returning from damnation.

"Had one of our fellas hold you down, got a rope around your wrist. Big pull and the ends popped together nice as you please. Sewed you up like a fine gent's jerkin. You'll do."

With the return of comprehension came the pain. That searing, pulsing agony, again unlike anything I thought possible threw me into unconsciousness. I was back in Hell. It could only have been brief because the sawbones was still there smiling at me when I opened my eyes. The pain was now huge but strangely manageable.

"Hurts..." was all I could say, master of the obvious.

"Drink," he said, holding a beaker of small beer to my lips. I slopped a lot, but the coolness and wetness over my tongue brought me fully to my senses.

"How long…" I wanted to know how much time had passed since my injury.

"A few weeks," he said, misreading my question. "If it doesn't mortify, of course. But, as I said, clean break."

"I want… to get back…"

He shook his head. "You'll just stay here, my son. Battle's over. The day is ours, and Torstensson has you to thank for some of it." He looked over his shoulder. "There are others who need me more than you." And he turned to a cot beside mine where a pastor was applying oil, an unction clearly not of any medicinal value to that patient.

There must have been something in the beer; the pain was still there, but it seemed to be in some other place. I lay and contemplated the strange thing I had seen. My mortal flesh had parted to show me my immortal bones. When we die and the worm takes us, the bones continue, expressing that once there was a life that moved them, that shrouded them. I had been vouchsafed a small vision of what I would become after my soul was called away. When I close my eyes, that image of whiteness jutting from my flesh is as clear now as it was then.

You don't often come across an old soldier with large, disfiguring scars. Big wounds to the flesh and the bones almost always mortify, and even when the skin has healed there is still rot within. Soldiers injured in battle die soon after, no matter what any surgeon, physician or apothecary can do for them. So a veteran who carries scars is a man whom God has decreed will remain in this life a little longer. I am one.

Perhaps I should have died. When I returned home after Klingenthal I wished with all my heart that I had.

After the day of the battle, when I had woken in the surgery tent, I descended into what abyss of Satan I know not. A fever grew on me, my entire body beat in time to my heart while waves of pain and horrible visions beset me. I was told that I raved and struggled against the surgeon and his men, tearing out the neat ligatures that he had inserted and risking displacing the bone. I was carried to the Benedictine monastery of Saint Mary near Chemnitz, and there I was nursed by the monks, while the army decamped and headed south west without me and others who had survived against all odds.

The fever peaked in two days, the waves of shuddering cold and steaming heat slowly melting into a lethargy so complete it was an effort even to breathe. There was a day, perhaps a week after the battle, when I woke to sunshine pouring in from a south-facing window and realized that I was alive and on the way to being healed. A monk in a white habit stood at the bedside, face shadowed, side hair haloed against the light.

"The Lord has made his decision, I see," he smiled. "We prayed for you, of course, but it is not for us to determine in which direction your soul will go."

I was fully aware of myself now. I remembered the battle, the fall from the horse and the vision of my own bones. I was able to raise myself from my paillasse onto my elbows but with a lancing twinge in my arm.

"Where am I?"

"In Chemnitz, not far from the battlefield. You were brought to us for healing."

"But... you're..."

"Yes," he nodded, reading my thoughts. "We're Catholics here, of course. The peril to your immortal soul and the state of your mortal body are much more important than mere catechism. Rest now."

He gave me some water. I drank deeply, slumped down and slept. When I awoke next I was able to get off the paillasse and relieve myself in a pot I found behind a curtain. I was full of questions; chief among them the whereabouts of my trumpet and other war gear. When another monk returned some hours later with a bowl of gruel and more water, I asked him. I think he seemed affronted that weapons and martial equipment were chief in my mind, and he told me he had no idea. I learned later that I had been brought here with absolutely nothing but my underclothes. Over the next two days Brother Albrecht, the monk I had first met on awakening, helped me to some clothes, a few small necessities, and a little money. I was able to set off south west in search of my lost army, with many blessings from him and heartfelt thanks from me.

"No thanks required, my son," Albrecht told me as I sat on a horse hired through the monastery's good offices. "Thank the Lord and do His good work, now that He has seen you well again. But think long and hard about what you do, and why you do it."

I rode slowly with much on my mind.

An army moves terribly slowly, especially one damaged from battle and depleted in sustenance and will. It was not difficult to follow the foul spoor of their march, and I hardly ever needed to ask the way, the evidence being all too obvious. I would ride by day, stop in the evening to buy or beg food where I could, and bivouac at night in a suitably concealed place. There was never any fear of assault or robbery; the population were too cowed, defeated and diminished to think of it, and any enemy soldiers who had escaped us must have headed south into Bohemia.

I was only two days on the road before I overhauled the tail of our army somewhere north east of Freiburg. I was greeted by my fellow

cavalrymen as if I had arisen from the grave—which in truth I had—
and when word of my return got to the higher command I was
summoned to Field Marshal Torstensson's tent. My trumpet comrade
Dieter had miraculously salvaged most of my gear while I was under
the surgeon's care, although the Sander trumpet was a crumpled ruin.
I thanked God that among all my stuff I found my beloved mouthpiece. That clunky old Sander I could do without; loud, obnoxious, but
perfect for its non-musical job. Doubtless I would be issued with
another of the same kind, but my better instrument was safe at home.

I donned my livery, the doublet still fouled with dried blood and
the shirt ripped on the upper sleeve, and reported to Headquarters. I
felt oh, so full of myself, a heroic figure bearing the stains and wounds
of combat. Torstensson was a massive presence of a man, even when
reclined on a couch as I saw him then. He had a commanding face, long
brown hair flowing over his shoulders, and neatly trimmed beard and
moustache. His eyes were riveting, but they were older than his years.
He never rode a horse and was often carried in a litter on account of
his gout. Although I didn't see her then, I heard that his wife was
travelling with him.

Torstensson was an enigmatic figure: Constantly in pain, hardly
able to sit a saddle, but continuously on campaign, ever the soldier,
ever on the move. He had power, he was organized and systematic, he
had presence, he commanded. Obedience was his due. But in spite of
all this, or because of it, he was virtually an exile from his own country.
It was said that Axel Oxenstierna was so enamoured of his military
prowess in expanding Swedish Imperial influence that he saw him as
his righthand man, Thor's hammer. In my opinion, Oxenstierna was
dead scared of his power, so the further away he kept Torstensson, the
more secure he felt. Torstensson had 'retired' once to Stralsund, a
Swedish possession, but had been persuaded back into action with
open flattery and veiled threats. Maybe Stralsund was just a little too
close to mainland Sweden for Oxenstierna's liking.

The portraits you see of Field Marshal Lennart Torstensson don't
do him justice; none of them show the shattered red network of vessels
covering his wrecked purple nose, the pendulous jowls and droopy lip
of a man wedded to strong drink. None show the tired suffering in his
eyes. Artists are just too damned flattering, but it's self-preservation of
course. Torstensson did speak German, but apparently not fluently, so
an aide translated for him. I heard tell that his Scots was at least
comprehensible. He spoke in the liquid, phlegmy way of one
marinated in a lifetime of indulgence.[33]

"The Field Marshal compliments you on your duty," the aide
translated, "and wishes you to know that the message you brought

limited our casualties and shortened the engagement."

I stood there for about twenty heartbeats in a lengthening silence before realizing the audience was over. I thanked him, saluted and turned about, somewhat chastened by the abruptness of it all, and returned to my comrades.

Chapter Twenty

In which I battle onwards, return home and find no home to
return to

*Selig sind die Toten, die in dem Herren sterben. Sie ruhen von ihre Arbeit,
und ihre Werke folgen ihnen nach*
Blessed are the dead which die in the Lord from henceforth... that
they may rest from their labours; and their works do follow them
Offenbarung/Revelation 14:13

We followed Lennart Torstensson on his campaign through Saxony
and beyond. He united briefly with de Guébriant and his Hessians, but
the tradition of squabbling that had started with Johan Banér
continued to the point where a proposed foray into Bohemia had to
be cancelled. Instead, that February we laid siege to Freiberg, suffering
so bitterly from cold and lack of basic provisions that sacking the town
and looting its stores were deemed essential to us. Many of us serving
men thought the thrashing at Breitenfeld would have had lasting
effects, but halfway through the siege word came to us that Leopold
Wilhelm and Ottavio Piccolomini had raised an army of some fifteen
thousand men in Prague and were descending upon us.

Torstensson raised the siege, although not without losing over a
thousand men, and retreated west, harried all the way by the Imperials,
until he reached Reichenbach. There we licked our wounds and finally
found enough to eat. This whole debacle was given a positive slant by
our commanders who insisted that we had scored a great victory by
drawing the enemy out in winter and thereby sapping his resources. In
fact, it was only through arguments between the Imperial leaders, and
the abrupt exit of Leopold Wilhelm in a mighty huff, that we weren't
set upon where we rested.

Besieging, sacking and pillaging was what I saw that year; military
service enough for a lifetime. I used my pistol in combat, I blew orders
on my trumpet... and I killed with my sword. The first time you kill
somebody is like no other. It all happens so suddenly in the heat of
battle; 'I have brought about a man's death' at first feels as unreal in
that moment as 'I have lain with a woman'. It's only afterwards, when
the frenzy has died, and the stable world overlies the wreckage of the
field, that the full import hits. You have sent a soul to Judgement. Life
is never so casually regarded, never so cheaply held, after you have
killed.

I was near death a couple of times myself, I suppose; once when a

ball zipped past my ear and I felt the wind of it, and another when I
made a fundamental mistake in a sword fight. I was off my horse in a
melee, fighting at close quarters with my sword while using my useless
pistol as a club. He came at me, this stinking specimen, with his sword
raised above his head. I applied the tried-and-true technique of the
boot in the essentials and nearly broke my toe. The bastard had sheathed his foretackle in some sort of metal armour. My boot went *whang*
and the sword swept down, but my kick had given me a little sideways
spin so he sliced through thin air. Once a stroke like that has missed,
the man is helpless. I clubbed the side of his head with the butt of my
gun, and was mighty put out when the man beside me finished him off
with his blade. He was *mine!* I had progressed to that point.

So, the army ranged through Bohemia, even to the gates of Praha.
I wouldn't call any of these engagements battles as such; they were
skirmishes at best, but because we faced little opposition and did great
damage, our hold was consolidated on a great swath of Habsburg land.
Or, I should say, *their* hold, because this was the rise of the mighty
Swedish Empire; the beginning of the end for the northward aspirations of the Heiliges Römisches Reich; the Holy Roman Empire. My
trumpet colleague Dieter Walser and I used to laugh over that title
round the campfire, comparing the ways in which it wasn't what it
pretended to be. To judge by the foul atrocities visited upon its
enemies and its allies alike, purportedly in the name of the Lord Jesus
Christ, 'Holy' would be the last description you could apply; Roman it
certainly was not, when the place whose name it took in vain was
thousands of miles away across ice, snow and soaring rock; and when
we were thrashing its armies, stained and frayed at the hems like a
whore's shift, it sure as hell wasn't an empire. But I'm sure someone,
somewhere will put this into better words than mine.

Once we stood down after duty, Dieter and I took to drifting over
to the other cavalry trumpeters, who would sit around in a group and
yarn. You could call it mutual interest, I suppose, but really we were
from different worlds, united only by our instruments. Some of these
men had served nearly as long as I had lived, dodging death by either
miracle, luck or some happy faculty for self-preservation. It wasn't my
place to talk; even though I knew something of warfare, I was still
young and green. So I sat, nursing my mug, and just took the wisdom
in. One day the talk got around to officers they had served under.

"Ah, Christian of Braunschweig," reminisced one old trumpeter.
"He was as mad as a bull in rut, that one. Christ, the idiots I've served
under!"

"Died young, didn't he," said a younger man to my left. "I heard
he lost an arm and it mortified. Physicians couldn't save him."

"Physicians, shit! More than useless on the battlefield. What'll they do: sniff your turds, taste your piss, or rub gobs of your bile and phlegm between their fingers? And then, of course, they'll bleed you. Stupid bastards! Just the perfect remedy for fellows missing their arms and legs. Nah, Christian didn't get killed by a stupid physician. Died years later."

"So the arm healed up?"

"'Course. Assign it to the power of music, my son."

"Music?"

"Yup. Before he had his arm amputated he had all his officers stand in a row and salute him, while he commanded us to play for him. Six of us there was—Christ, I'm the only one left now, God rest their souls—and he called us into the tent with our trumpets and kettle-drums before he'd let the sawbones touch him."

"You played fanfares while they were chopping him up? You have to be joking!"

"Are you calling me a liar, sonny?"

"No, no. But even so…"

"I tell you, it's as true as I sit here. Mind you, he must have had a few drinks on board, and he was biting down on a stick o' fuckin' kindling, but when this surgeon chap sawed off the broken end and sliced away the hanging rags of meat, he never made a sound. At least, I didn't hear him, 'cos we was playin' a sonata just as loud as we could. Daft bastard."[34]

In the spring of the year 1643 Torstensson was recalled from the south by Axel Oxenstierna to undertake an invasion of Denmark. The hated Sound Dues, which King Christian IV had foolishly increased, were a goad to Sweden.[35] All nations bordering on the Ostsee were sick of the taxes levied by the Danish crown for passing through the Øresund and the other smaller channels called the bælts, and they had had enough of the threats of bombardment from the fortresses at Malmö and Helsingborg on the eastern shore. Remember; at this time what are now the Swedish provinces of Scania, Halland, Blekinge, Bohuslän and the island of Ven were all Danish territory, so the Danes had a complete stranglehold on the seaway. The Dutch, a strongly seafaring nation, were keen to ally with Sweden, and signed a pact offering naval assistance, which went well with the Swedes, who lacked a convincing navy. What finally tipped the balance was Christian's incessant meddling in peace negotiations with the Holy Roman Empire, in spite of the Treaty of Lübeck, which expressly forbade him. The Swedes saw this as an obvious attempt to minimize their influence in the region. A pincer invasion was planned where forces from Sweden under Gustavus Horn and Lars Kagge would move west towards Danish territory, while Torstensson attacked Jutland from the south.

So Torstensson headed north from Bohemia, a slow and arduous journey that lasted through an unusually hot summer. While *en route* my squadron, now diminished to fewer than two hundred horse, were instructed by our Duke to leave the army and turn for home. We had done more than enough to help cement the religious self-determination of the Protestant north, and to harden the hold that Sweden had over our lives.

One useful thing that would serve me well in the future was my determination to learn Swedish. I saw the way the wind was blowing and realized that it would be useful if ever there could be a time for me away from warfare. It was not as difficult as I had at first imagined; there was a lot about the language that reminded me in rhythm and cadence of the fisher folk's speech around Breserwitz and Stralsund. I took the opportunity to speak with the Swedes in our companies of cavalry whenever I could, and before long I could join them at their campfires and follow their rough speech.

This next part of this journal is almost too hard to write. I had seen death, destruction and wastage at men's hands—and had done enough killing myself—so I thought I was hardened, immune; steel forged in the fire, bright and immutable. When I arrived at Schwerin again, tired beyond death and sick in mind and body, I was greeted by a somber Hartmund Breitkopf. I had been called upon to return home some weeks past, and he had waited impatiently to relay the message to me. Like the summons from Michael before my father's death, my heart was clutched and my world shrank and spun.

I rode home, not on dear old Jürgen; he was a tired old steed and spent his days in pasture, and I needed speed. The sun was low in the west on the second day—it was now into the autumn and the nights were beginning to come early—when I came to the place that used to be home. The farm was gone. Bare wasted fields, burnt-out buildings, the stinking bones of slaughtered livestock. A pillow, ripped open, feathers blowing in the wind...

I walked away in a sweet, gentle rain. Almost without knowing I walked to the church at Belitz. The pastor; he would know... As if by instinct, as if I already knew where to go, I found the new-turned place in the grass of the churchyard. I found the wooden marker. I didn't weep; I didn't cry out in anguish; I did nothing. I settled slowly onto my knees, gripping the damp grass in my hands.

They are awaiting me in Heaven. I know that. We must believe that, because if we do not believe that, we believe nothing. Then we are no more than the beasts of the field. My poor little family had stood no chance. I could see Hans and Michael and Lukas in my mind's eye, beset all around and heroically defending what was theirs, a bulwark between the marauders and the house and the farm and the women-folk. I saw them in my mind's eye as they fell, fighting to the last, but I dared not see any more than that. I dared not even think of the fate of Mama, of Annamaria and Clara. I refused to let my mind go there. How I wished Jürgen had been there! Jürgen was indestructible. No sword nor pike nor lead ball could have brought him down. My big, heroic and loving brother would never have succumbed. Not he! But he wasn't there, and I didn't know where he was. And now there was nobody in the world who was mine.

The pastor found me there. I felt a hand settle lightly on my shoulder. I stood.

"We brought them here," he said gently, "and gave them the rites. It was done properly and with all due reverence. *Ratgeber* Schleef in Rostock has all the papers…"

Chapter Twenty-One

In which I visit vengeance upon those who have sinned

Rächt euch nicht selbst, meine Lieben, sondern gebt Raum dem Zorn Gottes;
denn es steht geschrieben, »Die Rache ist mein; ich will vergelten, spricht der
Herr«
Dearly beloved, avenge not yourselves, but rather give place unto
wrath: for it is written, Vengeance is mine; I will repay, saith the
Lord

Römer/Romans 12:19

"Who? Who did this thing?" I whispered as soon as I had my voice.
I knew; I didn't want to know. I had marched with Banér, with de
Guébriant, with Torstensson. I knew. I had seen this so often. Who
did this thing? The crude cards that the great and mighty play in their
games of chance and then discard. That's who. I knew only too well
because I had seen it over and over again. I wanted no reply from the
pastor, but he answered me nonetheless.

"They came some weeks past, laying waste and taking," he sighed.
"They have a headquarters not three miles from here. There is nothing
we can do!"

"They are still here? The animals who did this are *still here?*" There
came a sudden upwelling of anger, suddenly focusing me in the here
and now.

The band of discarded soldiers that had descended upon our
holding was a rag-tag collection of filthy Scots clansmen slung off their
land; impoverished Pomeranians; broken labourers from across the
German realms; and other assorted disaffected with not the slightest
interest in who or what they had been fighting, or even why. They were
a cast-off band of scum, of dregs, of offal. Rubbish of humanity
trained in the most basic arts of war, armed, paid nothing, and released
like rabid dogs on the world.

"They rule us," the pastor wailed, clasping his hands together. "We
dare not resist." I had pity for him then, a small, elderly, well-meaning
shepherd totally lost in the horror of the world.

"And there is no help from Rostock?"

"Rostock pulls its skirts about itself. There is enough trouble there
without inviting more."

"Güstrow? What about Güstrow then?" He only shook his head.
"How big is this army of scum? How many men now *rule* you?" I
stressed the cowardice of the people, poor man.

"There are not above twelve of them, but they go everywhere armed and they kill at the slightest provocation. And they take the women…" he couldn't continue.

"Then they must die." Something hardened in me then, and, you know, I don't believe it has every really softened since. "They will pay!"

"Please, please do not do this," he begged. "It is to the peril of your immortal soul. It is written in Scripture that God ordains the time of judgement, and it is not for us to divine His will. Be assured, there is a place reserved in Hell for them in their due time."

"Their due time is *now!* Is it not also written in Scripture that if there is harm, then you shall pay life for life, eye for eye, tooth for tooth? Isn't that what Scripture says? Hand for hand, foot for foot, burn for burn, wound for wound, stripe for stripe? Isn't that what Scripture also says?"

He couldn't answer me then, and I wanted no answer anyway. "Where is this place?"

"Prebberede; a short way…" He pointed. "Not the big house. Smaller, a farm. To the north. But, please…"

By now it was fully dark. I turned without another word, mounted my horse and rode north. I thought I knew the house; it wasn't the big place, but a somewhat smaller family dwelling attached to a substantial farm. I remembered it from when I was a boy; it was owned by a family named Bauchen back then. I came to within half a mile or so, tethered my horse in a small copse, and approached the place on foot, keeping to bushes and other cover. Candles and lanterns were lit throughout the place and there were sounds of great merriment. There was one guard posted at the front door; he was sitting on the threshold and appeared to be resenting the din from within. I stole round to the rear of the house. No guard there, and only one door and a small window. A great haywain, half loaded with straw, was parked in the yard that backed the house. On one side of the house was a small, high window with an open shutter, perhaps to provide fresh air for a kitchen.

I did nothing then. I made my way quietly back to my horse with this intelligence in my head, and rode for Rostock, arriving there with scarcely a halt deep in the night of the second day.

I walked to the *Rathaus* early next morning having hardly slept at all, wasting money on a hostel cot I had scarcely used. I was looking for *Ratgeber* Schleef, the city councilor and notary who had been a friend of my father's and who dealt with all our papers. I found him at his official desk and when he looked up and saw who his visitor was, his expression turned my heart. He took me by the hand, more squeezing than shaking, and showed me to a chair. He must have been fifty-five or sixty years old and, though stooped, his grip was strong.

"Anything I can do. Anything at all. Anything within my power. Please ask."

"I want a harquebus and sufficient powder and shot to despatch a dozen men."

"But… but you can't…" He was shocked and dismayed; thrown utterly off his path, "…You can't just take… vengeance into your hands." He had expected to deal with weeping and to commiserate, giving condolence and assurance, but he saw cold anger, resolution and purpose instead.

"You'll…" a shake of the head. "You'll make matters worse."

"Why shouldn't I act when Rostock does nothing?"

"These are distracted times." He was retreating from his promise, falling back on excuses. "We have more than enough worry and concern. The Watch must concentrate on defending the town. Much has changed since you went away. We answer to Sweden, and their soldiers spare no thought for us."

"Yes, I see it. A wide streak of self-preservation has entered the council's deliberations. Who feeds you?"

"Feeds…?"

"Where does the food for the town come from, except the farms? Where does the fodder for your horses come from, except the farms? Would you cut off the hand that feeds you?"

"We cannot protect everyone in these times," he sighed, "and our farms are mostly wreckage."

I sympathized with him then, but my purpose could not be deflected.

"Then lead me to someone who can lend me the equipment I need with no questions asked, and I will lift this onus from your shoulders."

He raised his eyes to me and frowned, and I could watch the thoughts running behind the eyes. He had promised me anything, anything at all. Was my demand within his power? I think perhaps he thought it might be. His brow cleared, and I saw now that he would be obliged to fulfill his promise. He gave a lopsided smile. Clearly, he had come around to the view that he would be happy to help; he could discharge an obligation to me and my family, and to my father in particular, to whom he had been a great friend. And, perhaps help rid the district of a scourge, although what he thought of my chances I never did fathom.

I was surprised at the extent of Herr Schleef's assistance. He wrote a note on a small piece of paper, folded it and handed it to me. "Take this to *Hauptmann* Schwinn of the Watch. God go with you."

Schwinn, a grey-haired veteran of wars gone by, commanded the Watch and probably prayed that no more action would ever come his way. Even so, he had a wicked twinkle to his eye, so when he read the note and had me expand upon my requirements, he chortled with glee. I rode back to Prebberede later in the day with not one, but three matchlock harquebuses slung at my saddle, all the shot I needed, and more than enough powder in a small keg.

You may think that one man against a dozen was complete madness. Yes, it was. Of course it was! But I was dead anyway. I was hollowed out. There was a huge hole where my soul had once resided, and I didn't care if I lived or died. But I was careful; oh, so careful. Madness, yes, but madness bound to a high and holy purpose. I was the mill of God and I would grind exceeding fine!

I tethered my horse in the same place as before, loaded my guns and refilled my powder flasks and shot pouches, then crept forward carrying two of the weapons. I laid them down under cover of the hedge, but as close to the house as possible, returned for the third one, and brought it back with the now half empty gunpowder keg. A long bladed knife was my only other weapon. Hiding in the hedgerow and keeping my back to the house, I lit the matches for the guns with my tinder and pyrite, and laid them close by to smolder. As before, lights were lit and merriment was in order. Their hopeless watchman was swine-drunk, almost asleep over a slopping mug. Oh, how I blessed the power of strong drink! And how I blessed the drunken fools who suspected nothing in their pig arrogance. I sidled sideways up to the front door and slid my knife almost without effort through the watchman's side ribs. He died with scarcely a murmur. One down. The haywain was enormously heavy and I thought I would never move it, but slowly as I heaved and shoved, it rolled forward until the back door of the house, and the window too, were blocked.

I seized a sheaf of straw from the wain, darted quickly around to the side of the house, and sparked the sheaf alight. I held it down so the flames coursed up its full length, then hurled it through the open window. The opened half keg of gunpowder followed. All I needed to do then was drag the guns and the smoldering matches even closer to the house, station myself at the front door and watch the excitement. It took many anxious heartbeats for the straw to burn its way to the spilled gunpowder, but a great roar and a spurting flame signaled the beginning of the festivities.

It was horrible.

As the flames spread through the house, those who could find the door emerged roaring and cursing, and one by one they died by my lead balls, thudding into them at almost pointblank range. I reloaded only twice. How I praised my training! I think five must have come out to their deaths that way; the sixth caught me halfway through reloading the third harquebus, reeling drunkenly towards me. He walked onto the point of my knife, an almost comical expression of surprise flashing across his face. The rest must have gone screaming from one hellfire straight to another, lost in the passages of the house. One man did find his way out of a small, high window I had missed on the other side of the house, slithering down a sloped roof to the ground. I let him go, almost gleeful in the thought that he would carry this horror through the rest of his life.

I had killed already in battle; it was me or my enemy, with no decision to be made and no regrets to carry. But those dozen I took down on that day? That was murder.

The pastor was right. Vengeance was not mine to mete out. As the fire died down and a thin cold rain blew in from the east, some great dike in me burst and I wept bitterly.

Chapter Twenty-Two

In which I put my affairs in order, return to Schwerin, and learn
the identity of a young lady

Ich bin so müde vom Seufzen; ich schwemme mein Bett die ganze Nacht und
netze mi meinen Tränen mein Lager
I am weary with my groaning; all the night make I my bed to swim;
I water my couch with my tears
Psalmen Davids/Psalms 6

I wrote to Hartmund Breitkopf from the *Neue Krug* where I was
lodging, explaining the situation and begging leave. Two days after the
terrible discovery I went back to the house for the last time. The walls
stood but the interior was open to the weather. I picked among the
wreckage, my boots crunching on broken shingles, wood and plaster.
A piece of damp paper caught my eye in one corner where a bureau
had been in which we kept papers; my hand-written sheet of *Sonata per*
un clarino solo. I folded it carefully, almost unthinking, and slipped it into
my scrip. I have it here now on the table as I write. It is a touchstone
to that lost world and it shares its origin with just one other thing; the
mouthpiece that has been with me all my life.

I crunched further, finding little things here and there: a comb that
was Clara's, a kerchief I had seen Annamaria wear, a quill that I am
sure had been used by Michael when he wrote to me. I found a heavy
leather glove that Hans must certainly have worn, and in what was
once my mother's room I picked up a miniature likeness of my father,
face down in the dirt. I could find nothing of Jürgen's.

I took all these little things to the churchyard in Belitz, dug a small
hole in the newly turned earth there, and buried them. I don't know
quite why I did this, but that cavity in my soul began to heal as I tamped
the earth down, and I felt able to look forward.

While I was doing this I heard a light step behind me on the flag-
stone path between the graves. I looked up from my work. There was
a girl there with some wild flowers. She was about my age, lightly built
with long, pale hair. Her face would probably have been comely, but it
looked as woeful as mine felt. She walked over to me.

"I heard," she said. It didn't really matter what she had heard; she
understood.

I rose from my small excavation and nodded. I had no words then.

"I always bring flowers for my people," she said, "but today we
can share them if you like."

She dropped a few of the blooms she must have picked from the late-flowering hedgerows onto my small pile of soil.

I nodded again. I wanted to thank her with words, but there weren't any.

That's all we did that day. Our meeting was chance.

I paid the pastor a sum of money to have prayers said for my family, and asked him to order a better memorial for them out there in God's acre, because I knew the weather would not be kind to a wooden grave marker. I left there and rode to Rostock.

I visited Herr Schleef at his business office in Wokrenterstrasse, just below the Oberkante. The notary informed me that Jürgen was titular holder of the land with the title deed, the family estate and the crest. He could only do so *in absentio* for a number of years, I cannot remember how many, then it would all revert to me. It was a matter of indifference to me, but I politely asked him to guard the papers—deeds, titles, letters, all those things my father had brought with us to Schwerin from that other world—and to see to it that the necessary official functions were carried out. He introduced me to his son Christophorus, who he was grooming to take over the business. I shook hands with a man my own age, and found an open face and a witty, almost ironic uplift to the lip. I had the impression that he could take things very seriously, yet paradoxically still find amusement and entertainment in them. I don't know why, but I took to him immediately, assuring him that my business would remain with his company.

I remember emerging from the Schleefs' door into weak sunshine, blinking my eyes and knowing, now, that I could return to Schwerin and pick up life where I had last laid it down. I rode back into that life slowly over two days, and arrived in Schwerin as the bells were sounding the last hour of the day. Fitting back into military routine and musical practice at Court was an immense reassurance. Just like that time long ago when the insect of home life was trapped in the amber of the past, so my earlier life took on a phantasm, seen dimly, fragmented and yellowed with age. Certainly, the routine or work and the intense and demanding schedules kept my body busy, but in my heart there was turmoil and no centre.

I hadn't known what to expect of my first meeting with Hartmund Breitkopf, but I had not anticipated his distant, businesslike demeanour. He was as supportive of me and my work as before, as critical and as encouraging of my progress, but there was a new barrier. Over my apprenticeship we had developed this weird, close while distant, confidential yet mannered, relationship, but at times of family crisis I had felt a bond that had crossed over rank. Now, with the most heartrending crisis of my life behind me, he was not there in a way I had almost expected he would be. He was not, and never would be, a replacement for what I had lost, but I did have a forlorn hope for some sort of support, some kind of firm place to rely upon and to go back to. It wasn't there, and I felt untethered.

Then I kept thinking of that girl; the one I had met in the church-yard at Belitz. She told me she had 'heard', but I wondered what she had heard. I felt unhappy that I had spoken no word to her, so she would never know whether her kindness in sharing her flowers had been appreciated or ignored. I wanted to contact her, just to apologize, but I knew in my soul that it was much deeper than that. I saw her often in my mind's eye, and at the most unlikely moments during the day, and my heart would trip a little. I thought of her every night after my books were shut and my candle was out. And when the lightening of the dawn sky woke me, I saw her then as well.

I wrote a letter to Pastor Haussmann, the pastor in Belitz, asking him in the most roundabout terms if he knew of any young lady who had relatives buried there. I hardly expected a reply so quickly, but within ten days a letter appeared in my slot at the front door. (Yes, since becoming field trumpeter I was privileged to have my own mail slot, although little arrived there now.) I tore open the letter and quickly scanned the slanted, spidery script of the Man of God. Her name was Elisabeth, he told me, and she had been coming to Belitz from Rostock every week to remember her parents, who had passed away some years ago. She was the only child of the Bauchen family of Prebberede. As soon as I read that sentence I was filled with horror; good God Almighty, I had burned down her family home, having first done foul murder in it! She had heard about the fate of my family, but surely to God she couldn't have heard anything else at the time I'd seen her! I was mortified to think of her discovering that she had shown sympathy and dropped flowers for an arsonist and mass murderer. She *must not* discover anything else.

I quickly dashed off a letter to Pastor Haussmann telling him it was all a mistake, that I had no interest in the woman, and to please not raise the issue with her if he ever saw her again. I still thought of her—how could I not?—but the catch in my heart was now one of anxiety and embarrassment.

I became a dedicated machine. I practiced my swordsmanship and my riding, knowing deep in myself that I had to be better than any of my comrades. I worked hard at the trumpet, signing out music from our shelves with an eye to difficulty and challenge, practicing wherever and whenever I could. I borrowed books from the court library in Italian,

French, English and Swedish, and I studied long into the night. My head became filled with music and words, while my body began to feel tuned like a fine instrument. I was soldier, musician, courier, man of the world.

I was bereft.

Chapter Twenty-Three

In which my Duke gives me orders and I visit the Danes

Ich bin ein Fremdling geworden im fremden Lande
I have been a stranger in a strange land
Mose/Moses 2:22

Twenty years on this earth and I had seen a great deal already. After the hard campaigning and conflict, the terrible return home and the shattering and rebuilding of my life, I would have welcomed more than anything else on this groaning earth some quietness and peace. I did enjoy some return to court and military routine in the opening months of 1644, including an excellent Easter service with music by Herr Vierdanck. But I had signed up to serve, so serve is what I was obliged to do.

Although we saw action in spurts, and returned to blessed home for periods, the war raged on. Jutland was attacked and overwhelmed by Torstensson with scarcely any resistance. By January of that year all that mainland part of Denmark was in his hands. But the Swedish army found crossing the bælts, the channels between the islands, an order of magnitude more difficult. Sjælland, where the capital Köbenhavn lies, is the furthest east of the islands from Jutland. Meanwhile, the attack from the east into Scania under Gustavus Horn and Lars Kagge was delayed until February, giving the Danes time to enhance the fortress at Malmö. We heard news in May of a heroic sea battle in Western Denmark at which only nine Danish ships, led by Christian IV himself, had driven three times that number of Dutchmen back into the deeps beyond the island of Sylt. But this was only a setback for the Dutch, who were now coming to the aid of Sweden in earnest, and most thought it only a matter time before a sea passage would be clear for Lennart Torstensson's army to cross to Sjælland and assault Köbenhavn by land.

The *Hoftrompeter* called me into his office a week or two into June. We had played some fine music over the past few months, in spite of the pall that hung over most of our celebrations. I was now occupying a secure place in the trumpet corps—he had assigned me some difficult high work, which I had performed most pleasingly—so I had assumed his summons was to discuss musical matters.

"We have a meeting with our Duke. Right now. A little job for you in Köbenhavn."

I was both mystified and a little frightened. Fearful of meeting the Duke again and having his huge presence bearing down upon me, but also intrigued by what he might have in store for me. But why to Köbenhavn, enemy territory, and very much more to the point, why me? Breitkopf walked me through the passages of the *Schloss* in silence, and I felt diffident enough not to try getting more information out of him. He seemed angry, worried...

The last time I had met Adolf Friedrich, Duke of Mecklenburg-Schwerin, it had been in the large reception room with the high windows. I was young and cowed and terrified then, and I felt not much older or wiser on this occasion. We were shown to a smaller council chamber with walls of bookcases, and dominated by a vast table surrounded by about a dozen chairs. The Duke sat behind the table at the centre in a large and ornate chair, and motioned us forward. Unlike the last time, we were quite alone.

"Be seated." He waved us to sit opposite him, a signal honour. "I am told you have acquitted yourself well in our service," he addressed me without preamble, "and that you are a good student of languages and warfare."

I was tongue-tied at first because I didn't know if he was stating facts, giving me compliments, or even expecting to receive a response. I found my voice. "Yes, sir," I replied, which seemed neutral enough.

"I am pleased that you think well of yourself, and that you agree with my assessment of you. Know any Danish?"

"No, sir. I know some Swedish..."

"And who told you to learn Swedish?" He sounded waspish. I had the impression their language irked him, reminding him perhaps of their dominance.

"Well, nobody *told* me to, sir." Now I was worried that I had somehow disobeyed orders through using my initiative. "But, while riding with the Swedish cavalrymen, it just seemed like a good idea."

"Pick up languages easily, do you?" The grilling continued.

"Not easily, sir. It's very hard work, but I find it rewarding."

The Duke looked over at Hartmund Breitkopf. "Picked a good one here, did you not?" Breitkopf nodded briefly. "Well, there's precious little time for you to cram any Danish into yourself, but needs must."

"If I might observe, sir," I began with suitable deference, "there is more to the rhythm and pronunciation than to the grammar. It might not take me long get the colour of it."

"So, you will do," he sighed. "You will do quite well."

Breitkopf's attention appeared elsewhere as if he had withdrawn himself from the discussion and wanted no part of it. What I would have to do for the Duke waited while he assessed me, eyeing me speculatively, pulling his moustache, and gently nodding his head. He came to a decision.

"I want you to take messages to His Excellency King Christian IV of Denmark and place them into his hands and no other."

Oh no, I thought, not again. Yes, I had studied hard to be a good courier, yes, I had worked hard to make myself the best I could be, but still I felt very small in a very large world. Physically I was capable, but in my mind... Perhaps I should not have felt this way; I had taken orders from Banér and de Guébriant, had been commended by Torstensson and vilified by Piccolomini, but to meet a king! To speak on behalf of my Duke to the King of Denmark! It was a heady wine and a frightening responsibility. The Duke must have watched these thoughts running across my face because he snorted.

"Not worthy? Not ready? Not capable?" He looked over at the *Hoftrompeter*. "What do you think, Breitkopf?"

"Ready as he ever will be, sir. Intelligent, versatile, courageous..." But there was still something about his attitude that I couldn't fathom.

"Yes, yes," replied the Duke with a flap of his hand, "we were well aware of this little bugger's balls on first acquaintance, were we not? Now let's test 'em in the fire."

The Duke reached over to a leather dossier at his elbow and removed several folded papers from it. He held them in his hands, seeming to contemplate their content, then unfolded the first one. He scanned it, paused again then made up his mind to continue.

"Christian IV is beset by Sweden. Surrounding him are other principalities that are at odds with his politics and his religion. Hamburg, Lübeck, Mecklenburg, all are opposed to his policies, his imposition of taxes upon their shipping, his meddling with the Papists. And now Torstensson, the hammer of Oxenstierna, has all of Jutland. He has only to find his way across the bælts to Funen and then to Sjælland, and Christian will fall. And we do not want that, do we?" He paused. "And now, of course, you are looking at me as if I have lost my mind." He raised quizzical eyebrows.

"We have been fighting alongside the Swedes, sir," I replied slowly, "against the allies of the Emperor." I was more than confused. "And, had we not been called back here, begging your pardon sir, even now we would be fighting with Sweden against... against the enemy..."

The Duke placed his elbows on the table and steepled his fingers. "Sweden occupies Pomerania to our east, holds Wismar, and has free run through Holstein to our west. And you know only too well its power in Saxony. And now, with Jutland occupied and forces pushing from the east into Scania, should København fall, then Mecklenburg,

Lübeck, Hamburg will be entirely surrounded by Swedish territory. We will lose any shred of autonomy we might at the present possess. Surrounded by Sweden, we will become a Swedish province. Thus, we cannot allow our enemy to be bested by our ally. Nice pickle, eh?"

My war had been a war of black and white; a war of us and them. When I had taken messages to the enemy, they had remained the enemy. When I had killed, I had killed an enemy. This I could understand, but it was a struggle to comprehend the enemy as other than the force of opposition. There came a strange stab of memory—coming suddenly to me out of nowhere—of Brother Albrecht in Chemnitz. He had told me that my soul was much more important than mere catechism. Perhaps the message he was sending me now was that enemy and friend were of less importance in the balance than peace and harmony. But on the other side, a dawning truth came to me that our Duke was fearful for the survival of himself and his house, and that his machinations were quite venial and self serving. Whatever the motive, I put my conflict aside; I was his servant to do with as he wished.

"These papers," and he drummed them with his fingers where they lay on the table, "spell out the terms wherein the Protestant Princes will offer support and show solidarity. Territorial demands, easing of Sound Dues, compensation, and so on. They are in cipher, and here is the key, which you will memorize and destroy." He handed me a small piece of paper with the familiar table of random numbers and letters. "Why are they in cipher Hintze?"

"Well, sire, if they were intercepted, they would be useless to an enemy."

He smiled broadly. "Exactly. They would be. But you will have the key. What do think would be the consequences *to you* of these papers falling into the wrong hands?"

I quailed. I knew the answer only too well, but I could hardly bring myself to express it. I recalled being tied to a horse and led by the neck with a rope, but that would be a stroll hand-in-hand with a pretty maiden by comparison. I glanced quickly over at my master, remembering those very words of his, and looked vainly for support. There was none.

"You know the answer," purred the Duke. "And worse would befall Mecklenburg. And worse still would befall... me." He picked up the folio of papers. "Here are the same messages in plain text. I require you to read them through and through, to memorize them so you will know our thoughts when you read the coded papers to His Majesty. Read these and then give them back to me. And this paper," he took a smaller leaf back from the pile, "is an authority in plain text, signed by me, that *should* give you free passage. Use it judiciously. Destroy it

173

if you have to."

He folded this leaf twice over, melted wax over a candle and sealed it with his ring. "This one I will seal, but watch whoever breaks this seal first, and be sure to retrieve the pieces as proof. Questions?"

I could think of nothing to say at first, overwhelmed by the enormity of what he expected of me, then thoughts began to order themselves.

"What route should I take to Köbenhavn, sire?" It seemed to me that if the enemy was my friend, and my friend the enemy, there might be no safe route.

"You must go by sea, of course, but not by Wismar; Torstensson with his artillery is too large a presence there." The Duke motioned to my master. "Take him; show him maps."

"Yes, sir." Breitkopf stood and I followed suit. "I have that all in hand."

"Take the papers. Go away. Prepare to travel. Time is of essence!"

And we were dismissed from the room. As I closed the door I noted the Duke was pulling at his moustache, a worried frown on his brow. It never even crossed my mind at that time that he might have considered me disposable. Or that Breitkopf, for all his aloofness and distance, hated the thought of me being tested in this way.

We left the Presence and went straight to the library, where Herr Rehnskiöld, the scribe, surveyor and archivist, took us to a map case along one wall.[36] The map he rolled out showed the northern coast and the many islands of the Danish archipelago.

"Here is Warnemünde," said Breitkopf, indicating the town to the north east of us. "Coastal town of Rostock. And here is Wismar where Torstensson is massing his artillery, awaiting transport to Falster and thence to Sjælland. His main force is across here in Kiel, in Holstein to the west. A successful passage all depends upon the Dutch navy. Although the Swedish navy is inferior to the Danes, the addition of the Dutch will probably tip the balance."

"Warnemünde is much closer to Falster than Wismar," I observed.

"And safer, too. I doubt if you could travel with impunity in Swedish territory; their patrols are highly vigilant right now. Even in Warnemünde you'll need to be careful. There is a Swedish garrison there, but nowhere near as well manned."

"It's our territory..."

"Of course it is, but our Swedish brothers are there only for our protection, don't forget. We pay them to protect us, do we not?"

I smiled at the irony of benign occupation. "Surely, with the present situation at sea there can't be many ships sailing from either port." I remembered our difficulty in finding a ship to England from

Hamburg, and that was in relatively safe waters.

"Since the Dutch threw in their lot with the Swedes there are very few merchantmen who dare to set sail. Would you take a ship through the Øresund if you didn't know who was manning the guns in the fortresses? But there will always be fishermen. Warnemünde is a fishing port. That's how you will go."

I prepared myself as best I could that day, both in my mind and my body. The treasury provided me with funds, some Danish and some in my own coin to pay for passage, and of course there were receipts and papers and vouchers to sign and swear. I had studied the documents I was to pass on to Christian IV, memorizing as many details as possible. The more I read, the more dangerous I found these papers to be. With my lingering black-and-white understanding of the world, I wasn't to know at that point that what I read was hardly unusual in diplomacy between principalities. 'Us' and 'Them' become blurred when you see to what lengths allies and enemies will go in assuring their own well-being. But, in truth, the Protestant Princes had been trying for many years to forge some sort of peace in the region, and there was a broken trail of dishonoured treaties to prove the point.

I slept badly that night, ate some morsels at Frau Walther's table at the first hour of the day, and began the first leg of the journey to Warnemünde. As I prepared to mount my horse, Hartmund Breitkopf appeared and gestured for me to wait. I had been hoping in my heart for a thaw in his demeanour, perhaps an explanation of why it was so important that I go on this mission and not he, but he was all business-like as usual.

"We have a habit of buzzing regularly to keep our lip in shape, do we not?"

I nodded. Of course: When I wasn't playing, an hour or two a day of buzzing was an essential exercise, even without a mouthpiece.

"Only when you are totally alone. Complete giveaway."

And that was all the parting advice I received.

To arrive at Warnemünde I skirted Rostock to the northwest. I had considered cutting my time with a hard ride, but decided a slower pace and a change of horse would be less noticeable. The most disconcerting thing of all was that I would go unarmed, except for a small and almost useless knife. I missed having my sword beside me, and felt its absence at my hip. I was travelling incognito and would pass myself off as a merchant, should I be challenged. There were always occasional Swedish patrols to watch for but, being on home ground and armed with documentation, I had no fears. Things would be more difficult in Denmark, although I was confident that I could find my way past any scrutiny. The Duke's signature would carry a lot of weight, and I was sure any official who accosted me would treat an enemy courier with due courtesy.

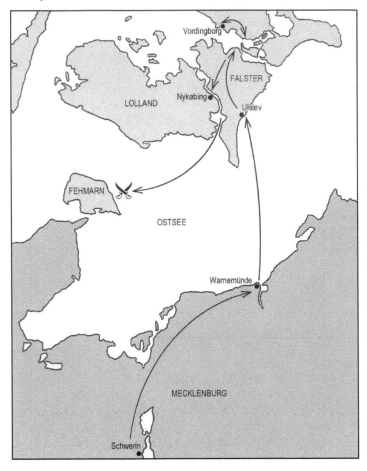

Jacob Hintze's first mission to Denmark

In Warnemünde, late one evening, I finally found a fisher captain willing to take me across the Ostsee to Falster. He was, I seem to remember, the sixth I had tried. I had been careful, but I knew that inevitably the fishermen would talk amongst themselves, so I was getting a little desperate. This man stood on the deck of what looked to me like a diminutive and unseaworthy vessel, draped all around with nets, his feet spread on planks glistening with fish scales, and eyeing me with suspicion. His name was Udo. His people had fished these waters for herring as far back as family memory went, and he looked like a smoked herring himself. It hadn't been easy to persuade any of the fishermen to consider me seriously; they were unwilling to take risks, cared little for anything outside fishing, and were highly averse to trouble of any kind, and especially young whippersnappers who brought it. The purse of coins I showed Udo turned his aversion into reluctant compliance. He agreed to bring me as close to shore as possible and then, when it was fully dark, to row me in close in his skiff, which was lashed upside-down on the deck. This would be a risky business, but a couple of months-worth of hard work fishing were jingling in that little leather purse of mine.

"And we are safe from warships?" I asked him, fearing that any sign of naval activity would drive the fishing fleet back to safety.

"We fish. We have always fished. We fish under the bows of their ships; under their God-damned guns. They will stop us how?"

A stark contrast to the paralysis among merchantmen while Denmark lay under siege.

His confidence had reassured me, and I stepped on board the two-masted smack early the next morning, skidding on slippery muck and gripping tightly to a rope in the absence of a rail. The fleet was due to sail and it wasn't long before I was out on the Ostsee, surrounded by small bobbing craft, as the sun rose above the water. My Nordsee experience came back to me then, so I fixed my gaze to the northern horizon, prayed to espy Falster, and did my best to keep out of the way. It wasn't long before the sharp rocking motion of the tiny vessel and the stink of fish began to work their magic. As the crew ran out their gill nets and held the smack's head off the wind, I found a place at the gunwale over which I could drape myself out of the traffic, keep my eyes on the edge of the sea, and heave into the water whenever I needed to.

It was a mercy beyond price when our little boat pulled away from the rest of the fleet and made towards the grey line of Falster, fading in the falling evening. Udo had selected a landing spot along a deserted sandy shore on the eastern side of the island, not far from the nearest habitation, which I believe was called Ulslev. The skiff was skillfully unshipped from the deck and slung alongside, and I stepped in with Udo, exchanging the rocking motion of the smack for one much worse, but thankfully only brief. After forty or fifty hard strokes of the oars our prow grated upon sand. I leapt into shallow water with my bag across my shoulder, and turned to wave goodbye and thanks to Udo, who couldn't wait to get back to his fleet.

Chapter Twenty-Four

In which I meet King Christian IV of Denmark in the most
unlikely of circumstances

Ich rede von deinen Zeugnissen vor Königen und schäme mich nicht
I will speak of thy testimonies also before kings, and will not be
ashamed
Psalmen Davids/Psalms 119:46

I ate a chunk of cheese and some bread I had brought with me, and
took a long draft from my flask. There was a hollowness about me that
needed filling, and I had the impression that it would be a long time
before I could look at another herring. There was no point in travelling
further as it was now full dark, so I lay down beside some dune grass,
pulled my cloak about myself and slept until the sun rising over the sea
woke me. It was a desolate place; wind-blown sand, bending grasses
and the cry of gulls. I walked inland, forming strategies and ideas of
my future progress as I went.

Riding for the first phase of my journey would not be an option.
You don't just show up at an inn in a remote place, assuming you can
find one, speaking the language poorly and asking for a horse, without
rousing a good deal of suspicion. I would have to walk north, and hope
to encounter on my way enough labourers and farm folk to test my
language, and hopefully gain some feel for it. This was a tall order, in
spite of what I had told the Duke. Only when I encountered officials
of some kind could I reveal my purpose and use my letter as a passport.
And who knew how far I would have to walk, and how much time I
had? For all I knew, Torstensson's invasion had started, and by the
time I arrived anywhere near Köbenhavn the town would already be
Swedish.

The first order of business was food, and for that I would need to
find a farmhouse in this desolate and underpopulated place. It was the
middle of the afternoon, with just a lingering memory of my morning's
bread and cheese, when I finally came across a low cottage fronting a
small spread of land where a few cows grazed. I didn't need to
approach the front entrance; a middle-aged woman emerged and asked
me what I wanted. Yes, it was Danish, but I had heard rhythms and
cadences like this along the coast of my own country.

"I am a traveller and I would like to buy some food," I said in what
I thought might sound like Danish. She looked quizzically at me so I

tried again, slowing a little and adding what I thought might be the right inflections.

"You're not from here. You from Sjælland? They talk different up there."

"Yes," I lied. "I have been visiting my uncle in Ulslev. Could I buy some food?" I had to repeat myself, but I think I was getting better at it.

"We have little food here and almost no use for coins, but I will see what I can find." She pushed back through the flap of sacking that passed for a door. While I waited outside a man emerged from the back of the house, the husband clearly. A rattle of rain pushed across from seaward but he seemed immune to it.

"Can use coin in Nykøbing," he remarked, hawking into the grass beside the path. "Can't buy ale by barter. Lot she would know," and he cocked his thumb towards the house. We stood in an uncomfortable silence; me reluctant to speak, he with no need to.

The woman emerged presently carrying a small loaf, an end of hard sausage and an earthenware jug. She poured small beer into my flask, and gave me the food to put in my bag. I had little idea what my money was worth, so I made a guess and offered her a coin. The delight in her eyes as she grabbed it from me, and the chagrin in his as the coin disappeared somewhere into her clothing, gave me my first lesson in the value of Danish money. I bade them farewell and thanks, and continued on my way, gaining a little in confidence.

Another day of walking brought me to the north coast of Falster and the need for another sea crossing, albeit a short one. The south coast of Sjælland was only three miles or so away, across the Storstrøm, and it was quite easy to make out the dwellings on the other side. I practiced a little more with my hoped-for Danish accent on some fishermen, one of whom took me across the inlet. He skirted the island of Bogø, and deposited me on the sand for about a fifth of what I had paid for bread and sausage. I was getting the hang of the currency.

It was close to Vordingborg on the evening of my second day in Denmark that I had my first encounter with the military presence that was quite clearly on high alert throughout these islands. A troop of cavalry came upon this stranger walking their roads, and hearing his inadequate grasp of their language, drew conclusions and arrested me at pistol point. They were a scruffily turned-out bunch; I had seen better nags between the shafts of a tinker's wagon. It was brought home to me then that every ablebodied man and horse that could be spared had been levied to resist the siege of Denmark. This troop was led by a mere subaltern, who directed his pistol at my chest. He was the only one, I noted, who carried a firearm; the rest had an assortment of swords, pikes and lances. I wasn't about to reveal my mission to such a lowly officer, but before I could do anything more than respond to their challenge, two troopers dismounted, seized my arms and spun me around to face their commanding officer.

"Search him," he commanded. I was sure that nothing good would come to me or to my messages if my belongings were rooted through by a bunch of provincial yokels. I was unarmed, pinioned by two hearty but ignorant soldiers, a gun pointed at me, and quite defenceless. When I look back at this incident, I think it must have been the first time I truly asserted myself; I summoned every shred of authority I could muster and shouted, "Don't you dare! In the name of King Christian IV of Denmark, *don't you dare!*"

The pistol wavered, the grip on my arms eased slightly, and I stared down the man in the saddle. He holstered his weapon and gestured for the two troopers to release me. Here was the point where babbling in relief would have been a huge temptation, but that was the last thing I would do. I stood my ground, feet firmly planted, and kept eye contact for many heartbeats. I judged to a nicety the point at which he would break the silence and try to reestablish his authority, and forestalled him by a breath.

"I carry messages to your King from my leaders. I am a courier and I demand fair treatment and swift passage." It was only two days since I had first heard Danish spoken, so my accent must have been barbaric beyond belief, but it appeared to do the trick. This stranger walking their roads was going to get his case kicked up the pecking order.

"Come with us." The subaltern gestured to one of his troopers to stay on the ground and motioned me to his vacant saddle. So we trotted into Vordingborg, a trooper running at my stirrup, and reined up at what appeared to be a temporary command post.

I was brought before an officer who was apparently the regional commander, a man with thinning hair, yellowing whiskers and old, tired and watery eyes.

"We found this man wandering to the southeast. He claims to have messages for the King." The disbelief in the subaltern's delivery was matched by the commander's expression. He looked up at me from his seat behind a trestle strewn with papers. My two escorts stood on either side.

"Messages for the King? Of course you have. And I'm Anne Catherine of Brandenburg. Who the hell are you?"

"I carry messages from my prince, Duke Adolf Friedrich of Mecklenburg-Schwerin," I intoned in my best official voice, although my slipshod pronunciation doubtless ruined the effect. "To be delivered personally to His Majesty King Christian IV of Denmark."

"Prove it. Show me the messages."

"I cannot do that, sir. I am sworn to place them in his hands alone."

"Who says so? Proof?"

I reached into my scrip and passed him the sealed letter; my passport, or so I hoped. He tore it open, scattering pieces of the wax seal onto the tabletop, which he then swept onto the floor with his hand. He scanned the letter quickly, squinting mightily, and looked up and me again.

"Appears genuine. I'll take your messages and pass them along." He held out his hand.

"I am sworn, sir, to deliver them personally."

"And what's to stop me taking them from you anyway?"

"Two things, sir. Firstly, our code of conduct stipulates free passage…"

"Welcome to the modern world, sonny," he interrupted. "If you vanished without a trace—and we would see to it that you did—nobody would be any the wiser. A foreigner skulking around in our territory. There's a bloody war on, in case you hadn't noticed."

Although I shrivelled inside at the threat, I tried to maintain my poise. "And, secondly, sir, they are in cipher and your King will expect me to decode them. Without that, the messages are useless."

His face flashed anger and then resignation seemed to take over. "Obstinate little son of a whore, aren't you?" *Søn af en hore* was very similar in Swedish.

"I am, sir. And I expect my obstinacy to be respected."

He bridled at this, but I felt certain he was unsure of the extent of his authority. He nodded, clearly choosing the easy way.

"All right. But, if you're so keen to press your precious messages into King Christian's hands, you won't be going anywhere close to Köbenhavn."

"Why not? Sir?"

"Because he's with the navy, and hasn't been in Rosenborg Palace for some time."

"So, how will I proceed from here?" This was a bit of a blow. The bastard was enjoying my confusion, and wanted to keep it going.

"You'll just have to wait 'til he sets foot on land, won't you? And who knows when that will be?"

"My messages are urgent, sir."

He sighed. He clearly just didn't have the energy for play-acting. He motioned to one of my escorts. "Take him to the mess hall. Feed

181

him, give him a place to lie down. I'll see if I can find the whereabouts of our King."

I saluted, turned on my heel and accidentally dropped my scrip. I bent swiftly to pick it up, scooped the pieces of wax seal into my hand, and rose. I saluted again and marched out.

It was two days of excruciating boredom and anxiety before I was summoned to the commander again. It appeared that he had taken my mission more seriously than I had at first thought, because messengers had been sent to various locations for intelligence on the King's movements. It was not good news: His Majesty was with the navy somewhere to the south east of Falster, and there was rumour of an engagement with the combined Dutch and Swedish fleet, which had set sail from Kiel in Holstein. How I would meet him and pass my messages along was a matter of conjecture.

"Supply ships are waiting in Nykøbing," the commander told me. "I know nobody there, I have no idea whether they will take you to His Majesty, but I will lend you a horse. One of my men will ride with you. Here..." He scribbled a note and handed it to me. It was more than clear that he was ridding himself of a problem, while ensuring that no censure would come his way, so I took his kind offer, mounted the horse and set off for Nykøbing.

Much as I would have liked to practice my Danish while we rode, I was assigned a taciturn oaf who replied to everything I said with monosyllables or grunts. We boarded a small ferry not far from the place I had crossed, and after that it was a long few hours across Falster to another ferry, and finally a sight of what turned out to be a mean little port town clustered around a long inlet. I was again greeted with suspicion when I arrived, my voluble riding companion doing nothing more than show me to the commandant of the Nykøbing region. I had to do the same explaining as before, but the note from the previous official, together with the chips of wax seal I had scooped off the floor to lend some veracity to Duke Adolf Friedrich's letter, seemed to do the trick. The letter from my Duke was by now becoming tattered and dog-eared.

A small ship would soon be setting sail, this commandant told me, with the intention of intercepting the Danish fleet and resupplying it with water and food. Ammunition they apparently had in plenty as no engagement had taken place. I was introduced by the commandant to the captain of the ship, and with some persuasion I was allowed on board.

I had a whole day and a night of trying to keep the horizon in sight, trying to swallow the constant diet of salt fish and precious little else, before the Danish fleet was sighted. My timing was appalling; the fleet was apparently on the verge of an engagement with the enemy. Under normal circumstances a supply ship would hold off, staying far out of harm's way while the action took place, but my urgent messages meant that our vessel would have to come as close as possible along-side the flag-ship, and transfer me by dingy. There has never been a time in my life when more people have been more irritated by me at any one time. Nobody wanted the inconvenience I embodied, but nobody dared to take an action that might later be censured. I was a nuisance to be passed off as quickly as possible. This was often the lot of the courier.

It was of some interest to me to hear the trumpeter on board our little vessel exchanging his messages with his counterpart aboard the Danish flagship *Patientia*, which loomed grandly on our port quarter. I didn't understand the signals, of course, but was amused by the large number of exchanges. I bet with myself that those signals were the essentials of an argument about me. I was escorted to the side of the ship and obliged to climb down a rope ladder to a dinghy that bobbed and heaved below me in the most contrary way. A few surly strokes of the oars took us across the distance between the two vessels. It was a harrowing experience climbing, or being half-hauled, up to the deck of the *Patientia* while it was underway, with my little boat bobbing up and down, the oarsmen cutting the water this way and that, and the rope ladder snaking around. Finally, with help from a huge tarry hand lowered from above, I was hoisted over the rail and dumped on the deck. My poise and *sang froid* were hard to maintain under such conditions.

Having heard the back-and-forth from my supply vessel, the captain of the *Patientia*, Jørgen Vind, strode over to me. "What is so damned important that we must haul-to and await *you* just as we are going into action? Who in Christ are you, and what do you want? Quickly!"

"I have messages, sir, from my prince, Duke Adolf Friedrich of Mecklenburg-Schwerin to King Christian IV of Denmark," I replied after scrambling hastily to my feet and saluting mightily.

Suddenly Vind's face changed from anger to smiles. "Excellent!" he shouted, not to me but to his second-in-command Grabow, who had come to stand behind him. He waved him forward. "Excellent timing! This fellow will distract the royal nuisance with his messages, and keep him below."

He pointed me towards a companionway, motioning to another of his officers to see me off the deck smartly. It was clear that the next command would be to clear for action, hardly the place he wanted me to be, any more than I wanted to be there. I had only just taken a step towards the safety of the below decks when the Royal Personage himself appeared from the companionway. The captain's face fell as his regent strode forward with every evidence of taking command, but a thunderous noise from forward signaled the first enemy cannon fire.

"Clear for action! Clear for action!" roared the captain as frantic activity began all around us. I shrank back into a corner between the rail and the ladder to the upper deck and wished to God I was anywhere else on earth.

Christian IV's heroic action at the battle of Kolberger Heide is well known. The way he appeared on deck in full royal regalia to rally his sailors, his gestures of defiance at the enemy, and especially the explosion that threw him down, wounding him in thirteen places and taking out an eye. Bleeding profusely, he had sprung back to his feet, shouting that all was well, and had urged his men again to continue the action. There are paintings that depict his heroism, and it is even celebrated in song.[57]

It is all rubbish. I was right there, shrunk into my corner and near pissing myself. I saw it all.

Amid the thunder of guns, the shouted orders to the crew and the general hubbub of a ship in action, I am pretty sure the King didn't hear what Vind said next.

"For Christ's sake get that God-damned idiot below decks!" was what I heard him say to his second-in-command. He was obviously terrified he would be charged with negligence if his regent was injured or, God forbid, killed. But it was too late for anyone to take action, even if they could. The King strode forth, unsheathed his sword and, damn me to Hell if I tell you a lie, started on an elaborate and flowery speech, waving his weapon and assuming a warlike stance.

There was no way in the world a king should have been aboard a warship in combat in the first place. He was a reckless idiot to think that royal leadership would make a damned bit of difference to the outcome; he should have been back in Rosenborg Palace in Köbenhavn where his people truly needed him. Instead, he went tearing off to do battle with the enemy, the kind of heroic posturing that leaders just didn't do anymore. Kings and popes and princes used to lead armies into battle, but more and more it was left to the professionals. But I have a feeling, amid all his heroic actions and antiquated lust for battle, that there was desperation as well. Denmark was surrounded and most wise heads said it was only a matter of time before the islands would be overrun and would have to surrender. I wonder if Christian saw the end in sight and wished to sacrifice himself before he was dethroned and humiliated. I had seen it myself; when life is not worth living, a death wish sets in that makes one take extraordinary risks. If you have no care for what happens beyond today, you will accomplish great deeds that look to an outsider like heroism. Heroism and the death wish are close bedfellows; they share each other's fleas.

Legend, paintings and song tell one story, but here's mine: the *Patientia* tacked hideously, keeling over almost to her beams as the captain brought her round, then righted herself, masts springing to the sky moments before the first broadside. I had been under the cannons at Breitenfeld, looking them in the mouth and in danger of instant death, but it was nothing like this. The gun blasts, the smoke and fire, the shattering roaring din, was like no hell I could have imagined. All the violence of hellfire and damnation was loosed on the deck of that ship. I saw guns spun like children's tops, great spinning splinters of wood, pieces of ship and men blasted into sawdust, blood foam and bone. And amid all this Christian IV stood waving his sword and yelling at his men to redouble their efforts. I know almost nothing of warfare at sea—and from my bolthole I saw very little beyond our own deck—but the *Patientia* must clearly have raked an enemy ship and then reloaded to engage the next ship in line. The descent into Hell was repeated; shattering blasts, smoke and flames, and then one of our own guns exploded. It was said later that a Swedish ball had hit it and caused it to burst, but I think that's close to impossible. More likely the gun had burst under the pressure of repeated firing, as poorly forged barrels often did. But this eruption was so close to the King that it should have been the end for him. As it was, by a miracle he was flung down and rolled to a spot on the deck not far from where I cowered. Blood poured from his face, his neck, his shoulder. He clawed at the wounds, spreading the gore over his hands and clothes, and I saw the vacant place where his eye had been. A dark stain spread across the royal breeches.

No, he did not spring up waving his sword and exhorting his men to battle. He writhed and sobbed like a child, until two hearty sailors acting under instructions from Jørgen Vind, hauled him uncere-moniously to his feet and dragged him below. Well, I've writhed and sobbed and pissed myself like a child too, but that is not how the action of kings should be recorded for the world.[38] But I know what I saw, and in his place I would have behaved the same way. But perhaps I would wish to be remembered the way he is now.

The two sailors returned from below, spotted me cowering and would have manhandled me down as well, except my willingness to go below forestalled them. As I ducked down into the companionway and sat against a bulkhead, a third wave of damnation began to rake the ship. I have been in danger of my life often, but never before have I felt my fate to be so far out of my hands. I would live or die that day, and nothing I could do would influence the outcome.

I don't know how many hours of din passed above, while below decks with no horizon to watch, my stomach began to heave and roil. I was so miserably ill down in that dark, stinking place that I scarcely heard the cheering, scarcely felt the ship come to itself, scarcely appreciated the dying down of all those appalling sounds. I was hauled out onto the deck again, soured with my own vomit, to a scene of rejoicing as the *Patientia* scudded before the wind with other ships of the fleet dimly seen about it. Sunset had separated the two fleets, making the battle a near stalemate, but even if victory might have been ours, I confess I was not at all sure who the 'ours' really was. I later heard that the Swedish and Dutch had been forced to retreat beyond the island of Fehmarn, with neither side taking significant losses.

The Danish fleet would eventually chase the enemy back to Kiel and blockade them there, but by that time Christian IV would have been removed to Rosenborg, where he truly belonged, to nurse his injuries. So, important though my messages might have been, the King's health was uppermost. A supply boat was summoned and Christian IV, lashed to a wooden bolster and attended by his physician, was swung outboard and onto the deck of the waiting vessel. I followed, my precious messages still with me, wondering whenever I would be able to rid myself of them and escape this horrible mission.

It was aboard ship on our voyage to Köbenhavn that I was finally brought into the presence of the King. He was a sorry sight, lying upon a couch in the largest cabin they could find, but still paltry accommodations, his physician beside him. Two servants stood back against the bulkhead, their expressions betraying fear and concern. The King's face and shoulder were swathed in stained cloths, one eye covered with a patch. He was apparently feverish and ill. Even so, simply being in the presence of so powerful a man—and one who had been legendary among us North Germans for so long—was an experience never to be forgotten. He was sixty-six years old at this time, far too old to be so active, but almost hectically unable to stop and rest. Even in illness, old age, and battle-wounded as he was, he struck me as a huge and dominating presence.

He bade me sit beside him. I took the by now worn and creased letters and had his physician break the seals. I read the letters to him, translating the cipher into German as I went, secure in the fact that I had memorized the plain text. He nodded and smiled. I could see by the whole change in his demeanour that I had brought him good news. It must surely be my imagination, but I felt that from this point onward he seemed to gain a new vitality. He motioned to one of the servants to bring him quill and paper, but it broke my heart to see how incapable he was of using them. He had to resort to dictation, the servant swiftly writing his words, then sanding and folding the copy for him. He asked the servant to assist with applying his seal, and when this was done he handed the letter to me.

"I thank you," he said to me, "for your courage in bringing me these valuable messages. Please convey to your masters my sincerest thanks, and my assurance that with their assistance we may prevail. Take this reply and guard it with your life."

I received the paper, bowed and left him, already thinking of my return. I had been hoping to return with only the spoken word but, like on the outward journey, I had been charged with carrying life-endangering material. However, I was sure the Danes would give me every support upon the way. Indeed, the return journey mirrored the outward one; once the *Patientia* had docked in Nykøbing, with much effort I found a fisherman willing to take me to Warnemünde, and the rest was easy.

It is true that the navy of Christian IV had at least held off the combined Swedes and Dutch at Kolberger Heide, at which I had placed so decisive a part! and had then blockaded their fleet in Kiel, but supremacy at sea swung heavily in favour of the allied Dutch and Swedish navies. In the summer of 1644, resounding defeats were dealt to the diminished Danish naval forces, including the decisive battle fought between the islands of Fehmarn and Lolland at the end of September. Denmark as a maritime force was exhausted to death at that point. Denmark should have fallen.

Now the time was perfect for a Swedish invasion into the islands from Jutland. However, before Lennart Torstensson could start any incursion, an Imperial army of fifteen thousand men under Count Matthias Gallas marched north through Holstein. So instead of an invasion into Sjælland, Torstensson was obliged to turn about, leave Jutland undermanned, and march south again. I have never ceased to be amazed at Torstensson's energy; he was at an age when all men want their peace and comfort, and ease from the travails of the world. Had he not done enough already? I know that when I saw him after Breitenfeld and Klingenthal he was unwell, and I heard later that his wife, Baroness Beata de la Gardie, had joined him on campaign to nurse and nurture him. Certainly, Oxenstierna could call on no other commander capable of doing anything close to what Torstensson had achieved; he was the man of the century. Still, he was obliged to do yet more.

I did not know what the effect of the messages I carried might have been to the fate of Denmark as a nation, and I will never know due to the covert nature of everything we did. At least, when I had left Schwerin and set out for Rostock with my messages, it was made clear to me that I might arrive too late, and that Lennart Torstensson might already have found his way across the sea with his army, and would have invested Köbenhavn. Had this happened, Denmark would have become part of a contiguous Swedish empire across the entire entrance to the Ostsee, and Sweden would have had a mercantile and political hold over all the nations that traded throughout the region. Instead, a protracted stalemate ensued, where invasion was supplanted by negotiation. In the end, through the Treaty of Brömsebro in early 1645, Denmark was forced to concede all the territories on the eastern shore of the Øresund, which included the critical fortresses of Malmö and Helsingborg, and so the crown of Denmark relinquished control of the Sound Dues. But, even though humiliated and diminished, Denmark remained a nation, and Christian remained a king... at least for a few years more.

It would be nice, here in my old age, to think that the messages of support from the Protestant Princes that I conveyed to Christian IV on that memorable occasion made some sort of difference to the outcome between nations but, as I have said, I will never know, and neither will anyone else.

Chapter Twenty-Five

In which I ride to Jüterbog with Torstensson and make matters
worse with my nemesis

*Der Herr sprach zu meinem Herrn: "Setze dich zu meiner Rechten, bis ich
deine Feinde zum Schemel deiner Füße lege"*
The Lord said unto my Lord, Sit thou at my right hand, until I
make thine enemies thy footstool
Psalmen Davids/Psalms 110:1

It would have been much deserved to return home to Schwerin and
occupy my time playing the trumpet for Duke Adolf Friedrich. The
trip back from Denmark was uneventful, thank God, and the messages
I carried were well received, but it was mid August before I saw
Schwerin again. The Duke met me as soon as I returned and was full
of questions about the state of Denmark and the invasion situation in
general. I had been out of touch with news, so I was surprised to learn
that Torstensson had not invaded, but had been ordered back south.

The daunting news for me was that our Duke had promised support
to the Swedish forces in their new campaign. I had a great deal of
difficulty reconciling the duplicity of this behaviour, having just passed
messages to and fro with our 'best friend' the Danish King, but of
course he was under enormous pressure from the Swedish overlords.
Even so, as I watched his face as he sat in the chair in his study, I could
see the care written there. A proud man, heir to a duchy and controller
of the lives of many, under the thumb of men who cared only for power.

So now it seemed highly likely that some number of our cavalrymen would be deployed and, yes, they would need trumpets. I had
signed up as a soldier and I knew that was my lot, but God help me if
I wanted to put my head back in the cannon's mouth just now. Nevertheless, late in October my troop of just one hundred and fifty cavalrymen headed south with the intention of joining the Swedish forces
south of the Eider in Holstein, where the Imperials under Matthias
Gallas had set up defensive works. This turned out to be an
incompetent piece of work by Gallas, because Torstensson was able
to outflank him and threaten from the rear before we got there. This
forced Gallas to retreat to Madgeburg, leaving behind a great deal of
his baggage and artillery. So, instead of meeting the Swedes fairly close
to home in Holstein, we were obliged to continue further south in
search of them.

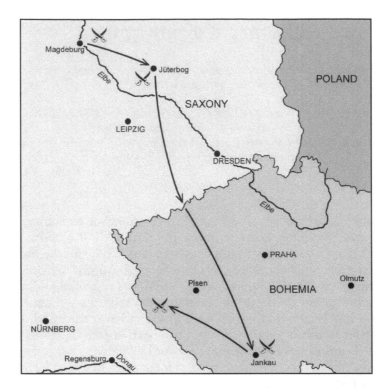

Jacob Hintze's second campaign with the Swedish army

It was on one of our nightly bivouacs that I got a full measure of the evil of Joachim Wadegahte. Although he treated me with loathing at every opportunity, after his failed attempt to put me into harm's way at Breitenfeld, he hadn't tried anything malicious. But it was common knowledge among us that his superiors considered him less than competent, and that it was family pressure alone that kept him in a position of command. I recalled often Heinrich's observation from those first days at Frau Walther's, that he would make an excellent cavalry officer as his stupidity and pride were exactly the qualifications required. Family connections had done the rest.

Foraging was a matter of course, but we were a small troop and keeping us and the horses fed was not difficult or particularly destructive to the farm holdings in the regions we passed through. We had been issued with enough small change that we could buy food from farms and villages, and farmers and merchants breathed a sigh of relief when horsemen came calling; it meant they probably weren't going to be robbed, beaten and their women raped in exchange for their wares. Infantry battalions, on the other hand, sent waves of fear rippling ahead of them. Mercenaries, shoddily trained pressed men, and the general human pus that gathers in any army, had no such compunction. They were paid a pitiful amount of money, sometimes almost nothing. And even if they had money, they would hardly spend coin on what they could take. Give men like that weapons and you create monsters.

One late afternoon I accidentally overheard Wadegahte and his cronies in their tent as I passed by. Normally I wouldn't snoop, but the tone of his voice made me pause and listen. He and his cronies had found a keg of wine, had been testing it for some time, and were now discussing a food raid on a small farm not too far distant. In retrospect, it was quite naïve of me seriously to consider this out of character for our cavalry officers. Perhaps I still held our behaviour above the standards of everyone else I had witnessed? I had to stop and listen further. I couldn't believe they would even think of this; surely even Wadegahte wouldn't, except for the loosening effects of that keg. The other two were toadies; I'd seen that type before, and the Wadegahtes of this world prey upon them.

"But I'm out of money. I don't have a *Pfennig!*"

"Me neither. Doesn't matter. We take." This was Joachim, well flown by the sound of him.

"What, just go there and…"

"You heard me. Christ, we need to eat! You scared, or what?"

The flap of the tent was flung aside and I dodged quickly away around the corner. I watched as they strode to their horses, mounted and galloped away. By now my misgivings were taking on solid form. I mounted my horse and followed them, a good distance to their rear. They crested a hill with me following, and as the view opened out I saw the farmhouse and outbuildings not three hundred yards away. They galloped into the farmyard, reined up and swung down from their horses. I wasn't sure what to do—they were superior officers after all, and I would be facing deep trouble if I intervened—but then I heard yells followed by the scream of a young girl, and that spurred me to action.

I galloped down the hill, pulled up outside the farmhouse wall and dismounted. I drew my sword before striding through the gate. A man and a boy were lying against an interior wall, bleeding from head wounds, but I think still alive. The two toadies held a struggling woman, clearly the mother of the girl I had heard, while Wadegahte wrestled the girl herself down to the ground. She was screaming as he tore at her shift. He was halfway into her by the time I strode over. Without thought for the consequences, I landed a flying kick into his hairy bobbing rear end with the point of my boot. It caught him right

191

at the root of his prick, just south of the arsehole, with a popping crunch that thrilled right up my leg. He rolled off her with a huge tearing intake of breath, then jackknifed around the farmyard clutching at himself and barking in agony. I think of all the blows I have struck in anger over my military career, this was by far the most satisfying. The other two cowards released the woman, and I held them off with my sword while she rushed forward to raise her daughter to her feet. With one arm wrapped around the girl's shoulders she leaned over Wadegahte, cleared her throat deeply, and hawked copiously into his writhing face.

I waved my sword point into the two cronies' faces, giving one a nick on the cheek that would remind him of his cowardice for the rest of his days. I herded them over to Wadegahte and they helped him up, slinking off to their horses. I heard them gallop away, and I imagined his arse on the saddle...

The woman bent to attend to her menfolk, who I think had been bludgeoned not stabbed, and would probably live. I sheathed my sword and returned to my horse, and it was only then a great wave of memory slammed into my mind. My legs failed; I knelt beside the horse shaking and retching with the whole terrible scene in my mind. I saw again that imagined tableau of my brothers fighting for their lives, but this time I went further into a place where my mind had forbidden me to go. I saw my sisters and my mother. That girl was my Annamaria. I saw... I cannot tell you what I saw. I lay there in the dirt in an overwhelming agony of spirit. In years to come that memory would return again and again, so even now, whenever I let my vigilance slip, I am back there. It never loses its strength, that vision.

Trotting slowly back to the camp and hour or so later, wretched in mind but upright in body, I thought of the stupidity of what I had done. I had attacked and wounded a superior officer in the presence of witnesses. On the other hand, if charges were to be brought against me, the whole sordid story would have to come out. I would see to that! True, it would be three words against one, but Wadegahte had incurred a bad reputation among the troops and with his commanders, while us members of the *Kameradschaft* really were treated with some deference. On balance, I decided he would be wise to keep his mouth shut. Shit sticks. Mercenaries and pressganged troops behaved that way of course, and had from the beginning of time, but gentlemen did not, or so I felt, and I was horrified and dismayed that these three had. On balance, I felt safe from official action, and as Wadegahte wished me dead anyway, I was in no more danger from him than I had been before. You couldn't be more dead than dead.

There are, of course, various ways that death can be brought about, so my vigilance around him had to be redoubled. When I think of him at this period, I can only imagine a burning hatred coupled with a seething impotence, which together must have driven him mad. I know he had started this war with me, but I was also fully aware of the way I had inflamed it. I had bested him at every turn, and I would pay the price.

It was a number of days more before we eventually caught up with the Swedish forces at Madgeburg. The city was surrounded and it was clear that it was only a matter of time before the Imperial forces were starved out of their defensive position. We heard afterwards there were no cats or dogs left in the entire town of Magdeburg, and that the populace had taken to eating anything that could be swallowed. We encountered Imperial soldiers breaking out of the encirclement, risking their lives to cross over and declare themselves new adherents to the Protestant cause. But these were pathetic specimens, with no loyalty to anyone except themselves, and so woefully undertrained and undernourished as to be useless as fighting men. It was a sad sight to see Swedish troops and their mercenaries alike laughing at these men and sending them packing. Some of these sad souls proved useful, though; under questioning it was revealed that Gallas had had enough, so rather than leaving his troops and the people of Magdeburg to starve to death, he was about to execute a cavalry breakout.

Commander Helmut Weitz called together the four subalterns of his troop, and the two trumpeters, me and Dieter, for a conference. A map was spread out on the trestle in his tent, and he stabbed features of it with his finger as he talked.

"Here, here and here are places where the defences are necessarily weakest, all to the south of the city. Now, when Gallas breaks out, which he must, he will head south to Bohemia. But he will not break out in any of these places. Why?" He scanned our faces.

"Because we will expect him to head south?" asked one of the subalterns.

"Exactly. In all likelihood he will make an attempt in a place we least suspect. Torstensson has detailed us to cover here, here and here," he whacked the paper with his finger. "Points east and north of east."

"Do we know when they will attempt a break, sir?" I asked.

"No. Dark of night obviously. We will post guards at all these likely spots, sunset until daylight, trumpets take watches turn and turn about. The slightest hint of activity must have us in instant readiness. They *must not* break free."

I recall my discomfort with night watches like that one; wearing full gear the whole time, the chafing of the cuirass, the weight of the helmet, the bladder that could only be relieved on the spot. I kept my mouthpiece in the trumpet the whole time, yet always worrying that this most precious property of mine might somehow become lost. The nights became a long monotony, waves of vigilance flowing into nodding inattention, until suddenly the moment came!

It was near the middle hour of a cold night in mid November that four thousand Imperial horsemen suddenly broke out of the encirclement. Sure enough, they had opted for a spot they considered least guarded, and they came out in force. Their full thundering, galloping exit took us by surprise. In truth, no matter where they chose to break out they would have found thin defencive lines spread out around the entire encirclement of Magdeburg.

An instant alertness; bringing my trumpet to my lips and blowing the calls to awake, to saddle and to ride. The unreality of the blur of activity, the noise and scramble, neighing of horses, shouting of men, clarion calls singing out in the cold air. Because it took a great deal of time to muster cavalry from points around the perimeter, the chase began with just our hundred and fifty men under Weitz, enhanced later as the rest of the cavalry caught up. So much for our aspirations to contain them and finish with the business then and there.

We chased them in the deep of night, dangerously unsure of our footing, through forest and scrubland that they must have scouted well. It was a heroic effort on their part. It worked at first, but it was doomed to failure.

On November 23, 1644, close to the town of Jüterbog, we outpaced their exhausted mounts. Almost the entire Imperial cavalry was wiped out. It was a sad, pathetic and brutal business. The men were half-starved and exhausted, their equipment was in ruins, and their horses were just this side of the knacker's yard. But they fought! Oh, my God, how they fought! I think what most affected me in this awful episode was my expectation that cavalry would behave in a way that infantry would not; that our esprit, our discipline, all our rigorous training, would have caused us to behave in a more chivalrous way. Even after the latest Wadegahte episode I still thought well of my comrades in arms. Of course it was us or them; of course it was all-out war. I knew that.

We took no prisoners.

The slaughter, the humiliation and misery of such a one-sided contest marked one of the low points in my military career. I blessed God who had made me a trumpeter and messenger, that I would not have to engage too closely in this sickening, sorry business of reducing fine fighting men to impotence. This is hard to write about, and I need not dwell upon it any further.

We captured three thousand five hundred horses that day, few of which were in any condition to use, and a wealth of war gear, similarly in an almost useless condition. I heard later that only about two hundred men, Matthias Gallas among them, had escaped further south to what he thought was the safety of Bohemia. Gallas was relieved of his command and never saw military action again. It was more than obvious to all of us on the field that Jüterbog was a loud signal to the Holy Roman Empire that this war simply could not be won.

By either side.

It was in December of 1644 that the great powers in this conflict met for the first time in the Westphalian cities of Münster and Osnabrück. Two cities were required because Catholic and Protestant emissaries refused to meet face to face. The Catholics did their work in Münster, while the Protestants settled on Osnabrück. It would be long years before any resolution was arrived at. Conflict would continue from Spain to Transylvania and all places in between, while delegates jostled for seats at the table, squabbled over protocol, and exchanged such volumes of paper, parchment and ink between the two cities and their respective principalities, that a special postal service had to be set up.

All this I learned much later when I played a small part in the machinations, but for now, as Christmas came and went almost uncelebrated and a cold New Year blew in, we rode even deeper into warfare.

Chapter Twenty-Six

In which I fight at Jankau, am spared by God's hand, and take an important hostage

Da ward der König sehr bewegt und weinte; und im Gehen sprach er: "Mein Sohn Absalom! Ach, daß ich doch statt dir gestorben wäre!"
And the king was much moved, and went up to the chamber over the gate, and wept: and as he went, thus he said, "O my son Absalom, my son, my son Absalom! Would God I had died for thee!"

2 Samuel/2 Samuel 18:33

We continued with Torstensson's rampage, chasing the remnants of the Imperial army deep into Bohemia. On behalf of his Swedish masters, Torstensson had forged an alliance with George Rákóczy, the successor to Bethlen Gabor, Prince of Transylvania, so now his desire to carry the war directly into the hereditary lands of the Emperor was well reinforced. We rode with him on explicit instructions relayed from our Duke. We were to finish what we had begun, and it was clear to all that the smell of ultimate victory was in the noses of our rulers. But now, on receiving news of Matthias Gallas's defeat, Holy Roman Emperor Ferdinand III appointed General Melchior von Hatzfeldt to assume command, reinforcing him with a hastily enlisted Hungarian force under Johann Graf von Götz, and Austrians and Bavarians, under Johann von Werth and Count Johann von Sporck respectively. (It seemed that Johann was the favoured name among these Habsburg generals.) So now, what we saw as a humiliated and defeated Empire seemed to rise from the ashes to face the Swedes with a numerically equivalent force. But this was more illusion than reality; although the Imperial army fielded probably three thousand men more than we did, mere numbers really don't tell the story. This was a last ditch effort by an impoverished Empire that had lost all credibility, and it was facing an apparently far superior army. We had a versatile and flexible artillery, highly mobile cavalry, and all of them under the most formidable commander this century had yet seen.

I say 'apparently far superior army' because at this stage we were actually far from our best fighting form. Feeding and equipping an army on the move is never simple. It is true that the previous successes of the Swedish forces had resulted in the capture of weapons, horses, supplies and other gear, but there was still the need for a vast amount of food. And in the despoiled and ruined country through which we marched there was precious little to be had. And it was cold, colder than I ever remembered. The cold was a biting, penetrating presence which, together with the continual hunger, sapped our morale. And everywhere we rode was clotting, slippery mud that splashed and stuck to mount and rider. By early 1645 we had been nearly six months in the saddle; we were filthy and lousy, and near the end of our resources. The flux ran through our troop, quite literally, and I longed with a passion for water to wash myself that didn't need the ice smashed off it first. When one of our squadron shot a deer it was a day of joy, although sharing it out amongst us all didn't leave much for anybody. I think we ate everything between the antlers and the arsehole, we were so hungry. And then, of course, all that gorging gave us mighty liquid bowels. Some of the infantrymen had bleeding gums and loose teeth, but for some reason that affliction missed us. Perhaps my nettle soup was of some benefit.

In the dull monotony of the march into Bohemia it was an exciting day if a stirrup broke and I had to visit the blacksmith; anything out of routine to break the dullness of it all, and the bonus of a warming at his forge. We grubbed for whatever broken food we could find, and argued amongst ourselves almost continually. As I trotted through desolation I looked back to that sunny day in the marketplace in Rostock; the trumpet, the fine uniforms, the glory of it all, and kicked myself in the heart for my stupidity.

In January we marched into the high hills of the Erzgebirge, only to be stopped at Kaaden by the appalling condition of the terrain and the loss of the bridge across the Eger at Saatz, which had been carried away by floods. Rebuilding the bridge was accomplished by February, so we broke camp and marched again to meet the enemy. The Imperial camp was finally sighted near Horazchowitz, on inaccessible heights on the west side of a small river. I think it was the Eger. Artillery was wheeled out and several shots were exchanged, but it became pretty clear that von Hatzfeldt wasn't coming down from his heights, and Torstensson sure as hell wasn't going to attack uphill. The two armies broke camp and continued to march parallel to each other, keeping to their own sides of the river, pausing only to fire useless shots across the water.

I still look upon what we accomplished in that march and marvel at our depth and resourcefulness. Lugging artillery, powder and shot wains, and all the other wheeled supplies through forest, sucking mud and half-frozen creeks was a titanic task. On several occasions Torstensson was spied on horseback exhorting his men to redouble their efforts. The man was indefatigable—how he could even sit a saddle was a mystery—but urge us on he did. At some point in our march the cavalry crossed the river by a ford, and by a dint of heroic effort the infantry, baggage and artillery were dragged across cracking and creaking ice.

It was some time in the middle of February that I was called to Lennart Torstensson's tent, realizing finally as I made my way there that someone in the chain of command thought me a useful and reliable messenger who could be called upon in delicate situations. This was not a bad achievement for one who had not yet seen his twenty-first birthday. I had become the trusty servant of my betters and superiors. It was flattering, but I tried hard to keep it all in perspective; I could be killed tomorrow…

The General was seated on a chaise longue, flanked by his cavalry commanders, including Helmut Weitz my squadron commander. They had clearly been working on messages. I wondered if Torstensson remembered me. Why would he, when he consumed and disposed of whole armies? These great ones must have been immune to sentiment; seeing their men as breathing beings, rather than chattels, would surely torture their souls. But he had changed, this great man. He was clearly in constant pain, and he swigged mightily from a mug of wine beside his chair several times during our brief meeting. His commanding face had shrunk into itself, and his powerful demeanour had shrivelled. I thought then that he was near the end of his life's work, and long beyond where a lesser commander would have folded his tent. Still, he exuded power.

"*Du talar Svenska, tror jag,*" Torstensson rasped.

"Yes," I replied in his native tongue. "I do speak Swedish."

"Good. Olmutz has been under siege by the Austrian army under von Waldstein. So von Hatzfeldt must be made to believe that we will make an attempt to relieve the town." He handed me a folded and sealed paper. "You will take this message to the enemy."

I was confused and he saw it in my face.

"We sue for peace with this message," Torstensson continued, "but you will spread the rumour among his men that Olmutz is our real objective."

"He must think we see no point," Weitz amplified, "in wasting men and material. In this message we are offering him capitulation and free passage."

This intervention earned a frown and another swig of wine from Torstensson. "He will absolutely reject this as laughable rubbish, of course," the General added, "but meanwhile you will have sown the seeds. You will have found occasion to speak to his men and spread a quite different story. Olmutz. That is our objective, tell them."

This was a dangerous game. With such subterfuge I would be

contravening the code of conduct of messengers. I had experienced Piccolomini's reaction to duplicity, and I knew if I was caught at this I was a dead man. I came down to earth; in truth, the trusty servant was really just a disposable chattel.

So here was my head screwed tightly into the blacksmith's vice again. Once more I prayed that the message and the messenger would be held distinct, and that the chivalry of war would give me free passage. But we had shown no chivalry at Jüterbog, so I wondered how much might be shown to me now. I left the tent quickly and went to the picket where the groom had prepared my horse. As I swung up into the saddle one of those turning points in my life took place, although just then it was simply an annoyance. As my weight went onto the stirrup the girth strap broke, causing the saddle to slide off the horse's back. Caught by surprise, with the saddle coming down on top of me, I fell under the horse and was kicked smartly in the head by the startled beast. I knew no more until I awoke in my tent with a savage headache and an open sore on my scalp.

"My God, what kind of idiot are you?" cried Dieter, our second trumpeter, who shared the tent with me. "They had to send someone else. Fellow from one of the Swedish lot."

I nodded, which sent a lance of pain through my head. "What happened?" My memory was a blank.

"Your girth strap snapped, down you went and got a kick for your pains."

"What idiot of a groom..." but I couldn't continue for the pain and swimming nausea.

"Don't piss on the groom. Poor bastard couldn't have known. Our equipment's in such shit condition."

The pain died down a little and left me wondering what disciplinary action might be taken. It was an accident, damn it, but how easy it would be to read it as cowardice. My courage had been under question before when I had had the temerity to disagree with the Landgraf von Hessen on my qualities as a messenger. As it turned out, I had no need to worry as no action was taken.

I recovered quickly enough—the scalp wound was skin-deep—but the full horror of the incident only came to me two days later. A report came to our command, trickling its way down through the ranks, that a messenger from our camp had been intercepted near Preisnitz, interrogated, and then executed by the enemy. There was seething anger amongst our men, cursing those Papist bastards and wondering why in hell they would do this. I knew. Oh, God, I knew only too well! I held my peace. Helmut Weitz took me aside some time after I had heard the news. I was appalled and devastated. I have often thought we are assigned a guardian by God who ensures our destiny, and as I look back now over the years I cannot help but believe the Lord wanted me to remain on this earth to serve some purpose. But for one to die in my place? That was hard.[39]

The misinformation fed to von Hatzfeldt caused him to split his forces, but by using a select and highly mobile cavalry unit he was able to follow our progress and be informed on a daily basis. Once he discovered our true line of march, he hurried to intercept us, so it appeared to me that the messenger's death had served no purpose at all.

There were many desertions from the enemy forces; quite a number of their infantry ran away on that stretch, a few of whom were scooped up by our outriders. One day, a week or so into our march away from fording the Eger, I was out on one of those patrols, as we took turns about and about. Those forays were a refreshing change from slogging monotony. We would ride in the wooded areas parallel to our line of march, always on the lookout for enemy patrols. That day we came across a group of infantrymen in a clearing, ill-equipped and ragged, and clearly on the run. I swung my horse in their direction, watching them scatter into the forest, but it was an easy matter to ride them down among the sparse trees. I leaned out of my saddle and grabbed one fellow by the collar of his jerkin.

"Friend, friend," he yelled in the barbaric mountain accent of southern Bavaria, half strangled as he was by my hold on his clothing. "Not enemy! Friend!"

A couple of the others were rounded up, and we came together in a clearing with our three captives held beside our horses. My captive was hardly my age; a farm boy filled with fear and wishing he was back in the Tyrol and that all this was a nightmare. In contrast to the mercenaries, like the highland Scots animals among our infantry, this poor boy must had been pressed into service, and had doubtless taken the opportunity to desert with several of his elders. It was an easy matter to disarm them, tie one wrist to a harness and trot them back to camp. They showed no resistance, poor sheep.

On questioning by the higher command, they revealed that the Bavarian commander, Johann von Werth, had declared to von Hatzfeldt that if the Swedes were not brought to battle within three days, he would take his troops home. He said they were needed for local protection in Bavaria and had been spared reluctantly to fight for the Imperial army. The deserters also spoke of starvation rations, particularly a lack of bread, which did not accord with our previous intelligence that the Imperial army was well fed and supplied. These deserters had clearly decided to head for home before they starved or before things became too hot for them. I don't know what became of them after this had been wrung out of them, but my heart went out to that poor farm boy, so far out of his world and such a short way along his life's path.

So, like Torstensson, von Hatzfeldt was driven to face the enemy and get the job over and done with as soon as possible. Looking back at what followed, I have the impression that Torstensson appreciated full well just how hungry, cold and demoralized we were, and he was therefore reluctant to take the huge gamble of a battle so far from home, unless he was absolutely sure of his territory. To see Jüterbog reversed and the Habsburgs back in control would be unthinkable. Here were the Swedes, lancing deep into Imperial territory with the people of Praha and Wien, and an anxious Ferdinand III, all watching the outcome and doubtless deep into their prayers. For our part, we knew that as invaders, foreign in speech and religious faith, far from home and cold, tired and hungry, if we lost this battle none of us would live. We would be eliminated to a man because that was the only message Ferdinand III would wish to send to the world.

It was a day's ride south of Praha at a place called Jankau that our two armies finally met. By the time we arrived the Imperials had occupied two hills at either side of the town. The townsfolk had scuttled away and not one mortal soul remained within the walls. We formed our battle lines behind the slightest of inclines with the enemy facing us on both flanks. The area was mostly forested, with few clear places where an overall view of the field was possible. Upon a hill to the left of the Imperial forces was a small chapel, an obvious vantage point and observation post, but curiously not occupied by the enemy. A few salvos of artillery were exchanged, especially when our horses were led to a nearby brook for water, but nothing came of this testing fire.

We fielded about sixteen thousand men, while the Imperials had at least nineteen thousand, including far greater numbers of cavalry. If anything, our superiority rested with the artillery. Large quantities of weapons, powder and shot had been captured along our campaign trail, so I believe we were better supplied than our enemy. It had been hellish lugging it all across tracts of untrodden country in the bitterest of winters, but we prayed the effort would pay off. That we were the more desperate side by far was obvious to all of us.

One of my last duties as a liaison with the enemy in time of war took place on the morning of February 23, the day before the battle. Once again, I was called into the commander's tent. I ducked under the flap and was confronted by the entire stern-faced Council of War; all the commanding officers of our entire army forming a semicircle around Lennart Torstensson's couch. Among all the faces I recognized his three chief lieutenants: Arwid Wittenberg, Robert Douglas and Caspar Cornelius Mortaigne.

I was obliged to stand and wait as their deliberations wound down.

"He is weak." One of the Swedish cavalry commanders was saying. "His foot soldiers, and his cavalry too, are running away."

"Yes," agreed Mortaigne. "Von Werth is getting impatient. He will leave and take all his men with him." Torstensson rubbed his hands at this.

"And no assistance will come from the Palatine," observed the tall, cadaverous Robert Douglas, a Scotsman who had served the Swedes as cavalry commander for some time. "Pope Innocent X loathes the Habsburgs. If von Hatzfeldt does not fight now, he never will. He is driven to fight. Fight he must."

"What is their state of readiness?" barked the General.

"Deplorable," replied Weitz. "Our scouts report no reconnaissance by the enemy at all. Götz was detailed by von Hatzfeldt to reconnoiter the whole country around, but he has done nothing. Our *éclaireurs*, on the other hand, now know the lie of the land in great detail."

"And, from our reports," added another cavalry subofficer, "his hurrying after us has resulted in leaving vital supplies behind."

"So!" Torstensson gripped the back of his couch and rose painfully to his feet, waving off with irritation an aide's attempt at assistance. "After mature deliberation with all of you generals and colonels, in God's name, we shall attack the enemy!"

They all applauded his words, clapping, cheering, thumping their chests and rattling their weapons. He waved them to silence as he sank back onto his couch. "Yet..." he eyed them all cannily, "if we were to offer him another opportunity for delay, he would certainly take it as further evidence of our weakness."

"He cannot delay!" said Wittenberg.

"No, of course he cannot. But if we make such an offer, he can only see it as a sign of unreadiness on our part. It sows uncertainty."

In all my experience serving under Lennart Torstensson, the chief thing that stands out in my mind is the subtlety of the man. Of course, he was a great general, strategist and leader of men—everybody will tell you that—but the games he played with his enemies' minds set him apart. His further action that night emphasized this point.

"Bring me quill and paper." An aide swung a small table up to his couch and placed writing instruments to hand. He wrote quickly, sanded quickly, and folded the paper. He sealed it with his ring and beckoned me over.

"Take this to General von Hatzfeldt," Torstensson instructed me, thrusting the message into my hand. "Out of leniency and goodness we offer him the chance to delay his attack. He will laugh us to scorn, of course," he told the assembled command, "but we have nothing to lose, do we?"

Nothing, I said to myself, except the mortal life of your courier.

I mounted and galloped into enemy territory. My horse's hooves crunched on stale snow drifted beside the path, a cold wind whipped at my face, and the plumes of panting vapour drifted back to me. The little devil in your mind nags you at times like this, telling you things you don't wish to know. I thought of pain, I thought of death, but the rhythm of riding somehow calmed me. It must have been a mile before I sighted the sentry outposts of the Imperial forces. Here, at least, courtesy made the sentries step aside, and I continued at a canter to the campaign headquarters tent.

I was surprised at the small stature of General Melchior von Hatzfeldt. You have the impression that the high and mighty are larger than life, but here was a short, almost fussy-looking man with curly white whiskers and a bald head that I could see over the top of. He took my proffered paper with a sniff, tore open the seal and scanned the lines quickly.

"Look at this," he laughed, motioning to one of his staff officers standing by. "The mighty Field Marshal is clearly afraid of a fight." The officers took the paper while he turned back to me. His eyes raked me slowly from boots to helmet, and as they did so I had the disturbing impression that he was able to look inside me.

"Hungry?" he asked. "Cold? Tired?" I nodded in spite of myself, caught quite off guard by this strange little man. "Go away and eat." He waved me away and turned back to his officers, saying over his shoulder, "Return in one hour."

The sentry who had shown me in took me to a mess tent where I was given a piece of hard sausage, a hunk of bread and some ale. All eyes were on me. It is a most disturbing thing, to be among your enemies, to know that for a pinch of salt they would kill you without mercy, yet to be eating at their table. I cannot recommend this to whet an appetite. However, it was only as I ate—trying hard to slow myself down and appear nonchalant—that I realized how famished I was, and how close to desperation me and my comrades really were. It occurred to me, as I tried not to wolf down the victuals too quickly, that this wily bastard von Hatzfeldt was sending a clear message. He was telling me that his soldiers weren't hungry, cold and exhausted. On full bellies they might give as good as they got.

I was called back to von Hatzfeldt under an hour later. By this time it was mid-afternoon and the light was slanting among the trees. Aside from the sentries, he was alone in his tent. He looked me over with that weighing, assessing expression but said not a word. I took the paper from his hand, thrust it into my scrip and saluted. Only when I turned to leave did he speak.

"Tell the Generalissimo that we see right through his horseshit. Tell him: *horseshit*. We will not delay. We are more than ready. And we will take no prisoners. Go!"

I saluted Torstensson, passed him the paper, and took great pleasure in giving him the 'word of mouth' in Swedish. "*Han tror inte din skitsnack, min herre.*"

He roared with laughter, winced in pain, then roared again. "Doesn't believe my horseshit! What a shame!" He broke the seal and scanned the letter. "No prisoners. So? We will take none ourselves." He looked directly at me then, and for the first time I had the impression that he saw me as a person, not as a utensil to use as he pleased. I wasn't sure if I liked this attention.

It was later in the evening, when the light had completely left, that Helmut Weitz called together his officers and trumpeters. "The word from Commander Douglas is that towards the first hour after midnight we sound our trumpets and make a great deal of noise. Tell your riders to goad their horses to whinny. We ride nowhere, but we make a great din. Get some sleep now."

He dismissed his officers but called me and Dieter aside. "Sleep in turns. One of you must be wakeful when the call comes. You will sound *Buttasella* as loudly as you can." *Buttasella* is literally 'throw your saddle', which means mount and prepare to ride.

Dieter was out and snoring, and I was nodding when the shout came down the ranks. We were both up in an instant—I had no need to shake him awake—and we began blowing like hell: *Pom, ba-a-ah, pom, ba, ba, ba, pom, ba, ba, ba...* Horses were neighing, men were shouting orders, and from some way to our right wheels were crunching over rock and gravel. There was no question in any enemy's mind that we were moving out. The only items actually moving out were the guns, but uphill in the direction of the chapel on the hill, while it was still dark. Meanwhile, a small troop of foot soldiers were detailed to head down the road by which we had come, so that at first light it would look as if we were retreating.

As the sun rose, Torstensson led our large contingent of artillery and cavalry to the right and quickly passed through dense bush and forest, taking possession of the chapel, an obvious strategic advantage. The guns were quickly dragged up from their cover in the bush and emplaced, ranging over all access routes from the valley below. The other portion of the army swung to the left, as if to attack the Imperial right. Von Hatzfeldt and von Werth immediately moved towards them to strengthen that position, only to see the larger portion of the Swedish forces emerge on their left, an area that von Götz should have been covering. So, although we had divided our forces, it was clear that the Imperials were taken by surprise. My section comprised thirteen regiments of cavalry and six infantry regiments, and I believe there were similar numbers on the other flank. The artillery, some twenty or so guns, was distributed evenly across the width of our lines, except for those around the chapel. I was close to the command centre and would be shuttling between these two forces all day.

It was terrible to see the folly of von Götz, realizing he had not covered his flank, then plunging into territory he had failed to reconnoiter. I was on the hill at that point, and watched his entire force became entangled in an area of dense scrub and forest, with numerous small lakes, streams and marshes. They were bottled up like sheep in a pen, crowded together as more and more arrived with no communication or orders. Our artillery, ranged above them, caused awful carnage before our cuirassiers and musketeers descended on them. In the slaughter that followed von Götz himself fell under a hail of ball. Their war cry of "No quarter!" was soon replaced by "Sancta Maria!" as if calling upon their Virgin Mary for help. There was none.

Our battle cry was, *"Jesus hjälpa oss!"*—"Jesus help us!" And He did.

I don't know how many miles I must have ridden that day. No sooner had one message been delivered than I was back in the saddle for the return, and setting out again without rest. It wasn't combat, it wasn't battle, but it was fatiguing beyond belief. Unlike those open terrains, like the wide grassland at Klingenthal where I had been injured, I was never in real fear of attack. There was always the cover of trees or bushes, and when carrying a message I could always steer clear of knots of combat. In the midst of battle it is impossible to know the ebb and flow, let alone the outcome, especially when it is being fought in forest and mountain. On one return to the command centre I was certain we had lost everything; a wedge of Imperial cuirassiers had penetrated our lines, begun sacking our baggage and, horror of horrors, carried away Baroness Beata, the General's wife! When we heard this, all the spirit was taken out of us. By the grace of God she was later rescued, unharmed of course, because such a prize kept intact would be worth a vast ransom. But it was many hours of uncertainty while the battle raged on before news came to us.

General Melchior von Hatzfeldt's fate was even more perilous, and there I had a direct hand. A number of the Imperial cuirassiers who had penetrated our lines had been driven back into the woods that flanked the chapel hill on the east side, and our riders were giving chase. I was returning to Robert Douglas on the left flank, when I heard shouts and the clash of weapons ahead of me. I slowed to a trot and rode towards the sound warily in case I needed suddenly to ride out of harm's way. I came upon an older man on horseback, finely dressed and clearly enemy, being harassed by two of our cavalrymen. Blood stained his sleeve from a cut to his arm, and his jerkin was ripped from his shoulder.

"God damn you!' he was shouting. "I've given you my purse, and here's my sword. I surrender!"

"Hey, look at this!" shouted one of his captors, shaking out the purse into his palm. "There's a wealth in florins here."

"So we kill the bastard and share the wealth," laughed the other. And when I heard that voice as I rode in closer, it shrivelled the hairs on my arse. None other than my lifelong nemesis! "Shit chance we'll have of getting any of his ransom money," he crowed, raising his sword to strike.

I galloped forward quickly, momentarily distracting their attention, and damn me if I wasn't looking into the face of Melchior von Hatzfeldt himself. Without a thought I yelled, drew my sword and held it to Wadegahte's throat. Von Hatzfeldt recognized me immediately, and as he realized his life was no longer forfeit he sagged in his saddle.

"It's von Hatzfeldt, you blind fool!" I yelled, waving my blade in Wadegahte's face. "Have you totally taken leave of your senses?"

Wadegahte stabbed, shot and poisoned me with his eyes. I could see from his tightly wound body and his rapid eye movements that he was assessing his chances of killing me first, before dealing with his captive. Suddenly I was in mortal danger. I backed my horse away, swiftly sheathing my sword and pulling out my musket. I pointed the weapon where the tip of my sword had just been. He eyed the muzzle, knew I could and would fire, and sheathed his own sword. He was bested and he knew it.

The General gained some composure, his pride and station coming to the fore. He sat upright again, faced his captors with a sneer, then turned to me.

"I am undone," he said, addressing me alone. "Take me. I do not even know who has won the day."

And then he smiled weakly at me.

"Horseshit," he said.

Chapter Twenty-Seven

In which I taste the bitter-sweetness of victory, fail to vanquish an enemy and ride with Major General Robert Douglas

Det var en mycket hård och blodig strid, såsom har inte setts under de senare
åren, och kommer inte att snart ses igen
It was a very hard and bloody combat, such as has not been seen
of late years, and will not soon be seen again
Lennart Torstensson

We won the day. And it was the most awful slaughter. We won the war that day, if any side could be said to have won it. The Battle of Jankau marked the point at which Catholic and Protestant, Habsburg and Swede, the Holy Roman Empire and the German states, finally realized they had fought themselves into poverty, ruin, pestilence and famine. There was nothing left to fight for. In effect, we dealt the war its mortal blow that day in Jankau, but it would be years more before there was peace.

Bone tired, deadly exhausted, sick, cold and hungry, we surveyed the blood-soaked fields around the burnt shell of the town of Jankau and wept as we rejoiced. We had lost two thousand men, but the enemy had lost everything.

The day following the battle, February 25, I was called to the tent of Lennart Torstensson, and went there in trepidation. I had escorted a seething Wadegahte and his crony, together with our prize captive, back to our chapel headquarters the night before, so I knew this was some sort of follow-up. I had spent a sleepless night knowing that Wadegahte and his toad would have already got their story to their commanding officer, and would have implicated me in the incident before the surrender. Blame would be squarely on me; they would see to that. But who would be believed? The more I tossed and turned, the worse things looked, and the light of day hadn't eased my mind.

I entered the tent to find not only Torstensson, but also Major General Robert Douglas and my own squadron commander, Helmut Weitz seated behind a trestle loaded with papers, maps and writing paraphernalia.

"Hintze," began the General in his own language as soon as I had saluted. "Tell us what happened during the apprehension of General von Hatzfeldt."

"Happened, sir?" I stammered, off guard in spite of trying to prepare myself. "We... we... he surrendered to us... and we escorted him to the... to our... your headquarters. Sir."

"You came upon him yourself?" There was ice in his voice.

"I... I joined two others. Officers... who had already apprehended him, sir."

There was serious trouble here. The intensity in their faces, their stillness and attention, all their eyes upon me.

"In what manner had these two officers apprehended him?" Torstensson leaned forward.

Now I was certain that the hostage von Hatzfeldt had told them the full story, and I was equally certain that if I didn't do the same I would never wear livery again. But to tell the whole truth would be to condemn Joachim Wadegahte to death. Maltreating a prisoner of von Hatzfeldt's stature was a hanging offence, no matter who you were. Blood had been drawn and death had been threatened.

Satan, as our old pastor used to tell us children, sits upon your left shoulder, while Christ sits upon your right. Never since childhood was this more apparent to me than at that moment. I could almost feel the Fiend's talons in my flesh, his foul breath on my cheek. The truth would dismiss my nemesis from my life forever. No more in the back of my mind would there be the fear of what he might do next. Sweet freedom, that's what Satan offered me that day in front of those three austere inquisitors. I had killed in battle, I had committed cold-blooded murder in retribution, but condemning this man to death was more than I could do. I raged within myself at the injustice, and would have wished away my conscience to escape this horrible dilemma, if only I could. But that, of course, was exactly what the Dark Lord lusted for.

"I really cannot say, sir." Oh, my God, I was back in front of my Duke again, a quaking little boy with dashed dreams.

"I really think you must," replied Torstensson with no thaw in his ice.

"Do we need more?" Robert Douglas spoke up. He addressed the other two in an excellent, almost unaccented Swedish. "Von Hatzfeldt has told us of these events. Before this lad intervened those two would have killed him and shared his purse. We know the truth."

"Do we? Do we know the truth?" the General growled. "You would believe our sworn enemy over word of our own officers? They say *he* was there first, and they came upon *him!*" He shot his finger at me. "I will hear the truth from his mouth! This man can tip the balance."

"I... I cannot say, sir."

Douglas spoke up again. "Your two cuirassiers tell a different story entirely, we know. But von Hatzfeldt has nothing to lose by the truth, whereas your officers stand to lose everything. Is the question really in balance? Does this man need to speak?"

"Yes, he *must*," growled Torstensson. "We do not condemn our own officers to death on the word of our enemy!" Then he leveled his finger at my face again. "But he chooses not to speak! So he condemns himself. Silence is guilt."

Just as I realized how badly things were likely to go for me, Douglas came to my rescue. "Silence might also be innocence. He is clearly loath to implicate these two, because he knows that to do so is their death sentence." He looked straight at me. "Am I not right?"

"I cannot…"

"Yes, I *know* you cannot," he interrupted testily. "You don't wish to be their executioner, but you also know the truth. Yes?"

Perhaps I inclined my head slightly; perhaps my whole demeanour shouted louder than words, but all three nodded, Torstensson last and reluctantly. A decision had been made.

"They are your men," said Torstensson angrily, addressing Weitz. "It is your decision what is to be done with them. I would hang them!"

"Yes, I am ashamed to say they are my men," sighed Weitz. "And this is not the first incident…"

"Then hang them up for the scum they are, and let the stinking flesh fall from their bones!"

"They will not hang without Hintze's testimony," replied Weitz evenly, earning a shrivelling look from Torstensson. "But they will have their emblems, their badges of rank, their insignia torn from them, their swords will be taken away and broken, and they will then be discharged from our service. I will send a message to Duke Adolf Friedrich appraising him of this decision."

This was a hard line to follow. The Wadegahte name carried considerable weight at Court, so Weitz could never have him executed, no matter what the transgression. It would be the end of Weitz's career. As it was, it would he hard enough for him back in Schwerin to justify the decision to expel Wadegahte from the cavalry. Yet, by allowing him to live for an offence that carried the death sentence, he was challenging Torstensson's authority as supreme commander. It was one hell of a balancing act. Torstensson was clearly still angry, but of necessity he nodded a surly approval. So my nemesis was punished, but was still in my life.

"And you, Hintze," Weitz took a turn at aiming a finger at me. "One word of any of this from your lips and you suffer the same fate. Understood?"

I saluted and left.

There it was: bitter-sweet victory at Jankau.

Some days later it was Robert Douglas himself who called me to attend him. The chapel and some outbuildings had been commandeered, and I found him ensconced in a small room within the building complex. I had a moment or two to study him while he finished writing at a small camp table; a long-faced, austere man, moustache and goatee trimmed meticulously, with red hair falling in waves across his shoulders. Down in the ranks we had all heard stories of this savage, rapacious and unbending Scotsman, and here I stood in his presence, singled out from all the others only by yesterday's incident. He looked up at me from his work with clear, icy blue eyes.

"Ye ken Angliss, laddie?"

My blank face told him he was speaking no language I knew. I picked up the word English, and I had heard the barbaric shoutings of Highland Scots, so I surmised that this was what he was speaking.

"I'm sorry sir," I replied. "I understand some English, but..."

"Aye, Ah mind ye hae Angliss, but ye dinnae ken a wurrd o' Scots." He smiled at the joke he was playing on me. "Aye, weel, that's the way o' it." Then he went straight into excellent German, in an educated accent of the North. With this, and his perfect Swedish, I realized I was in the presence of a formidable intellect. "I'll come straight to the point. I like the look of you, and have petitioned Helmut Weitz for your services."

My heart sank. What the hell did he want with me? We were finished, were we not? All I wanted was to go home. I held a blank expression at odds with my heart, and this made him smile again... and now the smile was ominous.

"The Holy Roman Emperor Ferdinand III of the House of Habsburg," he intoned in a mocking voice, "King of Hungary and Croatia, King of Bohemia, Archduke of Austria, blah, blah, blah, has scuttled from Praha under disguise in the dead of night. So terrible were the roads of his realm that he abandoned most of his baggage near Plsen, continuing to Regensburg with nothing but his crown and some ten thousand Ducats with which to pay his troops. He now cowers in safety behind the protection of the Donau. His most precious possessions remain under the guard of one Count Schlick."

"This is news indeed, sir," I replied, "but—if you will excuse my forwardness—why are you telling me this?"

"Because it is our plan to liberate some of his abandoned property, and I think you would be a serviceable addition to my company. Weitz is in agreement, as I told you."

Now my heart was in my boots. Douglas was one of those zealous bastards that the world is too full of; the sort who are filled with an enthusiasm they naturally assume everyone around them shares. Hip-

hip-hooray and off we go, and damn you if you don't sign on and give your all. We were exhausted. The whole army was tired to death, hungry for food, hungry for home and warmth and surcease from want. We were cold and dirty and lousy and sick. Some of us were dead. We had beaten the bloody Papist Holy Roman Empire Habsburg bastards into submission, humiliation and ridicule. So, for the love of God, let us go home!

None of it. Oh, dear, the Emperor had forgotten some of his baggage, and if he wasn't already scuttling defeated like a roach under a wainscot, we were going to go and poke at him with a stick. The Douglases of this world have no conception of when enough is enough. But that's what leaders are made of.

"I am honoured, sir, that you consider me…" My God, the words were like cold ashes in my mealy mouth.

He waved my words away. "Three small, handpicked squadrons. We need speed, excellent horsemanship, and a signaler who can perform under duress. You come well recommended. We will gather here for briefing at the tenth hour."

With that, I was dismissed.

"The entire baggage train became bogged down," Douglas was telling his hand-picked cavalry squadron commanders later that day. "The Emperor removed scarcely anything from it before hurrying further west. We have it from our *éclaireurs* that the populace were forbidden to recognize his passing, for fear we would hear rumour, discover his whereabouts and attack him. Yes?" to one of his officers.

"But our scouts *had* discovered his whereabouts, sir."

"Sadly, only after he had passed. By then he was safe south of the Donau. Now…" Douglas unrolled a map onto the trestle table in front of him and traced a line with his finger. "Here. The place is eighty-five miles to the north, not far from Plsen. Three days if we travel hard."

"Sir," one of the officers raised his hand. "Do we know the strength of the company guarding the train?"

"Yes. Not great. It is expected that reinforcements will be sent from Regensburg, to both protect the train and assist in moving it further west. We have to be there first!"

"Sir," spoke up another, "as cavalry we can hardly carry much away…"

"Yes. Good man! We travel light. Each of your men must bring two saddlebags. We want no kingly rubbish. We look for bullion, coin and insignia in particular."

So it was that three squadrons of cavalry headed north at all speed, emerging upon the Praha-Regensburg road just west of Plsen in the middle of the third day. It scarcely stopped raining the whole time we rode, so we could only imagine the mess of the main roads between towns. As we came over a short rise between two large stands of trees we encountered what our scouts had told us of: a row of wagons thoroughly bogged down with their horses unhitched and grazing, and picketed about by only a couple of squads of armed men. Douglas barked out his orders, I sounded the calls and we galloped down the hill *en masse* with swords unsheathed, while the guards and waggoneers scattered before us. A few of their harquebusiers had their weapons shotted and ready, but we were so quickly upon them that not much lead came our way before they were put to flight. We so outnumbered them that death or desertion were the only options. It was a pathetic guard for such a valuable cargo, but the fleeing Imperial army believed our track to be far to the south and east and had no idea that an enemy force could be so near. Douglas's rapid double-back upon our route south had taken them quite by surprise.

The ransacking of the Emperor's baggage was a festive occasion. We had fought his armies, we had killed his soldiers, we had put him to flight, but here and now was a direct poke in his eye. We rooted through the personal Imperial belongings for specie and bullion, but found very little. The Imperial toad scuttling from Praha had brought furnishings and tapestries, paintings and bed curtains, and all sorts of other trappings (no unwilling musicians, I noticed) most of which were flung aside or smashed. The mud around the wagon wheels received the cast off and trampled treasures with joy. It was a comprehensive sacking. Then, just as I was tearing the lid off a wooden chest in search of valuables, I was back again in the ruins of my own house, crunching on broken tile and plaster, sifting ruined house chattels through my fingers.

All the heart went out of me and a lump rose in my throat.

There was a triumphant shout down the line when insignia, flags and regalia were discovered; much more important for inflicting humiliation than a wealth of trinkets and baubles. I don't know how much more destruction our squadrons might have accomplished in their search for riches, before our scouts returned with a warning that a mighty relief force was approaching from the west.

We stuffed our saddlebags as quickly as we could with as much portable treasure as possible, leaped into the saddle and were away. The force that Ferdinand had sent back was considerable, but they only encountered the scattered runaways of the guarding companies to the west as the light was fading. The sole concern of this force had been in rescuing the baggage train, and it can only have been when they approached next morning that the full and awful truth became -

known. By that time we were long gone, night had passed, and a chase with a day's delay would have been hopeless.

So ended my brief acquaintance with Robert Douglas. The world is filled with people like him, and I thank God I am not one of them. When I returned to my squadron I learned that we were recalled, and that a long ride home was planned as soon as we could make ourselves ready.

We all attended divine service that night and thanked God for our deliverence.

Chapter Twenty-Eight

In which Christophorus Schleef and Elisabeth Bauchen come into
my life again

*Ich bin der Weinstock, ihr seid die Reben. Wer in mir bleibt und ich in ihm,
der bringt viele Frucht, denn ohne mich könnt ihr nichts tun*
I am the vine, ye are the branches: He that abideth in me, and I in
him, the same bringeth forth much fruit: for without me ye can do
nothing

Johannes/John 15:5

Schwerin never looked so appealing as we approached its walls in a
soaking and freezing downpour in late 1645. Our Duke had called us
back because protection of his own realm was as important as fighting
the enemy far away. As we patrolled the length and breadth of Mecklenburg-Schwerin in the year that followed, my soul would be squeezed
with sharp regret that patrols like these could not have been instituted
sooner. In concert with our Swedish allies and 'protectors' we rounded
up renegades and mercenaries, we stamped out any military presence
that was not our own, we imposed order. My duties as a court trumpeter
were always at war with my duties as a seasoned cavalryman. Precious
little fine music got played while I sat in the saddle, slept where I could,
ate what came to hand, and played the life of a soldier. The war
continued in France, in Bavaria, in Holland and Spain, while our
Ostsee principalities continued their incessant pleas for peace while
trying to clean their own houses.

I had kept my room at Frau Walther's all along. She certainly allowed
me a great deal of flexibility in my living arrangements, and as long as
I paid what she asked there was no problem. I never really knew if
others used my room in my absence, but I didn't notice any change in
the disposition of my meagre belongings. As long as the bed covers
were clean, I really didn't care.

I often failed to check my postal slot at the entrance gate of the
Schloss because nobody ever wrote to me. I was passing through one
February day in 1646 when the gatekeeper called me and waved me in.

"I know you don't stop in all that often…" he began. The last part
was left unsaid; only bad news came for me by post, and he had seen
it.

This time, however, it was a request from Christophorus Schleef,
son of the Rostock notary. There was paperwork to be dealt with and

signatures to witness, so it would be necessary to have it done in person. He indicated that there was no great urgency, but the sooner it was completed the better. My heart ached as I read the paper; this could only be the legal formality acknowledging that Jürgen, my lost and dearest brother, would never come back. I would sign, but I could never accept. I wanted nothing to do with the land, nothing to do with the farm; I wanted all of it not to be.

I had been in the court's service long enough now that a certain amount of freedom was granted me—especially as a member of the *Kameradschaft*—but no more than others with a similar or longer service, I suppose. It was late March before I found time to visit the stables and get good old four-footed Jürgen saddled up. He was always waiting for me after my patrolling, and he always knew me. His memory of me matched my memory of his namesake. He was not a young horse by now, and was used mostly for exercise at home because of his intelligence and training, but he was mine to ride on those brief excursions where he could take his sweet time.

I rode slowly back to Rostock, recalling the last time I had come this way *en route* to Denmark. It seemed almost to have been in another lifetime, or to have happened to somebody else. It was a melancholy journey because I rode through lands that had once been prosperous but were now either unpopulated, or worked in poverty and desperation. Ten years ago, when I came this way with my father, I was sure it had seemed better than this. I tethered my horse in a small copse late in the evening of the second day and wrapped myself in my cape to sleep. Early the next morning I was riding into Rostock.

Herr Schleef the Younger greeted me at the door to the office on Wokrenterstrasse and ushered me in. "My father is unwell," he told me before I could ask, "and he has largely passed the work over to me." I said that I hoped it was a passing illness. "His illness is the illness we all must suffer," Herr Schleef replied. "He is nearly sixty years old and his time is measured."

The office I remembered from my last visit seemed more ordered. The books and rows of document boxes, the papers, the parchment rolls and all the writing paraphernalia still overwhelmed the small space, but their disposition seemed more rational. Christophorus Schleef sat behind a high desk and motioned me to a stool. He had a few sheets of paper in front of him, and a rolled parchment, which I think I recognized.

"Now, Herr Hintze," he began, "we have the matter of your estate." He appeared hesitant to continue, so I helped him along, appreciating only too well how painful he would find it, as a young and inexperienced man, to discuss this with me.

"I assume, Herr Schleef, the time has come to declare my brother Jürgen no longer heir to the estate." I couldn't put into plain words either what we both knew would have to be expressed. On his part, he fell back on legalese to ease the embarrassment.

"The time limit according to the statutes laid out by the legal and administrative bodies of Mecklenburg..."

"My brother must be assumed to be dead," I finished. There; it was out. He said nothing. "Look, Herr Schleef, I will sign the documents you have ready for me as I am legally required to do, but I will ask you also to prepare a deposition to the effect that no proof of Jürgen Hintze's demise exists, and that I am signing with this proviso. Will you do that?"

"I most certainly can. I can only hope that your belief..."

"Call it faith." Our eyes met and an understanding passed between us.

He spread out the documents to be signed, fiddled with the quill, which needed no sharpening although he did it anyway, and squinted into the inkpot. He then stepped to the foot of a stair and called up. Herr Schleef the Elder descended slowly, saw me rise from my stool, and came to shake me by the hand. The grip was still firm but the hand trembled.

"It is good to see you again, Jacob Hintze, and to see how you have become the image of your father. Please excuse me but I am unwell. My son does well in my stead, as you are doing in your father's."

We signed the papers, Schleef the Elder's inked witness shaky but acceptable. He then took his leave and returned painfully to his room, saying to me with a smile before putting his foot to the stair, "You see, I am still of service, and I still keep an eye on this young upstart. Just like you with the ladies, eh?" and he winked. I had no idea what this was all about, but hardly felt able to ask.

As Herr Schleef the Younger was returning the papers to their document box, I decided to unburden myself of something that had been on my mind since he had first written to me. "Look, Herr Schleef, I cannot have anything to do with this land, this house, all these papers..."

He eyed me quizzically as I stumbled to a halt. "It is all yours by right, assuming your brother..."

"No, no. Let me explain. I am a soldier, I am a trumpeter, I am in a different world now. I want none of this. It's too... painful. I wish it didn't even exist. Get rid of it!"

He nodded. "I understand. However, it is highly unlikely that there would be any interest in purchase in these troubled times. For now, I would suggest that you leave all these holdings in escrow." My expression told him he needed to clarify. "I can hold the property as notary, administer it for you, deal with rentals, should any arise, and you need have no further care of it."

"You're right, of course. But just now…"

"I know. I do understand. There can be nothing but painful memories now, but in the fullness of time there will be healing." For a man of only my own age, he showed a compassion beyond his years. I was content for him to be my Simon of Cyrene, and I did indeed feel the lifting of a burden.

Our business done, the younger Schleef asked me if I had eaten, and if not, could I be induced to take a midday meal with him. I readily agreed; I had eaten sparingly when I woke and it was now past noon. As he closed the outer door behind us, I had a feeling the understanding that seemed to have passed between us might lead to friendship. In Schwerin I was among a group of highly skilled court players, and an equally prestigious group of seasoned cavalrymen who had seen much together, but I counted not one friend among them. There was no man there with whom I could share anything but the most mundane of conversation, or the foulest of jokes. In short, within a huge group of like-minded souls with a common purpose, I was desperately lonely.

I thought I had seen enough of fish in my short life, but the meal we were served in a small tavern on the quayside was excellent. The proprietor of *Der Cogge* knew Herr Schleef well and welcomed us both with dishes of herring, sole and onions, accompanied by grainy bread and a fine ale served in glasses. We finished everything on the board.

"Thank you, Herr Schleef, for your hospitality and kindness," I said, raising my almost-empty glass, and quietly belching fish and onions. "I had expected an experience of some formality, but I am pleasantly surprised by the after-office service."

He raised his glass in turn. He had that look in his eye that had so intrigued me the first time I met him; it was serious yet filled with jesting irony. "I have done my duty as a notary, and now we are off duty. May I call you Jacob if I ask you to call me Chris?"

I smiled, realizing that this was the first time a ray of happiness had settled on me for what seemed like an age. We tapped our glasses together and finished the ale.

"There was one other small matter," my new friend said in what I thought was still a light tone. "There is a young lady who has been asking after you."

"Hah! The only 'ladies' who ask after me are…" I shut up quickly. What happened on campaign was of no concern to anybody. Then an awful thought came to my mind. "Who? Who is this?"

"Pastor Haussmann at Belitz was approached by a lady who insisted on knowing who you were. He was apparently under instructions to divulge your identity to nobody. She insisted, so he contacted me. Us. My father."

This was fearful news. I didn't know what to think. It was surely the Elisabeth Bauchen who had come upon me in the graveyard that day. But by now she must know everything! The memory of that woman had hung over me these years like a poised sword, forcing its way into my mind unasked; unfinished business to dog my footsteps. So why would she wish to contact me? To revile me? To take action against me under law?

"What did she say?" I asked in panic. "What did she say? Was she angry? What?"

He waved me to calm myself. "None of that. I only saw her in passing. She was with my father for a short while, and she seemed in a serene enough state when she passed though the office. My father simply asked me to mention this."

"You know what this is all about?"

"Well, of course I do, you idiot! The whole of Rostock and the countryside around knows what it's all about! Some anonymous saviour rid the place of vermin, and rode away into the west."

"But nobody knows who I am! How could *she?*" Had the pastor broken his word?

"She *doesn't*. My father knows. And old Schwinn of the Watch; he knows. No one else. What happens out there," and the wave of his arm encompassed the entire world that was not Rostock, "is of no concern to folk here. All they hear is rumour. She knows *of* you, of course, but not who you are."

"Then why does she wish to find out who I am? What does she want with me?"

He gave me that great broad grin of his and said, "Why don't you meet her and find out?"

"I burned her house down!" I yelled, causing the other patrons to turn their herring-chomping jaws towards me. "I am an arsonist and mass murderer, God damn you!" I continued in a vehement whisper.

"Who can fathom the minds of women," he laughed, which nearly broke our fine new friendship right there. I was so furious I couldn't speak, which was a Godsend because his next words repaired the rift. "See her. Meet her. If she meant anything bad to you she would have employed a lawyer, not consulted my father and me."

I nodded, recognizing that I would have to meet with this woman, give her whatever she wished by way of apology, and with luck have her haunting shadow out of my life.

"So, where and when?"

"In your time and at the place of your choosing."

"I have to be back in Schwerin, so it must be soon. The day after tomorrow then, at the second hour. I cannot ride my old fellow hard. And where else but the churchyard in Belitz?" I was pretty sure this was now a relatively safe place and that she could come to no harm riding there.

"I will send word. Where are you staying?"

"Oh, anywhere my horse and I choose. The soldier's way."

"You are welcome to stay with us." It was tempting but I needed solitude.

"Thank you. It's very kind…"

We parted at the door of the tavern with a firm handshake. I knew I would see more of Herr Schleef… Chris, at some time in the future. Just knowing he was looking after my affairs would be a balm to my heart.

There was a pony tethered at the gate to the churchyard in Belitz when I arrived. I tied Jürgen some way distant in case the beast might be skittish, and passed slowly through the gate. She was sitting on a stone bench beneath a tree, a small posy of flowers in her hand. She was dressed in a plain shift of light blue stuff, gathered at the waist with a belt of the same material. On her head was a white kerchief, a searing reminder of the one buried close by. Long, pale hair, caught at the nape with a tie, spilled over her shoulders. She looked up as she heard the gate creak. The face was not as careworn as I remembered, her blue/grey eyes bright and a half smile playing around her lips. Not a pretty face, but filled with the inner beauty that comes with knowledge and confidence. But now, as I was in front of her, I could see doubt cross her brow.

It was absurd. Again, I was unable to speak. I stood before her, she sat, and that is how it was for many heartbeats, until she rose and stood. Her eyes met mine, a little below my level, and still we stood. She broke the spell with a gesture, and we sat beside each other on the bench, a space between us.

My tongue-tied state broke in inanity. "I… I burned your house down."

"My father's house, not mine. I only lived there."

There was much left unsaid, but who was I to probe any further? Another silence as birds sang and the wind wafted the trees.

"Why did you want to see me?" I asked in a small voice. "Do you wish to hear my apologies? My confession?"

"Far from it. You did a brave thing." She turned her head to me and held my eyes.

"I didn't know who I was," I told her. "I was not me." I would not have believed as I rode up here that morning that I could possibly open my mind to a stranger, but here I was on a sunlit stone bench in a graveyard, opening my heart to a girl holding a bunch of flowers. "I was nobody when I did that. I was dead. I became a murderer."

"You are a soldier. You took vengeance." A huge load was lifting from my shoulders, a load I hadn't even known was there. I thought it was a shadow; it had been a burden.

"The pastor tried to dissuade me with Scripture. But I was too angry."

"He told me. Refused to say who you were, but sniffed at your willfulness."

"Ah, I bested him, that's why. 'An eye for an eye' I told him."

"He's a simple man, but kind."

Another quietness descended. We had now come as far as we could go with this talk; I had 'confessed', she had 'forgiven'. The mission was over and now it was time to break camp, a truce made.

It was she who broke the silence this time. "You're Jacob, aren't you?"

"Yes. Jacob. Jacob Hintze."

She inclined her head. "We knew your people slightly. It had to be you." She paused, eyeing me from the side, a slight smile on her lips. "Jacob," she said as if testing the name. "Jacob. I'm Elisabeth."

"Yes, Pastor Haussmann told me your name when he wrote…"

"You must have thought the worst of me."

"The worst of myself. When I knew what I had done. And who I had done it to…"

She laughed lightly, and that was a pretty sound. "So, now I know who you are. You know who I am. All done." And then that sideways smile again. No, it was not all done. I could not, would not, make the next move, but would she? Impasse. And so we sat again as the day passed, as a hare hopped into our quietness and went about his business, as a small songbird perched on 'Hans Engelbrecht who passed this life in…'

"I want to see you again," she murmured.

My world came suddenly to a sharp point, and twisted me. I am a soldier. I have ridden to meet the enemy and I have killed. I have no place here, and there is blood on my hands. There is blood in my soul! We are at war, and as long as we are at war I am nobody's but my master's. She would tear me from that fixed place. She saw all this in my face and the shadow crossed hers.

"I *will* see you again." There was a force behind her eyes and a firm line to her lips. I have no idea even now what love really is, but as I

220

felt her will and looked into those blue/grey eyes, I had a vision of a path that might be taken. Perhaps. Not yet. It frightened me.

"I am a soldier. My life is in death." I was harsh, deliberately so. "I will not take you there. I *can not* take you there."

"You will. I see it in your eyes. You will."

Yes, I thought as her eyes melted mine, I might. How could I not? No woman had captured me this way before. I had absolutely no experience of a woman as more than a vessel for my pleasure, as a sheath for my sword. This woman sitting beside me might have been another kind of being, so different was what I felt.

"This war…" I began.

"Cannot last forever," she finished.

"But while it does…"

"I will be here."

She rose lightly from her seat and turned to face me. I rose and faced her. We stood for I don't know how many heartbeats, looking into each other's eyes. I don't think either of us made the first move, so well-tuned were our thoughts, but there we were with our lips together, arms around each other. No kiss I had ever felt… Well, enough of this soft, unsoldierly stuff.

I rode back to Schwerin deeply divided. I regretted yet also revelled in that kiss. I should never have kissed her; a kiss is a dangerous thing, as Iscariot showed Our Lord. Yet, the sweetness I still felt on my lips! How could that be wrong? I saw her face in my mind's eye continually, knowing there was no going back, as I agonized over dragging her into my violent world. But she knew what I was and she accepted it; wasn't that enough? Round and round my thoughts went, with no resolution. I don't remember much of that journey, and I don't think I fulfilled my tasks as conscientiously as I should have done on my return to duty.

Sufficient to say that a kiss seals a vow more firmly than ever priest or notary or lawyer can.

Chapter Twenty-Nine

In which Elisabeth Bauchen becomes my lover

Sie ist lieblich wie die Heinde und holdselig wie ein Reh. Laß dich ihre Liebe allezeit sättigen und ergötze dich allewege in ihrer Liebe
Let her be as the loving hind and pleasant roe; let her breasts satisfy thee at all times; and be thou ravished always with her love
Sprüche/Proverbs 5:19

Letters now came regularly to my mail slot in the gatehouse, and the old keeper would smile and laugh as he handed them over. My address was written in her rounded script, and I think he knew from her hand that there was a woman in my life. Those letters I wrote, and hers that came back in reply, tell of our love in a way my words here cannot. I would keep her latest letter by me all day, never dreaming of opening it until I returned to my room, bursting with anticipation. When on patrol I would ache for our homecoming, when I would immediately look into the mail slot and find the paper I knew would be there. In absence, written words carry wonderful power.

For a year that dragged on forever, I could never break away from duty along the borders of Mecklenburg-Schwerin to visit Elisabeth in Rostock. And perhaps I was even fearful to do so. Our letters had to suffice. I was still terribly torn about dragging her into my life, and I knew she was filled with fears for my safety. She often wrote that she awaited the arrival of the post in agony, and was wracked with worry if an expected letter didn't arrive. I told her often enough that my duty took me away for days and even weeks at a time, but still she worried. She had no need; I knew how to take care of myself. Most of my work at that time was routine, and on only two occasions did I take messages to other heads of state, and neither was in any way hazardous. Breitkopf was still charged with most of the sensitive messaging work, and while I itched and lusted to do what he was doing, I did understand our Duke's desire to keep all such work with the most experienced hand.

Finally, on one wonderful occasion duty took me to Elisabeth's home town. It was the wedding mass in March 1647 of a Rostock city councillor's daughter to a merchant's son, which was to be celebrated in the *Marienkirche* with organ, choir and many instrumentalists. Herr Nicolaus Hasse, the cathedral composer whose trumpet piece I had encountered while in Schwerin, had been commissioned for this work. He had scored for three trumpets and kettledrums in the choral sections, and it was a great pleasure to have been selected by *Hoftrompeter* Breitkopf to ride here and perform with Friedemann, Albrecht and Wolfgang, who was one of our two kettledrummers. It is not often, Friedemann confided in me, that one so young would have this honour. It said much, he told me, of Hartmund's faith in my ability.

I wrote to Elisabeth as soon as I heard this news, and she told me that if I wasn't already billeted I would be welcome to a room at her uncle's house. She had lived with her uncle, her mother's brother, and her aunt since the death of her parents, in a nice house near the harbour, where the uncle had his shipping business. As I read those words a thrill passed from my heart to my loins, an amalgam of fear and passion. We had now been writing to each other for almost a year but had kissed but once. Would I simply sleep in a room in her house? Would she have invited me if only to sleep alone? Should I take a step that would be impossible to undo? My God, how I lusted to! My, God, how I feared to! I raised the possibility of this billet with Breitkopf, and he agreed to the arrangement with a broad grin. He was clearly a lot more certain than I was.

I did not contact Elisabeth on our arrival in Schwerin; we were all business, and that is the way it had to be. At rehearsal the day before the nuptials we discovered that Herr Hasse was a stickler, even though his trumpet parts were really quite timid. The *Kameradschaft* and the chapel used different pitch standards in our region, a not uncommon occurrence wherever you went. The pitch we would use was set by the organ, which had been installed in the *Marienkirche* many years ago. It was at a much higher pitch than our instruments. Traditionally, this wouldn't matter at all because the trumpet corps never played in concert with the other instruments, but when it came to bringing trumpets into the church as musical instruments in their own right, all sorts of tuning and transposition compromises were necessary. We trumpeters found this pitch issue an irritant when we travelled elsewhere, and as trumpets were being scored increasingly in both chapel and secular music, it was common to travel with a bag full of miscellaneous bits and pieces, and be expected to transpose when necessary. There was one occasion while in the Duke's service when I had to borrow a local instrument—a ridiculously high-pitched thing—and I ended up looking a bit of a fool. Thereafter I always brought several instruments on these visits, as the others did. Nowadays, I'm told, trumpeters own three or four instruments, but it wasn't common then.

The *Marienkirche* performance was not as fraught as most because we had brought high-pitched trumpets, but even so it took some fiddling with bits and pieces of tubing before we—and more to the point, Herr Hasse—were quite satisfied. The parts written for us were simple enough; the trumpets in the choral sections were more for emphasis than music, while the kettledrums rounded out the mighty and glorious effect.

Elisabeth was able to attend the ceremony on the strength of a friendship with the bride. And so, for the first time, she saw her Jacob in a quite different role. I say 'her Jacob' because when we wrote we shared our thoughts, our life and our love. I was hers in all but formality. She later said that she found the wedding service overwhelming, but had loved hearing me play. And now a path in our entwined lives led before us, because she suddenly saw me as more than just the soldier. She had seen the art.

We met in the *Hauptmarkt*, just near the church, after I had entrusted my trumpet to Friedemann and agreed to meet him at our stabling on the morrow. Elisabeth's apartment in her uncles's house was on the top floor, up a tight stairway, and quite separate from the rest of the house. It was there we went after the wedding service. I didn't meet the aunt and uncle then, so I knew not whether they condoned, condemned or were kept in ignorance. As we went to bed that night, we lay down as court musician and lover. Any more than this you do not need to know.

It was some time before I finally pinched the candle and rolled back to wrap her in my arms again. "I want your child," she whispered. If Wolfgang had struck a mighty thunderclap on his kettledrums right outside our bed curtains, the shock those few words gave me could not have been greater. My heart thumped like a hammer mill and sweat broke out all over me. I had hoped, or perhaps assumed, she had been doing what women do to prevent such things, and the thought of her slipping her vigilance was frightening. My first—unworthy—thought was that, one pregnancy out of wedlock and they'd drum me out of the corps as quick as lightning. Then, hard on this came the true moral dilemma.

"No, we cannot!" It was a huge effort to match her whisper. "At any time I could be taken from you. Every time I left you, you wouldn't know if I'd ever return. I cannot leave you alone in the world with a child."

"I will not be alone."

"Who will be there for you if I die? Who? Your aunt, your uncle?"

"You will never die, Jacob."

"Why do you say this? Why do you cling to some stupid hope that I will always evade death? I have been preserved so far by God knows what luck."

"Don't you understand, you stupid, protective sweetheart? With your child inside me you would never die!"

I rolled onto my back, fully awake with my heart pounding amain. This was a terrible turn of events. Love through a woman's body I had had before, but this was the act of love pushed into the future, a love with entanglements, with obligations. How naïve and stupid I had been not to see all this; not to see that the kind of love we had encountered in the churchyard in Belitz would obviously lead to this. All the letters we had exchanged, all the protestations of undying love! Childish! Now, by my lust in entering her body, I had joined myself to her in both spirit and flesh.

Next morning, while the light was only pale in the eastern sky, I stole with Elisabeth down her stair. We went quickly to the place where my horse was stabled not far away. She knew I would have to leave that morning. As we hurried through the cold streets there was a shyness and a distance between us, mostly brought on, I admit, by me. My mind was in turmoil and all I wanted was to shut my thoughts out, escape and not think of the future.

"Must you go back so soon?" It was a silly question, but there was still sleep in her eyes.

"I have to go back to Schwerin," I said as I slung my saddlebags over my mount. "You know that. And I'll have some explaining to do if I linger any longer."

"I know," she sighed. "But you'll come for me."

I couldn't look into her eyes, and once again I had this vision of the two of us together. The path ahead was filled with fear and fore-boding. I feared for her if she was with me—her safety, her loneliness away from her people, her ability to care for herself—but I think I feared more for myself. I feared entanglement, I feared a loss of my independence, I feared responsibility. None of this could I bring out in words.

"I don't know when I might see you again..." I began.

"I will wait," she replied simply.

"And if I die?"

She fixed me with steady eyes. "I told you last night, for me you will never die!"

I found a voice for some of my thoughts, and my speech was harsh. "I am a soldier. I am my own man. When I go into danger, it is only me. But from now it will all be different." I still couldn't meet those eyes, and she heard the doubt in my voice and felt the doubt in my mind.

"But you *will* come for me!" she flared, pulling me round to face her. And now I was seeing a new Elisabeth, one with steel. My raising the spectre of my death was not intended for her protection—she knew that—but just a ruse for me to slide away from responsibility.

"After last night, you will come for me!"

Now I met those blue/grey eyes, and as our gazes levelled her steel melted all away and tears formed. My steel melted with hers. This woman could see inside me, and I was naked. I knew then that she had me, and that her love for me had defeated my selfishness. But now I feared what would become of her when I was killed in battle; not if, but when. I felt a doom clamp its cold hands around my soul. Could I throw the two of us together, only to have her left alone, weeping, desolate…? My heart was torn, she looked so forlorn. But whatever happened from this time onwards, we would be one.

"I will come for you." Just her face at that moment, the memory of our first meeting, and the feeling last night of her most intimate parts around me, resolved all. "I love you, Elisabeth. I will come for you."

That was the tipping point. That was the moment the skeins of our lives twined together, woven on God's loom, never to untangle. I would leave her on many occasions over the years to come, sometimes for weeks and months at a time, and she would never know what cannon's mouth I had put my stupid head into, but I would always return. I saw all this just at that moment in her eyes. I leaned down to her and kissed her long and hard on the mouth, tasting her, drinking her in, so as to carry her away with me, to feel and savour in lonely months to come.

She walked quietly out of the yard with several backward glances, while I returned to my preparations. She had only just passed the corner when Friedemann, Albrecht and Wolfgang emerged from their lodging above the stable, throwing me lascivious looks and broad smiles. I said nothing. We rode out of the yard, set our horse's heads to the west, and returned to duty as court trumpeters to the Duke of Mecklenburg-Schwerin.

Chapter Thirty

In which I lose my mentor and serve the cause of peace

Gehe hin, mein Volk, in eine Kammer und schleuss die Tür nach dir zu;
verbirge dich einen kleinen Augenblick, bis der Zorn vorübergehe
Come, my people, enter thou into thy chambers, and shut thy
doors about thee: hide thyself as it were for a little moment, until
the indignation be overpast

Jesaja/Isaiah 1:18

It should not have been a difficult mission. I would go over it in my mind again and again. I knew the outcome, I knew the result, so why must it play again and again across my mind? There are no might-have-beens; our destiny is but one track through the wilderness, and it is what it is. Yet still I tortured myself.

In the spring of 1647, not long after I had returned from Elisabeth's bed, Hartmund Breitkopf and I were charged by our Duke with carrying two critical messages to Friedrich William, Elector of Brandenburg-Prussia in Berlin. One of the messages would require an immediate reply, while the response to the second would be relayed further south to the Elector in Dresden. For reasons I never understood, neither message was in cipher. It was likely I would return with the first reply, and Breitkopf would continue south. Alignments leading to alliances were taking place, with Brandenburg-Prussia playing a key role in consolidating the Höhenzollern holdings that wrapped around Mecklenburg from the south and east. This was one small part of the mighty peace talks continuing in Westphalia, and the content was sensitive enough that it should not be allowed to fall into the wrong hands. No postal service could be trusted.

We rode south east. It had been an unusually wet winter, but it seemed we were now being smiled upon as the weather was fair with a warm wind from the south. We kept to forest tracks where we could, avoiding heath and open ground wherever possible. Travel across country was not as dangerous as it once had been. On our cavalry patrols we travelled as a unit and the way was cleared for us, but the smaller the unit, the greater the risk.

This was the first mission I had ridden with Breitkopf since I had taken ship to England with him. I looked forward to perhaps getting a little closer to him, as the closest I had ever been was on that overseas trip. I wasn't open with myself then as to why I strove to know him better—to find some way behind the facade of the man to the person himself—but I know now that it was because I was not yet ready to step into the world as a man. For all my experiences, the boy was still inside me.

It was some short distance from Berlin, on the third day of our travels, that we heard five or so horses approaching rapidly from behind. Thinking they were perhaps troops in the employ of the Elector we slowed and pulled over, either to let them pass or for them to stop and question us. Our bona fides were sound and we had no fear of capture or interrogation. But no sooner had we pulled aside, than three more horsemen appeared in front of us. We were flanked behind and in front, with no open way into the thickets beside the route. They had clearly tracked us and set up this ambush. The three ahead of us had bared swords, so it was equally clear they were unfriendly. Among the others I think there were three raised pistols. Their dress was non-descript; no uniform or insignia of any kind. Of the eight now surrounding us, one who seemed to be the leader rode slowly forward with his sword straight before him.

"Give me your scrip!" he demanded of Breitkopf with his left hand extended, sword pointed at the face. "Now!"

Hartmund moved his hand towards his sword in its sheath, but the others spurred forward, tightening the circle, and so he desisted.

"Your scrip! Now!" The sword was waved in his face. "Slowly. No false moves."

These were not just brigands out to rob travellers of their goods and a few coins. These men were not going to kill first and rob the corpses. There was no interest in our saddlebags where the best of our goods would be. They were after our messages. We had been targeted, but we would not die until our messages had been verified.

Breitkopf slid his hand slowly down to his waist where his scrip was buckled to his belt, holding the aggressor's eyes the whole time, and slowly extracted the paper. Seeing what he had come for so easily gained, the man relaxed his vigilance slightly. Everything went suddenly mad. Breitkopf whipped out his pistol and blasted the man out of his saddle, flinging the pistol in another's face as they spurred forward to surround us. Two guns barked—I didn't see where their shots went—then they were upon us. I shot one down as he rode at me, flung the pistol down and whipped up my sword, swivelling in the saddle as I did so. It was useless; we were immediately on the defensive and outnumbered. I ran one man through, I am sure, while taking a cut on the shoulder, but Breitkopf was beset. Holding off one assailant from the side, he received a slash at his sword arm that thudded home. How he did it I don't know, but holding off a second man with the injured arm, he spurred to me and thrust the paper at me.

"Take it!" he yelled at me. "Fly! Fly!"

I hesitated. I had to stay and fight. I was utterly without thought. I slashed at the man beside me—brow, eye, nose, cheek—and he fell back with a scream. Another was on me from the other side, and I parried his first stroke.

"Go!" roared Breitkopf. "Go, my son! *Go!*"

I seized the paper from his hand, wheeled, hacked at another, forcing myself past his mount, and rode. A pistol blasted and I felt hot wind.

I didn't see Hartmund Breitkopf fall.

I rode as if all Hell was opening its foul mouth behind me. I rode as I had never ridden before. I rode in fear, in anguish, in yellow cowardice, in unthinking horror. I don't know how I managed to outpace the two who galloped after me, but I was in among trees, dodging bushes, splashing through water and marsh for what seemed a lifetime. I rode south, I rode east; if I was able to think of anything at all, I thought of Berlin. By God's mercy, little of that horrible ride remains in my memory. I rode into Berlin, practically fell from my horse, and was carried almost insensible to some place of rest. I think the fever that took me, and threw me into the damnation I thought I had escaped, was more of my spirit than my body. I prayed to God in my terrible waking dreams that He would punish me and damn me, that He would take my soul away and throw it down into Hell, where it belonged.

I recall one dream most clearly, because it was the dream that brought me back into my right mind; the dream that returned me from Hell below to the living hell of this life above. Elisabeth came to me, dressed all in flowing white, not saying a word but smiling and standing beside me. I asked her what she was doing in Berlin, and as I spoke the woman of the house in which I had spent my recovery smiled and welcomed me back to the world.

"You have been near death's door these last three days," she said as she gave me water to drink. "It is good to see you in your right mind."

I stirred, and my shoulder lanced sharp spears where I had been cut. The pain brought me to full realization, and the horror of it all came back. What of Hartmund Breitkopf, I asked, what of him? She shook her head gently from side to side. A troop of the Elector's cavalry had backtracked on our route, she told me, and had discovered his mortal remains. As she told me this, my heart tightened, my world shrunk and I wished I had died beside him. It was only slowly I came round to the knowledge he was no more, but at that moment my guilt at not helping him—guilt at running away—tore at me. She saw my tears, mistaking my anguish at my own failure for grief. Her sympathy only made matters worse.

Friedrich William, Elector of Brandenburg-Prussia, called me to attend him when I was more fully recovered. He was seated in a large audience chamber in the palace, surrounded by attendants, guards and the usual toads who gather round authority. He looked down a long, uncompromising nose at me standing before him and fixed me with his eyes.

"You did well to bring us these messages. We commend your heroism. You must understand that in flight from your comrade you served a higher cause. His death was not in vain, and through you his purpose has its vindication."

I have to tell you that, as he said these words, I thought that no cause on this Earth, no petty dealing between princes and dukes and electors, was worth one single lump of the stuff I used to shovel out of the sties in my youth, compared to the life of *Hoftrompeter* Hartmund Breitkopf. I wished again, right there in audience with the mighty Elector of Brandenburg, that I had died and my master had lived. I bowed, thanked the great man and was dismissed.

I accompanied my mentor's body back home, while a messenger from Berlin took our second communication further south. At some point in our travels (the wagon, the waggoneers and me) thoughts of my Elisabeth came to me, and a balm came over my soul. We were in life, the two of us, and we would go forward together. My master, my mentor, my tutor must now be in Heaven, and perhaps his soul looked down upon us and smiled in remembrance of the day I had told him of my womanly billet in Rostock.

And he had smiled.

Duke Adolf Friedrich was heavily involved in the organization of Hartmund Breitkopf's funeral. It was only then, I think, that I realized how close these two men of quite different stations had been to each other. The Duke commissioned Johann Vierdanck to produce a *Musikalische Exequien*, and Vierdanck outdid himself. It was magnificent, moving and heartfelt, and because of the deceased's role, and as the Duke thought so highly of him, there was lots of work for the trumpets. Vierdanck followed the style of his teacher Heinrich Schütz in the form of the service, and added florid trumpet parts in an essentially Italian style, something quite new to us in the north. The diminished musical forces at Court meant that the Duke had to bring musicians into service from quite far places, and no expense was spared. I looked with regret during rehearsal at the motley group of string players brought from elsewhere, and wished I could have seen my friend Berthold among them.

Strangely, I remember almost nothing of the service itself. I think I was still in that state of disbelief, held in a world that was not mine, suspended somewhere like a prisoner awaiting a judge. It was only at the end, as the last chords of the final glorious choral section died among the ceiling beams, that I felt the glory, the power and the might of what we had just done.

And then I was torn all to pieces.

Right after the service (it seemed to my dilated imagination that the echoes were still playing in the space above me) Duke Adolf Friedrich beckoned to me to come with him. I was numb and unthinking, and followed him without understanding what he wanted of me, or why he had singled me out. He conducted me in silence to a small and comfortable sitting room, where there were soft chairs, tapestries on the walls, rich carpets, and a large globe on a stand. We sat opposite each other in an undreamed-of intimacy.

"You played from your heart, my boy," he began. "Trumpet music is the highest honour we can bestow upon a military man."

This had been such a glorious, heartrending and final experience for me that I could find no words. I nodded and blinked the tears from my eyes. He looked down at his feet.

"I use you," he sighed almost to himself. "I use you couriers to do my business. I send you into danger. Troops; they are just men, some men, any men, to use in battle, to tally as won and lost…" He paused and sighed again. "But you, Breitkopf, Hoffmann…" He looked straight at me then, and his eye was moist.

"You were close to him," he recovered himself, "but, oh, you cannot know how close he wished he could come to you. His affection for you became in many ways too strong. You know nothing of him, do you?"

"No, sire." I found a shaky voice around the lump in my throat. "We were close, yet we were also distant. I could never fathom him."

"His life was founded in tragedy. He had a son, you know; a wife, a daughter, a household. This was before he came here to Schwerin. He never spoke of any of it, and I gleaned it only in conversation with others. And even then, it's not all that clear. They died during the opening years of the war—it must have been sixteen-nineteen or twenty—somewhere in the south. He was *Stabstrompeter* then, and it was not long before his talent became obvious to me. And because he knew the country well, I used him for many missions…" He paused and closed his eyes briefly. "I think, as he had lost everything he cherished and cared for, he was a man who would risk danger far more than others. Death for him would be a reunion."

I silently remembered the dangerous executions I had undertaken in Prebberede, and the death wish that had inhabited my soul. The cold, automatic way a body can behave when the soul is deadened with anguish.

"He was dealt another blow when his very good friend and colleague Thilemann Hoffmann was murdered. Do you know of him?"

"Hoffmann, the Berlin trumpeter? Yes, sire. Herr Breitkopf spoke of him, but I didn't know they were close."

"They were, very, and it wounded him. Hoffmann was a messenger as well. I often thought that Breitkopf almost wished he had died in his place, and that he felt guilt he was still alive." He looked closely into my face, as if knowing. "He never took on an apprentice until you came along. Did you know that?"

I hadn't known, and all my speculations over how he had treated his other apprentices became moot. And his distance and aloofness began to take on a new aspect. I was riven suddenly with the memory of his last words to me: "Go, my son! Go!" My son...

"It was not long afterwards," continued the Duke, "that Herr Pinklemann brought him news of your rare talent."

"What!" I was thunderstruck. I was so surprised I lost all thought of deference. "Pinklemann! How did *he* know about Pinklemann?" It had been common knowledge in our family that Pinklemann had gone outside the law of the *Kameradschaft* in helping me. This could not be true!

The Duke smiled. "Networks of information don't stop at matters political. Why would the *Hoftrompeter* of the Court not have a finger in musical affairs elsewhere?"

"But... but when he rode up that day... He had heard me play, and he and his troop drew aside from their path..."

"So you were led to believe. He had known Pinklemann for over four years at that point. They first met when they had cooperated over a wedding mass in the *Marienkirche*; a loan of players from the *Kameradschaft*. So when Pinklemann discovered your talent he contacted Breitkopf immediately."

"He lent me a trumpet. He tutored me for *four years*."

"He did. You were far too young to be brought here, but far too talented to be wasted in the town band. He knew that. That's why he undertook your tuition. And not simply in music, of course."

"Not simply...?"

"He was charged by us to assess your other capabilities. It was clear from his reports that you had a fine intelligence, and that a facility with languages would be within your grasp."

"And... and four years later the cavalry rode up..." My world tumbled upside down as this new intelligence took root. I saw my revered first tutor in a quite different light, and was struck with a pang of anguish that I had never thanked him for what he had done. I would offer prayers for him as long as I lived, knowing in my heart they would find their way. It was little enough.

A suspicion settled into my mind. "That day, sire, when I first played for you at Court..."

"Yes," he smiled, "we did so enjoy our play-acting, the *Hoftrompeter* and I." He laughed lightly, recalling that time.

All this took some time to digest, during which there was a long silence that neither of us felt to break.

"When your father died," continued the Duke eventually in a sombre tone, "Hartmund stood in. He was your stability. But when your family perished it was too hard. He dared not come close, because he feared losing you in combat, as he had lost his own son. He dared not."

My son...

On every occasion I had gone away, on a mission or to war, Breitkopf must have agonized over the parting. But each time there had been a nonchalant dismissal or a studied indifference. I remembered my mission to Christian IV.

"When you sent me to Denmark, sire...?"

"Yes. He was angry with me. Very angry. He insisted he should go, but I told him you needed testing. I overruled him. I sent you into danger against his advice. How else was I to know your worth?"

Dear God, I had known so little! I would offer prayers to Hartmund Breitkopf too; another debt I would carry to my grave, and one that burdened me with heavy unfulfillment.

"Thank you for telling me this, sire. I am in debt to so many people. Debts I can't possibly..." The tears stopped me, and there in front of Adolf Friedrich, the mighty Duke of Mecklenburg-Schwerin, this seasoned soldier, hardened campaigner, fearless cavalryman wept like a baby. The great man let me.

"Debts are paid here on earth," he finally said. "Every time you put your trumpet to your lips, the ledger becomes more balanced. He hears you. He is rewarded in Heaven."

I knew now that I had been selected, tested, groomed and polished since I was a child blowing on a smelly bone. Now it was time to make full use of me. Having been assayed in the crucible of warfare, my service to my Duke took on a more personal nature. I was still field trumpeter in the cavalry, still trumpet ensemble player to the ducal court, but now the more clandestine activities began to take on a new importance. I don't think the Duke was quite ready yet to thrust me into this new role, but the death of Hartmund Breitkopf gave him little choice. My open military and musical service was now punctuated by periods of absence, which were remarked on and noted, but never commented upon by my colleagues and messmates.

Chapter Thirty-One

In which Elisabeth Bauchen becomes my wife and peace is in the wind

Wenn jemand neulich ein Weib genommen hat, der soll nicht in die Heerfahrt ziehen, und man soll ihm nichts auflegen
When a man hath taken a new wife, he shall not go out to war, neither shall he be charged with any business
Deuteronomium/Deuteronomy 24:5

Slowly, as the months went by and Elisabeth's letters continued, my fear of the commitment I had made by sharing her bed was only a memory. It had given way to a sense of security and a feeling for the future. I still felt discomfort for my loss of independence, but I knew now that she would come to me here; we would be together. Soon the days of returning to my lonely room in Frau Walther's house and reading by candlelight for want of company would be gone. That marriage ceremony in the *Marienkirche*, when she had first heard me play, had done more than cement the lives of some Rostock city councillor's daughter and a merchant's son. It had cemented ours as well. Even so, there was still the huge hurdle of my acceptability in the eyes of her guardians. I was patrician in name only, I was a serving soldier in time of war, and it became clear that nothing about our relationship could be taken for granted.

Elisabeth's home life had not been a happy one. I recall, when we met in the churchyard in Belitz for the second time, she had said: "My father's house, not mine. I only lived there." I wondered then what she meant. She was an only child; her mother had miscarried a number of times until finally succumbing to a fever when Elisabeth was just ten years old. Her father had never reconciled himself to having no heir, had found no woman willing to be his wife, and had instead 'adopted' a young man, a relative in some way, to carry his name. The boy had died while in service at the Battle of Wittstock in 1636. Her father slid into drinking, violence and foulness, and died soon afterward. Elisabeth never told me if his death was of excess or a broken heart or, God forbid, that he might have committed the mortal sin of taking his own life. Uncle Otto and Aunt Griselda had taken her in and had given her a loving and stable home life, while the property in Prebberede passed through many rental hands, slowly falling into disrepair. The burning of that house was the funeral pyre of miserable memories.

It was many months before we could be together again. I travelled back to Rostock again on duty in the autumn of 1647 and it was then that I finally met her guardians. At first introduction they liked me well enough—this dashing young trumpeter and cavalryman—but under their guardianship she was surely destined to be the companion and helpmate of a merchant, a trader, a man of standing. One did not marry for love in Uncle Otto and Aunt Griselda's world, and there was conflict between the debt they owed her deceased parents and the obvious attraction they saw between us. Aunt Griselda, though, was torn by indecision but, as we found later, there was a soft heart in her.

Uncle Otto was not torn. He was quite sure of himself; a puffed up and self-important man, massively whiskered, large in stature and bearing, a big noise in the town council, a sponsor of events and donor to charities. I knew him as soon as I met him, one of my father's colleagues at the *Rathaus*. He would have none of her dalliance with me and his moustache bristled at the very idea of it. I was invited into his room—a deeply male place where no foot of the fair sex was ever allowed to tread—and given a grilling that almost made me wish I was back in Ottavio Piccolomini's tent. Much less than an hour of having me under his guns convinced him that nothing good would come of our union, even though I was in effect a patrician and heir to an estate. Should I renounce my nonsense at Court, on the other hand, return to 'my' land, and commence the life of a landholder, then he might be persuaded to smile upon my suit. Even in the desperate, war-torn mess of our country he held to this line. He didn't have to survive out there beyond the sturdy gates of Rostock, the purblind fool.

In Otto's final assessment, I was just too damned dangerous to be around Elisabeth. I had to agree, but not to his face. I had said often enough to Elisabeth that the life of a soldier was no life for her, but we both knew we were driven by an attraction that overshadowed all fears and misgivings. And I would never, ever go back to that land. Ever. I left the interview in a very sorry and miserable state.

Aunt Griselda saved us. It turned out that her righteous, upstanding man of the town was actually clay that she could work in private on a wheel of her own devising. She had come to the realization that we were beyond the point of no return, and that denying their charge's dreams would condemn her to misery and spinsterhood. Against her Otto's better judgement—and God knows what words or wiles she wielded—we were betrothed, with my good friend Christophorus Schleef providing the official function of witness and notary. He was delighted to undertake the office and I think it brought us even closer. Elisabeth carried a considerable dowry, while my landholding, should I ever do anything with it, would give us considerable security.

We would never be able to have the wedding Elisabeth deserved, and that her aunt and uncle would have liked to insist upon, so it had to be a quiet affair. After signatures and witnesses at the Schleef office in Wokrenterstrasse, we rode as a small party to Belitz where Pastor Haussmann united us in the sight of God.

Otto drew me aside after the service, leading me quite forcefully by the elbow into the churchyard, stopping not a yard or two from the stone marker of my own family, although he didn't know it. He gripped my upper arm and looked me directly in the eyes. I returned the same direct gaze, not flinching from his scrutiny.

"Our Elisabeth deserved to marry well," he told me. "It has been our bounden duty to her parents to see that she did so. On you rests her happiness. You know," and here the grip intensified and the eyes drilled holes, "that I consider you below her station. You are a mountebank, sir, and, I strongly suspect, one to take advantage. But you also know that I hold high expectations of you. You, sir, had better guard her well, love her, respect her, keep her from want."

"Yes, sir!" I replied as I took his orders, resisting at the last moment the reflex to salute. "I will do everything in my power."

He thrust his proud, whiskered face into mine, eyeing me closely, not quite sure if he was the victim of an irony bordering upon insubordination. "You will. By Heaven *you will*. You will raise yourself. And mark you this: I will be watching."

Poor man. For all his importance among his cronies of the town council, he had been twisted around a woman's finger, and he knew that I knew. He could have smiled upon me, but that would be too much of a step down. We left the gravestones and returned to our small group waiting by the church gate. I had received my marching orders.

I rode home with my wife across the stricken fields and the blasted landscape of Mecklenburg with a lightness in my heart, but some heaviness in my mind. The delight and wonder of her company, her presence—the full and still incredible reality of her darling existence beside me—was underlain with a growing onus. No longer was I my own man, responsible only to my superiors and biddable by them. I was being pulled from the fixed place… but by joy and wonder.

Everything about that return to Schwerin at the close of the year 1647 was different. I had found a place for me and my wife. Wife! It was a modest place, upstairs in the middle of a row, just along the Ritterstrasse from my old lodging. I took pleasure in having an address on the Ritterstrasse, the road of the horsemen, cavalryman that I was. The place I found was close to markets and a supply of good water, a continuous worry in any town. It was extremely sparsely furnished with the few items I possessed, and would only be better appointed when Elisabeth's considerable belongings arrived by wagon from Rostock. Nevertheless, I had bought a few items of furniture, some copperware and a couple of rugs, so when I brought her into the house it would not be too unwelcoming. It was so strange to see her standing there in the centre of the room, scanning with appraising eyes. I had retained a serving girl, Anja, to assist Elisabeth with running our little establishment. She was a round-faced farm daughter of about thirty years, with a sunny disposition. Like many folk from the surrounding countryside, she had drifted to the town from a farm with too many offspring, not enough food, and danger from roaming brigands. It was not long before I was made to feel that things were in good hands, thank you very much, and to please keep out from under foot.

I bade farewell to dear old Frau Walther, and there were tears and hugs aplenty at the old rooming house. She gave me packages of sausage and bread and cheese to give to my wife, and instructed me under pain of her displeasure to bring Elisabeth to meet her. The meeting, when it came a week later, was a happy affair and it became the start of a friendship that provided Elisabeth with resource and support during my many absences. There was one disquieting moment as we sat and talked around the hearth. Giselle the slop maid, older by far but still easy on the eyes, came into the room from the kitchen carrying a bucket, paused and caught my eye. Fear shot through me as she cupped a breast from below with her free hand and jiggled it, smiling a saucy smile, and then crossed the room to the stair. No one else had seen her.

The first month of the year 1648 was when Elisabeth sat me down, held both my hands in hers, looked into my eyes and told me about our son. I knew it was a son. Or did I really, then? How can any man know what lies waiting in a woman's womb? How can any man really know what seed he has planted there? But Elisabeth knew. As soon as she felt the quickening she knew. He would be Michael. Michael was coming back into the world.

The huge absence of *Hoftrompeter* Breitkopf was a void that could not be filled. On a demand from Duke Adolf Friedrich to the *Kameradschaft*, Friedemann was promoted to *Hoftrompeter* and took his part admirably in the music of the court, but we all knew it would be a long time before we could play without pangs of memory. Although Friedemann Alltid enjoyed this post at the highest level of the *Kameradschaft*, he never failed to acknowledge that he would have enjoyed promotion to *Hoftrompeter* in any way but this.

My routine of military, musical and courier life continued as I fulfilled my official duties in Schwerin, and was then absent for weeks at a time. Peace was in the wind and there was much back and forth for me between home and the towns of Münster and Osnabrück where the peacemongers had gathered. Many of the messages I carried were in open script and could have been delivered by anyone, but there were others whose contents were covert, potentially embarassing and quite often dangerous. Those were the real reason for my travels.

One day I chanced on my erstwhile tutor, Herr Doktor Martius, when passing him in a corridor. He beckoned me to his study. "Do you have some time?"

I entered the book-lined space with the globe of the world, and found even more chaos of paper than I think I had seen before.

"We haven't talked for a while," he began in French. "Sit, sit."

"It's been a year or so," I answered in Italian, shifting a pile of books off a chair.

"How then progress your language study?" In English.

"Jag talar Svenska ganska bra nu."

"Hah, now you have me! Never did take to Swedish. They're too damned close for my liking! Threatening."

"It has been extremely useful to me," I replied, also reverting to our native language.

"Tell me, what are your views on the coming peace?"

This put me a little on my guard. It was an open secret that I was in the service of our Duke in a covert capacity. I had conveyed many letters and documents of an uncompromising nature, but there had also been sensitive material that was not to be discussed. Although I trusted Herr Martius, I had to think carefully before answering.

"I think negotiations are going well..."

He laughed and swung a leg up onto his desk. "Of course, pointless to ask because you don't know what to say and what not to say. So, let's throw the discussion onto philosophical grounds."

"Philosophical...?" Here I was again, back at the beginning, nonplussed in front of my tutor.

"Peace from warfare is but one aspect. Peace to pursue one's faith without censure is another. But for me, the third aspect crowns all: peace to pursue my thoughts and studies without officious interference."

"Yes. People have been imprisoned and put to death for views that oppose church teachings," I said.

"Yes, Catholic teaching. But not anymore. Peace and resolution will open the way to a new age, where the finest minds, like the late-lamented Galilei and Kepler, will not be hamstrung by Scripture."

Again, I felt myself on unsure ground. We are taught the truth of Holy Scripture, and we gainsay it at the peril of our immortal souls. That, at least, was my upbringing; but you don't send a man to war, maiming and killing other Christians, and expect him to come back questioning nothing.

"There is no word in Scripture that says the Sun is at the centre," I replied, understanding where his line of thought was taking him, "but you are implying that perhaps we should be free to make other interpretations?"

"Of course. Scripture is not the beginning and the end. God has given us minds with which to think and question. Would He be so cruel as to scatter evidence of His mighty work before our eyes, yet deny us the capacity to wonder at it? To discern its meaning, if we can?"

"God is not cruel..." I began.

"No, but perhaps He looks the other way? Was this a holy war? Was God on your side? The other side? Any side at all?"

He was throwing me into deep waters. Hartmund Breitkopf had quizzed me on my motives after my first campaign. I knew then, as I knew now, that the Holy Roman Emperor had to be stopped, but I also knew that it was more political than religious. It was about our right to be independent; to be ruled by our own princes, to worship as our pastors showed us, and to be under no other power. It was all too complex to put into words. And, frankly, I was fearful of thinking too deeply; there was a great pit of unwanted knowledge yawning at my feet.

"No, this was no holy war," I began tentatively. "I don't think I was fighting for God. I think I was fighting for our Duke... For his right to rule us, for us to be free to think and worship as we please. I don't know..."

"Exactly!" he interrupted. "It had nothing to do with slaughtering young men because they run beads through their fingers. Christ would be disgusted. It was a war for the right to be free of outside interference." Now his voice was rising. "The Habsburg power monger and the meddling Pope will be put in their places, the Protestant princes will be free to rule as they please, and scholars will be free to question the very fabric of the universe!"

This was high flown stuff indeed. I felt the need to bring him back to earth just a little bit. "We are still in thrall to Sweden," I remarked.

He nodded and sighed. "Yes, the talks in Westphalia leave political freedom in... hah!... God's hands. But we can at least score two out of three: freedom of worship, freedom of thought."

"It will be a different age. Both of us have seen only warfare all our lives. Maybe we don't even know what peace will look like."

"It will be a wonderful discovery. And with that, I must let you get back to your duties. God bless you, my favourite pupil!"

We shook hands, and I left his office perhaps a little wiser and certainly warmed by his friendship and praise.

Chapter Thirty-Two

In which I work for peace, meet a saint, and a son arrives

Seid fruchtbar und mehrt euch und regt euch auf Erden, daß euer viel darauf werden
And you, be ye fruitful, and multiply; bring forth abundantly in the earth, and multiply therein

Mose/Genesis 9:7

The immensely complex process of peace-waging began to reach its conclusion early in 1648, although it would be autumn before the ink was applied to the documents. The two Westphalian cities of Münster and Osnabrück had been pretty well taken over by the delegates, who naturally lived in very fine style. One hundred and ninety-four states were represented at one time or another, and their plenipotentiaries were supported by an army of functionaries, all of whom had to be housed and fed. I rode to both towns, and frequently between them, on a number of occasions that year, carrying messages, documents and private correspondence, and was shocked every time at the spoilage and desolation of the countryside I rode through. For miles around farms had been ransacked, livestock slaughtered and the land wasted to feed the negotiators. Opulence, luxury and excess ran riot within the town walls, while the country for miles around starved.

The only places outside these two centres that saw any benefit were the inns that provided stabling for the multitude of messengers and postmen shuttling back and forth. It was a long day's ride between Münster and Osnabrück, with changes of horses if needed at Greven or Tecklenburg. The innkeepers were in heaven. I know what it's like to hold travellers to ransom; they have to stop, they have to change horses if they're in a hurry, and they usually have a thirst on them as well. That well-trodden track between the two cities was a green swath of plenty across a wasted landscape.

The Holy Roman Emperor was represented in Münster by Maximilian, Graf von Trauttmansdorff, said to be a wise and powerful negotiator. However, once you're on the inside you see that 'wise and powerful' actually means the man is a clever, manipulating bully. Fabio Chigi represented the Papacy only, I suspect, so he could curry favour with the College of Cardinals on his way to becoming Pope. The French sent Henri II d'Orléans, duc de Longueville, although everybody knew the real power lay with Jules Raymond, Cardinal Mazarin. Henri was there for the pomp and the show, and he made much of it.

Our faction, the Protestants in Osnabrück, were pretty well dominated by the Swedes under John Oxenstierna, son of Axel, and John Adler Salvius, although Johann, Graf von Sayn-Wittgenstein of Brandenburg spoke for our Protestant states. Mecklenburg was a weak partner in all this, but Duke Adolf Friedrich still needed and desired representation as there was much to lose. On the great scale of influence dukes were much lower than kings, princes and electors and he felt his vulnerability acutely. Sweden occupied Western Pomerania, pressing on our border, and also held the port town of Wismar. If things went badly, Mecklenburg would be absorbed and become a Swedish possession, with our Duke ousted in favour of some foreign administrator. Autonomy was at stake and, the essential access for our merchants to the Ostsee through Rostock.

Denmark had almost no representation. After signing the Treaty of Brömsebro in 1645, Christian IV's territory was curtailed, and his influence in the region was virtually gone. After his losses at sea, the greater part of his power as King was passed on to the *Riksrådet*, the council of the Danish realm, which was dominated by his two sons-in-law, Corfitz Ulfeldt and Hannibal Sehested. There was no love lost between him and that pair, since the Swedes had ousted them from their comfortable nests in Norway, thanks to their father-in-law's bungling. But I had seen Christian just after his injuries in the Battle of Kolberger Heide, and I don't think anyone present saw him as anything but a damaged, tired, spent old man. When he died early in 1648, the throne was taken by his drunken oaf of a son, who pissed away a fortune and ended up in an early coffin.

It was easy to see why there was so much work for us messengers. When you reckon the number of people involved over the years of negotiations, and the necessity of keeping absent masters abreast of developments on a regular basis, the paperwork generated proved to be prodigious. The delegates were influential functionaries who could be spared for a long duration, yet whose independence of thought and judgement could not be fully trusted. The volume of correspondence that travelled between those two towns, and elsewhere across the entire continent, was incalculable. I heard tell from one functionary that at one stage they were actually running out of paper and ink, so couriers had to be sent to Hamburg for more! Oak galls became a solid investment.

There was actually one saint among all these self-interested potentates: Alvise Contarini of Venice. He was lauded in the official document: "By the Mediation and Interposition of the most illustrious and most excellent Ambassador and Senator of Venice, Aloysius

Contarini Knight, who for the space of five Years, or thereabouts, with great Diligence, and a Spirit intirely impartial, has been inclin'd to be a Mediator in these Affairs."[40] He alone, in my estimation, is deserving of praise for his part in putting an end to this appalling and destructive mess. And the appalling and destructive mess I refer to could well be the negotiations themselves. How he tolerated, month after month, year after year, the excruciating detail and petty demands, I cannot begin to imagine. He even had to mediate between puffed-up toads who argued about who should enter a room first!

I was privileged at one point to meet Contarini, so my assessment of him carries some weight. It began with Duke Adolf Friedrich calling me to his office one day in late March. I was currying my horse when the messenger came to me, so I passed the comb to the groom, washed my hands quickly and followed him. The Duke was seated in his small sitting room—alone, as he always was when I was called there—and he waved me to a chair with little formality.

"There are more messages for von Sayn-Wittgenstein," he began. I knew this wasn't all, because such routine messages were normally passed along to me through Herr Schlauklug, the clerk who penned the Duke's dictation. "I also want you to find a way to eavesdrop on the Swedish delegation in your usual way, or at least on whatever functionaries of theirs you can ingratiate yourself with."

"What particular intelligence are we after, sire?" I so enjoyed the intimacy of 'we'.

"Wismar, Stralsund... The Swedes surround us," he whispered. "I need to know what Oxenstierna is really bringing to the table. I need to know this *before* it comes in front of von Sayn-Wittgenstein. He speaks for us, yes, but look what huge advantage Brandenburg could gain at our expense. Von Sayn-Wittgenstein has the power, and he's an acquisitive bastard. He's in it only for himself."

Well, who isn't, I thought. (I hadn't met Contarini then.)

"Keep your ears open. Listen. Keep me posted. Use regular postal couriers, but use cipher. We'll arrange the keys between us."

Once again, on a windy day in early April, I set out for Osnabrück, a week-long journey, buzzing on my lips as I went because no trumpet would accompany me. I skirted Hamburg to the south, crossed the Elbe before Lüneberg, and passed through Soltau and Neinburg. The weather continued wet and windy, so I was relieved to find road houses where I could stop at the end of each day. I carried legitimate messages for several of the delegates other than von Sayn-Wittgenstein, but they were bland enough to be taken by any post rider.

Once in Osnabrück I made for the hostelry that I knew most of the Swedes frequented. Not the mighty plenipotentiaries—they were housed in luxury—but their armies of servants, scriveners, lawyers and notaries; the real people behind the scenes who knew more than they even thought they knew. Although I spoke Swedish well, and boasted a vocabulary far better than almost all soldiers like me, I still had a noticeable accent. I reasoned that I could pass myself off as a Dane; a neutral figure from a nation that had little involvement in the peace process. A Danish merchant selling paper, ink and quills. Perfect!

I spent three futile days, visiting functionaries, talking trade, buying drinks and generally trying to soak information out of the lower levels. My line of horseshit nearly ran aground when some clerk started quizzing me about paper quality and fillers, insisting on a product that didn't snag on the quills and cause blots. I waffled and withdrew before I thought suspicions were aroused, but there I think I was mistaken. It was only on the evening of the third day that I hit an ore-bearing seam.

"What's your business here?" asked the old clerk with the inky fingers. I had spotted him sitting by himself in the corner of the common room in the hostelry, a beaker of red wine in his veined hand, and had sat across from him with a nod. He looked like a lonely drinker; I had watched him pour himself three beakers from the jug at his elbow. I sipped at my wine, suppressed a shudder—supplies of good wine seemed to be drying up, although I didn't doubt the high and mighty were better supplied—and told him my fabricated tale.

"Hmm. Dane. Always need supplies. You should talk to our quartermaster, he might deal with you." I looked around the room inquisitively. "Not here now. Have to be tomorrow. I'll tell him."

I took another shuddering try at my beaker of wine vinegar while a silence developed between us. "Close to the end now," I remarked. "Peace must come soon."

"Danes," he replied with a sneer. "Nothing to do with you, is it? Got you cornered and nicely gelded, we have."

"True at the moment. But we are free to come and go, and we can still be a power in the Ostsee. Don't take us too lightly; nothing's settled yet."

He snorted at this. I knew it would goad him. "We Swedes control the outcome. We are the masters, and once the treaties are inked we will have all the Protestant states in our power."

"But you already hold Wismar and Western Pomerania. And Bremen-Verden to the west."

"Yes, but Mecklenburg is in our plans. Rostock. And Lübeck. We intend to exact tolls on all your ports. Control of trade across the whole German coast."

"From what I hear," I ventured, trying to still my thumping heart, "you'll have to face von Sayn-Wittgenstein because he'll have Eastern

Pomerania. But he fights with a vengeance for the freedom of his Protestant allies."

He laughed at this and sloshed more wine for himself. "He's in our power. Oxenstierna gives him Eastern Pomerania, he gives us the port dues in Mecklenburg. Done!"

Here was certainly material for my Duke to work upon; and also to cause him even more anxiety. There was nothing more to be got out of my wine-soaked clerk as the drink took hold, but as a lower level operative I dare say he had no further details of any plans. I had enough to make my visit worthwhile, however, and I felt sure my Duke would now have sufficient intelligence on their machinations to spike their guns. I thought it might be too late to code a message and find a messenger, so I went to my paillasse determined to do it as quickly as I could next morning. I regretted, when I was woken abruptly, that I had not taken the time and trouble to find a messenger the night before.

The door crashed open before it was light. I didn't need to rise from my bed; the two soldiers who burst in did that for me. Arms gripped painfully above the elbow, I was hauled down the stairs and out into the street with my belongings left behind me. I tried to protest my innocence, put on outrage and bluster, but they paid me no heed. Deep in the *Rathaus* they took me, and threw me into a small room, damp with mold and lit by the tiniest slit of a window near the ceiling. While I pissed against a wall I took stock, and there was little to be optimistic about. Clearly, I had raised suspicions, and the more I thought about my actions over those three days the more stupid I looked. Stupid, stupid, stupid! The Duke was hasty in trusting me; I was too young and green and naïve to be trusted. Breitkopf would never have been so rash. As I chastised myself for a young fool, I suddenly came to the realization that today was my twenty-fourth birthday. Then I thought of my darling Elisabeth and the child inside her, and all the dreadful ghosts of my warnings to her came back to taunt and haunt me. I was near to tears but I bit back my despair. Well, I thought, I've come this far... A few deep breaths... Chin up, you've been in the manure pile before and found your way out somehow.

I don't know how many hours I sat, slumped against a damp wall, mood swinging between anguish and hope, before the door crashed back on its hinges. Is there nobody, I thought, as the same two soldiers hauled me to my feet, who knows how to open a door gently? Up the stairs we went, to a higher level in the building where light streamed into my slitted eyes. I was brought into a high-ceilinged room where a large gentleman sat behind a massive oaken desk. Two men who looked like clerks paused in their work to stare at me from their tables to one side. The soldiers returned to each side of the door while I was examined slowly and carefully from head to foot by the large gentleman. Wise eyes dominated a long nosed and rather dour countenance, with well trimmed face furniture and long, flowing hair.

"Who the hell *are* you?" he asked me in German. I should not have reacted, should not have let my guard slip, but I was anguished and fearful. He saw the comprehension cross my face swiftly. "You're no Dane. Speak! Who are you?"

I knew if I told him anything at all my Duke would be compromised, and all would be lost. I could not speak, and resolved there and then to keep quiet at all costs. I had stood still for a good long time in silence when he rose from the desk, came around to me, and peered closely into my face, and specifically my mouth. He smiled slowly. He waved the guards and his two scriveners out of the door, and once it was closed behind them he smiled.

"*Sei un trombettista. Posso dire con le tue labra!*" Again, he had caught me flat footed, and he could see that I understood my profession had been discovered. My lips—*mi labra*—had given me away.

"*Il n'y a pas besoin de s'inquiéter,*" he said, and all my resistance fell away. German, Italian, and now French… I was truly exposed. And then, I don't know from where, a little imp of hope and naughtiness tickled me.

"You see right through me, squire," I replied in English, saluting mightily, "and I place myself at your tender mercy."

When I said earlier that I thought he was a saint, it was at this moment that the impression first came upon me, although I didn't even know who he was then. He laughed uproariously and shouted, "Good one! Good one! Oh, well played back, sir!" and slapped me between the shoulders.

You can imagine my confusion and the sense of unreality this man had created. A short while earlier I would have considered myself under sentence of death, or at least dishonour, and here was this buffoon laughing away and bandying languages at me. What *was* I to think? He saw my confusion, but also saw, I think, that I was equal to the occasion and not about to be cowed or beaten down.

"Sit," he commanded, returning to his seat and indicating a chair in front of the desk. "My name is Alvise Contarini and I have exiled myself from Venezia these last five long years to attempt the task of beating peace into this land. During that time I have dealt with knaves, poltroons, cowards, criminals, turncoats… and spies. And perhaps one or two wise men, although there I am not certain. You are not the first person I have encountered who is not what he says he is. You are not even the twentieth."

Why, I wondered, was he so concerned with me? I was nothing

in the greater scheme of his work. As if in answer, he continued.

"You are a petty detail. But I didn't get this far without attending to details, no matter how trivial. And in all this time, did you not think I might have established a network for information gathering? Was it not possible that a Danish paper and ink merchant, who knew nothing about his products, would go unremarked? Well?"

I nodded, realizing again how stupid I had been. My shame showed in the heat rising in my face.

"So!" he continued, rubbing his hands together. "Right back to my first question: Who the hell are you?"

"I do not wish to compromise my master, sir…" I began.

He swept his hand around the four walls. "I sent 'em out of the room. You. Me. These four walls." He placed a finger beside his nose. "You have my word on it." I knew then I could trust him.

"I am a messenger from Mecklenburg-Schwerin. My duke, Adolf Friedrich, is concerned that Sweden will win his territory, and he is not convinced that our allies will support him."

"Mecklenburg-Schwerin is a very small player in these affairs. Rightly fearful. Sweden wants to keep Stralsund and Wismar, but she also wants control of the entire German coastline. But tell me, do you consider yourself securely in God's hands?"

The sudden change of subject threw me again. I paused and thought back to the times I had been close to death, remembering particularly that courier who had died in my place on the road to Jankau. Yes, I was in God's hands, but I sincerely hoped He didn't want me with Him just yet.

"The reason I ask," he continued smoothly, "is that by God's grace I am here only briefly in Osnabrück, having come here from Münster on an urgent summons. And I must return quickly to see to the ratification of the treaty between the Dutch and the damned Spaniards. So, by pure happenstance I am here. But what, do you suppose, would have become of you if you had been brought here in my absence?"

"I dread to think, sire," I answered.

"You dread to think. My counterpart here would not have been so… lenient. You would, by now, be hanging by your neck out in the yard as a spy *and a weasel!*" My heart shrunk and a sweat formed on me. "But I am not quite so devoid of taste. I look at you and I see a musical talent, I see a gift for at least four languages, I see a courageous mien and a high devotion to duty. I see a young man who has much yet to do in this world. Hanging one such would be a pitiful waste."

"Sire, if there is anything I can do to pay you back for such clemency, I beg you to ask me."

"Nothing. Just go back to your master and tell him all will be well.

Tell him… no, don't tell him. Let me." He seized a quill and pulled a sheet of paper towards himself across the desk. He wrote quickly, sanded, folded and sealed the paper, and passed it to me. "You have guts. God go with you."

I rode back with this message myself some days later. Duke Adolf Friedrich refused to tell me what was in the letter I placed into his hands when I passed it to him. He simply smiled broadly and muttered, "Balls."

A puffing messenger boy from the town called me back home from the *Schloss* one wet afternoon in late May. The baby had begun and Elisabeth was asking for me. I thanked God I was here in Schwerin and not on some mission and all unawares. I ran through the streets, hard on the heels of the boy, not caring about the rain on my clothes or the puddles soaking my boots and hose. I could hear my darling Elisabeth's travail from the street before I even entered our door. The screams were terrible to hear. I know we are told in Scripture that this is woman's punishment for original sin, but as I stormed up the stairs I prayed to God the pain would cease. She was lying on her bed, head thrown back, face ashen and sweating, with Anja gripping one hand and the midwife the other. Two other women, neighbours I think, were busy with cloths and pillows and water. She heard the door open, and as I entered the room the pain mercifully died down.

"Jacob," she panted as I approached the bed and sat on its edge, "hold my hand. Hold me."

I gripped a damp hand and squeezed gently, and she gave me a wan smile. We stayed that way for some time until a spasm crossed her face. Her teeth clenched, her grip redoubled and a great cry erupted from her.

"Help her!" I pleaded to the midwife. "She cannot endure this! It will kill her!"

"Oh, don't be such a worrier!" replied the midwife, waving me away from the bed. "It gets easier, the more you have. She's young and tight. Give her a few years."

"Yes," said Anja on her other side. "When the Duke's Marie Katharina drops them she hardly notices. Maria Elisabeth is her sixth, you know, and she practically slipped out when her ladyship coughed."

"Now, out of the room," cried the midwife, shooing me to the door. "This is no place for men. She has seen you and she knows you're here. That is good enough."

It was terrible. I stayed in my room all that afternoon and well into the evening, sitting, standing, sitting again, picking up books and putting them down, while next door the screams became more and more frequent. I couldn't imagine how she could endure such pain, and several times I was on the verge of going next door. I stopped myself because I knew it would be pointless; this was the way it had always been. What could I do? I don't know if it is normal for men to feel guilt for inflicting such pain on women in this way, but I certainly did. We are complicit in the original sin, yet we are rewarded with pleasure and are not punished.

There was one final shuddering scream, and then a long, drawn-out silence that went on and on, almost worse in its portent than the sounds of pain. My world stopped for however many hundreds of heartbeats I cannot say. A thin, piping cry brought the world to motion again. I jumped up and went to enter her room, only to be barred at the door by one of the other women.

"Out, out, out! This is not your place. We'll call you when it is seemly."

"But I need... I have to..."

"It's a boy. You have a son. Now go!"

So I waited again. That thin little cry had stopped, and I worried and fretted that the little life that had made it had expired with it. How long again it was until a knock on the door! Elisabeth was propped up on her pillows with the tiniest sleeping bundle in her arms, and such a look of peace on her pale face that my heart melted. I sat. I pulled the woolen stuff back slightly from the little head and looked into the face of my son.

He would see peace.

Chapter Thirty-Three

In which I continue to work for peace and receive a horrible shock

Nun danket alle Gott mit Herzen, Mund und Händen
Now thank we all our God, with hearts and hands and voices
Martin Rinkart, Johann Crüger

Now that I had become a family man, I wrote to Chris Schleef in Rostock, simply to appraise him of the news. I received by return post a long, detailed and friendly letter that quite surprised me. So began a long correspondence where we put into writing many thoughts that otherwise would not have been expressed. Over the months that followed I would share his life, as he shared mine; I would learn of his love, his wooing and his marriage—Alena, her name was—and on infrequent occasions we would visit them in Rostock. In one letter he passed along the news that his father had passed away quietly in his sleep, and I made sure to pray for his soul at the next holy service. So our correspondence continued, building the friendship that both of us had sensed on first acquaintance, although it had taken this long to mature.

It was probably not long after the birth, although it seemed like an age, before Elisabeth and I could take pleasure in each other again. Even so, there were areas well beyond the field of play. I watched with awe as little Michael went for her tits, saluting a kindred spirit, but not without a little jealousy. It was my good fortune over the next few months that I could be more of a domestic body than ever before. I could return from day duty at the *Schloss* to a meal, quiet conversation, and the endless little discoveries and joys of watching a baby grow. These were fragile weeks, though, because we both knew that some small ailment could take him from us in the blink of an eye. The worry only passes when the child becomes stronger and able to resist the fevers that descend on all of us. A year, they say, and then you can breathe again.

Domestic bliss came to an end too soon. My Duke called me to attend him in his office in late August.

"The Peace is very near," he began before I had even sat down. "Mecklenburg is secure. I will rule here, and I will rule for my nephew in Güstrow until he comes of age, and be damned to his mother."

It is clear from these words that Duke Adolf Friedrich felt quite easy with me when we were alone. He trusted my judgement in keeping what was said between the four walls. Now that the Peace process was drawing to its closing point, he was much more comfortable, more affable; the man I knew when he had told me the story of Hartmund Breitkopf.

"I want you there in Münster. There is a mass of detail, which will be communicated to me by von Sayn-Wittgenstein and his toads, but I need inside information as well. I am worried about the port tolls that the Swedes are threatening to demand. Von Sayn-Wittgenstein knows I want the sees of Schwerin and Ratzeburg, and I want equal rights on properties for my nephew in Güstrow. So, nose around. See to it that I get what I want."

My heart sank. Yes, I was his to command, but perhaps I had become too comfortable in my domestic life these past months. And I also sincerely believed that he had nothing further to fear. Von Sayn-Wittgenstein had his interests at heart, although as his lowly servant I could hardly tell him so. And what could I do anyway?

I prepared the following day to depart again for the ride to Osnabrück. I thought to take my trumpet this time, thinking I would probably have time and occasion to practice. The parting with my Elisabeth was hard. Until I actually held her in my arms beside my stirrup, I hadn't really known how it would feel. It was hard.

Osnabrück was abuzz with activity as years of work were coming to a conclusion. The scores of delegates, the armies of functionaries were all hard at it, and a sense of excitement pervaded the place. Everywhere one went the talk was all of the coming Peace; in hostelries, inns, markets and taverns speculations and prognostications were all I heard. But I wandered functionless and despondent. There really was nothing of any major importance to report, and I am sure the encrypted messages I did send told the Duke nothing he didn't know already. But the non-news I sent was, I suppose, better than silence. Return messages from him indicated to me that he was satisfied and not overly concerned.

Aside from the major effort of preparing the treaties, there was great activity among artisans, scores of whom had been brought from far away to prepare paintings, engravings, sculptures, medallions and, of course, musical celebrations. A massive flowering of art was taking place, as the great powers represented at the tables tried to outdo each other in splendour and opulence. In an idle few hours I thought I might wander to the rather squalid quarter of the town where the workshops and studios were clustered tightly together. I spent the time poking my nose into workshops, drawn by the smells of oils and gums, fresh-cut wood and burning charcoal. It was an eye-opening experience on what lengths people will go to celebrate and commemorate. When I returned to my lodging that night I wrote to the Duke in plain text that all was well with the peace negotiations, and I enquired delicately if he intended to be present for the signing. If he came, there would be music aplenty.

The visit to the artisans was the only interest in a week or so of little activity. I did happen upon something close to my heart the following week when I was wandering and wondering whatever else I could do to amuse myself. I was strolling past a large building with an impressive flight of steps leading to an imposing door, when I heard trumpets within. Trumpets playing, stopping, repeating passages. A rehearsal. I quickly returned to my accommodation, retrieved my trumpet and hurried back. I wondered if I should make so bold as to just walk in, but there was nothing to gain from holding back, so in I went. There were eight of them and a kettledrummer, attached to the court of Brandenburg, working through some fanfares and sonatas. In a pause I approached the *Principal* trumpeter, who I assumed, quite rightly, was the leader of the ensemble.

"Might I be so forward," I said, "and ask to play a little with you? I am alone here in Osnabrück and sorely need to keep in shape."

"Where are you from?" He was a red-haired bulky man with wayward moustaches and heavily veined jowls.

"I'm from Schwerin, with Duke Adolf Friedrich's corps."

"Your duke not here yet? How is it you're all alone?"

"My Duke has sent me ahead to reconnoiter." It was the first thing that came into my head but he seemed satisfied. He thought for a moment.

"Don't see any harm in it. All friends here. Take *Flattergrob*, double the other fellas, and nothing fancy." And with that he swung on his heel, waved to his men and said, "From the beginning."

It was that easy. The festive feeling infecting everybody overrode the traditional jealousies between factions of the *Kameradschaft*. We were all brothers together; at least for now. The parts I was given were dead simple and I acquitted myself well, of course. So began a regular appointment with the Brandenburgers, an excellent opportunity to keep my lip in shape, a wonderful way to assuage boredom, and an opportunity to share a drink with like souls.

By the end of September the pressure was mounting. Simultaneous signings in Münster and Osnabrück were aimed for some time in the middle of October, although it was still impossible to assign a date. Activity among delegates, functionaries and artisans was reaching a mighty crescendo. The actual act of signing was to be celebrated in paint, metal, drama, verse and music.

The communication that warmed my heart came as a thin, cold October rain descended upon Osnabrück. I went to the post bureau, as I did each day of the week, and received the usual bundle of letters for von Sayn-Wittgenstein—which by now I was sure he was getting heartily sick of—and an openly written letter from the Duke. Immediately the Peace was signed I was to return from Osnabrück. I would be reunited with my *Kameradschaft* colleagues because much music was planned.

An encounter that shook my world and was nearly the death of me followed only a few days later. I was passing through a narrow way between two buildings on my way back from the postal station to my lodgings, carrying nothing, not even my sword, when a terrific blow from behind turned the world to blackness. I was in a dark, wet and cold forest in the Hartz Mountains; a tree was lying across my back and I was pressed into the ground. The tree turned into a horse. My head thumped time with distant approaching drums. I knew Imperial soldiers were marching and that they would come across me and hurt me even more. They would drag me out from under the horse, banging their drums and tying my arms behind me with its guts, and then they would run me through with their pikes. I rolled over onto my back and the pain roared out, spreading over my head. I was on a cold, hard floor in a damp and poorly lit room with my hands tied behind me and my boots lashed around with rope. A figure was standing in front of me, hands on hips with the light from a small, high window behind him.

"So, rising from the dead, are we?" sneered an oh-so-familiar voice. "If I had my way you'd never have woken."

I was to recall many times in the days that followed the combined sense of relief and foreboding I had had in Jankau when Joachim Wadegahte had been banished from my sight. But it was three years ago and the worry had receded in my mind, replaced with the activities of wooing, loving, marrying and creating new life. My vigilance had slipped. The man I was then was not this man now. And this man now was ill prepared for what had happened.

"Now you're just where I want you."

I had no thoughts at all; everything was pain and confusion.

"But before I finish you off, my masters need information."

"Masters…" I muttered, trying to balance in my mind my hated nemesis standing there, and my presence here in Osnabrück. It made no sense at all; it was a nightmare and I would wake up. My mind focused slowly, the pain receded slightly, and he was still there.

"We need information, and you will stay here until we get it. Then we'll see."

He moved out of my line of vision, a door slammed and a bolt rattled. Slowly, oh so slowly, my mind reconciled my present state with the horrible truth. He was here, he had kidnapped me, and I was in mortal danger. What was it about Osnabrück that some of my least enjoyable experiences involved cold, damp floors and small, high windows? I struggled with what little energy I had, but the ropes were too tight, my head began to pound and sharp yellow flashes played in my eyes. The light from that high window was fading by the time he returned. He grabbed me by the collar of my jerkin, dragged me over to a wall, and tied me to rings set in the stonework. Once I was propped up he shoved a beaker of water at my lips and I drank as much as I could, although a lot spilled down me. He crouched low and looked me in the eyes.

"We need to know about your Duke and Christian IV."

"My Duke… Christian…"

"Don't play for time! We need to know what they discussed, what terms were offered, what promises were made."

With the water to help me, I began to gain some presence of mind. "I don't know what you're talking about. Let me go. You'll get nothing out of me."

"Oh, yes, we will. A man will always break under pain, and I would take great pleasure in seeing you break."

"Set me free! You can't believe this will work!"

"Nobody knows you're here. If you're missed they'll assume you have left for home. And who will miss you anyway? And don't yell because nobody will hear you down here. You are here until we get what we want. Think about it!"

And with that he swung his boot and kicked me on the side of the leg just below the hip—that place that sends bone-screaming pain down the leg—and left the room again. As the pain receded I swore to myself I would never betray my Duke. Or would I? I thanked God that Wadegahte had made no mention of Elisabeth and baby Michael, because I knew in my heart that any threat to them would achieve what no end of pain could. I had seen too much of the death of my loved ones to even consider more. Humiliating though it was, I knew I would betray Duke Adolf Friedrich to save them. God be blessed, then, that there was no mention of them! But I needed to know more. I needed to know where he had surfaced from, who employed him, and what they hoped to gain. The commerce between Schwerin and Köbenhavn had been highly sensitive, but who in the world wished to use it?

It was a horrible night as the light left the cell, my bladder and bowels took control, and the pain of my tied hands waned into a frightening numbness. All this and the cold, hard floor began to win what threats of injury could not. When the light showed again in that dim little slit near the roof, I was almost ready to tell everything. Almost.

The door burst back, and the presence of the bastard, along with one of the toadies who had been with him at Jankau, hardened my resolve.

"Well? Ready?" he taunted. "Or is your pathetic sense of honour going to lead you into Hell? You always were a moral little slug, weren't you?" And he kicked me again, this time on the other hip. Through my pain I noticed the expression on the toad's face. Unlike his pal, he was not enjoying this. Wadegahte motioned him to hold the beaker of water to my mouth, while he dug into a bag he was carrying with him and brought out pyrite, tinder and a candle.

"Behold, the humble candle. Such an innocuous invention to cause so much pain."

He struck sparks and blew the tinder alight, lit the flame and held it close to my face. I felt the heat, and I felt fear. I glanced over at the toad, and he was looking even more uncomfortable. The following hours are ones I wish I could forget, but every time we cook pork over our kitchen fire the aroma takes me back. He loosened my wrists from behind my back and retied them at the front, then took the end of the rope and lashed it to another ring in the opposite wall. So I was now lashed against one wall with my arms stretched out in front of me, and tethered to the other. While I strained with all my force against the bonds, he told his toad to immobilize me even further by gripping the upper arm. Slowly, he worked the candle flame under my left arm from wrist to elbow, pausing every two fingers breadth or so, until a row of blisters marked its passage. His continual refrain while he did this was the content of my messages to Denmark. The arm had been numb from the overnight binding, but the flame soon woke sensation, and for a while I thought I might tell him everything. I bit down, I bit back screams, I struggled against the toad's grip, and I tried to look Wadegahte in the eyes. Yes, I had resolved to die without talking, but when the pain starts the best intentions fly away.

He stopped. He put the candle aside. "Not ready to talk? Guard him, Walter," he commanded the toad. "I'll be back later. Think about this Hintze, and ask yourself if you want more!" He slammed out of the room. The pain slid from points of agony to an overall searing fire. The toad glanced my way.

"You hate this, don't you?" I said, holding his eyes through my pain. "You hate what he makes you do, don't you Walter?"

"Shut up! Just shut up!" and he turned to the wall.

"He's going to torture me until I die," I continued, "and you are going to watch."

"I told you to shut up!" He moved towards me and made as if to kick, but I knew he couldn't bring himself to do it.

"You're going to help him. I'll die, while you hold me down. You'll help him to kill me."

He said nothing. He looked anywhere but at me.

"You were with him at Jankau, weren't you?"

Silence.

"And before that, near Magdeburg. I gave you that scar on your cheek."

No reply, but a shrug of the shoulders. I tried several times more to get a reaction but he refused to speak again. So we spent the day. The light from the window moved round. My jailer pissed against the wall and ate and drank from a bag, and I fouled myself again.

Wadegahte returned towards the close of the day and did my other arm. The less I write of this the better I will feel. They both left then and I spent another unspeakable night in darkness and agony. You crave sleep to take the pain away, but the pain stabs and sleep is impossible. A shallow rhythm of waking and not-quite-sleep is the best that happens. And the night is long.

"So, we continue," he addressed me the next morning. Paradoxically, as he and his henchman pushed through the door I felt a sense of almost relief. Something would now replace the terrible throbbing nothing, even though the something was likely to be horrible. "We'll have the information today, and then my masters will be happy. Must make our masters happy, hmm?"

"Who? Who are they?"

"Why in Jesus' name should I tell *you*?" Then he thought for a little. "Ye-e-s, why not? You can take it with you to your grave. That time, when you showed what a little shit you really are... Remember? Could have shared the booty, but no, you squealed. Coward!" And he slapped the blisters on my bare arm with his riding glove. "We turned traitor, thanks to your squealing to Weitz! Trotted off to the enemy, didn't we Walter? But there's no enemy, is there, really? Not in this business. We're all enemy. You, the Catholics, Denmark, the Swedes. Friends of convenience, enemies under the skin. John Adler Salvius wants information, we get it. And when I've got it, I'm taking your duke down."

"You evil traitor! What the hell were we fighting for? Where's your loyalty?"

"Loyalty? Loyalty! They sign treaties one year and piss on them the next. You talk to me about loyalty with your Adolf Friedrich sucking up to Denmark behind everyone's back. You hypocrite! They have no allegiance, any of them. Only concerned with their stinking hides. The treasonable words your duke wrote to King Christian will doom him."

I thanked God that Wadegahte couldn't resist a sermon. Salvius was second in command to Oxenstierna, so clearly the Swedes were assembling dirt in a last ditch attempt to control Mecklenburg. At stake was Duke Adolf Friedrich's autonomy, or at least his control over the commerce of our ports. I was under no illusions that I could escape from this horror, but I now saw how critical it was for me to keep my mouth shut. My poor stinging and throbbing arms showed me how close I had come to talking already, and I knew this was just the beginning. On my left shoulder there was a nagging devil who whispered in my ear, telling me I couldn't resist, that I would break, so why not talk now. I didn't need an angel sitting on my right to tell me that whether I talked or not, Wadegahte would kill me when he was finished. He lusted to.

"And now, back to business." He rubbed his hands in anticipation. "Let's see what happens when we do the legs…" He picked up his candle and tinder. "You! Roll down his hose and tie his leg to the wall."

Walter lashed me up, seized my hose—slowly, reluctantly and almost apologetically—and exposed my bare thigh. The candle was lit and the trial continued.

I was saved by the toad.

"Stop, stop!" he cried. "He'll talk. We'll find a way. Leave him alone. Please!"

My torturer flung down the candle and shoved his henchman against the wall. "What? What? You turned coward on me as well?"

"Don't make me do this. Please!" cried Walter.

Wadegahte stood before him with his fists up. It looked as if Walter might stand his ground and fight, but Wadeghate turned away in disgust, clearly not wanting to come to blows over me.

"Right! If you're too God-damned cowardly I'll fetch Leo! He's no crybaby." He stormed to the door. "Guard him. Don't let him move. I'll be back."

"You can't let me be hurt, can you?" I said to Walter as soon as the door closed. "Can't bring yourself to see it. But if he tells you to hurt me, will you?"

"Shut up! Just shut up!" He turned his back to me.

"Won't happen, Walter. As long as I can speak, I'll continue telling you the things you already know."

Silence.

"You know in your heart you can't do this."

"I've killed before! I've hurt people!" he shouted defiantly.

"In battle, yes. In self defence, yes. But in a cowardly cellar with your victim tied down?"

Silence, and a shuffle of feet.

"You don't have to do this." I had no idea when Wadegahte would return, and it could be at any moment. I dared not beg, but I had to put all the power I could muster into persuasion. "Once you've done this, you're his for life."

Now I knew I had hit the spot. He shifted his weight then paced across the room. He was clearly weighing his options.

"He'll have such a power over you, Walter!"

"If I let you go he'll kill me," he cried. He had seen where my words were taking him.

"He'll kill you anyway. You know too much."

"I'm dead!" And the poor boy started to cry. "He makes me do things. He's got me. I can't get away. There's nothing else…"

"Then run. With me. Now!"

"Where? Where can I go?" he wailed.

I thought hard and quickly. "Listen. I will use all my power and persuasion with my Duke. I will persuade him to give you clemency."

I don't suppose I believed this, but I would have offered the moon. The poor boy had avoided hanging on my word back in Jankau, so perhaps he thought I could provide another miracle. I doubted it, but at that moment I decided the future would have to take care of itself.

"Cut me free! Quick!"

Still he hesitated.

"You're dead if you don't!"

I waited in agony until finally he came to a resolution, pulled out his knife and began sawing at my ropes, tears streaming down his face. I tried to stand but my legs crumpled under me. Useless legs, useless arms. I beat at my legs with my fists to make the blood waken, crying out as the skin on my arms stretched and the burst blisters wet my shirt sleeves. Finally, I could stand. Walter opened the door and I saw a long stairway rising up into darkness. Up we hurried, me leading in a hobble, to a short landing where there was another door. I had only just grabbed the handle when it was pulled out of my grasp. Light flooded in, silhouetting Wadegahte and another of his bullies. Without thought I ran at him, lowering my head, and rammed him full in the belly. The air roared out of him as the man beside him swung his sword. I rolled to the side with a scream of agony at my raw arms, just as Walter stepped forward, took the sword blow on an upraised arm, and sank his knife into the man's chest.

Now Wadegahte was on his feet, sword in hand, and swinging for me. Walter spun round, dragging his knife from the other man's ribs, and threw himself between me and the sweeping sword.

Walter died for me.

Unarmed, defenceless, in burning pain and stinking like a midden, I staggered as fast as I could down a narrow, slippery passageway between high walls. I knew I would be no match for Wadegahte, and any moment I expected his sword to find my back, but my head butt in his guts must have slowed him. I burst out into a sunlit street where a market was in full swing, and by dodging and weaving between the booths and stalls I threw him off. I was certain he wouldn't dare attack me in public. Leaning against a wall, cradling my sore arms and heaving and panting, I took stock.

It wasn't too long before I found my way back to my lodging, having been rebuffed twice in my enquiries by people holding their noses and reeling back gagging. Once I had cleaned myself, I persuaded the concierge to tend to my wounds, bribing her with coin to keep her thoughts to herself. She tut-tutted as she applied salves and cloths, and gave me admonitions as to how to dress and treat the wounds.

Poor Walter; he was disposable. I couldn't have intervened for him. A mere staff trumpeter persuading a duke that a disgraced traitor, suspected rapist and torturer should go free on his say-so? He was a dead man, whether it was hanging by us or murder by his friend. But he must have gone to Heaven knowing in his last moments that he had stood up and fought for what he thought was right, and with that I had to be content.

Now that I knew Wadegahte was at large, I resolved never to let my guard down again, although, realistically, there was no possibility of keeping high vigilance while walking abroad. He had caught me from behind at a vulnerable moment, and he could do so again at will.

Chapter Thirty-Four

In which there is peace and fine music, and a tearing at my soul

Wenn eure Sünde gleich blutrot wäre, soll sie doch schneeweiss werden; wenn sie gleich ist wie rosinfarb, soll sie doch wie Wolle warden
Though your sins be as scarlet, they shall be white as snow; though they be red like crimson, they shall be as wool.

Isias/Isaiah, 1:18

I was born in warfare. I had seen my land torn to pieces. I had seen my whole world torn to pieces. I had taken up arms and killed, a small straw caught up in the cold north wind of conflict. I had seen the God of my faith used as a playing counter in a vast game between principalities. Outside the walls of towns, and all across the country between, everywhere I went I had seen desolation and fear and sickness. I had absolutely no idea what peace would look like. So, the celebrations in Osnabrück and Münster in October of the year 1648 were like nothing I could have imagined. The great ceremonies of ratification took place on the fourteenth of the month. The two documents, signed simultaneously in Osnabrück and Münster, were immediately enclosed in specially made lock boxes, which were conveyed as speedily as possible:

> To the most Serene and most Puissant Prince and Lord, Ferdinand III, elected Roman Emperor; and to the most Serene and most Puissant Prince and Lord, Louis XIV, most Christian King of France and Navarre.

The next day, in a thin rain, with great pomp and ceremony, the trumpets cried out in the centres of Osnabrück and Münster, and a short version of the terms of the agreement was read to a gathered multitude amid cheering, celebration and revelry that went late into the night. Gallopers were immediately despatched to all corners of the many warring realms with the command:

> To all and each of the chief Officers Military and Civil, and to the Governors of Fortresses, to abstain for the future from all Acts of Hostility.

It would be many days before the news was received in far places, and doubtless many men fell for nothing during this time of virtual peace. One could wonder what 'falling for nothing' actually meant when you saw what had really been accomplished in thirty years of warfare. People say the war was the start of a new order, but as I look around me now, I don't see it. I see a lot of richness in high places, I see a lot of acquisition of property, but the lives of little people are exactly the same as they always were. I do know that Pope Innocent X was absolutely furious with the treaty, not so much because he saw all those Protestant souls hurtling to damnation, so much as his inability to loot their purses to fill his coffers before Satan took them.

An approximation of how Jacob Hintze's world would have looked in 1648 after the signing of the Peace of Westphalia

Every delegate, every plenipotentiary, every ambassador, every highborn dignitary who had ever come to either of the two cities to wager, bargain, wrangle, bully and threaten wanted his day in the sun. Masses, *Te Deums*, and songs of rejoicing were scheduled for every church or meeting place throughout those last days of October. Duke Adolf Friedrich of Mecklenburg-Schwerin was no exception. He had won the rich yields from the sees of Schwerin and Ratzeburg for himself, and other properties for Güstrow. He had won rights over port dues, taxation and shipping for his main ports, but most of all he believed himself to be his own man. He had as much cause for celebration as anyone. Bells boomed themselves to pieces from every church tower, and we played fanfares on street corners, market places, on the steps of buildings and on bridges, until even the veterans amongst us began to feel taxed. Wolfgang had never beaten his kettledrums harder, nor had I ever blown so stridently, so high, so exquisitely loud.[41]

Reuniting with my comrades was a joy, but it was only when Friedemann, Albrecht, Wolfgang and the rest met me in our trumpeters' domain that I realized how much I had missed them. There was much work for us to do during the general assemblies, banquets and other occasions where a show of pomp and power was required, but none of this was out of the ordinary. We often felt we could play in our sleep, and there was danger of becoming complacent. As the cavalry was now standing down, there was little need for horseback trumpeting either. This was before the time of those horse ballets that became popular in France and spread east.

One day, around that time, Friedemann called me into the little office-cubbyhole off the trumpet room. He had papers spread before him, some of which I recognized, and a quill and ink. He rose from his stool and stood to attention before me.

"*Feldtrompeter* Hintze," he began with some formality, "you have served your time and shown your worth in the field. Now, in time of peace, the *Kameradschaft* is ready to reassign your status in the ducal trumpet corps."

This was the rise in stature I had often wondered about, but never had the nerve to ask about or persue. I knew it came in the fullness of time, and I was quite prepared to wait on the decision of my superiors. That it came so early in my career was a surprise.

"Sign here, *Stabstrompeter* Hintze," said Friedemann, thrusting the quill in my direction. And there I was—a swish of ink and a dusting of sand—staff trumpeter to the ducal court, a rank that would be mine for life.

I looked into Friedemann's eyes and we held the contact. It's a strange thing, but among musicians there is occasionally a profound communication that does more than words could ever do. He knew my thoughts and I knew his, but had either of us expressed them, they would have been dimished. Hartmund Breitkopf was present in the space between our locked eyes. Slowly and gently Friedemann nodded, and I smiled.

It was towards Christmas that Duke Adolf Friedrich called upon our special services, for which we thanked God. He had received some recently published music from Moravia by a composer named Andreas Rauch. Mecklenburg-Schwerin was too small a duchy to employ any composer of high standing, and we had lost Herr Vierdanck who had died two years before in Stralsund. Our Duke was always on the look-out for new music, and several times on my missions I had been instructed to return with the latest works from wherever I was visiting. The Rauch publication he had acquired contained thirteen great motets, and he selected a massive *Te Deum*, specifically, as he told Friedemann, because it had excellent parts for trumpets and kettledrums. There was much wisdom in this choice because wartime austerity had made him strip his court of all musicians except his choir and trumpet corps, so in this way he could stage a flamboyant and glorious performance without dipping into his purse for more players.

In the week following my return, we worked over the parts a number of times by ourselves, before working with the choir. We had to get some of the musical ideas into our heads first. Here was a composition melding trumpets with voices in a new and exciting way. I recalled the *Jubilate Deo* written by Michael Praetorius that Hartmund Breitkopf had shown me. It had been published not twenty-five years earlier, yet the division between the trumpets and the singers was absolute: when the trumpets played, the voices were silent. Here in Rauch's work we were brought in and required to play in concert, and although we had played in church and chapel before, it was still quite new to us. The book by Fantini had always been highly useful to us, and also showed us how backward we still were in the north, compared to the innovations flowing out of Italy. The techniques he outlined for playing our trumpets in tune with a choir required great skill and dexterity, but they showed the way. Those nasty odd-numbered harmonics that Nature has placed on our scale had to be wrestled down and obliged to sound well. The lower players had few problems, but *Principal* and *Clarino* were quite challenging. I took huge joy in fighting this music into shape, feeling an intense satisfaction. I thought a lot of my friend Berthold during those sessions, remembering how we had worked on these problems, and wondering where he was and what he was doing. He would have taken as much joy as me in weaving trumpet and violin to the glory of God.

One day, the practice room door opened during one of our sessions, and to our great surprise our Duke entered. There was a general faltering as all eyes looked his way, but he waved us to continue and seated himself on a chair to one side. We watched the satisfaction in his face as the great harmonies thundered out.

"Alltid," he beckoned Friedemann over. "Damn me if this music doesn't need strings and woodwinds."

"It is not within my remit as *Hoftrompeter...*" Friedemann began, but the Duke silenced him as he stood up.

"Yes, yes, yes, but you've got ears, haven't you? Remit be damned! Strings, winds and the organ too."

The chapel organ was a sore spot with the Duke; it had fallen into disuse after the musical ensemble had been disbanded, and it rankled. Adolf Friedrich said no more, but sat down and waved us to continue our work.

"Right!" said Friedemann at the end of our session, long after the Duke had taken himself away. "I think we're ready for the choir. Tomorrow. So, let's go and drink."

Zum Freischütz was the favourite drinking place of the corps, although I rarely went with them, preferring to return as soon as possible to my family.

"Coming with us?" This was old Wilhelm eying me. "Or you have to run home? Apron strings, eh? Still tied to yer mother."

In all the time I played with the corps, Wilhelm never did take to me. Until he died in harness he was the one player who treated me as an intruder. He had a way of getting inside me and, yes, I usually did go home as fast as I could. All I loved and cherished was there, and when you're given a second chance at family comfort, you take it. But I was nettled. He knew about what had happened in Belitz, but it didn't stop him from being nasty. One of those people who know how to find the tender spot. The mirror opposite of a lover.

"Yes, I'm damned thirsty. Let's go."

Elisabeth, I knew, would understand the ale on my breath, and my hours were irregular enough anyway. In those days I confess I took her devotion much for granted, and it was only later that I came truly to appreciate her qualities. I wish now I had told her more often... Aye, well.

A quick walk in thin, misty rain and we were comfortably seated in front of brimming mugs.

"Hey, Friedemann," said Alex, one of the *Principals*, "how come we're playing stuff written for the Emperor? God damn his Papist balls!"

"Yeah," put in another. "Just because we're at peace, doesn't mean we have to like the bastard."

It's strange what your memory does. Just then I had one of those eye-opening moments from the past, and I was back in that tent in Breitenfeld looking into the face of the feverish Italian musician—I couldn't even remember his name—before the present came back with a thump. I suppose it was the association with Ferdinand III and his brother's cruelty in taking a musician to war.

"First of all," Friedemann replied, "you have to admit that it's great music." We all agreed with that; nothing anyone in our region could do would come even close. "And if it's any consolation to you, it was written by a Protestant."

"A Protestant! What possessed him?"

Friedemann rolled his thumb across his fingers in that age-old gesture. "That, and an enormous reputation across Europa. That work was published at great expense in Wien, and if our Duke acquired a copy, you can be sure many other principalities did the same."

"Still," said Alex, "you'd think the Emperor would want to keep it for himself."

"Far as I can tell," replied Friedemann, with an ironic smile, "there wasn't a lot of celebrating in Habsburg circles. Played it once; over and done with."

They all laughed at this, a couple of them looking pointedly at me. Some of the older men had seen action against the Emperor, and there was camaraderie between us. I had come back; some had not. Among those who hadn't served there was a little of... almost envy. Young as I was, they looked to me as a veteran—and now a *Stabstrompeter*—so I had to be careful not to make much of it.

"Breitkopf always insisted," I said, to put the conversation on another tack, "that art crosses boundaries. There is no such thing as Catholic music, Protestant music..."

"It's all to the glory of God," cried Albrecht. "And I'll raise a drink to that!"

"Horseshit," rejoined Wilhelm. "It's all to the glory of enough ale and bread and meat to keep us. High flying hog turds!" He gimleted me with his eyeballs and raised his mug. "I'll drink to hog turds."

Our preparations paid off well because when we met with the choir and worked the *Te Deum* over, it was clear that little improvement was needed. Those astonishing triadic harmonies—the three notes together that underlie so much of our music—when rendered with trumpets and voices, were transporting. Harmonizing the *Clarino* parts perfectly with the voices, especially the trebles, showed us something new and quite exciting.

Although the Peace had been signed over a month before, the *Te Deum* in the chapel of the *Schloss* in early December was our first official celebration. Duke Adolf Friedrich and the Duchess Marie Katharina attended, and I think I saw three of their children, Juliane Sibylla, Friedrich and Christina as well. The Duke's awful sister-in-law, Eleonore Marie, had come for the event, bringing her son and her entourage with her from Güstrow. She must have been in some sort of celebratory mood as, thanks to her brother-in-law, the terms of the Peace included much for the duchy of Mecklenburg-Güstrow.

The ceiling of the chapel rang in glory that night.

And that night my life turned. Standing there in that great resonating hall, surrounded by voices and instruments raised in praise of God, I was struck by a revelation. Suddenly, it seemed to me that all the experiences of my life shook themselves down, reordering themselves, so I saw all my past as if it was written about somebody else. I had always known that each one of us is born to a destiny, an immutable path that God decrees we will follow but, to me, that knowledge had been hitherto unquestioned. Now, I felt opened out, and all the grains that made my life were shaken through a sieve to a show me a new order.

As soon as my childish ears had heard the sound of a trumpet all those years ago, I was beguiled. From that point my whole life had been directed by a power greater than myself, and I had thought it must be God. But, as a cavalryman, if I had to kill in order to play the trumpet that's what I would do. I would serve that end at the cost of the lives of others. In the battles I had fought, in the war we had wasted ourselves upon, there was no good side, no bad side. Though I tried to reconcile it, the truth remained; I had dealt death for my own selfish needs. In my mind's eye I saw again that young Bavarian farm boy at my stirrup, starving and cowering in fear; I saw the mortally wounded Italian musician; I saw an ashen-faced boy clutching his love's vial; I saw all the slashing, howling faces I had dispatched with my sword, the dismembered human souls who had stood in my way. My high art had been purchased at an agonizing cost. I had brought my music to this high place through spilled blood. Herr Martius had taxed me with this, so had Breitkopf, but I had shied away.

Central to this revelation was the question Martius had asked me: Where was my God in all this? Did the God of my fathers, the God of my family and my people, the God of Martin Luther, have a hand in all the killing? Did He not direct me as I had believed all my life? Or had He stepped aside and watched aloof as His Creation tore at each other's throats in His name? Until this point, I had believed most sincerely that my destiny had been driven by God but now, in that great hall surrounded by glorious music, doubt had clawed at my soul.

I was in spiritual torment.

For one long week I kept this soul-withering doubt to myself. I told no one, and my silence tore me like a dry vomit. I don't want to dwell long on that week in living Hell, except to say that although the weight of it bore me down, I could not, would not, speak to anyone about it; not my comrades, not my pastor, not even my beloved Elisabeth. No one must know.

Perhaps it was coincidence, but as I look upon it now I am certain it was the ineffable workings of the Lord: the very Sabbath following that miserable week of doubt and sorrow, our pastor chose to speak from Isaiah: "Though your sins be as scarlet, they shall be white as snow; though they be red like crimson, they shall be as wool." There is always forgiveness of sin, he told us, if we cleave to the Lord and behave according to His law. Here was the offer—gladly given with nothing demanded in return except service—of a clean slate, an opportunity to be washed in the blood of the Lamb. There is always salvation, always rescue from eternal damnation. His hand is steady and it extends to help us and guide us.

I came away from divine service that day in great comfort and with a change in my heart.

Chapter Thirty-Five

In which there is sadness mingled with joy, followed by terror

Der Herr hats gegeben; der Herr hats Genomen. Der Name des Herrens sei gelobet!
The Lord gave, and the Lord hath taken away; blessed be the name of the Lord

Hiob/Job I, 21

It was in the New Year of 1649 that Elisabeth told me a child had quickened in her again. The joy of knowing Elisabeth was with child lasted through the birth and a mere three months beyond. Our little daughter Annamaria came into the world in April, far too early, and she was born sickly. She left this life as a tiny bundle who had failed to thrive and weakened day by day. I would come off duty to a home in anguish; each day there was only news of steady decline. There was no help from physician, apothecary or the old wives. To watch this downward progress was to realize the mercy of God when he quickly took her from us. The pastor of the *Schelfkirche St Nikolai* in Schwerin administered the last rites, and though our Michael was still too young to understand, we knew he was aware that something terrible was happening in his world. At least, when the last breath had finally passed and the tiny body was lifted from the crib, he clung to Elisabeth's leg, fists gripping the stuff of her dress, round eyed while we wept.

We carried the little one back to Belitz; our people lay there, and we felt it was right. We put her in the ground between our family markers, and asked old Pastor Haussmann to pray for her little soul. Chris Schleef and his new wife came with us, and our grief was mingled with joy at Alena's news of a quickening in her womb. Our friendship blossomed, growing from two men to two couples.

There were financial and legal details of our estates to discuss with Chris, so we made our way to his office later in the day and sat down together. While in Rostock, we took the opportunity to visit my uncle-and aunt-in-law. Elisabeth visited through love and devotion, of course; I went through duty. I must say, though, that since our first meeting Uncle Otto had… not exactly warmed to me, but at least was not quite so condemning. He saw my secure position at court, saw Elisabeth's obvious contentedness, beyond her present grief, and responded with pragmatic acceptance. We both wished they could have met young Michael, but he was not yet ready for such adventures, so he stayed at home with Anja. Even though we were visiting Otto and Griselda at a sad time in our lives, we went away happy, and were somewhat relieved that I had passed muster.

When Elisabeth and I went to bed that night in the Schleef house, we came together for the first time in many months with great tenderness.

It is easy to write that once the documents at Osnabrück and Münster had been signed and sealed, peace immediately prevailed. Easy to write; nonsense in fact. After thirty years of lawlessness, destruction and famine it would doubtless take an equal time again to see the beginning of what might pass for peace. I haven't seen it yet, not truly. And, as I told you right at the start of my story, signatures on parchments are nothing: people will carry on hating other people until the end of the world. How many times had we seen accords, agreements and treaties trampled upon as soon as the wind turned? So, while Mecklenburg was not over-troubled within its own borders, foul rampages, invasions and slaughters continued in the surrounding principalities. Sweden and Denmark, our two close neighbours on the sea, had their own hatreds and conflicts, still unsettled: Denmark, a waning maritime power with dreams of a grandiose past, and Sweden with aspirations to make the Ostsee a Swedish lake.

Comparative stability within our own realm meant restoration of many features of our lives that had been missing for so long. There was more and better food in the markets, and goods from other regions were appearing again. Their availability still depended upon shipping, so while wars of occupation continued to be waged at sea, merchants were often reluctant to leave port. Fish we always had; heroes like Udo, who had taken me to Falster, went fishing and be damned to anyone. Outside the towns, reconstruction, building and a return to order were taking place amid green fields. But it would be generations before the wastage and destruction were only a memory, but the start being made was heartening. Every time I sampled some food from elsewhere, or rode through farmland, or saw newly laid mortar and brickwork, I thought that this was what peace must feel like.

Among the most wonderful and immediate developments was the reinstatement of the court ensemble. Musicians were employed again, organ-makers were brought in to bring the chapel instrument back from disuse, and much energy was expended on new entertainments and divine services. That terrific *Te Deum* by Andreas Rauch had set a standard. I did so wish my friend Berthold would come back when calls went out for musicians, but he never did.

—

I was away several times during the spring and summer of 1649, and it was then I really saw how the trumpet corps managed without one of its junior members. Very well, as it happens. I was far from indispensable, but it was interesting that when I returned from a mission, no questions would ever be asked, no comment made. I remembered those times long ago when I had asked after Hartmund Breitkopf and had received neutral, offhand responses. This was how our 'profession' was dealt with among the vast majority of members of the *Kameradschaft* who simply played the trumpet. At the same time, I never felt resentment or coolness against me, except from old Wilhelm, of course; my closeness to the Duke, and the need to convey his personal corresponddence, simply needed no remark. This was just the way it was.

I had known from that first voyage I took with Breitkopf that chosen trumpeters were engaged in covert activities. I recall his exact words to the keen, green little apprentice I was then: "That's what we do. When we're not playing the trumpet for the court and the army, of course." I can see his smile now. Over my years in the war I had carried messages, secret documents and word-of-mouth communications over a wide swath of country, using either my immunity or a disguise to ease my way. However, I had somewhat naively assumed that once peace parchments were inked, these activities would diminish. Far from it. The undercover network was alive and vital, and I had become a small part of an enormous skein. Widely travelled couriers like me were only part of it; there was no reason why others who travelled abroad and became intimates with courts and palaces should not be employed to nose around and carry private messages. On the surface we were messengers, couriers, musicians, artists, writers, while below, in the cellar of our world that people never saw, we were a clandestine legion. For all I knew, those artisans I had seen in Osnabrück were snooping for their home countries.

I remember when I was about six years old, Jürgen had taken me to a patch of mushrooms out in the lea. "Y'see little bro," he had said, "every year they come up at the same place. How do they know? It's 'cos underneath there's secret things going on we don't even know about." We—our whole covert army—were like those mushrooms. Pluck one away, like my dear *Hoftrompeter*, who I still miss, and the network is none the worse for it. And now, close to the end of my time in this world, I can tell you at least that much. Perhaps I have revealed too much, because so many lives and reputations hinge upon these words. But who will take the word of a *Stabstrompeter*... if anyone, aside from my loved ones, cares to read it anyway?

Mecklenburg-Schwerin was itself an insignificant player in these grand affairs, but because of my travels, and Breitkopf's before me, we became known as a reliable waystation on the route; a small but useful place for passing the baton. Matters of great import that were none of our business and had no effect upon our little duchy were often carried in my scrip, or my head.

One evening in the autumn, when I had only just returned from a mission to Hamburg, I emerged from the gatehouse of the *Schloss* to almost pitch darkness. It was scarcely the eighth hour, and yet the sky was a dark yellow, almost brown, and no ray of sun could penetrate. A wind was blowing hard from the east, enough to make footing on the bridge insecure. The further I walked toward the town, the greater was the struggle. The few citizens still outside were huddled against the gale, or reeling and staggering as the wind took them. Suddenly, it seemed as if the sky and the earth were joined, as a great wall of cloud and rain pushed across the Innensee and fell upon the town. There was scarcely any shelter to be found in the streets as the wind and rain forced their way between the buildings. Pieces of wood, roof tiles and loose fittings flew like cannon fire. I saw a roof peel back from a low building and go flapping like an immense and lethal eagle until it crashed into the road, reared up and was picked to bits. How I got home without injury I don't know, but soaking and shuddering I shouldered through the door. Anja was waiting there just inside the door, a look of terror on her face.

"Frau Hintze is not back!"

"Not back? Not back from where?"

"She took Michael to the market," Anja wailed, "and it's hours ago!"

"Why? Why?"

"It wasn't like this! We didn't know…"

I turned. "Wait. I'll get them." I went back out into the tempest and was almost blown to the market square, two streets away. There I met a scene of chaos. Everything that could be overturned was. Stalls, produce, boxes, carts were scattered willy-nilly. People were huddled against each other in the pelting, sideways rain, soaked and shivering. I found them. They had been forced into a corner between two bales of hay. Elisabeth had her cloak about the child; all I could see was the fair head of plastered wet hair.

It was impossible to speak, but I motioned her to stand, clasping her to me against the gale, and wrapped our boy more tightly in her cloak. It was then I discovered why I had been blown so easily here. The wind howling from the east, pouring between the houses, was like a vast watery wall that pushed and pounded and punished. I soon regretted leaving the shelter of the hay bales, but I felt committed.

How I dragged her along with Hans in my arms I do not know, but I know now that if I had left them there they would have perished, as quite a few did that night. After an age of pummeling I thought we could never survive, I burst our door open and shoved them in.

We dried off as best we could with cloths that Anja had laid out. She was weeping hysterically, with relief at our arrival and frustration at having failed to light the fire. The wind down the chimney had defeated all her efforts, and the house was cold and dank. The whole building creaked and rattled, while outside sounds of destruction could be heard above the roar of the tempest. We sat in the cold kitchen shivering, eating what little bread and cheese we could find, while Elisabeth gave a crust moistened in milk to our son. It must have been nearly midnight when the wind eased and the moon could be seen briefly skipping in and out of the clouds. By this time our clothes had mostly dried and the shivering had ceased. Anja got Michael tucked into his cot and retired to her room. Elisabeth stood as I stood and clasped me tightly to her. We went to our room, knelt by the bed and thanked God for deliverance. We pulled blankets and furs over us and rolled tightly into each other's arms.

I don't know if our son Hans was started then, but I like to believe he was.

In the following days there was a great deal of clearing up and rebuilding to be done. The army was called out to assist the Watch, as every capable pair of hands was needed. All the places of worship in Schwerin were occupied with the interment of the dead and the consecration of their souls. Elisabeth, Anja and I took little Michael to holy service, where we were joined by Frau Walther, Giselle and some of their tenants. It was a congregation of mourning and thanksgiving; souls speeded to Heaven, and gratitude for the continuation of life.

Storms like this were unusual, and I heard some of the older folk say they had seen nothing like it. Ignorant folk blamed witchcraft; others that it was a call to heed our sinfulness. Me, I think it was just a bad storm. This was a time when winters could be terribly cold, and during the war privation from want of food and warmth had accounted for more souls than ever were lost in warfare.

Chapter Thirty-Six

In which a child stirs, I visit Dresden and encounter a strange
travelling musician.

*Du Narr/ du bist ja nicht eingesperrt oder angebunden/ die gantze weite Welt
steht dir ja offen.*
You fool; you are not locked up or tied up; the whole world is
open to you.

Simplicissimus

It had been a bitter winter. The sea even froze in the ports, curtailing
trading and fishing and leading to hunger and want. Our household
managed well enough, with stocks of preserved vegetables, grains and
cheeses laid away when the yields were good. Even so, keeping us well
fed and warm were tasks that kept Elisabeth and Anja constantly busy.
Michael was becoming quite the adventurous handful, which added to
the busyness of our little ménage. I was away on a few small missions
over the cold winter months, but the spring of 1650 opened with one
glorious day in March, usually noted for its cold winds from the east.
On this day the sun shone down on the exercise yard, and finally we could
practice our cavalry evolutions without seeing our breath and numbing
our fingers on the reins. I recalled that day particularly because when I
returned home, I was greeted at the door by Elisabeth and taken by the
hand upstairs.

"Feel," she said, placing my hand on her stomach. She had told me
in the winter that there was business afoot again in her body, but it is
not a child until the quickening.

"Feel," she said again. "He moved today. Wait… Oh, come *on!*"

We waited, poised. There it was! A tiny tremor passing across her
flesh under my hand. I wrapped her in my arms and we stood with the
evening light over the rooftops bathing us in happiness.

"He?" I asked. "How can you be sure?"

"Just… I don't know. We seem to know."

I have to say that no trumpet I played on at the court of Mecklenburg-
Schwerin came even close to the first one I ever blew. Those experiences as a ten-year-old when I played for Herr Pinklemann, and later
when I read the inscription MACHT CONRAD DROSCHEL IN NÜRNBERG
1617, had stayed with me my entire playing life. Nürnberg and its
wonderful instruments had been in my mind constantly, almost as an
inner disloyalty. Nothing made in the Catholic south could be openly

declared as equal, let alone superior. I recalled the day I had rejoined my unit somewhere near Freiburg after the battle of Klingenthal. Among the possessions returned to me was the crumpled ruin of my Sander field trumpet, and I didn't give a damn. Since then I had played several of the same style by Anton Benninck of Lübeck, and they were no better and no worse. Conrad Droschel would be long dead now, but I had hopes that I could one day go to Nürnberg, find his successor, and discover that his manner of instrument-making had been passed along.

The Peace was secure, as was my place as staff trumpeter in the court ensemble. Still, my desires for a better instrument might have been left unsatisfied if Duke Adolf Friedrich had not required me to ride to Dresden in May with messages for the Elector Johann Georg of Saxony. I was also to present to the Elector and his spouse, Magdalene Sibylle of Prussia, a pendant of Ostsee amber set in silver. As usual, I was to keep my ears and eyes open, and to poke my nose where it didn't belong.

Parting from Elisabeth was now becoming a regular occurrence, but it never got easier. With a child growing in her again, I resolved to get back as soon as possible, but the proximity of Nürnberg to Dresden made me wonder if a side trip was possible. She looked so forlorn when I raised the subject, but made me swear to be back by the end of June at the latest. First, I would have to petition my Duke for permission to extend the trip, and also raise the subject of a southern-made trumpet with Friedemann.

It turned out that our *Hoftrompeter* had no concerns: "If it makes you play better, so be it. And if the Duke agrees, of course. Not sure if you could play any better than you already do, though."

I wasn't sure if I should accept this as a compliment, but I looked Friedemann in the eye and saw no guile there.

"It's just the way it makes me feel. Maybe I'm trying to capture a dream."

"Well, that's as maybe. But you do realize your dream won't come cheap. We may be at peace with the buggers, but I don't see the Purser releasing any funds to buy foreign instruments."

"But we buy fiddles and lutes from Italy all the time!"

"Who makes comparable ones here? Brass workers we have, and good ones too, no matter what you may think."

"You have served me well, Hintze," the Duke told me as I sat with him. "I see no issue with extending your visit to Dresden to include Nürnberg as well, and your request comes at a good time. As you may know, there is a great congress there in celebration of the Peace, hosted by Count Palatinate Karl Gustav von Pfalz-Zweibrücken. He is the commander of the Swedish army and in line for the Swedish crown. You must present yourself at the *Schloss* and act as my emissary in relaying my compliments and good wishes. I will give you letters."

I saluted. "Yes sir, it would give me great pleasure to serve you."

"And while you are there, I want you to look for some music. I am particularly interested in getting a copy of *Magnificat Octavi Toni*, in Kindermann's *Harmonia Organica*.[42] Write that down."

Having promised Elisabeth a safe return by the middle of June at the latest, and having been clasped and held and kissed as if I were never coming back, I mounted my trusty old Jürgen and took the road south by way of Berlin. This would be a slow and steady journey with no great urgency, so I felt that Jürgen could cope, although I knew that long distance jaunts would soon be things of memory for him.

The weather continued fair so I avoided road houses and camped soldier-style whenever I could. I skirted Berlin to the west, mindful of my last experience there, and continued through Jüterbog where awful memory again rang in my mind. But as I rode on I became lighter and happier than I had been for a long time. Yes, I was happy with my wife and my lovely son, with my fulfilled life at court, all the good things the Peace had brought, but here on this ride I finally felt war and horror and death lifting off my shoulders. I had not even known the weight was there until it was eased, but this is the way with me. I seem to carry pain and woe in ignorance. Seeing all the greenery, growth and industriousness that was going into the fields, my soul was cheered and refreshed. True, every so often I would pass through places where terrible things had taken place; I would see ruined buildings, blackened ground, the smashed wreckage of country people's lives, but these areas came not too often and were well separated, and they left no scabs on my mind.

One Sabbath I stopped in a small village somewhere south of Schönewalde—its name escapes me—and there I joined the people in simple worship. As we sang *Ein feste Burg ist unser Gott* I was taken back to childhood, into that little church in Belitz, before… all these things that have happened. You can never turn back, but you can allow a tear to wet your cheek for all that was, and will never be again in this sad world.

Dresden makes a fine sight as you approach from the north. It sits on the south bank of the Elbe, a natural barrier, crossed by the Elbbrücke, which has been in place for as long as people have lived there. A dozen or so spires and towers prick into the sky, framing the long roofs of the grand Dresdner *Residenzschloss*. It's a pretty town, and prosperous and busy. You don't just trot up to the *Residenz* and present yourself after many days of travel. After I had found a suitable hostelry for me and my horse, I ordered up a basin of water to clean myself, and with a brush I went about the dust and mud on my clothes. Then it was off to find a barber; I needed my cheeks smooth, and my rakish goatee and curling whiskers just so. I decided on a whim to sling my trumpet over my shoulder on its bandolier. I would do this quite often when arriving on horseback at an enemy camp, but rarely while presenting myself at court. I had a feeling it would make my presence feel slightly less petty.

On presenting my cleaned and barbered self at the gate of the *Residenzschloss*, I was met by a flunky and shown, not into the larger audience chamber where the Elector received his guests, but to a smaller room off to one side. Johann Georg was alone, seated in a large enfolding chair and reading a book; a large, red faced portly man who breathed harshly even in repose. He was then around sixty-five years old, silvery haired and bearded, and with a veined countenance that failed to conceal discomfort, petulance and irritation.[43]

"A messenger from Mecklenburg-Schwerin, sir," roared the flunky as if addressing a multitude in a vast chamber, "bringing communications to your highness, and a gift for her ladyship."

"Yes, yes. Leave us." The Elector waved him away impatiently.

The room seemed to be a *Schatzkammer;* a treasure house for curios that Johann Georg collected from far and wide. Lying on tables and hanging on the walls was a surfeit of swords, armour, musical instruments and baubles, all of the strangest and most exotic design. It was the first time I had encountered such odd-looking stuff. The Elector put his book aside and peered down his nose, a slight supercilious smile crossing his lips but failing to make itself further north. It was clear he was amused by my curiosity.

"*Turquerie*," he remarked. "From all over the Ottoman Empire." He seized a wicked curved sword from a table at his elbow and flicked it through the air. "A gift from the Grand Turk. Trying to buy peace. Now, give me your message."

He popped the seals off the first of the two papers I handed him and scanned the contents quickly, nodding and muttering. The second one was treated in the same way. "Hmm. Your duke has tastes that far exceed his modest reach. His petition for the secondment of Meister Weckmann must surely have been made in jest. You must tell him that we are only now rebuilding our musical establishment, and we can hardly spare one of his stature.[44] He wants folios of the man's music. Those we can send. This other message: I will reply in good time, but he must understand that agreements made and signed are not necessarily negotiable. Where is this gift?"

I took the pendant of Ostsee amber in its silver setting out of my pouch, unwrapped the soft leather that enclosed it, and passed it to him with a bow. The little eyes in the fleshy, venous face lit up as he swung it to and fro to catch the light.

"Equerry!" he roared. The flunky stepped through the door almost before the end of his utterance. I would have bet his ear had been against the woodwork. Nosy bastard. "Fetch her ladyship here!"

While the man went in search of his mistress, the Elector picked up his book and resumed reading as if I was a wall hanging or a particularly unremarkable sideboard. The slight amusement that my ignorance of his *turquerie* had aroused had entirely evaporated. Presently the door opened again and Magdalene Sibylle of Prussia flounced into the room, accompanied by a host of ladies in finery, servants in livery, and several others who looked like hangers-on. The room was packed, which made me wonder why my presence had not been delayed until the Elector was back in his large reception hall. His disgruntled expression told me he thought so too.

They were a fine pair, Magdalene Sibylle and her husband; her expression of petulance matched his exactly. So did her embonpoint, to put a nice term to it.

"Whatever is so urgent that you have brought me here?" she demanded, chins jiggling.

"You, and your multitude," he answered, waving the pendant. "A gift from our good friend Adolf Friedrich of Mecklenburg."

Her eyes lit up as she seized it, laying it in her palm and scrutinizing it shortsightedly.

"How kind of him!" she cried, her petulance and irritation temporarily set aside. "We must write to thank him."

No sooner had she said this than she laid the pendant aside on a table. I had the strong impression that such trinkets and knickknacks soon became boring; the act of receiving them, rather than their beauty or worth, was what attracted her.

Elector Johann Georg of Saxony took his attention away from his wife, noticed I was still present, and motioned to his equerry.

"Take him to the kitchen. See he's fed." And to me. "I'll have letters and books for you at day's end. Wait downstairs."

I saluted smartly. Much too smartly—almost an act of insolence, although he paid it no attention—turned on a heel, and passed into the corridor. I left behind me two fat, tired old rulers who had everything they could ever need or want, and were girt around by luxury, ease, trappings and gabbling bodies. But withal, they were clearly waiting only for the Grim Reaper to slice through their boredom and take them to their just reward.

I was shown to a large refectory, bustling at this middle hour with serving people of the lower ranks, all taking their refreshments. A serving girl seated me at a trestle and brought me bread and meat on a trencher, and a flagon of wine all to myself. This was unaccustomed luxury; I looked around and saw that only one other person had been graced with wine, small beer being the routine drink among the serving staff. The food was good and the wine drinkable. I had had some horrible experiences with the grape, but this wasn't the worst, considering the rotgut I had been served in Osnabrück. The other man who had a flask at his elbow caught my eye, noting the trumpet still slung at my back. He was in his mid thirties, I would say, with flowing black hair about his shoulders and as neatly barbered about the upper lip and chin as me. He beckoned me over to his bench with a wry smile.

"Here, have some of mine," he said as he topped up my tumbler. "They don't give lowly guests the better stuff. Where are you from?"

"Schwerin. Carrying messages." The wine was indeed better and I was quite content.

"Ah, trumpet and courier. Spy too, I don't doubt."

"I have been delivering messages and a gift to the Elector and Her Serene Highness."

"Oh, most surely. But not snooping around, eh? No covert mission, hmm?" My oaken face betrayed nothing. "Most unusual. Look, have you finished eating? Come up to my room. Let's talk music, even though you only play the trumpet. I am occasional organist to the Elector."

"I have to await return messages from him." I was reluctant to get too taken with his obvious charm, and a bit irritated at his presumption.

"I'll see to it they know where you are. It'll be hours anyway." He grabbed our flagons and rose from the bench. "Bring those," he continued, indicating the beakers.

Perforce I followed him. We ascended a number of staircases, passed through several hallways, and eventually came to a small door at the far end of a passage. My new acquaintance motioned me in and showed me a chair. The furnishing was rather sparse, and a pair of saddlebags and a backpack against a wall gave me the impression he was a short-term guest.

He raised his beaker. "Welcome to this most curious establishment, and may your visit be as short as mine."

"Short? But aren't you the organist at court?"

"No, indeed. No, No. Occasional is what I said. That's Weckmann; Matthias Weckmann. I am merely passing through."

"And going where?"

"Who knows? Where the wind takes me." He took a long draft of his wine, eyeing me over the rim. "But I want to know more about you."

"What if I am in no mind to tell you?" I was feeling enclosed and irritated, yet at the same time beguiled, and the testiness came out in my tone.

He laughed, and it was pleasant, open and honest. "I am so sorry. I do apologize. I'm sure you are all you say you are, but I have such a nosy, suspicious mind. So, let me tell you about me instead, just until you soften up. More wine?"

"I would love to hear your story, Herr... but I don't even know your name."

"Froberger. Johann Jakob Froberger, at your service."[45]

"I'm Jacob Hintze. Staff trumpeter in the Mecklenburg-Schwerin cavalry."

"Well met, sir!" The mug was raised again.

"As I said, I would love to hear your story, Herr Froberger, but..."

"Johann."

"Johann... But, I hope you will excuse me asking, why do you wish to tell me?"

He thought for a few moments, sipping his wine. "Two reasons: firstly, I crave the company of a fine lad like you; there are precious few other people here to talk to. Secondly, you strike me as being a gentleman as well travelled as I am. I want to soak information out of you. But in the nicest possible way, naturally. May I top up your mug?"

"Yes, I have seen many places," I replied as wine reached the rim, "and mostly under less than pleasant conditions."

"So. I travel now out of necessity. I had a good position with the Emperor in Wien until Empress Maria Leopoldine died in childbirth last August. Ferdinand suspended all music—poor grieving bastard; she was only seventeen—so we all had to leave and fend for ourselves."

I had heard of her death, of course, and wouldn't have wished such a thing on my worst enemy, which the Holy Roman Emperor had been through my entire warfaring career. This news had put a sensitive face upon him.

"So I came here," he continued, "because it's the next best place for a musician to be." He sighed. "But when you have a man as good as Weckmann..."

"So, no love lost there, eh?"

"No, no! Far from it. I love the man. Excellent musician. Great friend. I beat him in a competition organized by the Elector, you know... or, at least, I think I did..."

"Competition? Musical competition?"

"Yes. Give each player a theme, sit back and listen to what they can do with it. Not something you trumpeters would appreciate, though."

This nettled me more than a little. Froberger was assuming I knew nothing of music; assuming, in fact, that I was merely a player of cavalry signals or a fanfare thumper. Not unusual at that time, I must admit. "I'm a musician, damn you!" said the wine loudly. "And we play great music with the whole ensemble, organ as well. We're fine musicians, and we praise God with our instruments!"

"Apologies again." He hushed me with raised palms. "But I'm sure we can agree that the organ is the instrument of God, not the trumpet. After all, it is the only instrument worthy of permanent installation in a place of worship."

"Ah, but the trumpet will sound at the Last Judgement. Surely, that's a sign that God favours it over the organ?"

"Not by any means," with a huge wag of a finger. "Only the organ can express the full majesty of the music that God has vouchsafed for us. The trumpet? Hah! One scale, and a flawed one at that!"

"But we trumpeters know with certainty that God alone favours us." I said this slowly with a tiny smile, dangling my bait. By now I was beginning to like and trust this strange man. I watched his expression soften into curiosity.

"Oh, yes?"

"Yes." I paused. "Because when we put it to our lips and blow, only God know what will come out!"

He roared with laughter, slopping more wine into my beaker. "I like you Jacob. I like you a lot." He placed his hand briefly over mine.

"But tell me," I asked, "why do you have this room if you're not employed by the Elector?"

"Oh, I get room and board as long as I amuse them. But I have to fawn and crawl for it. The letters we have to write! 'To the most supreme Elector Johann Georg of Saxony, prince and ruler, blah, blah de blah, the undersigned sues to place his humble, meagre and most unworthy talent at the service of your august majesty...' Christ's bones! I'm the finest organist in Europa! It burns my arsehole to write that stuff."

"But it works. He keeps you on."

"Oh, Johann Georg loves collecting things, curios, works of art. That's what I am; a curio. He uses me occasionally, like in that competition, although I'd swear he was bored to sleep after the first five variations."

"But you're hoping he'll take you on?"

"No. This is a wonderful court, wonderful musicians, but one organist too many. I'm eating his food and drinking his wine until I can get up the energy to leave. I'll go soon. I'll head north. Perhaps I'll come with you?"

"I'm riding to Nürnberg before I go home. You're welcome to ride with me."

"Nürnberg. Horrible place. Kindermann's there I suppose… No, I want to go north. Köln maybe, Antwerpen, Paris, London…" He eyed me over his beaker, seeming to come to a decision. "I haven't told anyone this yet, so consider yourself privileged. I will travel, and everywhere I go I will describe my adventures, but not in words. In music!"

I had no idea what he was talking about, but I nodded encouragingly. "How will you live?"

"Did I not tell you? I am the finest player of keyboards in Europa. In the world. Everywhere I go I will be feted and retained, but I will always move on. I want to see the world, and I want to make musical essays of all I see. Magnificent plan, eh?"

"I must say, I am almost envious. All the travelling I have done has been in warfare. The present trip is the first I've made where I can ride in peace."

"Tell me. You're a courier; what languages do you have?"

"I speak Italian, French, Swedish and English fairly well, and make a complete mess of Danish."

"English! I *must* learn English. Have you visited England?"

Now I realized my mouth and the wine had carried me too far. My visit to England had been covert, as had most of my other travels. I was opening myself up dangerously to a complete stranger. He saw my hesitation.

"Ah, you may well deny it, but you *are* a spy. No, no, no!" he cried, holding up his palms again, "I am not about to expose you. Why? Because I am one myself."

"What!" Wine slopped. I put the beaker down; enough was enough.

"The Emperor treasures his remote eyes and ears. I report to him, and will continue to do so. You, of course, will not expose me either. That's our bond."

It followed. He was one of us mushrooms, and he would hold his peace. Even so, I held back from full confession and just smiled.

"Come with me!' he shouted suddenly. "Teach me English while we travel. We'll see the world together."

"You can hardly tempt me. I'm bound to my Duke, and answer to him."

"Yes, but doesn't your duke use you as a chattel? Wouldn't you rather be free of such servitude?" He shifted forward in his chair and placed both his hands over mine. "Travel, see the world, be your own man."

"I honour and serve my Duke," I said rather formally, carefully withdrawing my hands. "Everything I have I owe to him. And besides, my wife would be most unhappy."

His face fell. "Ah, wife," he sighed. "Yes, you're not the one to travel with me." [46]

I stood and made to shake his hand, but he pulled me to him and enfolded me in his arms. "Go with God. Make lots of children. Think of me."

I held his embrace. In such a short space of time I had come to feel a companionship with this strange man, and I felt better for having met him.

As I sat on my bench back in the refectory, quite fuddled by drink, I half wondered if I had been dreaming. Presently a messenger came, not to summon me back to the Electoral presence, but to thrust sealed papers and a package into my hands and to bid me go on my way.

I rode out of Dresden the next day, southwest in pouring rain, wondering where Johann Jakob Froberger would find himself.

Chapter Thirty-Seven

In which I find a trumpet that is utterly to my liking

An gut und bösem Schall kennt man das Herz-Metall
By good or bad sounds one can judge the finest metal
Christoph Weigel

Nürnberg was a mythical town of towers and pinnacles and fluttering flags; it was a place of pilgrimage, far distant and exotic in a boy's imagined world. Now, as I reined up on the rise of a hill somewhere south of Erlangen, and saw the Imperial city nestling below me, the *Lorenzkirche* and *Sebalduskirche* each with their twin spires framing the river, and the castle glowering over them upon its rock, I was not disappointed. Suddenly an imagined place became real. Most often, reality breaks the spell of the vision in the mind's eye, but not this time. I was transfixed.

I rode quickly into the city through the great northern gate, and the place was a madness of activity. Peace celebrations were seen everywhere in festive banners and flags, smiling faces, music wafting from buildings, and the all-too-evident effects of strong drink. The chances of finding anywhere to sleep were scarce, but I had no desire for lodging. Even though it was into the eighth hour of the day, I wanted my Nürnberg trumpet *now!* The Duke's errands could wait. Stopping at a wicket near the gate I asked a uniformed man, who I took to be a gatekeeper or sentry, where I would find the Guild of the Trumpet-makers. I was directed to the Obere Schmiedgasse where craftsmen made a huge variety of utensils, from pots and pans right through to fine jewelry. Some workshops had windows opening onto the street, and in some of these the finer craftsmen had set their tables across the space so as to take advantage of the light. In other premises there were open doors looking into dark interiors. Thundering, hammering and shouting echoed throughout the street.

I found a trumpet-making workshop through one door, drawn to that section of the street by the ringing din of anvils. I peeped in the open door; my silhouette against the light was enough to draw the attention of a man banging at an anvil. He put his hammer aside and came to the door.

"Perhaps you can help me?" I asked. "I had a trumpet by Conrad Droschel years ago. Do you know who succeeded him?"

"Hanns Hainlein," replied the man curtly. "Three doors up." He indicated with his thumb and returned to his bench.

I poked my nose into the indicated workshop and caught the eye of a man sitting at a rough bench. He laid down his work and came forward. He was a tall man, in his mid fifties I would say, although craftsmen's ages are difficult to judge because they give their bodies such abuse.

"Herr Hainlein?" He nodded. "I'm Jacob Hintze, from Schwerin in Mecklenburg. I play the trumpet with the cavalry. I had a trumpet by Conrad Droschel years ago. I understand you were his apprentice, and that you carried his patterns and style forward."

"Yes, God rest him. My *Meisterbrief* was in 1640 and then I started on my own."

"It was a lovely trumpet, and I would like to find another that plays as well."

"So, just the one? You're not an agent? Buying a batch?"

"No, just one instrument that played like my Droschel…"

"So, you liked the work of my master, eh?"

"It was the first trumpet I ever played. I've never really found another that feels the way that one felt."

"What do you play now?" he asked, eyeing the bag slung over my shoulder.

I pulled out the Benninck and passed it to him.

"Hah! Clumsy northern work. Heavy. You play these things in your cavalry?"

"Until the Peace these were the preferred kind. The only kind."

He hefted it in his hand. "Well, a bloody horse could fall on it, it's solid enough." He should have seen the Sander after Klingenthal. "But you've come to Nürnberg to buy a real musical instrument, eh?"

"As I said, the Droschel…"

"Hah! Typical. First trumpet you blew on, you fell in love with. I'll wager five *Thaler* the first woman you lay on, you fell in love with. Eh?" He fixed me with a gimlet eye.

I didn't know where to look. My mind went back to Giselle, and there in the middle of the clangour of anvils, the ringing of hammers and the roar of bellows, I had a vision of her athwart me with the sun shining on her from behind. And all my silly little romantic fantasies… But no, Herr Hainlein had no inkling of my Elisabeth; not the first, but beyond compare.

"See, that's the way of the world," he continued as my mind snapped back. "Everything's rosy when you're young, then it's downhill. First piece you ever had and you think she was the best. Always comparing, never satisfied. Listen, I could blindfold you, give you a trumpet, tell you dear, dead Conrad had made it with his own two hands, and you'd fall in

285

love all over again. Same with a woman; blindfold you, pop you in, how would you know?"

While it was interesting, but a bit disconcerting, to hear his philosophy laid out in this way, it wasn't advancing my search for a trumpet.

"Well, if I could just recapture the feel of that instrument…"

"Feel? Hmm. Feel! You feel more for a trumpet than you do for a woman? Trumpet, that's your first love. Women come second."

"That's as maybe, but my present mission is one of brass, not flesh."

He barked out a short laugh. "Look, I'd like to help you," he said, not unkindly, "but we're as busy as all buggery right now. Yes, we follow the old pattern. Yes, I could give you something that would please you mightily, but not for a good long while. Single commission; takes a back place to stuff ordered through our agents. Can you wait three weeks?"

My crestfallen face told him I couldn't. He sighed and waved his hand around the workshop. "See, I'm short-manned right now. One of my bell men has damaged himself. Sick in the arm, he calls it—he's from Bohemia—so my best bell man is up to here." He passed a hand across his throat. "All these trumpets," he said, indicating rows of nearly finished instruments on a table against the back wall, "are commissions. We've got people here for the conference from everywhere, and while they're here they all want instruments. Sweden, Brandenburg, Holstein, it goes on and on."

He thought for a moment. "Look, I could send you on to my apprentice. Wolfgang Birckholtz has just taken his Meisterbrief and he's damned good. Better be or I wouldn't have signed off on him. See how busy we are."

He waved an arm, indicating a worker slamming a rough, newly hammered bell onto a horizontal steel mandrel, shaped to the finished bell form. He had three of four roughed-out bells on one side of his bench, and a small pile of finished ones on the other. He would pick up a rough bell, swing his arm back and virtually hurl the piece with full force, almost the way you would see a spear being thrown. As he banged the thin metal onto the form you could almost see it spread, conforming to the shape. He then took a heavy steel bar smeared with tallow and rubbed the surface vigorously, repeatedly slamming the bell onto the form. As I watched, a crumpled, hammered and rough-formed piece of brass became smooth under his hands. Herr Hainlein noted my interest, and in a pause in the action called to the worker.

"Michael! Here!" The worker put down his steel and came over; a short, dark haired man with enormous muscles and a wide, easy smile.

"This is… Jacob was it? Yes, Jacob, from Schwerin. Michael is my best bell man."

"Ja. I like best to make bells."

"I'm sending him to Wolf. I've told him how busy we are here."

"Ja. Wolf makes good bells. Good bell, good trumpet." He bowed slightly and returned to whacking the next crumpled bell onto his mandrel.

Hainlein showed me to the door of the shop and we shook hands. I stood blinking in the sudden light, such a contrast from the dim interior.

"Wolf is two shops along, up there," he pointed. "He'll see you're alright."

I poked my nose through the door of another dark space. Three workmen were at benches and a forge, one soldering tubes over the fire, and the other two smoothing them out on a steel rod and drawing them through a die. A young man, I would guess a few years older than me, was working at a trestle closer to the door in comparative quietness. He got up from his work and came over to greet me.

"Herr Birckholtz?"

"The same." He had a wide, generous mouth and a crushing handshake. "How can I help you?"

"Hanns Hainlein thought you might be able to sell me a trumpet."

"I am certainly in the business of doing just that. Please step inside."

He gave me a stool to sit on while he returned to his place behind the trestle.

"Unfortunately, I am very pressed for time," I began.

"You're actually fortunate, not the reverse. I'm just starting in business now so I am not yet overflowing with orders. What are you looking for?"

"Years ago, I had a trumpet by Conrad Droschel, and I have never found its like since. I'm from the north; we play these..." and I extracted my Benninck and passed it to him.

"Yes, I've seen these. Not to our style at all."

"Herr Hainlein said similar words."

"And mostly foul, I am sure. Most of his words are foul." He stepped over to a table and picked up an instrument. "Would you like to try one of mine?" It was not yet bound with its cord and had the wood block held in place with a canvas ligature. "Try this. It's accounted for, but you can have a blow before I finish it and sell it."

It was only when he passed me the trumpet that I realized what I had been missing. It was light! Its balance on my outstretched hand took me right back where to I had begun all those years ago. It was a beautifully finished instrument, and had silver-plated fittings, delicate decorations on the ferrules, and fine engraving around the garland. I plugged my mouthpiece in—the same mouthpiece that had been everywhere with me—and played. Oh, yes! This was my first love, come back to lie over me again. I played for a good long while, rolling in nostalgia.

"Yes!" I cried to him, handing the instrument back. "I've come a long way, but this is exactly what I need. Let's discuss details."

"This one is very finely finished; a special order. But none are off-the-shelf. I'm not so organized yet that I can work to make stock. Also, strictly speaking, the Guild says we should only sell through agents, but we all bend the rules a little if someone comes to the workshop and wants just one. But with all these delegates in the city... Lots of demand... So, it would be some few days..."

"How many days?" I interrupted, sensing my dream evaporating. "I have to be back in Schwerin by the end of June at the latest."

I could see the calculations crossing his face. He was balancing my journey north with his workshop time, and not coming to a happy conclusion. However, I knew he wanted the work so I felt I had the upper hand. He sighed. "If I started right now, and you delayed your departure until... Hmm... Oh, it's difficult. So difficult."

"Tell me, who is this one for?" I asked, indicating the instrument I had handed back to him. "And how... *flexible* is he?"

Again, his thoughts were painted across his face, but this time I could see a happy resolution emerging in the lift of his mouth and the rise of his eyebrows.

"He'll just have to wait, won't he?" he smiled. "He hasn't looked in yet, so when he does I'll show him a pile of bits. Have to have some parts silvered..." He frowned. "He might be angry and cancel the order though..."

"Unless?" I could see it coming.

"Unless I were to receive a small financial compensation. Which," he continued hurriedly, "I could then pass along to him as a discount to assure him of my good intentions."

Yes, I thought to myself, Meister Wolfgang Birckholtz will go a long way in his profession. Here's a man who knows how to satisfy a customer and seal a deal.

"Doesn't your guild have strict directives regarding prices?" I asked in all innocence, knowing damned well that it did.

"What appears on paper is what matters. Here it is simply *Sie berauben Peter, um Paul zu bezahlen.* Isn't that so?" I had last heard the phrase 'robbing Peter to pay Paul' in the mouth of a Protestant reformer in a London tavern.[47] This Birckholtz had depths.

So, with the addition of a tightly wound red cord with tassels, and a handful of tuning bits, the deal was completed. My hand was again crushed as I bade farewell at the workshop door, lighter by forty *Reichsthaler* but floating with joy.

I would have to camp outside the walls for the night; I didn't even bother enquiring after accommodation in the packed and rejoicing town. I rode out of Nürnberg to the east in darkness, stopping beside the River Pegnitz and camping soldier-style below a wall with the sound of falling water not far off. I usually rise with the dawn, but it was not yet light when I was hurtled out of sleep by a terrible thumping noise reverberating through the ground. My immediate thought was of guns. Nothing so sinister; I had spread my blanket almost within touching distance of the outside wall of a hammer mill, and the mill master had chosen that moment to open his sluices and set the wheels in motion. I gathered my things amidst the din and rode back to the city, pleased to have learned where Herr Birckholtz got his sheet metal from.

Searching for the book Duke Adolf Friedrich had asked me buy was easier than I thought. A man at the city gate directed me to a street not far from where I had been the day before. Booksellers, printers, stationers and makers of inks and paints and brushes populated the narrow way between buildings. It took a few enquiries before I found a seller of music who had copies of the Kindermann book, and had just opened his shutters.

I had left my duty of visiting the *Schloss* until last. It was brief but could have been briefer. I recall it was June 4 when I climbed the hill in the mid-morning light, passing though the *Hauptmarkt* in all its busyness, and presented myself at the gate of the *Reichsburg*. I was shown into a cold anteroom where I waited for a considerable time, seated on a hard bench. It must have been nearly an hour before a second messenger reappeared in a fluster.

I stood to attention quickly. "I bring letters to his Highness Count Palatinate Karl Gustav von Pfalz-Zweibrücken from Duke Adolf Friedrich of Mecklenburg-Schwerin."

"I will send your communications to his Highness," he told me coldly. "Give them to me please."

"Would his Highness not wish to receive them into his hand?" I asked. "I am sure my Duke would wish me to have done so." This was untrue; I had no word-of-mouth from the Duke so there was no reason to be present when they were delivered, but I was annoyed at this high-handed little shit.

"That will not be possible. His Highness is extremely busy. There is much work and organization to attend to for tonight's festivities."

"Festivities?" I asked. "I would very much like to attend in lieu of my Duke, and perhaps convey my messages and good wishes then."

"That will not be possible at this late stage," replied this snotty little bastard. "Places were assigned many weeks ago."

I was not happy with this. In fact, I was seething but holding it inside. I had been kept waiting on that hard bench for nothing. "And the first messenger could not have returned and informed me of this an hour ago?"

He relented a little and made a weak smile. "I am sorry, I really am, but it's absolutely hellish around here."

I could have pushed my diplomatic privilege, I could have torn him up one side and down the other, but I decided God damn them, I've got my trumpet, I've got the Duke's book, so what more do I need? Besides, I was actually busting for a piss. I thrust the letters into his hand.

"Please convey my Duke's best wishes to Count Palatinate Karl Gustav von Pfalz-Zweibrücken." I saluted, turned and headed for the gate. On the way, I stepped into an alcove just beside the gate arch and watered the wall with a hot stream of contempt.

I was angry at the snub I had received but much more than this, I was sad. I felt sad for my Duke because here was firsthand evidence that a mere *Herzog* from a small principality in the north was of little account, his name and title not enough to give even his messenger audience. I resolved not to tell him, and if he asked pointedly I was prepared to lie.

I stopped in a tavern near the *Hauptmarkt* and bought something to drink, and food for now, and more to stow in my saddlebags. A fellow at the bench beside me—one of those flat-faced, square-jawed Bavarians with jolly eyes—was stuffing a clay pipe with tobacco. He offered me a fill, which I declined, and we struck up a conversation.

"Where you from?"

"Mecklenburg."

"Ah. Mecklenburg."

I could see he had no idea where this was. "North. Near the Ostsee."

"Ostsee, eh? Hmm. Long way then… Staying tonight?"

"I might. I heard there was some sort of festivity," I replied. "But I have no invitation."

"No invitation needed. Outdoors, in a field beyond the city. There is music followed by a showing of *Feuerwerk*."

Out of curiosity, even with the thought of Elisabeth waiting and hoping, I stayed that night to see this *Feuerwerk*. I stood with thousands outside the fence of a great field that had been set aside and prepared for the occasion. God had not smiled upon the organizers; there was low cloud, rain and a strong wind from the east. Even so, there was laughing, joking and singing among the mob as drinks, nuts and spiced cakes were passed around. I had never seen fireworks before; throughout my military career our hoarded gunpowder could never have been spared for mere entertainment, and there had never been any cause for celebration. There was a buzz of talk all around me as the sky darkened, then with the sight of a burning match being carried to a structure at the rear, the crowd fell silent. I had no idea what to expect until the first explosion shot a ball of fire into the air. The artificers must have been using some sort of mortar to project this thing so high. When it exploded with a terrific clap high above the heads of the crowd, I was amazed. Fire rained down, fizzing around us, the crowd cried out in surprise and wonder, and then another explosion, another flaming, burning thing shot aloft. It was wonderful. Such a new thing then; more common now. The show went on for a considerable time until smoke and rain and ashes descended and the explosions ceased.

Johann Jakob Froberger might not have liked the town—"Nürnberg. Horrible place"—but as I rode north in a gentle rain through Erlangen, I felt torn. Through me, my Duke had been snubbed, dismissed and diminished by the cruelty of power and pomp and majesty. Little did I suspect then that I would meet this bastard Highness Count Palatinate Karl Gustav von Pfalz-Zweibrücken again under frightening circumstances. But, on the bright side, my saddlebags were filled, my errands accomplished. Two trumpets in their bags tapped gently at my back, and I had seen wonders. My expectations had been fulfilled and the magical place of my childhood dreams was untarnished.

Horrible place? Maybe. But they make very nice trumpets there.

Chapter Thirty-Eight

In which I return home, try to settle into family life, and take on a
strange apprentice

*Ich kam nun mit meinem Recommendation-Schreiben... / und wurde selbiger
Musicus oder Trompeter meiner froh / weil er eben eines Lehr-Jungen
bedörfftig / und weil ich bey Jahren und verständig / nahm er mich auf 3.
Jahr ohne Lehr-Geld auf / die Kunst zu lernen*
I now came with my recommendation papers to the musicus or
trumpeter gladly because he needed an apprentice, and because of
my age and my knowledge he agreed to three years of tuition
without the need for payment

Daniel Simplex

Oh, it was touch and go! What if Elisabeth went early and I failed in
my promise? I rode north as hard as I could, but it was the end of the
third week of June when I finally reined up outside our door. I should
have reported immediately to the *Schloss*, and there was a risk of disciplinary action if I was discovered, but I didn't care. I would swear
Elisabeth held on and held on, so when I pulled her into my arms, still
sweaty and horsey from my ride, she decided to let go. She was right;
it was a boy. But how ever do they know? Our little Hans came into
the world less than half a day after I got back. I held the little fellow in
my arms while Michael looked on, wondering what in the world his
parents wanted with this squalling new plaything. The child's baptism
in the *Schelfkirche St Nikolai* on a glorious warm day was a joy.

We both realized that a brace of young lads would soon become a
burden, so I employed a maid and a manservant to assist Anja in running the house. Now we were becoming a real household, perhaps one
rather elevated in view of the breadwinner's status as a *Stabstrompeter*.
But the income from our two properties, well managed by Chris
Schleef, provided the supplement to sustain our living. There were also
other monies paid in contracts between me and the Duke for services
above and beyond my military and court duties, but these remained
covert and not discussed.

The end of the Thirty Years War signaled a breakdown in the way we
did things in the *Kameradschaft*, at least in Mecklenburg, although it may
not have been the Peace itself but a combination of many factors. We
were still jealously protective of our right to play the trumpet, and still
rigid in our systems of deciding who could play the trumpet and how

the candidates would be trained, but now the trumpet was no longer the exclusive domain of the cavalryman. More and more we were seeing composers scoring for us in perfectly integrated and homogenous works, and it became clear that musicians employed by the court, and paid for out of its revenues, could just as well be trained in this craft. A military background and all the discipline and strictures that went with it was no longer a prerequisite. Playing in those glorious masses that celebrated the Peace showed the way forward, and during this period of relative calm within our borders, we were increasingly gaining enormous satisfaction from our craft.

Playing outside of cavalry and horseback was not for everybody, however. The new compositions required a deeper knowledge of music and an ability to read notation. A good few of our old-school trumpeters played by ear—they knew no other way—and for them the life of cavalry calls, court fanfares and entradas would continue to be their mainstay. Others, like me (as I blessed again the wisdom of Herr Pinklemann) went in this new direction. I didn't come across much jealousy among our group, even though there was extra money to be earned playing with the chapel choir and the court musicians. Any grumbling appeared to be good natured, with the exception of old Wilhelm, of course, but he was a curmudgeon through and through.

Friedemann had embraced the new direction, and when three trumpeters were called for he would quite often choose me and Albrecht, along with Wolfgang the kettledrummer. We had played together since that memorable wedding in Rostock when Hartmund Breitkopf was still with us. The music had come a long way since then, and with it the demands, so the Hasse piece we had played in the *Marienkirche* now seemed rudimentary stuff. But Friedemann was careful and fair, so the others who could well qualify for these jobs got chosen as well, especially as I was still away on missions for lengthy periods.

All this as an introduction to the next new challenge in my life.

"Hang on a moment," said Friedemann as we were putting away our equipment at the close of a practice session. "Got something I want to talk to you about."

He ushered me into the little cubbyhole that constituted the office space of the *Hoftrompeter*. He had a sort of assessing look about him, and he seemed to be assembling his words before uttering them.

"You're, what... twenty-seven years old now?" I wondered where this was heading. "Well-seasoned, well-practiced, excellent player. Ever think of taking on an apprentice?"

"What!" A thunderclap. Nothing, absolutely nothing, could have been further from my thoughts. "Me? Why in God's name do you think I could? I don't know... I never... But I'm..."

He let me run down to a stop.

"Not exactly an apprentice; more a trainee really. You see, the Duke has been approached by this man. Brother of a young fellow from Breslau. The boy apparently has some talent as a musician, has been trained as a trombonist, and brother would like him to become a trumpeter."

"So, why me? Surely, some older man. Jiri, Albrecht… the mature fellows…"

"Don't bullshit me Jacob," he said. "You know as well as I do you can play the hose and drawers off any one of them, and you have the musical smarts as well."

"But I don't feel…" I stopped and thought. What didn't I feel? Ready, perhaps. Old enough? "Well, who is this lad?"

"He's fifteen years old, an orphan, reads and writes, and was a pupil at the Lycée Maria Magdalenen, very prestigious. Plays the trombone, wants to play the trumpet. According to the older brother, all he needs is guidance and a firm hand."

"In other words, a bright, talented little bastard who his brother wants shot of before he gets himself into trouble."

"Could be. But the Duke is favourably inclined, so perhaps you would be wise to be as well. Just training. A few hours a week. New perspective…"

"Can I meet him; decide? Or is this cut and dried?"

"They arrive tomorrow, by coach apparently. We'll get a call."

"Well, thank you! Thank you very much. I think…"

The following day Friedemann and I were led by a page to a receiving room in the lower reaches of the *Schloss* where a portly, red-faced gentleman and a young boy were seated beside Nicholas Schlauklug, the same ancient and timeless functionary who had welcomed me and my father to the court bureaucracy. There was a wooden box on the floor in front of them; doubtless the boy's trombone. Friedemann introduced himself as *Hoftrompeter* and the gentleman puffed up out of his chair. Friedemann then stepped aside and waved me forward: "*Stabstrompeter* Jacob Hintze."

The gent bowed to me. "Friedebert Speer," he said. "Pleased to make your acquaintance, sir. My protégé, raised by hand; he's my brother, we were orphaned…" He waved a paw in the direction of the youth, who remained seated in a posture of extreme indifference bordering upon insolence. "Georg. Here's the gentleman I told you about, Georg."

The youth unwound himself a little from his pose but seemed in no mood to rise. I thought of the Duke's recommendation, I thought of Friedemann's imposition and my reluctance to be pulled in. I looked over this slumped, insulting specimen and suddenly I became blazingly angry. Almost without thought of the consequences I yelled at him.

"*Get up!* Get up off that damned chair! Who in hell do you think you are?" Shock crossed his face. "Stand, God damn you!" I roared. "Stand here in front of me."

All in the room—the page, the brother, Herr Schlauklug, Friedemann—were struck into frozen poses, while the youth slouched upright with a spoiled little smirk on his face that just burned the hairs off my arse.

"Back straight! Stomach in! Chest out! Chin up, you bag of offal." I leaned close to him, wagging a finger in his face and spraying him as I yelled. "I've seen boys younger than you blown to splinters and gristle and giblets, and you dare stand in front of me as if you owned the place, you insolent little bastard."

I got through in a way I would wager nobody else had before. At the closing "bastard" he began to look downright frightened. It was most gratifying to watch the façade crumble and to see the true boy behind it; a child who been given everything he could ever have wanted, except guidance, direction and authority. And in particular, correction. My words had to suffice in doing the business that canes or belts should have done years before. But my anger, I realized much later, was directed as much at the brother as at him. Pompous fat sod.

"Never again!" I continued loudly, but in a more level tone. "Never again in your life will you dare to insult your betters and superiors! If you are to stay here beyond one hour… one single hour, you will do so in humility and deference. Do you understand? Well? *Do you?*"

He nodded in his fright; no words escaped. Silence enveloped the room; no one present dared so much as clear a throat. I got the strong impression that this was the first time in his life that young Master Georg had been yelled at. I suspected that the brother had taken over from the parents, although who knew what the two of them had been through.

"Now," I continued, "we will all sit down and discuss this application. Now, Herr Schlauklug, have you had occasion to examine this young… gentleman's papers?"

There was much shuffling, folding and unfolding, scanning and nodding, while Friedemann slipped out of the door with a huge grin all over his face.

"The term of the apprenticeship," said Schlauklug, "is for three years. Due to the applicant's financial situation, the usual apprenticeship fee is waived in return for service in the Duke's establishment. This will be mostly kitchen duties of a menial kind. You, *Stabstrompeter,* will be responsible only for tuition, the remaining duties to be assigned by the *Haushofmeister*."

"Thank you. We'll speak alone for a few minutes now," and I waved Friedebert Speer and the scribe out of the room.

"So, *Herr* Speer," I said to the boy. "Welcome to a new world. Before I have anything further to do with you, I want to assure myself that you will not be wasting my time. Your brother says you are a musician? Hmm?"

"I... I..." He looked at me with huge round eyes, unable to speak.

"It's alright. I'm not the ogre you believe me to be. But I can be, and will be if you don't satisfy me. Music?"

"I... I play the trombone. Sir. I started first on kettledrums. My brother says..."

"I'm not interested in what your brother says. I want to hear what you say."

"I love it, sir. The trombone. But... my brother..."

"If you mention your fucking brother one more time I'll throw your arse out of that door! Is that clear?"

"Yes! Yes, sir." There was a long pause, which I saw no reason to break.

"Well?" The pause continued as I watched confusion in his eyes.

"I don't know what I want... My bro... I... I like the trumpet a lot."

"Liking's fine. But you have to want to be here. Do you want to be here, bound here to me? Well, do you?"

I watched the confusion begin to resolve itself; I am almost certain I watched a decision coming forward, a breaking away from a thrall of always being told what to do and never having to make a decision. I like to think that young Georg Speer decided right then to take serious control of his own life.[48] Mind you, I would soon find that coming out from under his brother's pernicious influence wouldn't necessarily mean he would be coming willingly under mine.

"Yes, sir. Yes, I want to be here." I believed him then, but I don't know if he believed himself. He hadn't seen the kitchen yet...

"Good. One huge hedge has been jumped. You like the damned thing. Can you play it? Upper register?"

"When I can. I... I hold my slide shut and practice high in the gamut. The mouthpiece is large, but..."

"Get it out." I motioned to the box on the floor. "Play."

What emerged was a battered old tenor instrument from Nürnberg, made, I afterwards noted, by Georg Ehe.[49] And yes, this boy could play. I had him work pretty hard, checking his intonation in particular, and found little to fault.

Presently I called brother Friedebert and Herr Schlauklug back in, and we sat for a long time reading documents and having Georg recite his vows. Documents were signed and witnessed, with much flourishing ceremony on behalf of Friedebert and some reluctance on the part of his protégé. When we were finished I threw myself back in my chair and pointed a finger at Georg.

"Now, when I started as an apprentice at your age..." Good God, I was sounding like an ancient "...you would be obliged to be a soldier. Nowadays, I can take you on as a day student but that *does not* mean there will be any lack of discipline. Report at the front gate tomorrow at the third hour. Dismissed!"

I was damned if I'd waste my time on any mediocre talent, but here was a candidate with a lot of promise. The remaining problem was the level of his commitment.

Chapter Thirty-Nine

In which children are born and my protégé strains his bonds

Darum gehet hin und lehret alle Völker und taufet sie im Namen des Vaters
und des Sohnes und des heiligen Geistes, und lehret sie halten alles, was ich
euch befohlen habe
Go ye therefore, and teach all nations, baptizing them in the name
of the Father, and of the Son, and of the Holy Ghost
Matthaeus/Matthew 28:19

I received an invitation by post from Chris Schleef to visit Rostock; it must have been in the early summer of 1652 because Elisabeth was pregnant again, but not so far gone that she couldn't travel. I petitioned both Friedemann and my commander for leave, which was duly granted, but for only a short visit. We set off for Rostock, just the two of us, leaving the two boys in Anja's capable hands. Chris's wife Alena had given birth to their first, and they would hold the baptism only when we came to visit. I was all for taking the coach, which had now been established in these more peaceful times, but Elisabeth scoffed at it, insisting she would ride. Even so, we took the journey slowly, stopping each night after fairly short riding days. Our last stop was the *Neuer Krug* in Neu Heinde, just one stage from Rostock. I had stopped there before and really liked the place.

The Scheefs greeted us warmly at their house in Wokrenterstrasse, above the office where I had first met old Herr Schleef and his son. This was a happy time, a piece sliced out of life and preserved, to be cherished as it unfolded and to be remembered fondly afterwards. I think Alena, in particular, was a little disappointed that the young Hintzes had not come with us, but we warmly invited her and Chris back to Schwerin so they could observe the little animals in their own nest. We were delighted and touched that their little one would be called Elisabeth. The baptism took place in the *Nikolaikirche*, quite a small affair with a few family and friends. The little maid yelled her head off all the way through, but one of the old wives observed wisely that the crying was a good sign, as the child recognized the presence of Satan and cried to drive him away. I did recall that when our Hans was christened he had smiled the whole time, a sure sign, the old wives told me, that he recognized the presence of Satan and smiled to laugh him to scorn.

Our women had much to talk about, compare and discuss, which gave their men the chance to wander on foot about the town and talk.

"How well is Sweden dealing with Rostock and Warnemünde?" I asked. We were walking along by the wharves on the south bank of the Warne. The two towns, the major port and the smaller seacoast hamlet, relied almost exclusively on marine trade and fishing. During the war the Swedish hold had been tight and trade had been heavily taxed. "Better since the Peace?"

"Could wish. Ye-e-s, in some ways. What they hit us with here is nowhere near as bad as the days of the Sound Dues. We've just changed Denmark for Sweden, that's all."

"We all had hopes that after the Peace, Mecklenburg would have more autonomy."

"Didn't we all?" he sighed. "The Peace granted them Wismar, and also Stralsund in Pomerania, which rightfully should be ours. The negotiations went badly, according to the merchants and bankers here."

I couldn't reveal, from my inside view of the proceedings, just how much worse they could have been. The scars on my arm itched at the memory. "True, but the duchy survived and Duke Adolf Friedrich is rich from the sees of Ratzeburg and Schwerin."

"So, he spends as he wishes to?"

"Oh, yes," I said. "Music, art, court life are all coming back."

"Happy Duke, happy duchy."

"Not really. It burns him that he has so little control over his own duchy and his own people. The income is all well and good, but his subservient status is not to his liking."

"So he spends himself into greatness. Or, at least, greatness as others see it."

It was not so simple. I had come to know my Duke as well as many of his close retainers, and he was never so easy to read. There were depths and subtleties I found hard to understand, let alone express. "He's a complicated character," was all I said in the end.

"You deal quite closely with him, do you not?"

"Yes. Yes, I do," I replied and left it at that.

"Well, it is what it is."

We strolled slowly back, stopping on the corner at *Der Cogge* for a mug of ale, just like old times. Sadly, our homeward journey was the next day and the ladies waited, so one mug had to suffice.

Before we returned home there was the obligatory visit to Uncle Otto and Aunt Griselda. This time I was happy to find that Jacob Hintze was finally accepted as a suitable match for their adoptive daughter, which, after two children and a third on the way, a permanent court post and income from land, was about time in my estimation. Uncle Otto had climbed down from his high horse and now treated me as one of his own gentlemanly company. He listened to what I said, agreed with my views, and appreciated my wide knowledge on many subjects. Strangely enough, it was only in conversation with him that I discovered how much I did know about the world and the way it worked. He was liberal with his wine, and pleased that I appreciated it.

It had been a short visit, but with much warmth and good cheer packed into a small, carved-out space in our lives. Elisabeth and I and the little Schleef family had grown close, while Christophorus became more of a friend and the shade of a brother.

Our third son was baptized in August of 1652. It was only on the very day of the ceremony that we finally made the decision about his name. It was a hard, tearing thing for me to do, but Elisabeth agreed: we would call our third son Jürgen. What's in a name? My brother had been gone for nearly fifteen years, I was owner and beneficiary of the family property under law, and... he wasn't coming back. Jürgen deserved more continuity than a name for my favourite horse.

"Ever since that day they told me he'd gone to war," I said quietly, "I almost knew I'd lost him for good."

She squeezed my hand. "He loved you above the others, didn't he?"

I agreed with a returning squeeze. "But I couldn't have him gone. I wouldn't *let him* be gone." Yes, I had loved them all in their own way, but he most of all played the fullest chord in my heart. "I kept him alive. Here."

"He's at rest. He did what he thought was right."

"He made my first trumpet. Never told you that, did I?"

"*Made* a trumpet?"

"A stinking bone," I laughed. "A hollow cow shin, with a mouth-piece he drilled and carved."

"And it played?" she smiled.

"There were some notes. Horrible. Enough for Papa to take me to the *Stadtpfeifer* though. And the rest, my love, is history."

"My trumpeter!" She hugged me close and we kissed gently. "After the baptism we must go to *St Nikolai* and pray for Uncle Jürgen's soul."

And we did that. Even then there was still a tiny place in my mind where he still lived and would return. No matter the length of time, the certainty, the inevitability, there was as yet no proof. Until that came, the small flame of my brother still flickered.

I was unhappy with Georg, my protégé. Well, perhaps not unhappy but certainly disturbed. He was without question an incredibly good musician, he studied hard and wrote well, and he could account for himself in conversation and discourse. In short, one couldn't want a more able pupil, yet he was restless and undisciplined. He often came up from the kitchen—where the poor bugger spent most of his time on his knees when he wasn't with me—with a scowl on his face and stains of food and trodden waste on his clothing. I heard from the *Haushofmeister* that he was surly, lazy and undisciplined, so he was clearly not happy with the price he was paying for free tuition.

Even though I remembered my stint in the kitchens with little fondness, as a military man all my adult life, I had a rigid idea of what constituted discipline. I expected him to be where I told him to be, and I expected him to do exactly what I told him to do with no questions asked. This was the cavalry way, and it worked. I suppose I thought this way because for us, indiscipline broke the fragile link between life and death. On his side, he seemed to feel no allegiance to me or to my routines and schedules, and the kitchen was clearly beneath him. I was sure the problem wasn't with me; I could dish out authority when needed. It was him; he railed against it. He would get things done, and often exceed my instructions, but he would do so in his own good time. But he was disarmingly charming and there were times when I was on the verge of exploding at him, only for him to do something that took the wind quite out of me.

One day about six months or so into our relationship, Georg failed to attend on time when it was clearly specified on his schedule. He had done this before and I was getting sick of it. I had other work to do, but the longer I waited after the tower bell had sounded, the angrier I became. He eventually sloped into my cubicle with no contrition on his face, trumpet bag slung over his back and a sheet of music in his hand.

"Sorry I'm late," he cried with no obvious regard for my near-detonating face. "I had to finish writing this trumpet duet. It's just for you. I knew you'd like it, but I had to get it done."

"Damn you. You kept me waiting again," I replied, but his attitude was so beguiling that the steam had already left my heart. "Show me," I snapped.

I looked over the hastily scrawled notation, the bottom line still not dry, and thought to myself: My God, if you can compose this *and* play it I don't know how much more I can teach you. I pulled my Birckholtz off the peg without a word, propped the sheet on my music stand, and motioned him to get his trumpet out of its bag.

"Top part. I'll take second. One, two, three…"

It was high, difficult stuff, beautifully lyrical, a duet of question and answer, refrain and counter refrain. It was a fourth octave conversation between two trumpets. He managed admirably but, you know, I found it quite challenging. We played the whole thing over a few times, each repetition helping us to learn the nuances of it. As the last notes ended I came to a decision about Master Georg Speer.

"Speer. What do you want?"

"Want, sir?"

"Yes. Want. You write this stuff…" I slapped the sheet "…and you can play it. But you really don't like being here, do you?"

"I… I do like it here…" He thought for a moment and I could see doubt in the slope of his shoulders. "It's just…"

"You don't like the kitchens. You are bound by my rules. You are bound by my schedule. You are bound by your labour in this place, and it chafes you. Be honest with me!"

He took a long, deep breath. "I don't want to be bound. My brother…" he glanced at my face. I nodded: it's fine. "He tied me up, he ran my life. I couldn't do anything."

"And now I'm your older brother? The *Haushofmeister* is your older brother."

"No, no, it's not like that."

"Oh, yes, it is. I told you to be honest with me. You have exchanged one slavery for another. So, answer my first question: what do you want?"

"I want… You might laugh at me." I waved him off and his face cleared. "I want to travel. I want to see Venezia, Constantinople, Roma. I want to visit the land of the Grand Turk. And everywhere I go I will play my trombone and my trumpet! I want to see the world, that's all."

That's all… As I looked into the bright face of this boy, I thought of my travels when I was not much older than he. A huge wave came over me of regret, failed aspiration and a kind of hopelessness. He would see wondrous places, do marvelous things under skies of a different sun, sail seas of blue warmth in the light of a moon that was not my moon. I had seen death, destruction, bodily agony and spiritual misery, and suddenly, in spite of all the good things I now enjoyed in life, I was deeply and embarrassingly jealous.

"Go," I told him. "Go. Sit at the feet of the Grand Turk. Play your music. And may God guide you and give you all you desire. Go, and be free."

I had a meeting with Friedemann a day or so later. "He left with my blessing," I told him. "I discussed it all with the Duke and I have written to Friedebert Speer as well."

"Don't feel too bad about it, Jacob. It wasn't anything you did or didn't do."

"I know. It's a different kind of discipline. Some of ours comes from upstairs; all of his comes from within."

"Do you think he'll make his way in this new world?"

"I've given him letters of introduction. He wants to go south, and with winter coming in I don't blame him. Whoever hears him play will pay for his services."

"I hope so," said Friedemann with a frown. "Better musicians than he have gone hungry."

"I expect Friedebert will underwrite the boy, but I would bet Georg'll wait until he's starving before he asks. Free spirit is our Georg."

Annamaria was born in May of 1653. It hurt me, but Elisabeth more, that I was away on a mission in Flanders at the time. I really wanted to beg the Duke to release me from this particular duty, but I knew that to do so would lose me his favour. I returned to find a delighted Elisabeth and beautiful little maid, already with some wispy fair hair. Oh, the smell of a tiny baby's head! The feel of the little thing struggling against the swaddling. The vision of what something so small and defenceless will become. There is nothing as heart-warming as the grip on your finger of a newborn's tiny fist.

Elisabeth had not, at first, wanted her to be named Annamaria. Our first Annamaria had passed away and using the same name again was considered ill luck. But somewhere in my mind there was a longing for order and symmetry, a longing to recreate in miniature all the things I had lost. This was never expressed, but it was understood. Bad luck in naming can go both ways. I believed, and I convinced Elisabeth to believe, that God made His judgements over our actions, our deeds and our devotion, and not in such small choices we made.

It was different with Jürgen. That wrenched me. He still lived. Somewhere...

Chapter Forty

In which horses dance poorly, and I take a trip to France

Entre tous les Triomphes et toutes les pompes des Anciens, il n'y a eu rien de si Auguste qui puisse estre comparé au Carrousel de la Place Royale de Paris
Among all the Triumphs and pomp of the Ancients, there was nothing so august as to compare with the Carrousel of the Place Royale in Paris

Marcus Vulson

"Here's something you're not going to believe." Friedemann had called me and Albrecht aside after a practice session. It was high summer, sometime in July, and all the shutters were open to the air. "The Duke has got all keen on horse ballets. He's been studying books and music, and I have a horrible idea what he's got in mind."

"Books," sighed Albrecht, "he's always reading books."

"Tell me about it," I replied. "I can't count the volumes I've transported from all over Europa."

"Well, like I said, now it's all horse ballets," said Friedemann. "He's been reading about the French *carrousel*."

"Bloody French stuff," said Albrecht. "Can't be all that hard, can it? Playing on horseback. All you have to do is cavort about a bit."

"We'll see. Judging from the diagrams I saw in the book, there's a lot more to it."

"Lissen. If my horse can keep his cool among the guns and blazing straw and rotting meat, he can dance a fuckin' *menuet*. He'll do just fine."

Friedemann nodded but there was a look of doubt upon his face.

Sure enough, two days later on a fine, blustery morning we were met by the Duke himself on the sanded practice ring. He called all twelve us to dismount and gather round while he spread onto the sand a paper sheet covered in lines and arrows.

"Now, see here. I have transcribed some of the routines from the French *carrousel*, and we're going to practice them. Alltid, you will lead out here…" And there followed an extremely complicated and intricate discussion; one of those discussions where each party possesses a set of information, but the sets are in no way similar, so the communication between them is nonexistent. Just as it was beginning to get boring for the eleven bystanders, the Duke threw up his hands and said to Friedemann, "Well, try it man! Try it!"

Now, if Friedemann and the Duke had failed to communicate, it can be imagined how Friedemann himself wallowed along in explaining what we had to do, especially as the Duke chose at several points to intervene with clarifications that often weren't. Our first attempt to perform a horse ballet—a carrousel in the true French style—was an utter fiasco, a word I had picked up in my speech with Italians, and I wished we had one similar in German. And this experiment was simply with the horses; the music to go along with it would add another level of complexity. Once we broke into complete disarray, with horsemen blundering into each other as they misread the directions or couldn't hear Friedemann and the Duke's contradictory yelling, we pulled up and dismounted.

"No battle was won on the first salvo, sir," puffed Friedemann.

Duke Adolf Friedrich, surprisingly, didn't look half as furious as I thought he would be. He seemed to be in agreement. "Yes, you'll need to study this in much detail. Get the *Rittmeister* involved. Work on it. I'll see you here in one week from now."

"And the music, sir?" asked Friedemann.

"Surely, you have enough on file. Those evolutions were for was a *sarabande*." Friedemann raised his eyebrows in disbelief but fortuneately the Duke didn't notice. "Sort one out, get your men to go over it. Got to be timed with the routines. Next week." And he stalked off.

It was hardly as simple as Albrecht had thought, and he was among the first to realize this. The *sarabande* we chose was dead simple; one of those pieces we could play in our sleep or more than half drunk. Matching it to the evolutions of the horses was another story, while getting the mounts to follow the steps was next to impossible. Friedemann was backwards and forwards to the Duke several times during the week. It turned out that the massive tome the Duke was using as a reference had not been written by a specialist, and although he could read French there was a level of obscurity that hampered him.[50] Nevertheless, he came back a week later to observe progress, and this time he really did lose his temper.

"It cannot," he roared, as Friedemann reined up beside him, "be this difficult!"

"Fact is, sire, we don't know what it is we're missing."

"Missing? Missing, man! You're missing everything! If that was a sarabande, what kind of horseshit mess are you going to make of a *menuet*? Or a bloody *bourée?*"

"I'm sorry, sire."

"Dismissed! Come to my study. Bring Hintze. Eighth hour tomorrow."

I wondered why the Duke would have asked me to accompany Friedemann, but it became clear when we were ushered in the office the next day. At least, I thought it did.

"How's your French, Hintze?"

"I read a lot but practice little, sir." I assumed he needed my help in translating the huge book that lay open on the table at his side, two glass paperweights holding the pages down. I moved to examine the book but was stopped dead by his next remark.

"I'm sure you'll get it all back as flawlessly as usual on your way to Paris."

Paris? Here was that feeling again. Until now I had done my Duke's bidding gladly, putting my duty as a soldier ahead of the other life when I was standing down. Hearth and duty were in separate places, each held in its own world. Now, again, my heart sank at being away from the home life. My two lives were trying to join hands, but were being pulled asunder.

I looked enquiringly at him. "Paris, sir?"

"Yes, indeed. If we are to make any headway with the *carrousel*, we have to consult with the experts. This book is useless!" He slapped the pages with his palm and one of the paperweights slid off with a thud. "Misleading. Author knows less than he claims and decorates it with flowery bullshit. Listen to this: '*Entre tous les Triomphes*... yes, yes, triumphs and pomp of the Ancients... hmm, hmm, hah... *rien*... nothing... nothing compares with the *Carrousel de la Place Royalle de Paris*'. So, they matched the spectacles of the Ancients, did they? Fine! Now show me how they did it, you bloody fool!"

"Then we are to consult with the royal court in Paris, sir?" asked Friedemann, still, I believe, coming to terms with what would be his first foreign trip.

"Yes. No. Not the court, although you might present yourselves there. You must meet their *Rittmeister* at the Academie d'Equitation and pick his brains. I have written already. Our *Rittmeister* will accompany you. And the music; you must see about the music."

"I speak no French, sire."

"That's why Hintze is going with you. He will be very useful as *Rittmeister* Kulikovski speaks no French either. Damn me, he scarcely speaks German!" This was unfair; Stefan Kulikovski was a Silesian who had settled in Schwerin at the beginning of the war, an excellent horseman and perfectly capable in our northern dialect. We did take the piss out of him because of his accent, though.

"And the route to Paris, sire?" said Friedemann. It became clear to me that, for all his musical sense and experience with the trumpet music of cavalry and court, he had not ventured far and his knowledge of the map was rudimentary.

"Go and see Rehnskiöld. He'll show you routes. You'll have to go by land but you'd better avoid Flanders; the French and Spanish are at it again. It's not safe by ship either; the damned Dutch and English are making the seas unnavigable. Prepare to go as soon as possible. Report to me before you leave."

There was a new crossness about the Duke, coming out in a sense of urgency and fuss. In hindsight, I suspect even then he was aware that his passing was not far distant, and that the great projects in his mind would allow no delay. I also wondered if there might be some decay in his mind that coloured his decisions. The mission to Paris seemed so extreme.

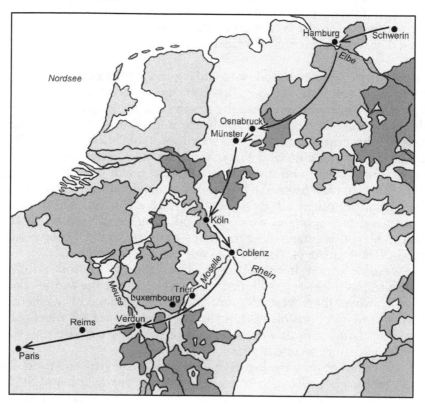

The route that Jacob Hintze and his colleagues took on their mission to Paris

So it was that I rode out of Schwerin one rainy summer day with Friedemann and Stefan, and two other members of our trumpet corps, Albrecht our steady man, and Hermann, who the Duke had assigned because he had not travelled much before. I was the only French speaker in our troop, Lord help me.

I had a new mount now, as dear old Jürgen had seen his last long mission. Treatment of horses in the cavalry is harsh; when their service is done and they can no longer be relied upon, they are sent away and seen no more. Hide, bone and glue are their destiny. This could never happen to Jürgen. I petitioned for his release and located stabling a short way outside Schwerin. There I saw to it that he had a field to shamble in, a covered place to rest his bones, and sufficient feed and comfort. Whenever I could find time, I would visit Jürgen, say a few words and offer him a treat. He would see me coming and raise his tired head, always ready for his apple or turnip. He lived a few years longer in this easy retirement. He had never been just a vehicle to ride, a creature to use; he was a companion and I loved him. When he passed, it was the passing of a friend.

The route we planned to follow would take us at least twenty-five days, more likely a month. We calculated on twenty to twenty-five miles a day, but it would depend upon the terrain and the length of our stops along the way. The road to Osnabrück and thence Münster I knew well, but beyond there it was new territory. Köln, Coblenz and Trier lay on our route, and who knew what slowdowns or problems we might face, what with the armies to the north and the general devastation in their wake. We hoped that at some towns along our route the authorities might ask us to play, so each of us brought as many crooks and tuning bits as we could. You never knew what pitch we'd have to play at, assuming other musicians were involved. Of course, such goodwill performances would add to our estimated travel time.

We rode armed. It was all very well to plot a route to avoid open conflicts, but there were still places of lawlessness in the forests along the way, where there were few people and fewer amenities. We carried both swords and pistols, although the latter would be more of a deterrent than a serious weapon. For lightness and comfort we wore no armour, so we were cuirassiers in name only.

Our saddlebags were loaded with letters, small gifts and food. We four trumpeters had our instruments slung on our backs, and Stefan brought a slew of writing materials for his own use, which we would all borrow from him when needed. I intended to write to Elisabeth once we arrived in Paris, when I would have a return address. I was becoming more conscious of how important it was to let her know where I was and what I was doing. I had told her this was a safe mission through peaceful territory and not to worry, but she knew only too well that in these unsettled times there was no such thing.

I was used to long-distance rides of this kind, as was Adolf, who had campaigned earlier in his career, but the others soon began to find it tiresome. There was a rhythm to it; plod, plod, plod all day; eat, drink, sleep; up again, plod, plod, plod. We were a strange troop: two officers and three of the lower ranks. There were times at the beginning when I felt uncomfortable about the level of camaraderie that developed amongst us almost without our realizing it. When I had first travelled with Hartmund Breitkopf, I had felt a disconnection between intimacy and rank, between deference to authority and familiarity during a common task. It was the same here, but I didn't feel at liberty to ask Albrecht or Hermann if they felt the same way. We would break the monotony of the journey with stories of past adventures—embroidered lies I'm sure, most of them—and with the singing of bawdy songs, of which we had an enormous repertoire. For me, to hear my superior officer joining in a canon and roaring out the words of *Leck mich am Arsch* was quite disturbing.[51] Friedemann: I had no idea... On the road divisions melted, so this disjointed feeling lessened as we travelled further, but I knew that such intimacies would have to be crushed when I returned to duty. I hoped the others realized this as well.

It was finally in Köln, perhaps halfway into our journey, that we had occasion to play some music. This doesn't include the many inns along the route whose patrons were either voluntarily or involuntarily regaled with our evening practice. Late one afternoon, 'fresh' from the road, Friedemann and Stefan marched up to the *Rathaus* and boldly presented themselves to the first officer of any importance they could find. The man they accosted in the front hall proved be a high official with the town council, and our brand of German was generally understood. As luck would have it, the *Bürgermeister* of Köln was in office, and when this official presented these two travellers from afar, he was quite keen to hear the rest of us. There would be a civic ceremony the following evening where merchants, church leaders and other dignitaries were to be presented with awards. Would we be interested in working with their trumpet corps in providing some music to herald the proceedings?

So it was we spent a day working with their six trumpeters and thanking God we had brought lots of ancillary plumbing to get our instruments in tune. Truth to tell, they were a dull lot whose bread-and-drippings was simple fanfares in four parts. For a city of the size and wealth of Köln, this surprised us. We more or less assigned ourselves, two to *Principal* and two to *Clarino I* and *II*, and improvised over their scores. The result was quite the improvement, and although I had misgivings about how they might regard us, I need not have worried. Over ale and bread in a tavern before our performance, the town trumpeters were all enthusiasm and support. I suppose they must have thought we were a fresh breeze, like the one that used to sift through the trees at the farm when I was young. We played together, we played well, and we developed an entente that crossed language, religion and boundary. The ale after the performance was even more convivial.

They paid us in *Reichsthaler*, and quite a lot of them too. We split our take five ways, but because we'd done all the work we made Stefan buy our drinks that night.

Chapter Forty-One

In which we learn how hard it will be to make horses dance

*Je veut en sçavoir non seulement ce qui m'est necessaire comme Roy, mais aussi
ce qu'il en faut por atteindre à la perfection de cét exercice…*
I would like to know not only what is necessary for a king, but also
those things one must do to perfect the exercise…
Antoine de Pluvinel

Our journey to Paris continued uneventfully. We had decided to avoid the Spanish Netherlands, so from Köln we followed the east bank of the Rhein upriver as far as Coblenz. We turned up the Moselle, through Trier, bypassing Luxembourg somewhere to the south. We crossed into France north of Lorraine, crossed the Meuse at Verdun, and headed due west for Reims. It all went rather tediously—it would have been more pleasant if the sun had graced us with his presence—until, over a month after we had departed, the twin spires of Notre Dame appeared in the distance. We came down from the east-northeast on a dull, overcast day in August and looked for a place to stay on the north bank of the Seine, a little down river from the Île de la Cité. We found an inn for the night and ate a good supper, thankful to have arrived. The next day we learned the location of the Academie d'Equitation and introduced ourselves at the gate.[52] A servant led us to the office of the Academie's superintendent, a thin ramrod of a man with fine whiskers and an elegant turn of leg.

"Yes, yes, welcome." He bowed quickly to all of us in turn. "René Menusière at your service. I have received a letter from Duke Adolf Friedrich and I will help you in any way I can."

"Thank you, Monsieur Menusière," I replied. "I have to speak for all my colleagues because they have no French. As our Duke Adolf Friedrich may have told you, we have been attempting to perform horse ballets with our squadron of cavalry, and it quickly became apparent that we would need expert guidance."

When I described to him what we had attempted he laughed out loud. "It's a wonder you didn't kill yourselves and your horses as well. Using war horses for this! Mon Dieu! Would you fill a trombone with gunpowder and lead shot? Non! Would you… oh… blow musical notes on the touchhole of a cannon? Non!"

I translated this and they roared with laughter. But I told them not to relay this little criticism to the Duke; he might not find it quite as humorous as we did.

"Please allow me to introduce our riding master, *Rittmeister* Stefan Kulikovski." The two bowed and appraised each other.

"So, you others are trumpeters and horsemen, yes?" I nodded. "Equitation we have here. Music is elsewhere. Let me think... The best documentation is perhaps from the wedding of Henrietta Maria and Charles, Prince of Wales. That was in 1625, and I know my master Pluvinel oversaw that and recorded it meticulously, as was his way."

"Where would we find it? This music?"

"It's with the English court. They keep all their own material."

"The English court?"

"Queen Henrietta Maria is in exile here while Cromwell rules in her son's land. They occupy the Château de Saint-Germain-en-Laye. It's not far. To the west, fifteen miles perhaps."

I knew, of course, that the English had executed their king, had fought a civil war, and that the land was under the thrall of Cromwell as Lord Protector. That the court was here in France was new to me. That we would have to travel further to find what we wanted was daunting.

"Now," continued M. Menusière, "I think your riding master, Monsieur Coulique... is it?... must visit the stables with me and see what we do. Not so much need for language; we'll manage well because it is things he must watch, and pictures he must see. I have a groom who speaks a little German." He thought for a moment with his chin his hand. "You trumpeters should go where the music is. The gate-keeper can point you the way. But first, Herr Hintze, before you go, what was the book your master was reading?"

"Um... Vulson?"

"Ah, yes, Marcus Vulson. Lovely book, beautifully printed, but not much use for what you want. Has he got Pluvinel?"[53]

"No, I don't think so."

"Well, I'm sure we can find a copy here in Paris for Monsieur Coulique to take back with him. Not the early edition; Peyrol did a poor job. Again, lovely pictures. We'll find you a copy of Menou de Charnizay's edition. But for now, we must go to the stables, and you should ride to Saint-Germain-en-Laye. Ask for Jean Savard, the archivist. Monsieur Coulique and I will need a day or perhaps more, so come back tomorrow evening. Bon voyage."

I told Stefan to make his way back to our inn, which was a short walk away, and that we would see him tomorrow evening. I was concerned that he wouldn't be able to find his way around, but he assured me that as food and drink were point, mime and grunt items, it would all be added to the bill, and not to worry so much.

The Chateau of Saint-Germain-en-Laye was a finely built place, surrounded by forest on all sides but the one facing the road, and lying in well-kept grounds. It occurred to me that there might have been a deliberate measure of distance between the exiled English court and the royal establishment of Louis XIV in the centre of Paris. Far enough away to avoid too much visiting, but no so far as to be seen as unmannerly.

We left our horses with a groom, asked for Jean Savard at the gate, and explained our purpose. We were shown to the rear of the premises by backways and passages that were clearly the domain of servants. M. Savard was a tiny, bow-backed man of perhaps seventy years with a twinkle to his eye that reminded me of Hauptmann Schwinn of the Rostock Watch. I pushed the memory back; not here, not now. He showed us into perhaps the messiest room I had ever seen. The floor was cluttered with piles of paper and books, rolls of maps and cartographical instruments, while shelves on all sides held more books, papers, folders, dossiers and envelopes. Among the scattered tables, trestles and chairs there was not a single useful level surface.

"Ah, the music of their Majesties' marriage!" piped Savard when I had explained our mission. "And the plans and routines of the *carrousel?* Oh, it's all here. Quite where…"

"If you can show us the music," I said, "that would be a wonderful beginning."

He strutted round the room a couple of times, darting at a shelf here and there, until he pulled a folder down, batted dust off ineffectually and brought it over to a small table. He had to sweep some papers and a small book onto the floor to make room. I stooped to pick them up but he waved me away.

"Now. Here's some stuff, probably by Henry Le Bailly," said Savard, riffling through the papers. "Never been printed, naturally; last thing he'd want is any suggestion he wrote anything for wind instruments. Let's see… it could match with these, which are the routines for the horses from Pluvinel." More papers emerged. "The marriage was in 1625 so, unlikely as it sounds, it's got to be Le Bailly."[54]

"Why unlikely?"

"Lute and singing, that's Le Bailly's forte. Trumpets! Hah! As I said, last thing he'd put into print." He pulled out more loose leaves of paper. "There are scores for oboes and fifes as well. Any good to you?"

"No. They're using them in the court at Schwerin, but we never had anything but trumpets in the corps. And kettledrums, of course."

"English still use trombones, cornetti, viols, but they're back in the past, and good luck to 'em. We're up-to-date here; everything from Italy."

He pulled down yet more papers from another shelf and piled them onto the table. The pile began to slip, and suddenly the air was full of sailing sheets of music, that settled in a dusty, yellowed snowfall. "Our files are such a God-awful mess. Wish we had someone here to devote his time to setting them right. You may copy anything you wish."

Between Friedemann, Albrecht and me we got all the papers gathered up. Hermann cleared a space on the table and we spread out the sheets that interested us. All of us could read music, so we swiftly sorted through the sheets we found useful and got to work copying, concentrating particularly on the scores with notation for the equestrian movements. I had forgotten that Stefan had our entire supply of writing materials, so we had to borrow quills and ink from M. Savard. The rigmarole necessary to find them was something to see.

"Write down all these things exactly as you see them," cautioned Friedemann. "Then we'll show Stefan what we have. I just hope he learns enough for any of this to be useful."

All the while during our copying the old archivist hopped around, making helpful comments and observations on the court and its function. At one point he showed us the necessary cupboard, which we all used gratefully as the day wore on.

"It's hellish trying to read this stuff," complained Albrecht at one point. "What do you make of this?" I translated for Savard who looked over the piece and offered some advice, sketching out a symbol on a scrap of paper with a stick of charcoal that he'd found somewhere. We knew then that we were in over our heads. It must have been past midday when we had arrived, and now the sun was setting in the smeared, west-facing window. That made us decide we had had enough. We had accumulated a considerable pile of copies, but there was more work for the next day.

"Come," said Savard, "let me show you something of the chateau before you leave through the servants' entrance."

We emerged from a small door beside a grand staircase leading to the upper levels, and were just about to ascend when harsh words in several voices came down to us from above. A dandyish man dressed in finery strode down the stairs, followed by an entourage of three servants with dark brown skins. This was something I had read about: the natives of the Barbary Coast and the slaves of the Grand Turk were said to look like this, but I had imagined those were just sailor's tales. I'm sure we all stared quite rudely when we saw the real things, as it were. The dandy was being pursued by an elderly man yelling unspeakable things at him in English. (I was pleased to add 'whoreson knave' to my vocabulary. All I needed now was an occasion to use it.) The whole ensemble swept past us and left by the wide front door, with the elderly fellow hurrying after with his hand on the hilt of his sword. In the silence after this apparition had passed, a serving man hurried down the stairs, ushered us quickly back through the door with apologies, and closed it firmly behind us.

"My apologies, also," said Jean Savard. "I chose poorly the moment to show you around. Perhaps tomorrow?"

The four of us had worked up quite a thirst by this time, and we needed somewhere to stay the night. Of course, my comrades all looked to me to find a suitable wetting and sleeping place. I knew exactly as much about the environs of Saint-Germain-en-Laye as they did, but at least I could ask directions. M. Savard told me of a couple of places whose repute was not so ill, and where we were less likely than most to get set upon and robbed. Taverns and inns were always my favourite places to practice the lower people's part of any language, and the one we chose in the maze of streets around one side of the chateau was no exception. Five mugs of ale in front of us, moustaches wiped with backs of hands, and sitting back with a long sigh; that was our work. Across from our table was another occupied by a small group of functionaries from the chateau, one of whom I recognized from the afternoon's debacle; he was the serving man who had ushered us away. While my four comrades chatted with each other in German, I swung my stool around and introduced myself in my best French.

"Oh, Germans, eh?" said the familiar man with a smile. "You speak well for a foreigner. You're the ones visiting the archivist, then. Heard you were stealing our secrets on the *carrousel*."

I smiled and assured them of our good intentions. "You serve the English court?"

"Yes. It's a job. It pays my way."

"But tell me," I asked, "if it's not too impertinent of me, what was all that fuss about this afternoon?"

"Oh, God, these bloody English." He looked around quickly as if suspecting an eavesdropper. "They've been camping out in France for Christ knows how long, they treat the chateau as a cross between a prison and a playground, and all they can think of is the Crown of England and how badly they want it back."

"But they were fighting. Almost coming to blows."

"Yes," said another. "You'd think, as Royalists, they'd all be on the same page. Think they'd hang together instead of hang separately. But Ormonde, Clarendon, Digby, forever fighting over something."

"It's a nest of vipers," said my man. "I don't know if there's one single person in that household who agrees with any other."

"Yes," put in a third fellow. "At each other's throats continually. Ruprecht's the worst; he goes around with that troupe of blackamoors at his heels, insulting, dueling and carrying on."

"Ruprecht?"

"Yes, him," replied my man. "That's the Queen's nephew. Trouble maker."[55]

"Swine," said the third man who had joined the conversation. "Ole Henrietta had to stop him fighting Digby, and then he had a go at Percy. Gored him, too. He's a fuckin' pirate. Swaggering around, showing all that side, but they'll be rid of him before long."

"Ye-e-s," replied my man. "Claimed he was back from the Indies or wherever with treasure, and when he was pushed on it, turned out there was none."

"You don't bring in coin to this lot, they turn you into a leper."

"There's a rumour Cromwell's treating with Mazarin to have the whole lot booted out of France. And good riddance to them."

"Oh, it's Charles he wants out of France. Henrietta can stay for all he cares."

"Hope she does. It's our bloody work that'll suffer if they're all turfed out."

So, it seemed a household that could produce the wonderful spectacle we had been transcribing was a squabbling, factional mess. After some more chatting, all the while refining my pronunciation and vocabulary, we finished our drinks, bade the people farewell and went upstairs to our pallets. Before I bedded down, I wrote a long letter to Elisabeth with quill and paper provided by the landlord, and entrusted it to him to post the following day. It irked me that I could not provide her with a return address. Tomorrow we should be back at the Academie d'Equitation.

We returned to the chateau the next morning, called for Jean Savard, and continued the work of the day before. It was boring, tedious and repetitive stuff, made even more so by our uncertainty as to how useful any of it might be. Towards midday we had had more than enough.

"If this doesn't do, I don't know what will," sighed Friedemann and he put down his quill for the last time. "Let's eat a little from our saddlebags and ride back to Paris."

We thanked M. Savard for devoting so much time to us, sure in the knowledge that our visit had given him something to do and was a welcome break from routine. Who knew, he might even make a start on organizing his files a little.

At the foot of the stair, as we were about to leave the chateau, a strange thing happened. A man emerged from a side room, looked me straight in the eye, and then swiftly swung upon his heel and turned away. He was finely dressed with long sandy hair, a pointed beard and clear blue eyes. He had a swagger about him than rang a bell with me, but before I could turn and go after him he had gone.

Stefan was full of himself when we called and collected him from the Academie at the end of the day.

"Christ, guys! Things I learn. Things I got to unlearn. Gimme beer God's sake."

We went back to the inn we had chosen on our first night and had a good supper while talking in generalities. We only got down to business after pouring the first of a few beakers of beer. Stefan had found more that was wrong than right: our posture was wrong, the signals we sent to the horses were fine only for battle, and our process of schooling was unnecessarily brutal and contradictory. He described a technique, new to him, of shoulder-in, and told us that their *volte*, which we were familiar with from practicing the *caracole*, was tighter and much more elegant. Many other aspects of training and riding had opened his eyes. It had been the most intensive and, in some ways humiliating, period of his life. The upshot of all this was that, although he was well versed in schooling horses for war—that was his assignment and that was all he knew—our mounts were completely untrained in these fancy arts.

Things began to get even more complicated when we showed him our transcriptions from the wedding music. In his two days with René Menusière he had learned to interpret some of the symbols and chicken scratches, and we thought that with study something could be worked out. He had been given a copy of Pluvinel; Menusière sent one of his men to a book seller to acquire a copy. The duke would treasure it, and it was hoped that between he and Stefan some routines could be worked out.

In some ways the training of our horses from weapons of war to instruments of peace followed the same path we trumpeters had taken from signaling our calls in battle to playing fine music in church. And in each case there would be much to learn, and quite as much to unlearn. I must say that I felt quite downhearted when I thought of my Duke's aspirations and the unrealistic plans he had. I worried for him.

I lay on my palette that night for some time before sleep, with the image of the man I had seen in the chateau behind my inner eye. I couldn't place him then, but the image of him faded as we began our return journey the next day, and I thought of him no more.

My memory of the road back is rather vague, probably because little happened that was out of the ordinary. We hurried more than we had on the outward leg, and I fretted for Elisabeth and my family, but I was at least confident that she would have received one letter from me. I hoped this would suffice, although she knew of the difficulty of communication while travelling.

One little scene does stay in my mind. The subject of our visit to Paris hadn't arisen much during our journey, but like looking through a little window, I see Friedemann on his horse with the sun behind him, turning to Stefan and voicing something we all knew but were reluctant to air out.

"Tell me, Stefan," he had asked, "will the Duke ever see his horse ballet?"

"I will do my best."

"That's not what I asked you."

Stefan sighed. "With our horses, now, it cannot be done. Can't teach old horse new way. We have new horses, not yet broken. With them, maybe we can school them this way... I don't know. It's the amount of time."

"So, not much hope?"

"There is one other thing." He smiled sideways, almost apologetically. "The horses, yes, we perhaps train them. But you trumpeters? I don't have such hopes."

Friedemann barked a laugh and we rode on in silence.

Gustav Adolph, our Duke's reluctant protégé, finally came of age in 1654 and became Duke of Mecklenburg-Güstrow. His long-suffering mother Eleonore Marie was mightily appeased by his finally coming into his estate, but still teeth-grindingly angry with Adolf Friedrich. It was a wonder that anybody from our court was invited to either his investiture or his rapid marriage to Magdalene Sibylle, who was the daughter of Duke Friedrich III of Holstein-Gottorp. However, invitations came, I suspect mostly so mother could gloat and preen and spear Adolf Friedrich with her eyes. They wanted trumpets to enhance their own corps—a pretty shabby lot if the truth be known—so our whole corps decamped to Güstrow with the ducal party. It was not so far from Rostock, so while I was busy with the ceremonies in Güstrow, Elisabeth made her way there by coach to visit the Schleefs, along with Anja, who was in charge of the three boys and our little daughter. Elisabeth was pregnant again but, she insisted, not so far along that she couldn't travel. I would follow after my duties.

It was there in Güstrow that we finally performed our first equestrian ballet. It says much for either our Duke's confidence in our abilities or his deteriorating mental state, that he decided this was the time and place. It was quite the gamble.

Frankly, it could have been worse.

Stefan Kulikovski had done wonders with the new horses, two-year-old geldings with spirit and verve, yet still schooled, willing and biddable. We were twelve trumpeters, with Wolfgang's pair of small, saddle-mounted kettledrums, and we held ourselves to a set of simple, well rehearsed evolutions. We were in a large, sand-floored yard across one end of which temporary tiers of seats had been erected, and by God's mercy the sun shone warm and bright. The place was packed with spectators, all of whom had been busy eating, and in particular drinking, for several hours.

We started with a walk forward playing a stately march, four trumpets wide and three deep, with the kettledrums at the rear. We reined up, sounded a great fanfare at the rest, then peeled away each side, right and left, trotting back to the rear. We assembled, all in a straight line this time, six trumpets on each side flanking the drums, then Friedemann sounded gallop solo. We echoed his call, all eleven of us, then thundered forward, turning at the last second left and right with a tight *volte* that *Rittmeister* Kulikovski had hammered into us. This manoeuvre had the appearance of the one in our warfare *caracole*, but with a *volte* so much more elegant and refined. Then we formed a circle, moving counter-clockwise at the walk and playing a simple *menuet*, turning then to clockwise and changing to a *sarabande* at the canter. We returned to the four-wide, three-deep configuration and repeated our evolutions. The performance finished with a twelve-wide gallop, reining up and sounding the fanfare.

All the music was laughably simple; it had to be because we had only ever played our cavalry calls from the saddle and even then, not at the trot, let alone the canter. The routines with the horses were quite basic too; there was only so much we could learn, or that Kulikovski with all his rapidly fraying patience could teach us. But very few, if any, in the audience had ever seen such a spectacle before, and the applause was thunderous.

Just seeing the joyful expression on the Duke's face made it all worthwhile.

Chapter Forty-Two

In which a strange man twists my arm to help in an enterprise that
is none of my business

Fürchte den wahren Gott, und halte seine Gebote. Denn das ist des Menschen
ganze Pflicht
Fear God, and keep His commandments: for this is the whole duty
of man

Prediger/Ecclesiastes 12:13

It was not long after my family and I had returned from Rostock that
I was called to an audience with the Duke. He was sitting in his small
retiring room, the intimate space where his missions for me were laid
out.

"How is your English?" he asked before I had even sat on the chair
he waved me to.

Oh, my God, I thought, here I go again; whenever he asks me
about language he's sending me somewhere horrible. "Functional, sir,
but it wants polish. I read a lot, but have had scarcely any opportunity
to speak."

"That will change," he replied, drumming his fingers on the table
beside him. "I have a request that I cannot very well refuse. I don't like
to send you into danger, but it is your duty to serve me."

I could only nod. My mind was suddenly filled with anguish. Yes,
it was my duty to serve—and clearly, I served well—but surely, had I
not served enough? More and more, home life and service life tore me
into pieces. I remember almost the first words I had uttered to Elisabeth
on the subject: 'I am a soldier. I am my own man. When I go into danger,
it is only me. But from now it would all be different'. It was all different;
had been for a long time. And now Elisabeth was eight months pregnant and I would be away for I knew not how long. The three boys
were a rambunctious handful—especially Jürgen, who was not yet
two—and one-year-old Annamaria was beginning to walk, talk and
find danger whenever vigilance slipped. While I knew Anja was a
capable helper, Elisabeth still needed me close and she cherished my
presence around our sons and daughter. And I would miss them all;
so much always happened in my absence. They grew too fast.

And I might not return.

"I see by your expression that this does not sit well with you."

"No, sir. I mean yes, sir." I wiped the expression off my face. "I
am yours to serve in whatever capacity you demand. My duty to you is

exceeded only by my duty to God."

He stared long and hard at me, but I kept my face stoic. "Very well. I wish to introduce you to a man who has urgent business with England." He picked up a small brass bell from the table, and the chimes had hardly rung out when his equerry entered the room. "Go and request Herr Ruprecht to attend me." Ruprecht? That name twitched my memory.

The equerry soon swung the door back and ushered in a man in his middle thirties who was dressed in travelling clothes. A slim, fit man faced me, with hands upon his hips and an intelligent and enquiring look in his eyes. He had full lips, a straight nose and waving brown hair that fell to his shoulders; almost too attractive to be called handsome. His carriage, his poise, every gesture told me that here was a man of power, a man to be reckoned with.

I had seen him before, during my visit to the château of Saint-Germain-en-Laye. He had been striding down the staircase with his blackamoors, yelling insults. I stood and stepped away from my chair while the Duke rose and came forward to greet him.

"Herr Ruprecht," said the Duke, "here is *Stabstrompeter* Hintze, of whom I have spoken."

The man turned to me, appraised me from head to foot, and then essayed a short bow. "Pleased to be of your acquaintance."

"I will leave you now to conduct your business," said the Duke, turning and preceding the equerry, who closed the door behind them.

As soon as the door clicked shut the man broke into a smile. "You will be the one to take my messages to England. Couldn't want a better man."

"I'm sorry, but I don't understand. You say I'm taking messages?" He nodded. "To England?" I couldn't grasp any of this. "How, if I may make so bold as to ask, sir, does this concern me?"

"Your duke tells me you are well versed in the carrying of messages, you know the networks and pitfalls of your trade, and you are an excellent speaker of English."

"But Duke Adolf Friedrich has no concerns with England. We're a small, insignificant duchy nestling under the blanket of Sweden!"

This was my usual line, used to deflect too curious an enquiry. I knew what he wanted, and I knew the Duke had already approved his mission for me, but I was damned if I'd make it easy for him.

"Exactly. What better place to travel from?"

"I'm sorry, sir, but I am confused. Who are you and where do you come from?"

"Who I am is of no concern of yours. Herr Ruprecht is the only name you need to know. I was recently at Saint-Germain-en-Laye, which you yourself visited scarcely a year ago."[56] So he knew of my visit, and what I had heard about him from the servants was neither to his credit nor to my peace of mind.

"But are there not many equally qualified messengers there? It's closer. Why me? Why Mecklenburg-Schwerin, of all places?" I knew, of course, that our obscurity was a desirable attribute, but I had no idea how much he knew.

"Because it is the last place anyone would think of."

"Think of…?"

"A merchant or businessman travelling from Mecklenburg to London would be beyond suspicion."

"Suspicion of what?" I felt as if I was already immersed in the cold Nordsee and sinking fast.

"Carrying messages," he said in a laboured tone, as if to a yokel, "of course." His tone changed suddenly. "What do you know of English politics? Cromwell?"

"Just what I read in the broadsheets, sir. What I hear…"

"You know then that this Cromwell has instituted a so-called Parliament and that he rules with a mailed fist clad in scripture?"

Everybody knew that. I had heard talk of Cromwell's plans for some harmonious Kingdom of God upon Earth, and I had heard of plots and executions. But I still had no idea what business it was of mine.

"Royalism is alive and well," he continued. As if I didn't know; I knew this from my visit to King Charles's exiled court the year before, but I also knew it was dangerous sedition to speak of it in England. "The King awaits in France, and it is a matter of time before he is restored to his rightful throne. And you will play a part."

Frankly, I thought, I would prefer to have my feet up on a log, toasting ends of bread over the fire and dipping them into hog dripping. That's what Anja and Elisabeth had promised me when I came home that night. But it would hardly be politic to say so.

"So, I'm to carry Royalist messages into the heart of Puritan England?"

"Yes. As I said, I couldn't want a better man."

Here we go again, I thought. This Herr Ruprecht was clearly another one of those zealous bastards like Robert Douglas. The ones who either naturally assume you'll sign on to their mad plans, or don't give a damn if you don't want to because they'll use you anyway.

I smiled. "I suppose I can't decline your kind offer due to an unfortunately conflicting engagement?" I thought of that warm, aromatic bread, salty and piquant; a much better prospect in my near future.

He roared with laughter. "There can be nothing that could draw a man like you away from so heroic an enterprise!"

322

"No, sir. It was indeed a jest."

"Now, you've heard of Thurloe, of course. John Thurloe?"[57]

"Well..." Of course, I had heard of John Thurloe, Cromwell's spymaster, the venomous spider at the centre of a web of intrigue, but I hardly wished to admit it. The less I spoke of covert knowledge and activities the more secure I felt. "What of him?"

"You can be open with me," he smiled. "Your Duke has given me *carte blanche.*"

Quite why my Duke had been unable to refuse this request was not clear in my mind, and apparently never would be. My duty was being sorely tried. I recalled the words of Johann Froberger: 'Doesn't your duke use you as a chattel? Wouldn't you rather be free of such servitude?' Now, yes, with all my heart.

"Well then," I replied. "A dangerous man to be confronted with, especially if you happen to be carrying Royalist propaganda."

He nodded. "The package I shall trust you with must not fall into Thurloe's hands. It is to be delivered in London to one Edward Sexby, and to *no other.*[58] He's to be contacted at a tavern called the *Sprig of Rosemary* near a place called Islington."

I knew the place; it was where Breitkopf and I had stayed... then suddenly it struck me; the man I had glimpsed last year in Saint-Germain-en-Laye: Robert Ramsay! I had last seen him all those years and experiences ago, and only now did I put a face to the name. He had known me, yet had clearly not wished any further contact. There were clearly depths here I couldn't plumb, but it seemed wisest to keep this intelligence to myself.

"The sprig of what?" I asked in innocence.

"Rosemary. The Levellers wear a sprig of it in the hatbands. It's for remembrance. You will await Sexby there. The message could compromise many who still toil for our cause in England."

"And, of course, you are quite free to tell me what this package contains?"

"There is a real plot underway to raise a rebellion and assassinate Oliver Cromwell!"

"A *real* plot?"

"You might not have heard of John Gerard? Vowell? No, perhaps not. Executed just this last month on a trumped-up plot on the usurper's life. Pack of lies. Innocent."

It was heartening to think I would be plunged into this den of wolves as an innocent sheep whose one qualification was that of doing his job well. And of living in a subservient little duchy in the middle of nowhere. Throw complacency into the fire.

"How was this so-called plot discovered?"

"A message in plain text was found in Gerard's baggage, purporting to come from Aubrey de Vere, Earl of Oxford. So obvious it had to be planted. Nobody would send such a message without using cipher."[59]

"True. That sounds more than inept. So, why would anybody be fooled?"

"Because they wished to be fooled, of course. The one characteristic of our enemies is the miserable paucity of their imagination. But a plain text message sufficed to convict."

"And so now a real plot is hatched?" If he noticed the ironic lift of my eyebrow, he didn't remark it.

"Yes. And you are to be the courier. Naturally, the messages will be ciphered."

I laughed out loud. "There's no cipher in this world that cannot be broken, given time." And a man can be broken too, although I didn't say it. He was clearly affronted at this; servants don't laugh in the face of their betters. "And besides, your weak link is always the man who has the key."

"You won't have the key."

Yes, I knew exactly where this was going. I knew who did have the key, and the knowledge filled me with dread. Robert Ramsay would carry the key to London, and I would take the encrypted text, each of us lacking the essential information, each of us prone to death under torture, unable to comply to save our lives. But now it was all changed. He had seen me; I had seen him. Everyone breaks, no one takes knowledge to the grave. I would betray him. I knew I would. And he would betray me. Everyone does.

"Oh, I *see*," I continued. "So, there I am stretched out on the rack in Thurloe's cellar saying, 'Please sir, I don't have the key', and he's nodding and saying, 'Oh, all right then, we'll let you go. Sorry about that, old fellow'."

Suddenly he was blazingly angry. He leapt out of the chair and faced me, his face working. "Who are you to speak like that to me? Damn you, you'll do as you're told!"

"Now hear this," I replied. I didn't rise to his anger, but kept my voice level, remained seated and swung one leg over the other. "You have just told me of heads rolling after a failed coup on his Olivership, and you are now inserting my cock into the blacksmith's vice and turning the pin. Who are *you* to speak like that to *me?*"

It was touch and go whether I had pushed him beyond a limit I had yet been unable to define. He stood there in front of me, jaw clenched and hands on hips, for the longest moment and then to my immense relief he smiled and laughed loudly.

"You'll do. Will you do it?"

Of course, I would. Dishonour, probably dismissal would be my fate if I refused. Duke Adolf Friedrich trusted and confided in me, but he would be obliged to dismiss me at any challenge to his authority. No *Hertzog* would tolerate such from a serving man.

"When?"

"As soon as possible. There's a Commonwealth frigate called *President* leaving Hamburg in about a week. The English Ambassador to Sweden is returning home courtesy of the Navy. You will be attached to his entourage."

"Attached? In what capacity?"

"You will be a guest, simply. There will be no duties."

"And this guest will travel under an assumed name." I don't know why, perhaps it was mention of the *Sprig of Rosemary*, but I reverted to an old standby. "I will be Herr David Lausmann, a trader in leather goods."

"Fine. Make sure to be in Hamburg well before the sailing. Take these." And he thrust papers into my hand.

I waited, absolutely still, arms folded, with no expression upon my face, until finally he said: "Thank you."

I left Herr Ruprecht's presence with a heavy heart.

As soon as I arrived home I sat down beside Elisabeth on the bench in the kitchen, held her hand, and told her I was called away again.

"It might be a month or more this time..."

"A month! Oh, not now, Jacob. Not now. Please!"

"I wish it could be otherwise, but the Duke has urgent messages."

"Where to this time, for God's sake?" she cried, pulling her hand away from mine.

"I can't say." Even if I did, I would have to tell her that I would be crossing the sea. To the best of our knowledge, the Dutch and the English were in the middle of a maritime war, and so any seafaring could be highly dangerous. The other dangers I would never, ever, allude to.

"Oh, of course you can't!" she cried, bursting into tears. "You and your duke and all this secret creeping around."

I moved to put my arms around her but she drew away.

"I can't just..." I began. "I have a duty..."

"Oh, duty, duty!" she shouted with tears running down her cheeks. "You have a family too. Do they not have a call on your *duty?*"

No words could come. I had never seen her like this; always she had said nothing, biting her lip and then kissing me God speed and safe return. She knew that in both peace and war I was never far away from danger. Now something had burst.

"I am a soldier…" I began.

"Yes, I know!" she flared back. "And I'm married to one, and I have to sit here and just take it." She broke down into sobbing, pulling a kerchief about her face, and only then was I able to fold my arms around her shoulders and bring her to me.

"I'm sorry," she said after a long, long time, "but this one is so hard. It sits in me like a stone."

"It's not…?"

"No, no. Frau Mencken says all is as well as it could be." Frau Mencken was the wise old dear who advised on women's matters. "It's just heavy and hard and I'm tired."

We sat, with her wrapped in my arms, until she relaxed a little and stole her hands around my waist. I could say nothing, and there was nothing I could say. She knew this, and together we sat, pulled into each other, resonating with each other's thoughts as only those who love can. I never told her anything, but she saw it in my face each time I returned. Years ago, she had seen the fresh burn scars on my arms, and had nodded in resignation with lower lip between her teeth when I had refused to tell her more.

Oh, how I longed to spill all the pent-up secrets and trials and worries. How I longed to unburden my spirit of the source of those scars, the constant pall of my nemesis hanging over me. I could not; if just one secret slipped out, down would come the whole covert edifice.

Finally, she sighed, pulled away and looked me in the eyes.

"When you are away I am a widow and your children are orphans. When you're back I'm a new bride. I cannot keep doing this."

"On my travels I think of you constantly."

"And I of you," she whispered. "I love you more than I can say, and I am filled with fear every time you leave me."

We sat again for some time, warm in each other's warmth.

"Tell me!" She suddenly perked up as though a candle had been kindled in her face. A smile lit up her eyes, tears now dry on her cheeks, and there was my Elisabeth back again. "Tell me a story. Tell me a story of the women in your travels. Tell me of temptation and wanton advances!"

I laughed. Yes, there were temptations and, yes, it was a mighty hard thing to stay true, but I always did. She knew I did.

"Oh, the women I have wooed," I said, "with my dashing cavalry whiskers, with the swish of my sword and a sweep of my feathered hat. They line up for my favours."

She pinched me lightly on the upper arm, a moue of feigned displeasure on her face. "And you fall for them, of course!"

"Nary a one! Why eat umbles and offal, when I can come home to a banquet?"

Another pinch, harder this time.

"No, no, my love. But do let me tell you of one love that I have succumbed to." A troubled wrinkle crossed her brow. "There was a man in Nürnberg who told me with great certainty... great certainty, I tell you, that my true love was my trumpet."

"Ah," she replied with a coy smile, "I wonder sometimes about your lips and tongue on my secret places, and how you play me as you play your music."

"Aye, but then, do I not satisfy you at the point of my sword?"

We would have had at each other then and there had circumstances been different. But, from that point onwards I was sensitive in a clearer way to the privilege of my marriage and the devotion and constancy of my wife. Never again I thought, as I swung up into my saddle the next day, would I take this wonderful woman for granted; her devotion, her strength, her courage.

I felt diminished, yet exhilarated.

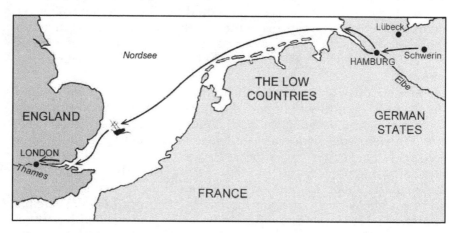

Jacob Hintze's second mission to London aboard Bulstrode Whitelocke's Commonwealth frigate, the President

Chapter Forty-Three

In which I find myself in peril at sea in two ways

*Siehe, die Schiffe, ob sie wohl so groß sind und von starken Winden getrieben
werden, werden sie doch gelenkt mit einem kleinen Ruder, wo der hin will, der
es regiert*
Behold also the ships, which though they be so great, and are
driven of fierce winds, yet are they turned about with a very small
helm, whithersoever the governor listeth

Jakobus/James 3:4

I felt uncomfortable on this mission. All the while I travelled I had
a sense of being watched, or tracked or followed. It was nothing I
could define, but I do believe that the more of this covert business I
was involved in, the more refined my senses became. I cannot explain
it, this nagging sense of unease, nor could I at the time put my finger
on exactly what it was that made me feel that way. But it was there on
the edge of my mind, and it unnerved me. I wondered if the spectre of
Robert Ramsay, glimpsed after all those years, had unbalanced my
senses.

I had ridden to Hamburg, scouted the docks, and eventually found
the *President*, a fourth-rate frigate of the Commonwealth Navy carrying
thirty-eight guns, destined for landfall in England at Gravesend. This
was a three-masted giant compared to the hauk that I had sailed in, it
seemed… oh, such a long time ago. The *President* would sail in the
company of another frigate, the *Elizabeth*, a name that heartened me
and made me think of home. In truth, even though our ship was large,
and I am sure our captain knew his way well enough, I didn't share his
confidence. No matter how often I was out of land sight with nothing
but water below me, I would never be at ease. The sea and me are as
dung is to honey.

Bulstrode Whitelocke, English Ambassador to Sweden, was my
travelling companion. I found the Master of the Ambassador's household as soon as I came aboard, and introduced myself as Herr David
Lausmann, trader in leather goods. He was fretful and busy with getting the entourage sorted out, accommodation assigned, and baggage
stowed. He bowed briefly, welcomed me aboard, and told me I would
take accommodation with the staff, and I would mess with the lower
echelon of the household. My berth on the ship was a favour to a guest,
and he asked me in the gentlest possible way if I would kindly please
keep myself to myself. I was only too happy to; the less I was with

others, the more secure I would feel. I was assigned to a small, cramped space, down several ladders, with one sloping side and a tiny port with a slotted wooden cover. Aides such as me were consigned to cubbyholes just above the waterline. There was a hammock to sleep in but I was tolerably certain its swinging motion would enhance that of the ship and induce instant spewing. I resolved to stay up on deck as much as possible.

We were obliged to stop halfway up the Elbe at a place called Glückstade because the weather out in the open sea was bad, which news hardly helped my peace of mind. The Nordsee, when we got there, was as horrible as I remembered it, but it could have been worse. I learned that the Dutch and English had signed a peace, so I wouldn't have to keep an eye out for the enemy and scuttle below to be ill. Instead, I could just hang over a rail and vomit. Damned either way. Memories of the Danish fleet came back to haunt me. A day into the voyage I was standing, or more accurately leaning, against the ship's rail during a rare calm, scanning the muddy, windswept banks of the Elbe as it widened to the open sea. A fellow passenger hove alongside, a tall, thin man with a flat nose and knowing eyes. My sense of being observed was heightened, and the last thing I wanted was this fellow prying into my business. I resolved that if he wanted to talk, he would have to talk about himself, and not about me.

"Good day to you," he said in German, casting his eyes around as if being watched.

"And a good day to you," I replied.

"I'm a functionary with the Ambassador to Sweden," he said with no bidding from me. "Noticed you the first day."

"I'm just travelling with the party, but not one of them," I replied, trying to be as noncommittal as possible. "What's your role?"

"Paperwork between us and Queen Christina. Well, Oxenstierna, really. He dips her quill for her and shows her where to sign."

"Us...?"

"The Commonwealth. You speak English?"

I nodded. "Papers to do with the Treaty of Alliance?" I asked, switching languages and relishing the chance to practice.

"Yes, indeed. Having the heads signing is the start of these things, not the end y'know. Lots of details."

"It's the old topic of the Sound Dues, eh?"

"Oh, yes. We English must have Baltic access. Lumber. It's mostly big pine for ship's masts and spars. Our tiny island is near stripped."

"So, you've just come from Stockholm?"

"Yes, through Lübeck and then across Holstein. We're on our way home after a winter in Sweden sorting out this treaty. And you?"

"Oh, nothing of any significance. Business in London."

He was quiet for some time, scanning the decks of the ship, and peering out to sea where the *Elizabeth* was keeping station with us. He appeared to have no duties to take him away. Presently he swung his gaze sideways to me, and he nodded slowly as if making an assessment.

"Nothing of any significance, eh? Business in London." He was quiet again for some time, while a fear began to grow in me. He nodded slightly. "I want to know who you really are and what you're doing."

Now my mind was filled with terror; I gripped the rail, hoping my sudden dizziness wasn't obvious as the blood drained from my head. How? How could I have been unmasked so easily? It took a long time before I could compose myself, still my racing heart, and form words.

"I don't know what you're talking about. You... you must be mistaken."

"Ruprecht... Cromwell..." He paused. "Come along. I wasn't born yesterday."

I looked wildly around. On a ship, in the middle of the ocean, nowhere to go, nowhere to hide. My worst nightmares rolled into one: to be defenceless, to be surrounded by horrible cold water, to have someone see right through me and call me for what I was. Still I prevaricated.

"Ruprecht? Cromwell?"

"Yes. Them. Royalist and usurper. Could I ease the burden on your heart by telling you that I'm on your side? Would this information help you to stop eyeing the briny swell as if you wished to jump into it?"

I said nothing. The sideways gaze came again, along with a slow knowing nod. "Y'know," he continued, "Whitelocke doesn't retain me just to do his paperwork. I have a nose for oddness, and I know you are not what you want people to think."

"Who the hell are you?"

"Let's just say that every eminent man has his eyes and ears. You know this for a fact."

I inclined my head dumbly, slowly regaining my poise and realizing that I wasn't quite dead yet. Clearly, he was another one of 'us'; part of that network of watchers and couriers that nobody ever sees, nobody ever acknowledges, but everyone of rank relies upon. But my relief at his assurance was tempered by distrust. I couldn't know if he might be working for the other side and setting a trap. I was truly 'betwixt the de'il and the deep sea', as an old Scottish campaigner with Douglas described such a dilemma.[60] I made up my mind; I would side with Royalist against usurper and let the dice fall where they may. I sighed and shrugged.

"I am carrying messages for... someone at Islington in London." There, it was out and I would live or hang for it. "I have no idea what they contain, and I do not have the key."

"And Ruprecht commissioned you?" I nodded. "Good. I suspected that much."

"So... so what do you want with me?"

"Nothing. I needed to know who you were and what you were doing. My master needs protection, and it's my task to see he gets it. And in Hamburg I nearly failed."

"Hamburg?" I was sounding like an idiot, still not sure what was what.

"Poison. Someone tried to poison him in Hamburg. Something in his beer. An enemy to the Ambassador. An enemy to England."

"Poison? Surely his food and drink are served with care?"

"New man; server our hosts had never seen before. Weren't able to find him afterwards. Wondered if it was you, but you're clear now. Near killed the Ambassador, but they gave him a rattlin' good purgative physic, so all's well."

"What reason would anyone have for trying to do away with Whitelocke?"

"Cromwell, our *Lord Protector*,"—he mouthed the title with great scorn—"sent him away. Sent him to Sweden to get him out of the country. He was being a nuisance with nagging about restoring the King. Open, public disapproval when Cromwell kicked out the Long Parliament. What if they don't want my master back? Cromwell's lot?"

"But surely Cromwell is a man of God! He wouldn't dream of ordering murder."

"So, what happened to his King then?" he asked with a withering scorn that I fully deserved.

"But that was conducted through due process... the law..." I was getting quite out of my depth.

"It was conducted through bullying, lies and subterfuge."

"Look, I'm just a servant on an errand from a small duchy. This is nothing to do with me. But I do know that nobody who cleaves so strongly to God would countenance such a thing."

"Course not. But his servants have no such scruples. Heard of Gerard?"

Of course, I had. Herr Ruprecht had told me of him. The concocted plot, the executions. Now I was really scared of what I had been thrown into. Deliver my bloody messages and run home, that was my plan. I nodded again; yes, I knew of him.

"Keep your eyes open. You and me, we're the same kind of

people. Know what I mean?"

With that we parted company, he to his master's suite of cabins and I to my more humble nook with its sloping side and tiny port. I paced the tiny space, thinking furiously. How could this man have seen right through me? Was I that obvious? And what about Cromwell, and plots? I was as rattled as I think I have ever been. I was at sea.

It got worse; much worse.

The calm sea didn't last. The wind grew steadily stronger as we rounded the point of Cuxhaven and skirted the long chain of islands that lie off the Lowlands. Once we had sailed as far as Texel, we would head for open sea. In a wind of this strength, having plenty of sea room from the lee shore was essential. As I tossed and turned on my paillasse that night, the wind continued to increase, driving the ship to the westward. Because my cabin was to larboard—on the lee side of the ship—the heeling under sail meant my port had to be covered at all times, but seawater still leaked in, soaking my belongings on its way to the bilges. I slept hardly at all, and decided to go up on deck for the rest of the night. I chose a spot in a corner, at the base of the starboard stair that went up to the quarterdeck. From this point onward I was on deck for the greater part of the voyage; the trick of keeping an eye on the horizon helped my stomach. I didn't dare believe my seasickness was abating, but so far I had been nowhere near as afflicted as before and could enjoy my food. From my vantage point I was able to overhear the orders and discussions of our captain and his officers, but I made sure to stay out of their way. By such quite benign eavesdropping I was rapidly improving my comprehension of spoken English.

We were about two days out, somewhere off Norderney or Borkum perhaps, and I was idly watching the crew up in the rigging one morning. One of the men reefing a sail caught my attention. He was a tall, heavily bearded man in ragged clothes, and he made a certain movement, a way of carrying himself, that reminded me of someone. It was a momentary impression but my heightened sense of unease made itself known again. Presently I watched this fellow swing down from the rigging and walk forward, away from me. My heart clutched. Wadegahte! A crew member? Impossible. He disappeared below decks before I could be sure. If it was he—and I knew I would have to make sure—the only reason he was here on this ship was because he was following me. It could not possibly be coincidence. He must still be working under cover, as he was when he tortured me. He must have been assigned to follow me, which meant this whole plot was probably compromised. Or at least his masters, whoever they were, were suspicious. I was committed, at least as far as England, and seriously considered hiding at Gravesend and finding a direct ship home. In my mind this was not cowardice but plain good sense, although I was certain it wouldn't be viewed that way. I decided to hold any decision until landfall.

It was some time after noon before this man returned to his duty in the rigging, and now I was absolutely certain. I looked in his direction as he walked aft, forcing my gaze to pass him with no hint of recognition. I had schooled myself in this all morning, but it was still one of the hardest bits of play-acting I had ever done. There was no doubt. Having followed me to Hamburg, he must have signed on as crew.

I resolved to find the Ambassador's spy; I felt I had to warn him there was an enemy aboard in case he meant harm to Whitelocke as well as to me. I had to wait until the evening meal before I had a reason to sit with the staff and perhaps catch a sight of my friendly spy. I messed with the underlings, but our galley was just across a companionway from where Whitelocke's staff dined, so I hoped to peep in and catch his eye. I finished my stew, bread and small beer quickly, stood up and poked my head in at their door. He was there but his attention was on his food and wine, and upon a lady to his right. I couldn't stand there for long before being shooed away, and I couldn't call his name because I didn't know it. A cabin boy passing through the door with some dishes was the solution. I caught his attention and asked him to take a message to the gentleman I indicated, saying I would be on deck where he had met me before.

"What do you want?" We were standing against the rail in the dark a short time later, with a wind picking up from the east.

"There's a man I know among the crew. He has worked against my master in the past. He means harm to me, and he might mean harm to your master."

"How? Explain."

"He must know about my mission to London. And he must be in the pay of the Lord Protector's henchmen."

"His purpose? To dog your footsteps? Have you lead him to your contact in London?"

"So it appears. But I can't be certain…"

"And I suppose you will be unable to point him out without exposing yourself?"

"I can't. He must not know I suspect him."

"So, an impasse. If there's a threat to my master I must know who this man is. I can't watch two hundred men, damn it."

"Tomorrow. I'll sit in my usual place, there," I pointed aft to the corner at the base of the quarterdeck stair. "You lean on the rail opposite. When I see this man, I will write his position with a lead stick on a small piece of paper, which I will tuck into a corner. He is taller than all the others, dark haired and has a full beard."

"That should suffice. We'll feed him to the fishes. Nice and quiet; a little man-overboard situation and nobody any the wiser."

Once again, I had Joachim Wadegahte's life in my hands, and once again I balked at ridding myself of him. Had I known then what anguish and pain I would suffer as a result, I would quite likely have set aside whatever moral scruples I had, and have done with him. But at that point, standing on the deck of a ship with the fearful cold sea all around me, I couldn't conceive of condemning a man to such a death.

"Just throw him in the brig, for God's sake. Just 'til the end of the voyage. I'll take my chances with him later." I was beginning to regret not keeping Wadegahte's presence to myself.

"Your choice, and more fool you. By the way, next time you want me, my name's Thomas."

We unrolled our plan the next day and it worked flawlessly. We had to wait most of the morning, with Thomas becoming increasingly impatient, before Wadegahte's shift ascended to the yards. He was furthest out on the second yard of the main mast, on the starboard side, and it was child's play to write his position in tiny letters, and quit my post, leaving the directions behind. I watched from a companionway while Thomas picked up the paper, consulted briefly with the boatswain, and then walked rapidly aft. The boatswain looked aloft, blew his whistle and called up. Thomas returned with two stout sailors as Wadegahte descended the ratlines and walked right into their arms, fury and incomprehension written on his face.

I began to kick myself for a fool; I had now alerted the enemy to my knowledge, and even if I hadn't I had gained nothing except time. I should have kept my peace and not got Thomas involved at all. Yet, even though I raged at myself, I knew it wasn't in me to have my enemy killed. In a fair fight, yes, but not through the cowardly hand of another. How this moral sensitivity had survived my war years I couldn't fathom. All around me since the age of sixteen I had seen terrible killing, merciless slaughter and needless death, but still I held to some shred of... decency perhaps?

But, as I said, regret wasn't far in the future.

Several days of strong winds followed by brief calms brought the *President* and the *Elizabeth*, still in eyeshot of each other, to the open sea off Texel. It was on a day late in June with the wind from the north-north west that I heard our captain say the voyage would now be swift and direct. All sails were set and the ship scudded along nicely. But that afternoon a fog came up so thick we could scarcely see the bow-sprit. The captain immediately ordered all sail down except for the main, which he had reefed so he would have some steerage way. He was clearly uncertain how much sea room he had and was taking no chances. I had glimpsed Bulstrode Whitelocke a few times in the previous days, taking the air and offering advice to the captain and the crew, and now he came striding out of a companionway in a great hurry accompanied by several of the gentlemen travelling with him and even his chaplain, Mr. Ingelo. I shrank back out of the way against the rail.

"Captain!" he cried. "Why are you not making way under these conditions? The wind is perfect from the east."

"We're not exactly sure of our position, sir. We haven't shot the sun since morning."

"Where were we then? Do you know?"

"Aye, sir. By dead reckoning our pilot says about sixteen leagues from Texel, twenty-four from Orfordness." Orfordness was the landfall on the English coast that mariners aimed for. "I took down sail and heaved to because 'tis far too hazardous. There are shoals and sandbanks off the Norfolk coast."

"But we are far out from land," replied Whitelocke tersely, "and nowhere near the coast of Norfolk. Lay on sail so we can make good speed. The wind is now rising as the fog clears."

"I agree 'tis a shame not to use such a good wind," said the captain with deference, "but darkness is falling, and needs must."

"I tell you to put on sail!" I could hear the temper in Whitelocke's voice rising.

"Sir," replied the captain, now in a pretty sharp voice, "I do know what I'm doing."

"Order sail put on *now*, damn you!" roared Whitelocke. "And if you don't, I'll find another who will."

The captain stood resolute for a moment then turned reluctantly, and had just begun to give the orders when Whitelocke asked, "What is our depth?" The boatswain swung round and called out to the sounding man to swing his lead. "Eighteen fathom!" called the man after a short while. "Eighteen fathom and steady."

"Well, then!" Whitelocke stormed back down the companionway with his entourage following. I stayed in my place, slipping down to sit with my back against the rail, hearing more than seeing the sailors aloft laying out the sheets. The wind thumped and cracked in the canvas, the ship laid over and lurched forward. I caught a glimpse of the captain's face; he looked sick and afraid.

We sailed on, scudding before the wind in full darkness. I was about to go below and see if sleep would come when the sounding man called, "Fifteen fathom, sir."

"Bring down sail!" yelled the captain. "Leave only the main, and reef it!" Orders were shouted and again there was great activity aloft.

The soundings continued. "Eight fathom!" called the lead-sinker man. "Four fathom."

"Tack! Tack!" yelled the captain. "Come about! Come about!" But he yelled too late.

There was a terrible grinding crunch that flung men to the deck, rattled the timbers of the ship and caused the masts to flex and sway. One sailor fell from the rigging to the planks and cried out in pain. Whitelocke came roaring back onto the deck in a terrible passion.

"Damn you, you bloody fool! You've run us aground!"

"I, sir? I?" shouted the captain. "You ordered sail!"

"You dare bandy words with me! You were supposed to be *navigating!* This is utter negligence. I'll see you…" Whitelocke was interrupted by an eruption from below of gentlemen, ladies, children and servants wailing, yelling and crying. Some of the sailors, too, shouted that all was lost. If anything, the seamen were more terrified because they had a fuller understanding of the danger. The ship shuddered again and ground further into the shoal.

"Fire guns!" commanded the Ambassador. "We must warn the *Elizabeth* and others of our peril. You…" to the master gunner who had come forward "…shot and fire your pieces!"

"But, sir, the guns are not yet unbraced…" he began before Whitelocke cut him off.

"Do. As. I. *Say!*" The master gunner thought to argue again but the Ambassador would have none of it. "Fire your guns or you'll be trussed up and flogged."

The captain came forward flapping his arms but was waved off. The gunners wavered, saw who was master, and did as they were ordered, working under threat of punishment, fear and reluctance in every move. Whitelocke hustled the women, children and servants below. The first concussion showed the error of what he had ordered. The gun, braced up tightly in its crib, had no means of recoil; the entire shock passed to the sides of the ship, shaking her from stem to stern splintering the mainmast and sending the main sheet flapping over the side. I cowered in my corner; I was back in the *Patientia* again, living through the hell of marine gunfire.[61]

"Halt! Halt your fire!" yelled the captain, coming to the fore and asserting his shattered authority. "Unbrace there! Unbrace!"

Seeing what he had done and clearly wishing to hide his face elsewhere, Bulstrode Whitelocke quit the deck, leaving the stunned seamen to make some sort of order out of the mess. The captain followed him below and, even above the sound of wind and waves, heated words could be heard. The boatswain ordered the remaining loaded guns to be unbraced and fired, but no evidence came that any heed was taken of them. The *Elizabeth* would be far astern if her captain had a modicum of sense about him, and would have reefed sail in the fog.

Our captain strode back up to the quarterdeck crying over his shoulder, "There I live and there I shall die!" Then he paused, looked about him and called the boatswain and pilot to him. "See here, I reckon there's a change of wind, and on the rise of the tide we might float her off. But we're in God's hands."

Many of the sailors were in anguish, some throwing themselves down on their knees and praying. They knew only too well that few ships grounded like us in a high wind stood any chance of survival, and few had heard the captain's optimistic comment. There were great lamentations from below decks as well, as the Ambassador's entourage bewailed their fate. I slumped in my corner and thought of death; of all the ways I had evaded my end through gunfire, sword, disease, starvation, freezing, hanging and torture, only to be brought to my Maker by the overweening puffery of some exalted donkey who believed himself born to command. I couldn't imagine why anyone would try to kill the bastard when he seemed so capable of doing it himself.

Amidst all the cries of doom and curses at fate, one of Whitelocke's assistants emerged from the companionway, went up to the quarterdeck and saluted the captain. "Sir, I have instructions from the Ambassador that you are to heave the cannon overboard to lighten the ship."

In spite of the predicament and the closeness of us all to death, the captain barked a laugh. "D'ye hear this?" he called to the boatswain. "This cockscomb wants to throw the cannon over the side!"

"Oh, sir, what a masterly plan! They land in the sandbar right beside the ship and the rising tide rubs our sides to buggery on them."

"Aye." He waved the messenger back. "Get down to your master and tell him no." He turned to the boatswain, who had stepped closer. "I rue the day that popinjay set foot on my ship. I'd be the one to poison him…" Then he spotted me not far off and shut his mouth.

Whitelocke presently reemerged on the deck with his chaplain Mr. Ingelo in tow, strode over to the boatswain—passing the captain as if he were a ship's fitting—and asked him why he had not done as instructed.

"My lord," he replied, "we can but drop the ordnance close to the ship's side where the water is shallow. The cannon will lie against the hull and the working of the tide will grind them against us and spring leaks." He was in a sweat to speak carefully and diplomatically.

I don't know whether Whitelocke actually listened to this good sense and would have heeded it, because at that moment one of the sailors at the fore shouted, "She wags! She wags!"

"Show me! Show me!" cried Whitelocke striding to the fore with almost the entire ship's crew behind him.

"See, see," cried the mariner. "She wags against the sand. She'll lift."

"She wags! She'll lift!" cried many voices.

The wind had definitely turned. The hull creaked and grated, rose majestically and began to float clear. The captain immediately had the boatswain call all hands to action and began getting the ship to rights, setting just enough sail to bring the *President* into deeper water before dropping the anchors. Whitelocke flung himself down upon his knees, dragging Ingelo with him, and praised God in a braying voice for interceding and saving his soul.[62]

I suspect that the captain, boatswain and pilot were praising a canny knowledge of the sea for their deliverance, but reserving some praise for God as well, whose ways we cannot fathom. Whether it was by the help of God or by the captain of the *President*, Death once more kept his scythe on his shoulder, preserving me for I knew not what.

Out of the cauldron, into the fire.

Chapter Forty-Four

In which I return to England and nearly drown on dry land

Wer aber von dem Wasser trinkt, das ich ihm geben werde, wird niemals mehr
Durst haben
But whosoever drinketh of the water that I shall give him shall
never thirst

Johannes/John 4:14

We limped into Gravesend under whatever sail it had been possible to jury rig. On landing, I received a horrible shock, another setback to add to the experiences of this mission. I had asked Thomas to give explicit instructions that Wadegahte be held back aboard the ship in order that I could hurry to my rendezvous ahead of him. As he was being held prisoner in the brig, this should have been a simple task. Thomas spotted me emerging from the companionway lugging my saddlebags and hurried over.

"Sorry. Bad news. The boatswain let the man out of the brig, but on mustering the crew before shore leave, he saw he'd slipped away."

"Slipped away?"

"Yes. Over the side perhaps, or like a rat down a hawser. Thought I'd better warn you."

Now my plan to go straight back home became more than appealing. How can you possibly continue if you have no idea where he is or what he is doing, observed the devil on my left shoulder. But I knew that to return empty handed would be the end of me. There was nothing I could do but thank Thomas for his help, make my goodbyes to Whitelocke's chief of staff, and step down the plank to the quay. My time at sea asserted itself and I weaved landsick into the little town looking for a place to rent a horse. My eyes were about me the whole time, but I didn't know if I was being watched. Once in amongst a few buildings, I thought of a ruse that might just throw Wadegahte off my trail. I was sure there would be a ferry across the Thames to Tilbury on the Essex side, so I entered the first tavern I found and asked about it. The landlord showed me how to make my way to Milton-next-Gravesend where a boat was made available by the lord of the locale. Doubling back a few times, sneaking along hedgerows, and generally playing the undercover agent to the hilt, I found a wooden jetty jutting from a shelf of grey mud. Tied up was a small sailing boat called a hoey with an ancient mariner at the tiller, who took me on board along with a reeking peasant and two sheep.

The last thing I desired was to be back on the water again, but it was a short journey under sail, and well worth the inconvenience if the ruse worked. Tilbury was, if anything, more destitute and in want of comforts than Gravesend, but I found an inn where I could acquire a horse, and I was soon on the first leg of my thirty-mile ride to London. By this time it was well past noon, so I rode west as far as I could before the light failed, and found a place slightly off the road to halt and rest until morning. The closer I rode to London, the more certain I became that I had evaded my enemy. I didn't know then how clever he had been, and foolishly had not asked the captain of the hoey if he had taken other passengers over the river that day. I therefore had no idea that my move had been anticipated and that I was riding into a trap; a trap of my own stupid making. There is only one road into London from the east and it would have been child's play to keep an eye out for a lone rider, to let him pass and then gallop across country and pass the message to have him intercepted. My assumption that Wadegahte was a lone wolf soon cost me dearly. He was one cog in a great mill, and I was the corn between the stones.

In a narrow way between fences, in sight of St. Paul's Cathedral on its hill, I was waylaid by two helmeted horsemen dressed in breast-plates over black surcoats, with grey hose and long boots. Each had a pistol trained at my heart. I turned my horse's head in reflex, only to encounter the other three troopers behind me, also with their guns out and ready to use. I spurred up and made an effort to escape, but they hemmed me in, not using their guns but jostling my horse until I was pinned immovable against a fence. They weren't out to kill me; they wanted me alive. My heart turned to lead. I was a dead man, and I knew my death would not be swift. They took away my sword, lashed my hands behind my back and my ankles beneath the horse, and escorted me into London. At times like this my loved ones have always appeared in my mind's eye. I recalled the set-to Elisabeth and I had had, the little one growing within her, and my other little sweethearts without their father, and my heart cried out.

It was a disgusting place they threw me into, a dank cellar some-where near the White Chapel. There I lay for more than a day, in half-darkness at best, while doubtless they rifled through my saddlebags, tore open my messages and tried to decode the cipher. I knew it was only a matter of time before they hauled me out and started asking questions. And now I was really assailed with doubts: what allegiance did I have for any of these creatures, Royalist or Commonwealth? None. None of this was any of my business whatsoever, and I had only been landed here by happenstance. I was an accessory; I had no interest in this affair, so why didn't I open up, tell them Ramsay had the key, and have them speed me on my way home as a cooperative third party? It was all so simple there in the dark on that stinking cold floor.

Nothing is so simple. 'Oh, all right then, we'll let you go. Sorry about that, old fellow'. That's what I had said to Herr Ruprecht, clearly seeing my destiny and knowing how laughable any kind of clemency might be. Speed me on my way? Oh yes, when pigs give birth to apples. I was dead whether I talked or held my peace. But what use to hold my peace only to prolong the time of my death, and the agony of it? But there were those who would die because of me. Ramsay first. Then this man Edward Sexby, the recipient of my messages, would be next. I would condemn these souls to death to ease my own passing. I had people's very lives in my hands. Aboard ship I had Wadegahte's life in my hands, and what had I done? Spared the bastard. Again. So, would I spare these souls, people I had never met or hardly knew, whose cause was not mine? Who had done me no harm?

You get some hard decisions to make while lying in the dark on cold flagstones, foul with your own excrement.

"Who was to receive your messages?" These were the first words the torturer asked me after he and an assistant had tied me to a table by my wrists and ankles. "Names please."

I said nothing. I could only make out his outline against the dim light from a sconce he had lit on the wall behind him. No features, no face. A shadow across my sight.

He leaned over me, breath foul in my nose. "You will break. You will tell us. We have time. You have not."

I knew then I was going to keep silent. I saw my loved ones in the miniature picture frame behind my eyes, knew I would never see them again in this world, and decided I would honour them by going out in strength, not in weakness.

He didn't begin to torture me then. They left me lashed to the table to contemplate what might be done to me which, in the hours that followed, was almost as painful as pain itself. I heard a bell in some far place sounding the hours, and I occupied my mind with counting in my head to predict when the next chime would sound. This was better than thought. Only when his flickering candle returned to light the room, and he had lit the fitful sconce on the wall, did he begin. He had brought a great oaf with him, a dull figure that blocked the light and appeared as a silhouette. I was expecting and anticipating pain by cutting, stretching or burning. It was much worse.

He set an earthenware jug down on a shelf beside the table. He motioned his assistant over while he unhooked a large copper funnel from a rack on the wall, the sort you would use to pour ale into a cask. The oaf forced my jaws open, shoving a stick of wood between them. I was filled with a terrible fear for my lips and teeth with his brutal squeezing and pinching. My torturer then jammed the funnel into my mouth and poured water from the jug. At once I was in the Nordsee, my other horror of horrors, and struggling to breathe. Terror crowded on me as I swallowed as much as I could, choking and gasping as I felt the water going to my lungs, knowing he would drown me. Timing to a nicety, he ceased pouring, pulled out the funnel and left me coughing, heaving and vomiting water upwards, only to have it descend and enter my mouth again. I strained against the bonds, rasping, belching and shaking my head like a dog while a red haze came down over my eyes.

"This just for a start," he said quietly at my ear once my heaving and panting had slowed. "Wait now. Think." He extinguished the sconce and they left me in the dark.

They came again. Twice, three, four times. I lost count. Each time, as the funnel crashed into my teeth, I would resist in terror for my teeth and lips, shaking my head and champing my jaws until I was forced to drink or drown. My belly bloated as I gulped madly, knowing that as soon as I stopped the water would wash into my lungs. Just on the verge of drowning, just on the edge of passing out, he would withdraw the spout and I would gasp and vomit, choking and retching, spurting through nostrils and mouth. Acid from my stomach mingled with spewed water. My throat and the insides of my nose were raw, almost bleeding, my lungs were on fire and my stomach ached and clenched. There was a jagged scrape across my tongue where the edge of a broken tooth had been dragged by the spout of the funnel, and my lips were swollen and bruised.

And each time the same question: "Who was to receive your messages? Names, please."

At some point he brought his awful breath close to my ear yet again. "Tell me," he asked in a tone that a lecturer upon Aristotle might use in questioning a Gymnasium student upon some obscure point of logic, "just how long do you think this cycle can continue before I hear what I wish to hear?"

I had no answer and I wasn't even sure my voice would ever work again. He was now close to killing me.

They repeated the cycle.

Again, as I lay shivering in filth and despair, I questioned my God and my faith as I had done so often since that day in the chapel when I had realized my path in life had been won through the death of others. If this was my destiny, if I had come to this awful place—to this miserable and ignominious end—by God's direction, why would I be made to suffer so, and to die? Or was I now seeing punishment for the sin of selfishness?

"You are an extremely resistant and stubborn man!"

I had been untied from my table, flung to the floor and kicked upright, then dragged up flights of stairs to a bare room with a few plain chairs and one table. There I stood, scarcely able to stay upright, in front of a seated man with long, golden hair flowing to his shoulders and a bright, inquisitive eye.

"But," he continued, "you would be dead now if you had not resisted."

He stood in a swish of fine coat and a flash of lace at the wrist, pulled a chair towards me and motioned me to sit.

"Drink," he said, pouring wine from a jug into two fine glasses.

I drank greedily, the wine stinging and wakening my torn throat, and held out the glass for more. While he poured again he looked me over speculatively and smiled. I knew only too well what game they were playing; this was the softening, the appeal to my better senses, the grease on the scotch of my resistance. He would talk to me so nicely, assure me of my imminent freedom, make promises. And if I failed to fall for the bait, I would be back downstairs again. He knew —they knew—how easy it is for the prisoner to fall in love with his captors. Oldest trick in the book. I felt insulted they would take me for such a gullible fool.

"Thurloe," I croaked. "John Thurloe. You'll be in Hell before I answer any of your questions."

He smiled widely. "You flatter me, sir. I am a mere assistant to the Secretary of State, who has far too many duties occupying his time to spend it in interrogation. Samuel Morland at your service."[63]

"Well, whoever you are, you can burn!"

He sipped his wine, set the glass carefully upon the table beside him, and steepled his fingers. "You refused to answer one simple question: Who was to receive your messages? That was all that was asked of you."

"And you'll never hear the answer from me. You or that monster downstairs."

"But you'll hear it from me. Edward Sexby."

Now I was at sea again. If they knew the name, why all the torture? What game was this I had been caught up in? He saw my confusion and smiled.

"You were to meet Edward Sexby," he continued smoothly, "at the *Sprig of Rosemary* in Islington and you were to pass along to him ciphered messages which contain details of an uprising against the Lord Protector, together with the names of many of the participants."

I was lost, utterly lost. Either they had broken the codes of the messages or Robert Ramsay had yielded the ciphers. He smiled again and upended the jug into both our glasses.

"I am playing with you, with your confusion. Let me lay things out for you. Firstly," enumerating with his fingers, "you were followed, somewhat ineptly, and led into a trap. Your mission was known by us from its inception, but we were slow to realize this. Secondly, on Thurloe's orders, that oaf downstairs tried to extract information from you in the most barbarous and inefficient manner. It is extremely fortunate that I heard of his work upon you and had it stopped. Also fortunate that I had extracted the papers from your scrip. And finally, the man carrying the key to the ciphers is in our hands."

Yes, Ramsay was taken. They knew everything. This whole stupid mission was a complete disaster from start to finish. It had destroyed the conspirators, and it had killed me. All for nothing. To have died in a noble cause, yes. To have died for this stupidity and waste? I cried in my heart for the misery and sordidness of it all.

"Still I play with you. Listen, you believe you have fallen into the hands of John Thurloe and that your mission is compromised and that you are as good as dead. This is not true. In fact, you are safe with me."

Again, he was playing the kind jailer, assuring me all was well, but I could not fathom what more he wanted from me. I was wrung dry. I just stared into his face.

"Has any enemy ever asked you, in your long career of carrying secrets and poking your nose into other people's business, if you would work for him as well as for your master? Have you ever been asked to play one side against the other? Ever been turned?"

What was this? I wasn't sure if I was hearing right. The wine had come like a battering ram at my head, a head already filled with fresh horrors of drowning, pain and death. Here was Thurloe's right-hand man talking of dissention and treachery, and it could not have been a ruse; he had extracted all he was going to get and more. Was I truly sitting in front of a self-confessed traitor? I was dizzy with these thoughts, but the better part of my mind told me to be careful.

"Temptation, yes," I whispered in all the voice I had. "But to fall, never. I serve my master and no other."

"I could wish I had the same master." He paused frowning, considering, I now guessed, how much he felt he could tell me. He came to a decision. "You know, of course, that this realm is under the thrall of a monstrous tyranny. That no man in high office knows any longer who his friends are. We supported reform, we supported change. We were ruled by a royal tyrant who took his cue from divine right. We removed a sovereign. We cut his head off rejoicing, in front of a baying mob. We now know that we have exchanged one tyranny for another much worse."

"So you work behind Thurloe's back?" He inclined his head. I was appalled that I had found my way into this card game of intrigue where the stakes were death. "You must be mad."

"Of course I am! We all are. But the very survival of this realm rests upon what we do here. He plots the murder of another king, to make his rule absolute."

"And the key to the ciphers?" I had to ask, but dared not mention Ramsay by name. But if I had survived, so must he. "How was it done so quickly?"

He gave me a long, steady look, then smiled widely. "Well, we could have broken them in time. Our man Wallis can crack anything.[64] But in this case 'twas hardly necessary." He smiled again. "Sergeant Robert Ramsay sends you his best wishes and condolences for the loss of your master, who was his good friend."

"So, he was…"

"Of course. One of our best. He's now on his way back to France. King's man through and through."

My relief was mingled with a new fear at my own predicament. I had stepped away from almost certain death down in that cellar and now I suddenly saw myself implicated in plots that were none of my business; being dragged into a new threat of death when a little sprig of freedom had been offered me.

"I have done what I was supposed to do!" I cried, pain surging up in my mouth and throat. "I'm not a party to any of this…"

"No, no, you are not," he cut in. "Of course you are not. You must leave, and we must find you passage." He paused. "But first wait. When did you last eat?"

At the mention of food my ravaged, empty stomach, my rasping throat and damaged mouth, all rose in a clamour, pain tore at me and I fell sideways off the chair into blankness. It was less than an hour, I was sure, before I found myself lying on a couch with my head propped up on a cushion. Someone had cleaned me and dressed me in a long linen shift. Morland sat beside me, saw that I was awake, and offered me water from a beaker. I sipped, slopping some, but feeling the coolness spreading through me.

"Can you sit? There's a little cheese here, and very soft bread if you can manage it."

I pushed myself up on my elbows and swung my legs to the floor. The food was good, although chewing and swallowing were painful.

My sore tongue played with the broken end of a side tooth and my lips felt huge and cumbersome. I finished the bread and cheese and he brought me more. I seemed to be emerging from of a long, dark passage.

"I owe you more explanation," he began after I had chewed the last morsel and finished a cup of water. "Yes, we work in secret and there are many of us. This present administration is a seething mass of plots and intrigues. I must confess, I followed this usurper when he first assumed the authority to lead, when he led his army in opposition to King Charles. Ramsay and I argued long and hard over this. Though he acknowledged his sovereign's folly, he cleaved to him when others did not. Why, even when our sovereign was executed, and his Queen and children sent into exile, I still supported Cromwell. Even then. But a line is drawn when our Protector wields absolute power, when he primes his son to succeed him, when that son would wish to ensure his promised throne by plotting to assassinate the Crown Prince on foreign soil."

"Why are you telling me all this?" I was such a small tool in these affairs and I simply did not want to hear these seditious words. "You have put me in mortal danger."

"Yes. How do I know that by dragging you out of that cellar I haven't opened Pandora's Box? But no, you are one of ours."

"Just let me go... home."

"You will. You'll leave here as a dead body... No, no, no," he threw up his arms with a laugh as I struggled out of the chair and came at him. "Calm yourself. Sit down. Please." I subsided with my heart pounding. "Subterfuge. Here's how it plays out: I hauled you up here to see what intelligence I could extract from you through guile, but you succumbed to your injuries. Your body will be conveyed downstairs in a box and buried in a pauper's plot in Spitalfields. Thurloe will know only that we failed in our interrogation, that you died under questioning, and that you had destroyed the messages you were carrying."

"And he will believe this?"

He shrugged. "He has no evidence to gainsay. Meanwhile, the messages and the key have been delivered to Sexby; your mission was a success."

"And I leave here in a *box?*"

"Not an infrequent occurrence, particularly from the cellars of this building. Although the occupants are almost always beyond caring."

I began to feel weak again as the food in my stomach and the knowledge of success in my head made my senses swim. Too much had happened to me, body and soul, and I believe in these circumstances the heart itself decides to close its doors to the world.

Once again I awoke on the couch, but this time a night had passed and morning light was streaming into the window with the clamour of steeple bells on its skirts. I sat up feeling battered but functional, found a necessary cupboard and then encountered my clothes, clean and neatly laid out over the back of a chair. As I was dressing quickly, Morland came into the room carrying a tray of food and drink.

"You, sir, live under a lucky star," he observed as he poured water.

"I don't hold with stars and such manifestations," I replied. "I believe my God has put me here for some purpose, and it is by His hand that I live or die." And at this point, and forward, I began truly to believe it was so; God's guidance was reinstated and I ceased to question the why and wherefore.

"Well, God has decreed that you will live," he said as he placed my cup back on the tray.

"And my lips, and at least my front teeth are still intact."

"Yes. Trumpeter, of course. Now, have you pissed and shitten already? I ask only because it is time to enclose you in a box so as to get you downstairs and off to Spitalfields."

"Yes, I'm ready. And I thank you, sir, from the bottom of my heart for rescuing me."

"Oh," he smiled, "I thought it was your God who had done all the work. Well, I don't mind sharing some of the credit with Him. Along with Ramsay, who has held you in his heart since he met you as a callow boy."

"Tell me one thing," I asked. "What do you know about this man who was following me?"

"Very little. His name's Wendingate, he's German, and he's one small bubo in the armpit of Thurloe's pustulent network. He has been employed by him... us... for a number of years. That's all I can tell you."

"Us?"

"We use him, and others like him, when we need. He's for sale; his services are for hire to whomever wishes them. He doesn't have your... sense of duty."

"That's all I needed to know. Show me this damned box!"

He led me to a back room where a rough wooden box lay open on the floor with its lid beside it. I climbed in and lay down, having almost no room to move, what with the sides pressing my shoulders and my head and feet pressed from above and below. Morland smiled, bade me bon voyage, and slid the lid into place. Mercifully, he didn't nail the box shut but secured the lid around with rope. It was quite a journey being carried down the stairs at a steep angle, the workmen grunting and swearing continually (more choice words to add to my vocabulary) out into the open and then thrust onto a cart. We squeaked and swayed and rumbled for perhaps half an hour, and then I felt my coffin taken down and placed in stillness. I waited. Horrors went through my mind. What if he lied? What if, in the next few minutes, I was to hear the first of many shovelfuls of earth dashed onto my box? I began to panic, to struggle as much as I could, but I dared not cry out.

By God's mercy the lid was suddenly off and light splashed in. A large workman gave me a hand out of the box, passed me the saddle-bags and sword I thought I had lost for good, took me through a street door and pointed to a ship. I was at the docks and the Thames oiled past beyond the hulls and rigging.

It was a long and tedious journey from Shadwell Dock across the Nordsee to Hamburg. How many times I lusted for quill and paper so I could write to Elisabeth and tell her all was well. But any letter would have to wait until we docked, and then no postal rider would be able to outpace me. So, once again, my dearest would know nothing of me until I burst in at the door.

And so it happened. After we had held each other close, each chin to each shoulder, she pulled back, looked deep into my eyes and saw the soul weariness and the vestiges of trial and pain. No words needed to be said, not even when we kissed deeply and she discovered with her tongue the sharp broken edge of a tooth.

Not even then.

Chapter Forty-Five

In which family relations take a new course, and I play the part of a
classical hero

Haec ait Horatius: Decrevit quam si superi, solus ego de ponte
Thus said Horatius: 'If the gods decree it, I will go to the bridge
alone'

Livy (Titus Livius)

I held our Jacob in my arms and looked into the blue depths of his
eyes. I saw me in him; saw me in all innocence before all the fear and
strife and bloodshed. But reflected there I also saw me before the
wonder of music, the wonder of the love of a woman, the beauty of a
life fulfilled. Those eyes redressed the balance; he lived, and everything
that had been lived before him led up to him, and was as it should be.

Jacob's birth, and the birth of our Clara who came the next summer, signaled a time of peace for me and my family. I was away a
number of times on missions, but not one of them had any danger, or
at least danger I would express at home. Of course, in those days every
time you left a city to travel you had the potential to come to harm,
but none came my way. Routine missions with open letters, gifts and
orders for the acquisition of books were a welcome change from
disguise, dissimulation and deceit. Also, I was able more frequently to
buy books for Elisabeth, whose reading was wide ranging and quite a
bit more intellectual than mine.

There was one homecoming more memorable than most. When I
started this life history of mine, I swore I would tell everything. I'll be
dead and gone before anyone reads it anyway, and I'm sure the living
will forgive my bluntness and honesty. This is a prelude to the reason
why Elisabeth and I have six children, and no more. And why she isn't
worn out with making them. I had just returned from a short visit to
Schwerin, entered the door to our sitting room and found Elisabeth
happy to see me but most forlorn.

"I'm so glad you're back. There are times when I miss you more
than others."

"What's the problem?" I held her in my arms. She rested her head
on my shoulder and looked up. I noted the little crow's feet around
her eyes, the silver now in her hair, and the fine wrinkles in the skin of
her cheek. "Tell me."

"I've been sitting with Hannah Derbfuss. She delivered a still child yesterday, and now she has the childbed fever. She's tired out with it. I don't know what else that useless husband of hers does except lie upon her. Eleven children, four of them dead… well, five now… and she's near to death as well. It's too much."

She cried gently while I held her. There was nothing I could say. Presently she looked up again, and I took my finger to her cheeks and wiped the tears aside.

"She took madder, savin, laurel—Frau Mencken advised it—but it was all useless. She is *dying* because he makes babies on her!"

I knew exactly what was coming. A long silence ensued.

"Jacob," she whispered. "I don't want to lie with you anymore." She felt me tense slightly even though I had primed myself not to. "No, no. I want you beside me always, but not in me. I don't want to end up like Hannah Derbfuss." And she wept quietly again.

What could I say? Nothing. Yet. It was the least I could do to hold her tenderly in my arms and gently stroke her hair. We stood like this for some time in a close stillness, while the bustle of the street resounded from below the window.

"I'll take you in my hand, of course," she continued from the muffled direction of my shoulder, "but I can't have your seed in me."

Well, I'd had a good long ride and no complaints. After all, this was just a reorganization of battle formation; merely a question of learning new manoeuvres.

"You just tell me what you want, my love; that's all that matters. And it's no cause for tears."

She looked up at me. "You've given me six wonderful children. Who could want anything better?"

I smiled. "Well, we old cavalrymen are pretty adaptable, y'know. Instead of riding my mount, I shall just jog along beside her stirrup."

She boxed me gently about the ears and I saw again that smile I loved so well.

Anyway, that's more than enough on that subject. It is only to raise the plight of women like Frau Derbfuss, who were reared among the farms and hamlets of our countryside, and who came to the city out of wartime necessity. They have an overruling duty to their husbands, or so the husbands understand. But Elisabeth is lettered, educated; she is her own person, not to do with as I please, and never has been. She is nobody's person but her own.

Along with peace at home and the joys of watching our family growing up, was the great satisfaction of trumpet work at court. Ceremonial playing had been set into a pattern for as long as I had played with the corps, and nothing ever changed in cavalry signals, but in the Duke's ambitious (but mostly overly so) horse ballets and in music for the chapel, lots of satisfaction was there to be had. My relationship with the members of our *Kameradschaft* tightened and broadened, with the exception of old Wilhelm who was a curmudgeon to the last. He finally had enough of the miseries, dissatisfactions and trials of this life and was found one morning cold in his bed, peacefully in the arms of Christ. There was a small funeral for him—he had no known relatives —and afterwards we blew our chops off in a private celebration for him, but more, I think, as a celebration of the fact that we were still here.

Friedemann had taken on an apprentice a couple of years previously; Reinhardt, a young lad with powerful equipment but slender self-control, and had modelled him into a fine addition to our corps. Now, on his admission to the *Kameradschaft*, how strange it was to stand waiting in our practice room, trumpets at the ready and Wolfgang with his sticks poised, until Reinhardt entered the room rigged out in his new finery. I saw me in him as we serenaded him mightily. The great wheel turns.

It may have been a relatively peaceful time in my life, and in Mecklenburg in general, for those few years following the signing of the Peace—aside from the usual domestic issues that kept the troops alert and on patrol—but things had been far from stable further east. I was called with some urgency to the audience room, the larger meeting chamber, in the summer of 1657, and found a large group of courtiers and military men already seated at a solid table, my cavalry commander Helmut Weitz among them. The Duke's chair had been pulled up to the head of the table.

"...so Karl Gustav's bogged down and looking for a way out," an officer was saying as I entered. "He's taken the Danes' attack as an excuse to turn back."

"Aye," said another, "he went east for venison and ended up with tripes."

"He didn't even try attacking Denmark through Scania, though. Too well defended, and he didn't have the shipping for it."

"True," said the Duke. "So now the Swedes must march through Mecklenburg from Western Pomerania as quickly as possible. That's the intelligence we have?"

"Yes, sir," replied Weitz at his side. "They have already marched from Bydgoszcz."

What brought this all about, as far as I understand, had started in 1655 with King Karl Gustav of Sweden—or Karl X Gustav as he liked to style himself, as if there were nine others before him—opening territorial warfare with Poland. He had succeeded Queen Christina, his cousin, in 1654 when she had turned Roman Catholic and abdicated. He was actually intent on marrying her, but she would have none of it, although she had apparently promised him the crown anyway. Rumour had it she abhorred the very idea of sexual union, especially with him, but having half promised him a share of her bed, she gave him her kingdom instead. Not a bad deal; there's no accounting for women stricken with the Papist plague. Whatever the case, Axel Oxenstierna —who pretty well ran Sweden while she played the harpsichord and fumbled her beads—was furious. Even though he rallied the *Riksrådet*, their Privy Council, against her she was adamant.

It wasn't long before Karl Gustav, as belligerent a warmonger as ever drew on hose, invaded the Polish-Lithuanian Commonwealth, ransacking, conquering and sending the Polish King Casimir scuttling off into exile with the Habsburgs. What had precipitated this emergency meeting of ours was the news that Karl Gustav had turned back from Poland; military setbacks, the return of Casimir, and a couple of forced treaties had made him look for an excuse to call it all off. Well, look at this! As soon as Sweden's back was turned, as it were, Friedrich III of Denmark decided to declare war. He had never been happy with the Treaty of Brömsebro—and the whole of Denmark with him—and he was another of those warmongering bastards anyway, so now he had decided to chance his luck.

All of this would have had nothing to do with us, except that Karl Gustav's retaliation involved rushing back through Pomerania and attacking Jutland. Danish Scania was too well defended for a direct assault across the Ostsee, while Torstensson had shown how easily Jutland could be taken. Of course, between Karl Gustav and his objective was little Mecklenburg, just trying to mind its own business.

Duke Adolf Friedrich was most disturbed by this turn of events; he knew only too well the devastation that over ten thousand fast-moving troops could cause, and he wanted none of it.

"He has marched already?" His voice rose, trembling. "Weitz, how far can he march in a day?"

"Eighteen miles? Twenty if he's lucky. Depends on the terrain..."

"So there is still time to intercept them!"

"Intercept...?" There were blank faces around the table.

"Armies have marched through Mecklenburg uninvited in times of war," shouted the Duke in a cracked voice, "but they will not do so in times of peace! Enough of the Swedes pissing in our faces! They'll not pass through *my* realm without they pay compensation. They'll wipe their boots before they enter *my* door!"

I felt great sympathy for my Duke. He had been unwell lately, and

I was frightened by the choler rising in his face. He trembled, his hands shook, and beneath the anger there was a new querulousness about him. I, like the others at the table, thought he had taken leave of his senses.

"But sire," said another of his military advisers, hitting the nail on the head, "Karl Gustav has nearly ten thousand horse and close to three thousand foot. How can we possibly stop them?"

"They will not force their way. We are allies, we are at peace, they will negotiate." He scanned the faces of the assembly and found much doubt and no agreement there.

"If they are desperate," observed Weitz, breaking a silence, "they may well violate the entente, such as it is. And if they do, we cannot muster one tenth their number. They can crush us with hardly a pause."

"We do not *stop* them," he quavered. "We do not even *delay* them. We give them free passage, but we demand compensation and we resist their advance until it is paid. And they dare not delay. They *must* move, and move fast, before Denmark realizes what is happening. Every day they fail to move is a day wasted. They will pay."

"But how would our... forgive me for saying this, sir... our modest forces delay them?"

"We choose our place. Have you not read your Livy? Have you not heard the story of Horatius and the Bridge?"

Oh, shit, thinks I, leaning against the doorjamb; I know exactly what's coming. That's why I'm the only serving man of lower rank in the bloody room.

"Get me maps," cried the Duke. "Where is Rehnskiöld?" Gert Rehnskiöld had retired from the Duke's employ a number of years before this and, I believe, was now dead. His replacement, whose name escapes me, stepped forward and unrolled a large map onto the table. "Here now..." said the Duke with his finger on Pomerania. "They've left Bydgoszcz. Give me dividers... steps of... twenty miles to be generous... hmm, march west, crossing the Oder then, far south of Szczecin. South of the Müritz, here, marshy country. There can be few firm places for an army to march. Hintze! What do you know of this terrain?"

I snapped to attention, stepping forward from the doorway where I had lingered. "It's some years ago, sire, so I can't be sure, but very difficult country for horsemen."

"Send scouts," he waved to his commanders. "Quickly. Find the most likely route. Find the most likely bottleneck. Report back to me. Go, go!"

One of the serving men left the room to arrange for a rapid foray into the east of our territory.

I wondered only for a very short time what all this had to do with me. The Duke beckoned. "Hintze, you will represent me. You will negotiate."

I found myself a week or so later at the head of a small troop of cavalry, spread out in a chevron across a spit of gravel amid marshes, lakes and waving reeds. I had told Elisabeth I would be on a routine mission of a few days at most, with no danger. I had always concealed the details of my missions from her—as I did with everybody—but now I was being untruthful. I was lying to her, and it didn't sit well with me at all.

Our scouts had reported that this spit of gravel was likely the only place the Swedes could cross, so it was here we would await them. A mild wind blew from the east and our noses detected the Swedish host at the same time their forward scouts appeared and galloped up to us. We were a dozen against an army. As I waited I mused again on the faith my Duke must have in me. He had made me troop leader, and really believed I could horseshit my way into some sort of agreement. As I spotted the first Swedish rider emerging from the scrub across the tarn from where I sat, I only wished I shared his faith.

He was a captain, an advance guard ahead of his army, scouting as we had done. He reined up in surprise, hardly expecting to be met by alien cavalrymen. Two others crossed the shallow water to the gravel and reined up beside him.

"What do you want? Get out of the way!" His eyes raked across the horsemen flanking me to the rear.

"You may not pass this way. I am an emissary and I require audience with your leader." It sounded so stuffy and stupid as I said it, and his reaction was predictable. He pulled his pistol out of its holster and pointed it at my heart.

"I have an army behind me, and we will ride this way."

"Then you will ride over my corpse, and those of my comrades." Good God, the things my Duke made me do! I'd had a pistol pointed at me before and found my way out of it, but how many times can fate be tempted? Even with knowledge that Swedish gunsmiths weren't up to much, and the chances of a misfire were better than fifty-fifty, it was still more than disconcerting.

"We will gladly ride over your corpses." I saw his finger tighten on the trigger, but I also saw doubt cross his face.

"It will be a sad day for your brief career as a captain when King Karl X Gustav of Sweden, Duke of Bremen and Verden, learns that you have slain an emissary of Duke Adolf Friedrich of Mecklenburg-Schwerin. I would be surprised if you avoided the noose."

He slung the pistol back into its holster. "Come with me."

I called my second in command forward. "Stay in the chevron formation. Let no one pass. Do as I did and lay your life on it." Poor bugger looked as scared as I felt, but he took it like a man.

The Swedes were not far up the track, and a canter of a mile or so brought us to them. My escort led me to the command unit, where I dismounted and stood beside my horse. Presently an officer on horseback came forward. My escort rode up to him, saluted and said some few words. The officer nodded, approached me and asked me my business.

"My business is with King Karl Gustav and no other."

"Do you presume to speak with our King? You'll deal with me or none at all."

"It would be a sad day when a fine officer such as you decided on his own initiative what was and what was not his King's business."

He turned with a snort and rode away, leaving me once again standing beside my mount. A short while later two horsemen appeared; the officer and another. The second man rode towards me, and there before my eyes was King Karl X Gustav himself, mounted on a fine grey horse and in full battle regalia.[65] It was he, or his lackeys, who had spurned me and my Duke years ago in Nürnberg. He had been Count Palatinate Karl Gustav von Pfalz-Zweibrücken then, and he looked as ill-favoured and boorish now as he was then. He spurred closer to me, swung down from the saddle, strode towards me and stood four-square, hands on hips. He was in his mid thirties then; straight nose, flowing black hair, a sensuous red mouth, and eyes frighteningly empty. There was nothing in there. Can you have a body without a soul? It's strange the things that pass through your mind at times like this. As I held his empty eyes, almost against my will, I could see why Queen Christina wouldn't dream of having his leg over her; like being bounced by Satan. Then I thought of Giselle and her repulsion at the thought of Wadegahte. They know it's unnatural...

"What is this? Who do you think you are? You dare summon me!"

"It is not I who summoned you, sire, but my master," I replied, coming back to the present. "These are not my words. I am here *in loco dominum meum;* I am my master's voice in all things."

He bridled at this, but he knew it to be true. "What's this about not letting us pass?"

"False. Duke Adolf Friedrich of Mecklenburg-Schwerin offers you free passage through his realm with the glad and open hand of friendship."

"And who in Christ's name does he think he is? His realm, be damned."

"Adolf Friedrich is, in law, the duke of this realm," I reminded him in trepidation. "And in goodwill and friendship he willingly offers to victual your troops and provide what other necessities you may ask in order to speed you on your way."

"And?" he sneered. "You're not finished yet, are you? Glad, open hand?"

"And he asks only a small compensation for this service."

"Ha! Thought so. How much?"

"Fifteen thousand Imperial *Thaler*."

"Fifteen *thousand*? Fifteen! In a piss pot! Be damned to you, and be damned to him! We'll ride over you."

"It will be a sad day…" (I was beginning to repeat myself) "…when such a mighty prince as yourself takes no advantage of the hospitality of a neighbour for want of some small recompense."

"God damn your impudence, you…" He almost exploded and for a moment I thought our gambit had failed and that we were as good as hanged. Then he spluttered to a stop, and I could see the mind working behind the dead eyes. Whether I and my comrades lived or died, whether my Duke was grossly insulted or not by an invasion of his realm, meant less than a nun's wet fart to him. But victualling, fodder, perhaps even powder, these were things worth parlaying for.

"Wait."

He swung around and strode over to a group of functionaries who had emerged from a covered wagon. I stood with great hope in my heart. He conferred long and earnestly with his accountants, as I assumed them to be, and then they retired to their wagon. The great man returned to his horse with not one backward glance, swung into the saddle and went about his warlike business. I stood beside my horse while the sun westered, near to wetting my drawers in relief. Finally, one of these clerks emerged from the wagon and came over to me.

"Twelve thousand. Not a *Pfennig* more," said this most unmilitary functionary, a wispy, tired little man with narrow wrists and veined hands.

"My Duke instructed me to demand fifteen."

"My King instructed me to give twelve. Do I return to him? Do you wish to risk his wrath?" He paused. "You must know he is not a patient man."

"My duke…" I began.

"Twelve."

"Let it be twelve," I agreed, hugging myself with glee but betraying not one shred of it. Duke Adolf Friedrich had instructed me to demand ten.

"Go on your way. We will deal with this transaction in three days when we are closer to your capital city. Here is our bond." And he handed me a folded and sealed letter.

I slipped the letter into my scrip, returned to my horse and rode back to my men mighty pleased with myself.

Jacobus at the Spit of Gravel!

Chapter Forty-Six

In which I visit Denmark again and make friends with an engineer

Durch Gottes Hauch entsteht das Eis, liegt starr des Wassers Fläche
By the breath of God frost is given: and the breadth of the waters
is straitened

Hiob/Job 37:10

My experience with King Karl X Gustav's business did not stop at the marshes of Müritz, much as I wished otherwise at the time. After passing through Mecklenburg and Holstein, the Swedish army, under the command of Carl Gustaf Wrangel, made short work of Jutland.[66] Towards the end of August they descended upon the fortress of Fredriksodde and laid siege to it, but it took until late October before the garrison fell. That was a good day for the Swedish army as they were able to seize a vast quantity of supplies, which would see them through the following months. Even so, having all of Jutland under their control still put them in the same position as Torstensson years ago; they could not cross the bælts—the channels between the archipelago—with their fleet because winter was setting in and the sea was freezing over. They were thus powerless to attack Köbenhavn and the Danish Crown. It was clear that the army would have to dig in and wait for spring before contemplating any kind of attack over open water. From where they sat, on a point of land overlooking the island of Funen, they must have been seething to be so close.

This balance of power swung dramatically as the harshest winter in anyone's memory descended upon the North. Exercising the horses, and ourselves, was an unbreakable routine no matter what the weather, so it was with huge relief that I was called away from the exercise yard one day in mid January. I took my horse to the stable, passed my bridle to a groom and slapped the steaming mount on his neck with a few murmured words. There was an unfamiliar horse in an adjacent stall, covered with a blanket and still sweaty from a hard ride.

"Just came in," said the groom. "Been ridden hard. Think he's a Swede."

"Yes, I can tell by his trappings. Probably why the Duke wants me."

I entered the door of the Duke's small office to find his son Christian seated with him. Christian was a year or so older than me and by now quite portly and florid. He had none of his father's attraction, none of that spark than made the old man so easy to admire, love and follow. I had seen him upon many official occasions since he was about fifteen years old, and knew he would be his father's heir in due course. We often wondered over our ale of an evening in *Zum Freischütz* what would become of the duchy under this fop's leadership, but such seditious talk never went further than our tavern table.

The Duke's face was grey and his breathing was not coming easily. He had a cough that failed to resolve and would leave him even more breathless. Since seeing him last, just after my encounter with Karl X Gustav, his condition had worsened. I guessed that Christian was now a fixture at his father's side as the reins of power were slowly relinquished. It made me sad to see him like this.

"Ah, Hintze. You know my son Christian, of course... who will succeed me... before very much longer."

I bowed to Christian and made some sort of deprecatory noise about the continuing long life of my Duke, but he waved it off with an impatient gesture.

"You know of Hintze," he said to his son, "and you know of his duties to me in various capacities."

"Yes, father. His services to you *are* known to me." With the face on him you'd think a gull had just shat in his hair. His tone of voice made me feel like a necessary but undesirable piece of furniture, a spittoon perhaps or a shitpot. I was sure that as a trumpeter he would hardly have noticed me, but it was clear my other services *were* known and not much to his liking. It occurred to me only a great deal later that he was jealous of my close relationship to Adolf Friedrich, a closeness he lacked.

"We have just received an urgent request from our Swedish allies..." began the Duke.

"Masters," interrupted Christian.

"Our Swedish *allies* for assistance in... in..." and he started to cough painfully.

"General Wrangel," continued Christian smoothly, "requires information that only we possess. His engineer, Erik Dahlbergh, needs explicit charts of the bælts. In particular, the depths of the water."

"Yes," said the recovered Duke. "The King wishes to cross on the ice."

"Impossible," I said without thinking.

"Who are you," shouted Christian, "to tell your superiors and betters what they think or what they do not think is possible?"

The Duke flapped a hand at him. "Hintze knows what he says, but perhaps he spoke in haste. It *is* damnably cold this winter."

"My apologies, your Grace, perhaps I did speak in haste." I

directed my reply pointedly to my Duke. This fat thing beside him did nothing to command my attention, although I was miserably aware that he would *be* my Duke in the not too distant future. "But in what capacity are we asked to help?"

"Dahlbergh was here as apprentice to Gert Rehnskiöld... years ago," continued the Duke.[67] "He is tolerably certain that Rehnskiöld was commissioned to make a survey of the bælts." He paused and coughed a little. "Particularly the depths. You must ask Rehnskiöld..."

"Rehnskiöld is dead, father. He lies buried in Stralsund."

"Yes, yes, yes! Go to the library Hintze. Get them to help you find the report. Take it to Wrangel's headquarters. You must hurry."

"Yes, yes," put in the large one, "speed is essential. Off you go, and report back here for your marching orders once you've found the report."

If the Duke had been alone in his study I would have had no qualms in asking why the Swedish messenger could not return with the papers himself, but the presence of his son made me reluctant. I faced the Duke and saluted him directly, turned and left, leaving behind me the premonition that I was about to embark upon my last mission for my master, perhaps my last mission altogether.

The librarian showed me to shelves stacked with dossiers, folders and rolled-up papers, trying to give me the impression he knew what he was looking for. "Herr Rehnskiöld did indeed make a survey, although it surprises me that Herr Dahlbergh does not have such figures."

"They probably exist in Köbenhavn."

"Might just as well be upon the Delaware, then.[68] What is his purpose?"

"Wrangel intends to take his army across the bælts over the ice and attack Köbenhavn."

"Really? Then he has lost his senses; it is impossible."

"Ours is to provide information, I think, not to judge." There was still a bit of a sting from Christian's tongue, so I passed it along.

"Yes, of course. So, he has to calculate the thickness of the ice and ascertain whether it lies upon the seabed or floats upon water? Hmm... And if the latter, how much water... Hmm, hmm..."

All the while he was removing files of paper, riffling through them and, I noticed, not necessarily thrusting them back where he found them. It looked a lot like that *kaos* that Herr Martius had told me about once, where everything in the world is disordered. I heard the tower bell toll twice before a jubilant expression told me the man had found something.

"Ah, ha! Ah, ha!" he cried. "Here's what we're after." He pulled open a tied ribbon, unrolled several tightly curled sheets of paper and pulled one out. He spread it with his hands and held it down with books and an inkwell. It showed the Langelandsbælt—the passage between the islands of Funen and Langeland—and clearly marked on it were figures in *Klafter*, which I think, were like the fathoms I had heard used aboard ship; about the height of a man. We checked the charts together and saw that they covered all the major bælts of the archipelago.

"I suppose there's no possibility of copying these?" I asked, certain the answer would be 'no'. I was having disturbing thoughts about our lending them and how they might be returned.

"It would take so long. The details are intricate..."

I shuffled all the papers together, retied the ribbon, and thanked their guardian. Originals it would have to be. I returned to the Duke's office with my roll of papers to find the two of them in deep discussion. They turned their attention to me, and I spread the papers out deferentially so he and his son could examine them.

"Excellent," said the Duke. "I am impressed with Herr Rehnskiöld's organization."

Christian opened his mouth to speak, thought better of it, and subsided.

"These are the originals, sir," I told him, "and there isn't time to make copies."

"There is no need," put in Christian. "You will take these."

Now I was pushed to be impertinent. "Couldn't the Swedish messenger take them back with him?"

"Certainly not!" shouted Christian. "These belong to us. How dare you question our judgement? The messenger has been sent back already, emptyhanded."

"You must guard these papers at all times," emphasized the Duke, "and bring them back in the condition in which we find them now."

"Bring them back, sir? Am I not delivering them to General Wrangel?"

"Of course you are delivering them to General Wrangel," interrupted Christian. "But he is not keeping them. Is that not clear? And you will stay with him until he has made full use of them. Only then will you return here with them."

"Yes, sir!"

I was in for a long, cold journey.

Even with my cape, a woolen wrap around my face and thick gloves, I felt the cold keenly as I rode in haste to the northeast, heading first for Lübeck where I lodged at the house of Herr Brehmer, a friend of Friedemann's who kept a small inn near the Burgtor. I hurried on to

Flensburg early the next day, driven by urgency. Everywhere I rode I saw the damage that extreme weather can wreak on people's lives. Livestock was kept indoors, fields were barren, roads were in places impassable with thick ruts of frozen mud and drifts of snow, and from every chimney smoke drifted while hoarded stocks of wood lasted. Adjusting stirrups, bridle and buckles would burn fingers made stupid with the cold. Camping outside was not to be thought of, so the stages of my journey were dictated by inns where I could stop, warm myself and rest my horse. Summer riding would have taken ten or eleven days, but in these conditions, even in a hurry, it was fifteen days before I rode into the spit of land called Lyngs Odde where the fortress of Fredriksodde stood.

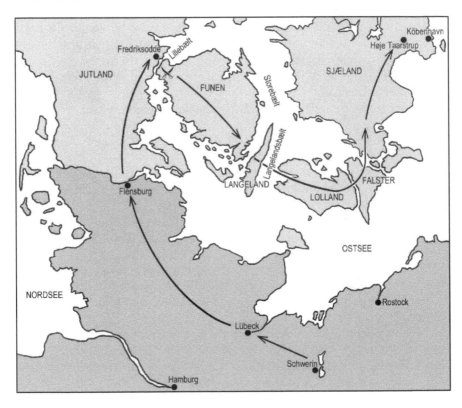

Jacob Hintze's second mission to Denmark

I had passed outposts and pickets throughout Holstein and into Jutland, always waved on as I explained my mission. As I came closer to Fredriksodde I passed row upon row of tents, wagons, wains, cannon, picketed horses; all the accoutrements of a massive fighting force. Now, as I reined up before the gate in the late afternoon I did my explaining for the last time. Inside the fortress the Swedish officers were doing very well for themselves, what with all the captured Danish supplies of food, drink and weapons. Still, waiting for spring must have been harsh punishment for their forced march through our territory and the long siege of the fortress while the weather turned.

I was led directly to the quarters of Erik Dahlbergh, the engineer charged by Karl X Gustav and Wrangel to do the impossible. He rose from behind a desk and smiled when he saw what I had in my hands.

"Ah, the man who might save my life," he exclaimed. "Or, at least, my reputation. Thank God you're here."

He was a tall man of about my age perhaps, with a mass of black hair and a fine, thin moustache very carefully cultured and waxed. To my ear his accent was refined but beneath it I detected his roots among the people. I had the impression, right there on first acquaintance, that here was a man who would make his way in this world by the force of his intellect, breaking his way through the impediment of birth.

"Schwerin, eh?" he said as he unwrapped the bundle of papers. He pored over them briefly, flipping from one to another, then smiled and turned back to me. "You know what? I wouldn't be where I am without Rehnskiöld, God keep his soul. Did you know him?"

I nodded. I had met him for the first time when he had furnished me and Hartmund Breitkopf with maps of Denmark, and that was a good time ago. "I first met him in… I think it was in forty-four, sir. Although I don't remember you then, I think you must have been with him."

"Certainly was. Torstensson was trying to find his way across the bælts back then. He was buggered then and we're buggered now. Well, maybe not. Let's see…" and he went back to the charts. I stood more or less at attention for quite some time before he looked up again.

"Oh, yes, pull up a chair. Want to talk to you."

"I am at your service, Herr Dahlbergh…"

"Herr Dahlbergh, bullshit! My name's Erik. Sit down. And you are?"

"Hintze. Er… Jacob that is…"

I sat on the other side of a trestle while he pulled the sheets out and examined each minutely, exclaiming occasionally. He pondered for a long time, occasionally writing figures on small sheets of paper, then looked up quickly. "It's all a matter of calculation. You've got the weight of a horse, weight of cannon… know how much a man weighs, with equipment…" He went back to the papers and wrote some more, muttering all the while. "Thickness of the ice is the key. And the depth of water beneath it…"

He lost himself again in the papers while I sat and waited patiently. After a while he seemed to remember I was still there.

"Look Jacob, why don't you go off and get sorted out? Tell them to assign you somewhere, get some food. Then come back and we'll talk." With that he went back to his studying and I left to look for whoever was in charge of accommodations. Some food and drink and a place to throw my saddlebags made me feel more at home, and in an hour or so I made my way back. Dahlbergh waved me over to the trestle, lit now by a lantern, with a huge smile on his face.

"We've got it! We've got it!" He motioned me over to the map and pointed to our location on the coast in Fredriksodde. "Look, here's the easy bit. It's narrow enough from here to Funen across the Lille-bælt, and the ice is good and solid. I've drilled it under cover of darkness; done the calculations. We could have moved across at any time, but we dared not cross if we couldn't go further. See, as soon as the Danes spotted us on Funen the rat would be among the grain. They would know what we planned. As it is, they think we're awaiting the ice break-up in the spring."

"So, you need to be certain you can go further?"

"Exactly! But not directly east. Look here." He pointed to a wide channel separating two islands. "See, it's more direct to march across Funen and then cross on the ice over the Storebælt directly to Sjælland, here. That's what Wrangel wants. But it's far too wide, and deep too, as I now know."

"You have a solution, then?"

"Yes, yes! The southern route through Langeland and Lolland. The ice will take us. I'm sure it will. Thank you, thank you Jacob for bringing the solution! We march tomorrow; the orders are sent."

Having done my duty, I was keen to bed down for the night and prepare my horse and equipment for leaving the next morning, but as I was about to take my leave, Dahlbergh looked up again from his studies.

"Do you go back right away?"

"Yes. As soon as you have finished with the papers."

"Finished with them? I will need them for the coming phases of our campaign. There is far too much detail here to copy, and far too little time."

"But surely," I replied, "you have the information you needed...'

"Yes, yes, for the second crossing only, and even then I must take measurements before the army crosses. But not the bælts beyond. I need time, and I don't have it. The delay in getting these charts to me has cost us dearly. Wrangel and the King have been leaning on me, but now the orders are sent; the army is ready to march. We *must* move!"

"My instructions are explicit. I must return with the papers."

"So you will. When we are in Sjælland and Köbenhavn lies in our sights!"

My heart sank. I had in no way anticipated this. I thought they would look at the maps and charts, take whatever information they required, and let me return home. For God's sake, winter had a mailed fist clutched on this awful country, and I was stuck with an insane project that most wise people thought impossible.

"So, I must ride with you?" He nodded enthusiastically. "Across the ice?" He nodded again. "Even when nobody thinks it possible?"

"Yes, even then. And it is possible, damn it! As long as the Danes think it impossible we'll catch 'em with their hose round their ankles." He paused and a quirk of humour came to one eyebrow. "Of course, they would get mighty shrivelled balls."

I couldn't help but smile. If I had to spend however long in this man's company it could be worse, and chances were the officer class would at least keep themselves warm and well fed.

"If you will excuse me, sir..."

"Erik! I told you."

"Erik... I will go and see to my horse and roll out my bedding."

"It's early yet. Sit, sit. I want to talk to you. Where did you learn Swedish?"

"While on campaign with Torstensson. I thought it might be useful."

"Thought so. You speak like a soldier; like my people. Oh, certainly, I can put it on and mix with the ruling crowd, but I began pretty low." He eyed me quizzically. "You too?"

"We were landholders, but very close to the soil." A vivid image of my father at the door of the *Schlachthof* with a bloody knife in his hand sprang into my mind. "Nothing high born about us."

"See, Jacob, I'm stuck in the middle. The rulers need me and use me because of my enormous ability." He smiled at himself. "But they don't *mix* with people like me. Then, on the other hand, I can't be seen to fraternize with the lower ranks either. So, that's why you're getting your ear bent. Here, have a drink."

He pulled out a flask and two beakers from below the trestle and poured wine. "Skål!"

This was stranger than bedding down with Breitkopf, stranger than singing with Friedemann. My sense of place was being strained, but as we drank some sort of bond passed between us; a level of comfort. He asked me about relationships with my colleagues and I explained a bit about the *Kameradschaft*, realizing what a privileged position I held there.

"This campaign will make or break me," he said at one point. "You see, if we get across the ice—and we will—the sun will shine out of my arsehole. Chances are good that I'll get a title. But if we fail— and I know we won't—guess who will have the same arse hanging out of his drawers?"

"So, just for obeying orders…"

"No, not quite. You see, this was my idea. Oh, the King takes credit for it, as is his due, but it was I who approached him in the first place. Tomorrow will be the test."

We talked long into the night, even though we both knew the next day was going to be one of make or break. It was so surprising to me that I had travelled this far into a foreign place, yet found someone with whom I could communicate with the ease of a Chris Schleef. I think Erik found it surprising too. Fortunately, the wine ran down before a degree of unproductive fuddlement could set in. I bedded down in my allotted quarters and slept like a sack of meal.

An entire army on ice: a set of measurements, a slew of mathematical calculations, an unknown quantity of unknowns. Erik Jönsson Dahlbergh was a brave man.

A sojourn in Denmark in his company might not be all that arduous.

Chapter Forty-Seven

In which I march on ice with the Swedish army and witness the
humiliation of Denmark

Dass Wasser sich zusammenzieht wie Stein und der Wasserspiegel gefriert
The waters are hid as with a stone, and the face of the deep is
frozen

Hiob/Job 38:30

The trumpets calling *Reise* woke me the next morning, the last day
of January with the cold gripping the land like a vice. It was unusual
for me to sleep beyond the sun, but the flagon of wine and the extra
furs I had been given may have been responsible. There was huge
bustling taking place; marching feet, shouted commands and neighing
horses as the army prepared to move. I emerged from the fort after
my ablutions and a bite to eat, to see the entire force beginning to
move toward the Lillebælt and Funen beyond. Erik rode up to me,
shouting for me to get saddled and follow. I returned shortly leading
my horse and chewing a heel of bread.

"This will be easy," he shouted as I mounted. "Wrangel was itching
to go and there's not much opposition. The Danes are waiting, but not
too many. We can at least get the infantry and cavalry over to Funen
today."

We rode in the company of nine thousand cavalry and three thousand foot soldiers. From our vantage point on a slight rise above the
beach where we paused, the troops could be seen spread out in a wide
square pattern almost like the view of a chessboard. Commanding
officers were stationed at the edge of the ice, waving men and horses
forward, counting them, waiting for set periods of time, then waving
more on and counting again. As we watched we could see an opposing
army on the farther shore, and the vanguard of our army already
engaging them. The popping sounds of muskets carried over to us on
a wicked wind from the east.

"I calculated the numbers and distance apart," shouted Erik. "And
I know the thickness of ice. So, no worry. It'll take us if we're dis-
ciplined."

We rode down from our rise and out onto the ice together, and I
think perhaps this was the most remarkably strange thing I have ever
done. I had expected the surface to be slippery; as boys we would slide
on puddles or frozen ponds, and once in Flanders I had seen folk

skimming along the surface on metal runners. But this ice was different; it was ridged and bumpy, with cracks going every which way, as if some giant hand had smashed it into pieces and flung it down to freeze. The horses clopped along quite steadily with the ice ringing and skittering beneath their hooves, while the wind whipped at us, finding its way through all our layers. This slow progression, no faster than a gentle trot, went well until about three-quarters of the way across. I could see that the rearguard surging forward, breaking the ordered ranks. Suddenly a great creaking, groaning noise, seeming to come right out of the ice below our feet, was followed by cracks like pistol shots and a deep rumble. Water began to flood across the ice as great slabs tilted and slipped.

"Shit!" cried Dahlbergh. "Too many men! Hurry! We're nearly there."

Commands were shouted and all around us men and horses forged forward, splashing in shallow pools of water and finding the going slower as the depth increased. The rearguard had water up to their knees before surging forward to the beach where the ice was solid and still intact. By the time we rode up off the ice the fighting was over. Blasted and gored corpses lay among the snow-girt reeds and grasses with their blood freezing around them. They would have to be smashed free or wait until spring for burial, God rest their souls. I remembered the last Danish soldiers I had come across, militiamen raised in a hurry to resist Torstensson. These men must have been equally poorly equipped and trained, assembled in haste to resist a surprise attack, and brushed aside by a vastly superior force. There had been only three thousand of them—some slaughtered and many run away—and I would bet that powder and firearms were in short supply.

Poor buggers.

Dahlbergh had reined up amid moving horses and men, and was having words with a cavalry commander. "We must keep order," he yelled over the din. "I know how many the ice can take. That's why you were supposed to be spaced out."

"I'm sorry sir. We kept order until the last, but the men feared the ice and seeing battle ahead, they lost discipline."

"Well, it had better not happen again when we bring the artillery over. We were lucky this time, but I'm not doing this with luck. It's calculation, calculation!"

A messenger rode up and called to Dahlbergh. "Sir, his Highness requires your presence. Please follow me."

Erik turned and rode over to me. "I'll be back. Stay with this squadron. I'll find you. Sorry I can't take you with me."

I was quite happy to stay back; I didn't particularly wish to encounter the mighty Karl X Gustav again, although I would have like to get a look at the famous Carl Gustaf Wrangel. I got to talking with the squadron leader who had had words with Dahlbergh. His opinion was that he would soon receive orders to cross Funen and prepare for crossing the Storebælt to Sjælland. I wasn't so sure in view of what Erik had told me, but I kept the knowledge to myself.

It was late afternoon before Erik returned. He had discussed the situation with his commanders and then had had to supervise the ice transit of some supply wains. Tents were being pitched and fires lit as the sun sank over Jutland, and a true bitterness descended upon the camped army.

"So, Wrangel and the King are all set to march tomorrow," Erik told me as we sat at our fire toasting bread, "but they'll have to be patient. First, the artillery has to come over. I have given explicit direct-ions about the loading. I told them that two hundred foot soldiers with wet boots was one thing, but sinking guns and ammunition wains was not be thought of."

By now I had some comfort with our strange relationship, so I wasn't shy in wondering what his commanders thought of this.

"Well, one look from the King can loosen your bowels." I had seen this but kept the knowledge to myself. "But I stood my ground. He knew I was right. Arguing the way forward was another thing. He was all for pressing east by the quickest route."

"When you looked at the plans yesterday you thought that wasn't possible."

"Exactly. Wrangel came to my rescue. I told them I couldn't see crossing the Storebælt; it won't hold. And now that the Danes are alerted, Wrangel's certain that's where they'll concentrate most of their forces. He thinks that if they believe we can cross the Lillebaelt, we'll be able to cross the Storebælt as well. Even more reason for an alternate route. That's why we head south east."

My knowledge of the islands of the archipelago wasn't great, but I did remember that going south meant crossing Langeland, Lolland and Falster before you could get to Sjælland. "Surely, there are three... maybe more ice crossings that way. Won't it be just as difficult?"

"No. Only the Langelandsbælt. Funen to Tåsinge will be virtually solid. Tåsinge to Langelland there's an island in the middle; Siø. Then Lolland through Falster, easy! No, only the Langelandsbælt."

I remembered my visit so long ago to Falster, and the little crossing of the Storstrøm with the island of Bogø halfway. Easy on this ice.

"How wide is the Langelandsbælt?"

"Ten miles only. The Storebælt is at least sixteen."

"And it will hold?"

"A few days and we'll know. I need to assess the ice. Come with me."

We drained our glasses and turned in for the night. Even inside a tent and covered with furs, blankets and whatever else could be found we had to snuggle close for warmth. I thought of the foot soldiers and cavalry outside, huddled around their fires, trying desperately to dry their boots and feet while the wind scraped its icy fingers down their backs.

We woke long before light but the army was already astir. The operation of getting the guns and the heavier wains over was underway. From where we stood looking west we could see the horse and oxen teams with their loads distributed across the ice, the gaps between them much greater than the infantry and cavalry of the day before. Erik nodded with satisfaction, pleased to see that he need not supervise as long as his instructions continued to be obeyed. Meanwhile, the rest of the army was preparing to march and with yelling, trumpet calls and the crunch on ice and snow of thousands of boots and hooves, the surge forward began.

Dahlbergh planned to hurry ahead of the army the sixty miles across to the other side of Langeland, assessing the ice on the smaller channels as he went. In these conditions it would be a ride of at least three days and there was no knowing what enemy forces might block the way. He detached a subaltern at the head of a troop of cavalry with the proviso that if we encountered any opposition, we would turn back and await the army. Along with the usual complement of weapons, one of the horsemen carried a great spiraled iron thing the height of a man slung horizontally to his saddle, while another carried a long wooden stave. We protected ourselves as best we could on that terrible ride but the cold and the wind were by far our worst enemies. I had suffered a deep freeze on my campaign with Banér and de Guébriant so I knew what was in store, but even so it was a nightmarish ride of a full three days of frustration before we reached the shore of the Langelandsbælt. We had met no opposition at all and had traversed the small bælts as if we were on dry land.

Erik called me and the two horsemen with the special equipment to his side. "We'll go out to about halfway. It's had three more days of freezing than the Lillebælt so it'll be plenty strong enough. We'll plunge the auger in and see what we find."

Out we went again, this time with not as much trepidation on my part. The wind whipping off the ice was pure misery, and when we stopped to set up the equipment it was even worse. That great spiral iron thing—the ice auger—was unslung from the horse and set upright with its squared end passing through the wooden stave. Eric seized the shaft and told the two men to take each end of the stave, pull down hard with all their weight and walk in a circle while he guided it. With a crunching and grinding the auger descended into the ice, throwing up shards that built around it.

"Keep it clear, Jacob," grunted Erik as he guided the shaft down, and I bent and shovelled ice chips away with gloved hands that soon became frigid. The auger bit into the ice and descended to the point where Erik could let go and stand aside. As it descended his smile widened. The two men were stooping, pushing down on the stave from above, when with a jerk the auger broke through and water welled up.

"Excellent!" said Erik in obvious relief. "A lot thicker than the Storebælt and with shallower water below. We can do this!"

We withdrew the auger, packed up the equipment and hastened back to the shore with the wind mercifully behind us.

We waited and froze on the beach of the Langelandsbælt for two days before the army hove in sight in the late afternoon of the second day. And what a relief it was. We had foraged far and wide for wood on this windswept wasteland and were down to a few sticks smashed out of the ice along the shore. Never before have four men so huddled over so few fitful embers.

Oh, what a fine sight that army was as they came over the crest of a dune and moved *en masse* to the beachhead. There is something noble and moving about the colours, the armour shining in a harsh sun, the weapons glinting, and the great rattle and roar of a mighty and well-disciplined army. The King's vanguard approached us, trumpeters sounded and we stood rigidly to attention beside our horses while he and Wrangel surveyed the scene. Erik Dahlbergh marched forward, saluted and conferred with them. After much discussion, pointing and checking of papers, orders from the vanguard were sent back by riders; the cavalry was to move forward and accompany the King, while the infantry and artillery were to camp and wait until the following day. Darkness was falling by this time but the King was keen to push ahead without delay.

So, on the night of February 5, Karl X Gustav, Carl Gustav Wrangel and all their cavalry commanders rode forward onto the ice leading to Lolland, with Erik Dahlbergh among them. Once they had set forth, squadrons of horsemen fell in behind them and, as in the crossing of the Lillebælt, spaces and numbers were counted out with precision. It was fully dark before the final cavalrymen started the journey. The detachment in which I was riding came somewhere in the middle. We rode in darkness, our mounts finding their way slowly through the tumbled and cracked ice. We made a great steaming host as we all assembled on the other side, picketed and lit fires for a short rest. Forage for the horses was very hard to come by in that desolate sandy place, and we were obliged to wait while they ranged far and wide looking for enough to at least stave off exhaustion. It was morning light before we could push off again. As we left we looked back to see the artillery and infantry setting out across the bælt, with the wagon train and camp followers in the rear.

Erik rode back down the lines looking for me; spotting me he reined up. "Come up nearer the front. Ride with me a while."

"Look Erik," I replied, "I have been thinking about my part in this. I've done all I needed to do and you don't need the plans any more..." In truth I was sick of war, sick of armed combat, tired of constant commerce with death and destruction. Yes, the army was a fine sight with its banners and blazons and tootling trumpets and, yes, I was proud to ride among them and be a part of their glory, but now shivering with cold, aching for home, I was done.

"Yes, go on..."

"I think I should turn around now. I'm a long way from home."

He smiled and nodded gently. "Yes, not your war at all, is it? You got pulled in. I saw your expression when I told you I needed to keep the plans."

"Right. It's enough now. Enough."

"Tell you what. Stay with us... me... just until we get to København. We'll have big fires, good food, lots to drink. You'll feel better then, be fitter for your return journey."

What he said made some sense, and I was reluctant to part with him just yet, so even though home and hearth hailed me, I agreed and we trotted together through Lolland and Falster, crossed over the Storstrøm—slightly familiar to me even in its grip of ice—and so arrived on the outskirts of København in a village called Høje Taarstrup. We talked and talked during those three days and I realized that even though he was the tool of our Swedish overlords, he had become a good friend.

The Swedish army had marched almost unopposed into the heart of Denmark. My impression from the ranks was that the stupid bastard King Friedrich III knew he had thrown the dice and lost everything. He was forced to come to Høje Taarstrup on February 18, with as much aplomb as he could muster in the circumstances, and sign probably the most humiliating treaty that a nation has ever had to bear. He knew that if he failed to appear, he would forfeit his crown and the very existence of Denmark as a nation. With a mighty army virtually on his doorstep, he had no option. One swish of a quill in a tiny rural church was all it took to lose the provinces of Scania, Blekinge and Halland, the island of Bornholm and all his Norwegian holdings. He was saddled with punishing renunciation of any inimical alliances, while the Danish navy, such as it now was, was charged with patrolling the Øresund and the bælts for shipping hostile to Swedish interests. From my point of view, the part of the treaty that really hit home was the requirement to pay the costs of the Swedish occupying forces; the hated 'soldier tax', which we suffered under in Mecklenburg and paid with extreme reluctance and venom.[69]

A final document, the Treaty of Roskilde signed some eight days later, made the Treaty of Brömsebro, which Christian IV had signed in 1645, look downright benign. I was on my way home by then, having bade goodbye and all God's blessings to my good friend Erik Jönsson Dahlbergh.

The journey back, retracing my steps almost exactly, was long, cold and unremarkable. At the front of my mind the whole time was my need to be back among my family again, and the nagging regret that my friendship with Erik had delayed me into giving them second place. I hurried as much as I could, but it was the second week of March, when the wickedest winter we had ever known was finally unclamping the world, before I saw Schwerin again.

Chapter Forty-Eight

In which my homecoming is marked by huge sadness and great joy mingled

Es ist allhier ein Jammertal, Angst, Not und Trübsal überall
Everything here is a vale of woe; anxiety, danger and trouble all around

Johann Leon

My Duke was dead. Schwerin was in mourning. An unkind sun lit a mild day as I rode through the gates on a morning to receive the news. *Hertzog* Adolf Friedrich of Mecklenburg-Schwerin had passed away on February 27, 1658 when I was still somewhere in Jutland. I rode straight home, fell into the arms of Elisabeth, the supporting pillar of my world, and wept for joy at my homecoming. I wept also on her shoulder for the loss of the other buttress of my life, the man who had made me what I was, had nurtured me, trusted me and placed his faith in me. I had ridden my horse to the edge of a precipice, but by the mercy of God, my wife caught me just before I fell.

She fed me, cleaned me, enfolded me, wrapped me around with love and family and food and fire. My children gathered about me and I hugged them in turn, took as many as I could on my knee, and smiled and laughed and wept with mingled joy and sorrow. I could not see into the future, could not see the past; I lived in the now, and drank in the wonders of my wife and children like a lifesaving draught. For the first night in recent memory I slept like a tree and failed to wake at first light. Elisabeth sent a message later that day to the *Schloss* saying that I had returned but was unwell, and it wasn't long before good, kind Friedemann came to call.

"We've missed you, you little bugger," was the first thing he said as he punched my shoulder. "Tough assignment, eh? And much longer away than we would have thought."

"Yes, too long. Too much…" I couldn't continue for a moment.

He squeezed my shoulder. "Hard for all of us. Expecting it, of course. But for you…"

"Sorry. Yes. It wasn't unexpected, I suppose, but with everything else it just came like a… like a… cannon in the face."

"Everything else? Can you tell?"

"Don't see why not. You've heard that Denmark has fallen?"

"Yes, yes, of course. The march across the ice is on everyone's lips.

It was galloped into town a week past. The whole world knows."

"Well, it's nice to have been a witness." He raised his eyebrows in amazement. "I went with them, with their engineer, helped to test the ice, watched them cross… It all seems like a dream now. Must give the papers back to the library."

"Papers?"

"Yes. I was responsible for the charts they needed of the water. Depths. That's why the Duke sent me."

"Well!" he said. "Quite the last assignment for His Grace. I'll take care of the papers. Want you to recover, get back to work. I'll come by tomorrow. We need to talk business."

He took the roll of charts—sadly somewhat dog-eared and creased, but they had got that way in a good cause—and thumped down the stairs. A good cause? Helping one bully to get the advantage over another bully; rich men playing with lives and weapons and realms. But while abetting these war-besotted brutes, I had found friendship in the most unlikely places. Talking, discussing, even philosophizing around a guttering fire in a windswept land of reeds and sand, biting wind and ice like iron.

It had been an interesting career, working for my Duke. I wouldn't have had it any other way, pain and misery notwithstanding. It had very clearly been my purpose here in this world, and I think I served it well.

Friedemann didn't need to come by again; I woke the next morning refreshed and ready for work. Of course, I still carried a stone in my heart for my Duke, but I could see the road forward. Over my morning bread I admired Hans's writing slate, listened to Michael's exercises in rhetoric, told a worried Annamaria that I would be home again this very same day, kissed Elisabeth goodbye, and rode my long-suffering horse back to his favourite stablemaster. My first duty was with His Grace, Duke Christian, a meeting I had been dreading since coming home. I reported to his secretary in the small outer office on the ground floor and was told to wait, while he bustled away. I sat on the wooden bench in that room for well over an hour, anger and resentment rising in me, before the new Duke's toad returned to tell me the great man would see me now. The interview was brief. It hurt me to see him sitting at that familiar desk, surrounded by those serried bookshelves, the globe of the world on its stand.

"So, you're back. Did you return the papers to the librarian?"

"Yes, sir."

"Good. Then all is well." He paused, looked down at some papers, and a silence descended between us. I stood. Presently he looked up, pretending to have just noticed me still standing there. Guileless fool. "Well, what do you want?"

"Just to report my return…"

"Good. Thank you. You may leave."

I snapped to attention with my back as straight as the proverbial ramrod, smartly saluted the empty chair beside him, wheeled around and marched out of the door with a great crash of heels. It was grossly insubordinate, but I didn't give a brass jeton. I had known this would happen before I left for Denmark, knew my days as a servant to dukes were at an end, but the way in which it was done hurt me. I went quickly up the stairs carrying my wounded vanity like a shroud.

My reception upstairs in the trumpeters' room cast the gloom away. A few of the fellows were there, going over some pieces on their music stands. They shouted out greetings, put down their instruments and shook my hand, or banged me on the back if the hand was already being crushed. I was a trumpeter first and foremost; this was my life, this was what I was here for, and it was more than enough.

"I'm glad you didn't linger too long in sunny Denmark," said Friedemann as soon as I had poked my nose round his door, "because we have a *Musikalische Exequien* to perform. Not a *Beerdigungsdienst*—a burial service—we had that already, but a musical memorial. We shall play our Duke out in style."

"When? When is it?"

"This Sunday, in the *Schelfkirche St Nikolai.*"

"Not much time. Less than a week."

"Have you been keeping in shape?"

"Buzzing almost daily as I rode, but I can't wait to get a trumpet on my face! Who wrote the piece?"

"The great Heinrich Schütz himself, no less!"

"*How?* How in heaven's name did they persuade Schütz to write for *us?*"

"Well, you know he had a very strong affection for Johann Vierdanck, and wrote to him often, especially when he was resident in Köbenhavn."

"Yes, but even so…"

"Well, as it happened, Duke Christian…" he paused. "Yes, I know it sounds strange… was visiting Wolfenbüttel—this was even before the old Duke had died—and asked Löwe if he would write something suitable when the time came."

"Löwe is *Kapellmeister* there isn't he?"

"Yes. Anyway, Löwe mentioned it to Schütz, just in passing, and to everyone's surprise, the *Meister* offered to do it himself."

"This is incredible! How did he find the time?"

"Well, these last two years, since the Elector died, he's been in 'retirement', and you know what that means."

"Oh, of course. He's writing just as hard as he ever did, but now it's for his own satisfaction and the glory of God, instead of for his wages and the glory of his Elector."

"Exactly. Under his present circumstances it was doubtless a great pleasure, as well as the discharge of an obligation in memory of old Vierdanck."

"Where is this piece? When can I see it?"

"Probably tomorrow. We all need to get our hands on it. It's in the library being copied. It came in manuscript—Schütz's own hand—so the parts need to be extracted and written out. Long job."

I was all agog to see it and amazed that so famous a *Meister* would write such a piece for us. I was dying to see what parts Schütz had written for trumpets. I knew of his earlier works where he made suggestions for their inclusion in choral pieces, but in his later years I hoped he might have written idiomatically for them.

"So, trumpets then? Stop teasing me!"

"Of course. Duke Christian explained his father's love for his trumpet corps, and *Meister* Schütz has done him proud."[70]

Our working lives were devoted to getting the *Musikalische Exequien* into shape for performance. The first phase had been to distribute the parts to the various vocalists and instrumentalists so they could become familiar with them. Only then would the second phase begin, where we would all come together and rehearse the piece in its entirety.

Reading over our parts the next day, I could see that this was an astonishingly new work; there was no talk of Schütz falling back upon familiar and comfortable stylistic formulae. In form it was a funeral hymn, each stanza having an instrumental accompaniment. Three trumpets with kettledrums were scored in two of the verses, and the whole corps played *en masse* in the final stanza. The writing was generally slow in tempo, stately and massive as befitted the occasion. It rose to joy, sank to despair, and climbed again to everlasting life.[71]

There was one particular section that caught my eye; in one stanza early in the piece, *Est ist allhier ein Jammerthal*, a solo trumpet took an arioso-like line, high, flowing and melodic. Friedemann was looking over my shoulder as I scanned the lines.

"It's yours Jacob." I couldn't believe what he had just said. I froze with the paper in my hands.

"No, Friedemann, no! I couldn't take this from you." I played the piece over in my mind, loving every note of it, and knowing it was written for the *Hoftrompeter* and no other.

"I want you to have it."

"But… this is *your* time to say goodbye."

"He would have wanted you to do this."

I couldn't speak. I looked at Friedemann standing there beside me, solid, supportive, reliable, and the thought of what he was doing for me stole my heart. He was passing to me the most poignant and personal statement a musician can offer.

I have always had difficultly remembering that day in the *Schelfkirche St Nikolai* when we played that *Musikalische Exequien*. It exists in another world, another place. I was as close, I think, to Heaven as I will ever come in this life when I played the solo trumpet part in *Est ist allhier ein Jammerthal*. I remember afterwards, as the last notes came back to me from the high ceiling, that I wept.

I wept for beauty, I wept for loss. I wept for our Vale of Woe.

I said goodbye to my Duke.

Chapter Forty-Nine

In which my future is provided for in a most unexpected way

You shall have your dinner served with trumpets.
No, no; sackbuts shall serve us
Thomas Middleton and William Rowley

I cannot count how many times after some horrible engagement or other, that I have taken a big deep breath and said, 'That's it. From here on all I want is regularity, normality, sanity'. It was the same after we sent Duke Adolf Friedrich to his well-earned rest. I went back to the trumpet corps secure in the knowledge that my life of sneaking and subterfuge was done, and that now I could go forward in serenity and joy, doing what I had always wanted to do. I had a secure position with the ensemble as *Stabstrompeter*, I played *Clarino* to a very high standard in church and court, and I had a fulfilling and loving family life.

There's a great fist up in Heaven that tosses the dice of your life.

When I reported at the front gate of the *Schloss* one bright, clear morning in late March, the old gatekeeper—the one who had been at that post at least since I was a boy of fourteen—handed me a summons to attend the Duke in the larger receiving room at the ninth hour, the room where formal occasions were held. I had heard that a family gathering was underway, and that it concerned the reading of Adolf Friedrich's will, but I had no idea why I was summoned. As I made my way down from the trumpeters' domain near the end of our working day, I assumed the Duke must have left me some little memento or trinket to remember him by, and was touched that he might have done this. There were several ranks of chairs facing a desk, the front ones occupied by family members and the rest by retainers and employees in descending order. I was assigned to a place near the back. Chairs behind the desk, facing the audience, were occupied by three legal-looking old files, pince-nez on their noses and piles of papers before them.

The reading went on for a considerable time as properties, chattels and gifts were apportioned, and I slid into a somnolent boredom. Suddenly I heard my name and my mind sprang back to attention:

And to *Stabstrompeter* Jacob Hintze, who has been my stalwart helper and servant in matters most personal and confidential, and who has never swerved from his duty to me, and by extension through me to the wellbeing of this entire realm, I leave free and unencumbered, in all its entirety the post inn, the *Neuer Krug* in Neu Heinde, and all the revenues that may accrue from it for as long as he and his offspring may live.

Thunderstruck doesn't do it justice. I sat there in a daze while others in adjacent chairs looked my way and smiled. The man beside me, an old servant I had seen innumerable times, took my hand and shook it. A woman on the other side patted my arm and told me how deserving I was. At the end of the reading I rose from my chair, still in shock, and came forward to the table at the front where the executors were dealing with paperwork.

"Here are the papers. There's a great deal to be done here. Would you like to retain one of us to guide you? Well?"

"I'm sorry... I don't..."

"I said, would you like one of us to deal with the intricacies?"

"Intricacies?"

"Signatures. Titles. Deeds. Well?"

"Perhaps it could wait?" I was coming slightly to my senses. It was like the aftermath of a blow on the head. "I think my accountant in Rostock, Herr Schleef, could help me..."

"Very well. Take all this documentation with you." He bundled the papers into a sheaf, tied them with a white ribbon and thrust them into my hands. "Don't delay."

A trumpeter had walked into the audience chamber that day; an innkeeper left through the same door.

Elisabeth noted this distracted Jacob Hintze when I had ascended the stairs and opened the door to our sitting room. She put down some work she had been sewing at the window, rose and came to hold my hand.

"What is it, my love? Bad news?"

"I don't *think* so, but I'm not sure..."

"What, then?"

And I told her. It was strange to watch the thoughts passing across her mind drawn so clearly on her face as I gave her all the details. This must have been what my face had looked like as I had passed from incomprehension through gratitude to joy and then to concern.

"This is incredible. What a wonderful gift! But it will be such a change. We'll need to go to this place, on the post road you say—we know it, do we not? We've stayed there, haven't we?—and see what accommodations it has, there'll be so much to do, and how are we going to deal with the..."

"Stop." I seized her hands. "Stop, my love. I have still to get this whole business into my head."

"Yes, yes, my mind was leaping forward. But it's so generous."

"It is. It is. But the first thing I have to do—and I should have done it before I came home—is talk to Friedemann."

"But he will let you go, surely? And the new Duke?"

"My love, that's not the point. I am a trumpeter. I am not an innkeeper. Can I become an innkeeper? Do I even *want* to become an innkeeper? Must I leave one to pursue the other?"

She paused for a long time with my hands in hers, her eyes locked to mine as if trying to look into my soul. Then she squeezed gently, looked down and nodded.

"Yes, you must have both," she sighed. "And if you can only have one, it's not the inn, is it?"

"I'll talk to Friedemann. Before we decide anything at all, I'll talk to Friedemann."

We decided I would sleep on it, although neither of us got the benefit of much sleep that night.

It wasn't an ideal arrangement, but we thought it might work. As Friedemann reminded me when I raised the subject with him the next day, once you were a member of the *Kameradschaft* you were in it for life. Only gross misdemeanours would cause you to be expelled, and running an inn wasn't one of them. He felt the situation was flexible enough that using me as a 'guest trumpet' when special occasions demanded might be the answer. In fact, during my cavalry service, and later on with my errands for the Duke, I had been absent for long periods. The trumpet corps had covered my place of necessity, wondering sometimes if I would ever come back. I would need to retire officially from the Duke's cavalry, but *Stabstrompeter* was a title that was mine for life. So, an absent trumpeter could be managed, Friedemann thought, provided Duke Christian approved. Christian, I was sure, would certainly approve of me leaving—the *Neuer Krug* was in his father's bequest—but the question was whether he would be happy to see me coming back. I was glad Friedemann would be the one approaching him because he might just be more favourable to his *Hoftrompeter* than he ever would be to me.

"I'm glad the Duke agreed," said Friedemann as we sat across from each other that evening in *Zum Freischütz*, our favourite ale house, "but I'll be sorry not to have you working closely with me anymore. I do know, though, that if I ask you to come and play you'll be ready and able. You might end up doing a lot of travelling between here and there."

"I thought I'd given up all that," I said. "Thought I was looking forward to a long time in one place doing one thing."

Friedemann sipped his tankard slowly, eyeing me over the rim. "I don't think you're done travelling. Never. It's in your blood."

"Maybe so," I agreed, "but for now, a few months without would do some good."

"Done a lot together, you and me," he observed. "I remember when you were just a young shaver. God, time passes..." He began gently to sing *Leck mich am Arsch*. And I joined in.

The inn was a shambles; the previous owners of the *Neuer Krug* had let it run down, and it was now taken care of by an elderly couple who could hardly cope. The last time we had been in Neu Heinde was in fifty-two, and when we had stayed at the inn then it had been a going concern. With the energy of Elisabeth and Anja it was clearly going to be so again. I was all for pensioning off the caretakers but Elisabeth would have none it. She gave them a living wage and a bedsitting room for themselves, and set them tasks they were able to perform without worry. Our two servants were given the choice of coming with us or finding other work in Schwerin, and neither of them stayed behind. Hans, our second oldest child, was only eight but already he was a willing pair of hands and I could see who would soon be the workhorse of the establishment. With Elisabeth at the helm it wasn't long before the *Neuer Krug* regained its reputation as a very welcoming road house, and then when Thurn und Taxis brought in the postal service we were very well situated.

It was joyful to know that we would be closer to the Schleefs, and could visit them often. They now had three children, the oldest a rambunctious six. I rode to Rostock by myself a day or so after we had arrived in Neu Heinde, taking with me all the *Neuer Krug* documents I had brought from Schwerin. Chris guided me through the intricacies, witnessed my signature and filed all the necessary claims, proofs and whatnot. I was hopeless at this stuff, still am. Elisabeth looks after all the daily accounts and reckonings now, and did from the word go. We parted at his office door with promises to get together soon and often.

We taught all the children their letters when we considered them old enough. Or, I should say, this was a task that Elisabeth took on more than me. Michael, at ten years old, was becoming serious about his violin; he had seen a fiddler playing jigs in the Schwerin *Hauptmarkt* and had got bitten by the idea, eerily familiar to my story. The *Stadtpfeifer* there had found an old fiddle for him among their castoffs, and I had found it quite easy to get it into good enough shape for him. I could see a musical life for him as he had my ear and temperament, although no interest in the trumpet. Before we left Schwerin, I had started to employ a tutor for him—a violinist at the Court—and I was now seeing if there was anyone available for the task in Rostock, or perhaps Güstrow. The other children were young yet for any educational activities and, having been town bred, they just enjoyed the open space, the horses and a new kind of freedom. I saw to it that they all sang in the holy service every Sunday in Belitz though, and were well coached in Scripture and observances.

It was strange to me that as the inn became more established, and as I became more of a personage in our small community, a certain prestige was accorded me. Neu Heinde was a tiny place, and in the absence of priest or mayor people would come to me with minor problems. 'Ask the trumpeter, he will know' became a refrain among the simple folk of the area. They came to call me the New Krüger, one in name with the inn. Why they thought I possessed wisdom or knowledge I do not know, but it's a fact that sitting down with disputants at the board with a mug of ale and a warm mutton and onion pie can often do wonders. I think the offer of food and drink is an excellent lubricant, a sovereign remedy for spiritual ills and simple human conflicts. After all, our Lord Jesus Christ offered bread and wine, and broke loaves and fishes for thousands who wished to listen to his Word. It's a good example to follow.

The hardest part of parting from the Court was not the absense of my colleagues, the withdrawal of all the privileges, pride and joy of service to the court, but the goodbye to my trusted horse. I remembered dear old Jürgen and I realized that, like my present mount, me and my horses seemed to develop strong bonds, greater I think than most cavalrymen. I said my goodbyes and hoped he would be well treated by his next master. I acquired a new horse to be stabled at the inn because, as Friedemann had predicted, I would travel a great deal between Neu Heinde and Schwerin to act as 'visiting trumpeter'.

It seemed that on every occasion outside the usual trumpet corps duties, Friedemann found a good pretext to bring me in. So, I played for Duke Christian's visitors, for marriages, seasonal celebrations, and some funerals as well. There were also playing opportunities at the *Marienkirche* and the *Rathaus* in Rostock, so although essentially retired from the profession, I kept my playing in shape and never let an opportunity pass to better my grasp and knowledge of developments. The trumpet was coming into its own now, and composers were specifying instrumentation much more. The Greek word 'orchestra' was being used to describe a group of musicians, whether in church or at the court. 'All together' it meant, and very appropriate.

So began and continued a very peaceful phase of our lives.

Chapter Fifty

In which I take my eldest son on a journey, and have an astonishing encounter

Ein treuer Freund liebt mehr uns steht fester bei denn ein Bruder
A man that hath friends must shew himself friendly: and there is a
friend that sticketh closer than a brother
Sprüche/Proverbs 18:24

Elisabeth and I decided that Michael had got to a level with his violin playing that we would try to find him a better instrument. He called the violin that I had refurbished for him his 'smelly old bone'—how he loved that oft-told story—so clearly it was time for us to take him seriously. On a visit to Hamburg I bought an instrument by a young man, Tielke, who was showing great promise in his craft.[72] (Were we in the North finally shaking off the notion that only Italians could make decent fiddles?) By the summer of 1662, Michael had progressed so far that we knew we would have to find him an apprentice position, preferably with a well-established court. He and I had been playing together for a year or two, and I could feel him going well beyond what I could do for him.

On one of my frequent visits to Schwerin I was able to borrow some of the music that Berthold and I had worked over so long ago. As I sat at home one evening, the candle lighting the weaving lines of violin and trumpet, a wave of longing for a lost time came over me. Ah, here was Andreas Bevernage again with those tricky, challenging keys! Oh, how we had worked on intonation, expression, tuning... How I remembered the common room in Frau Walther's hostel, the rapt faces of the other lodgers, the saucy smile and jutted hip of Giselle the slop maid. The springy press of her tit... Ah, we old trumpeters do go on a bit, don't we?

Michael was the same age as me when I had been sent away, so he was more than ready. He had become a strong young man, fine and wiry, and such a contrast to powerful Hans, who was younger by two years but topped him in muscle and stature. I enquired first for a place with the violinist of the *Stadtpfeifer* in Rostock, who had been tutoring him intermittently for some time, but he couldn't take on the commitment, nor could any of his colleagues. We wrote letters to several other musical establishments with no success, and it might have stayed this way without a little bit of luck followed by an astonishing encounter.

I was sitting with Friedemann, Albrecht and Wolfgang in the old familiar trumpeters' domain, and feeling quite nostalgic about this present visit, when I mentioned our problems.

"You know that Johann Löwe is *Kapellmeister* in Wolfenbüttel?" said Friedemann.[73] "We've had some really fine trumpet music from him recently. Tough stuff."

"The boy plays the fiddle," I observed pointedly. "It's a wooden thing with guts stretched over it."

"I prefer copper with skin stretched over it, meself," replied Wolfgang our drummer.

"Me," said Albrecht, "anything with skin stretched over it!" They all laughed.

"I'm talking about the violin, you arseholes."

"Yes, yes," said Friedemann. "You did actually tell me the boy plays the fiddle. Point is, some of Löwe's *capriccios* have really tough violin parts, so he's writing for some very fine talent there. Why not send him a letter? You never know."

I wrote a letter as soon as I got home, introducing myself and describing our wishes for our young man's future. I included a page of music with my letter; it was an example of the sort of music Michael was working through, and it would show Löwe that a tutor's attention would not be wasted upon a mediocre talent. The letter was the usual mixture of praise, fawning and false modesty; the way we do these things. The reply came only a week or so later (it helps to own an inn on the post road):

> *Stabstrompeter* Jacob Hintze salutations. It is with great pleasure that we have received your request and are both delighted and honoured that you should consider application to our humble musical establishment. Our first violinist, Herr Steiner, has examined the music examples you kindly sent to us, and is of the opinion that if the boy is playing these works his talent might warrant further examination, leading to an assessment of his suitability as an apprentice. We encourage you to prepare yourself to travel at your earliest convenience, bringing your clearly talented son with you. We remain, Herr Hintze, your most obedient servants in this matter.
> Johann Jacob Löwe,
> *Hofkapellmeister* to Augustus of Braunschweig-Lüneburg.

There was great rejoicing in the Hintze household and much bustle to prepare for a long journey. I took a treasured flask out of the cupboard in our sitting room, took down glasses that we scarcely used, and poured the boy his first glass of wine. Elisabeth had some too, and so the youngsters would not feel left out, we poured them barley water into tall glasses with great formality.

"To a journey!" I said as we raised glasses. "To the future!"

I watched my son's face with interest as he took the first sip. There was a momentary flash of distaste followed quickly by a stoic expression that said, 'I'm a man now; this is what men drink'. And then he drank again, more this time, rolling it a little round his mouth while his eyes took on a faraway expression. In an instant I was with him, looking out of his eyes, dressed in livery, surrounded by the denizens of the court, playing my music for them, hearing their applause. The world's great wheel turning full circle.

Elisabeth was not sure what this visit really entailed, and I was not too much the wiser. It was an assessment of his capabilities only, so whether they found him acceptable rested with the audition and then, if he satisfied them, would he return or stay? Elisabeth didn't know whether to bid her oldest son goodbye or just farewell. There was a great deal of hugging and kissing at the door of the *Neue Krug* as we prepared to set out. The whole family, all the servants, and a couple of folks from the nearby farms stood and waved us on our way.

It was strange to me, sitting on my horse, saddlebags filled with provisions, papers and spare clothing, trumpet slung on my back, while beside me rode my proud son looking to the south but waving back until mother, brothers, sisters and the whole household were out of side beyond a bend. It was a fair day in June with a gentle breeze, the sky populated by fluffy little clouds that meant no one any harm. Wolfenbüttel is over one hundred and eighty miles from Neu Heinde, a little bit west of due south, so an estimate of ten days seemed about right. I was certain of the route we would take, but not sure what lawlessness we might encounter, especially in the tracts of forest or wasted land between the towns. For myself I had no qualms—years of just this kind of travel had made it easy for me—but now I had a responsibility like none I had ever had before. I carried my sword at my side, of course, but I also took a pistol and sufficient powder and shot, although the chance of this being more than just a deterrent were slim. I had Michael buckle on my spare sword, although I had never thought to school him in it. We traversed a few tracts of land where we had to be vigilant, one in particular where we encountered three vagabonds with cudgels. One look at our swords and the pistol at my waist was all they needed to keep their distance.

My trusty Birckholtz trumpet in its leather bag bumped gently on my back, while Michael had his violin in a satchel at his side. Whenever possible we would keep in shape by playing scales in fine weather as we rode (we must have made a fine sight) or duets when we were stopped. Our conversations on that journey ranged over many topics, and it was here when there were just the two of us to keep each other company, that I learned so much more about my son. I resolved to take all my other sons in turn on adventures like this so I could get to know them better. I took to coaching and instructing Michael on his deportment and behaviour when he met his future tutor, then stepped back a little as I recalled my father doing exactly the same thing to me. No, experience showed me that I should keep my counsel to myself; he would stand on his own merit.

We crossed the Elbe at Dömitz about a third of the way into our journey. We had intended to find a hostel in Braunschweig but fellow travellers told us of an outbreak of plague, so we skirted the city to the east. I had tried to find us inns for meals and rest, but often we had to camp out soldier-style and buy food from farms or the small villages we passed through. I think Michael liked this best, because for many days into our journey I had been telling him stories (mostly true) of my campaigns in war and peace. He lived my adventures in his imagination, a grown lad with a future laid over a little boy with dreams of spires and ramparts and fluttering banners.

"Tell me again of the ice," he would plead or, "did you *really* sail across the Nordsee in a ship?"

I was telling him things then that I had kept locked away. I was opening my covert life to the world, feeling that I no longer needed to be secretive. It was the unloading of a burden, another of the legion I hadn't known I was carrying.

As you come down to Wolfenbüttel from the north you see the town nestled around its little river with the chapel dome and tower of the *Schloss* pricking the sky. The massive *Schloss* dominates the clustered dwellings. We crossed a bridge—the town is ringed around with water —and rode into the centre looking for a place to stay. I impressed upon Michael the necessity for a high level of cleanliness in body and clothing before we rode to the *Schloss* to present ourselves. We found good beds and food, and stabling for our horses a stone's throw from the *Rathaus* and the wide *Hauptmarkt*. No matter where you stayed you had a good chance of getting infested with lice, but this place seemed free of them. Cleaned, well dressed and presentable we walked the short distance to the *Schloss*. Michael carried his violin and bow in a bag across his shoulder; I brought my trumpet just in case a duet was called for, and I slipped a folder of papers under my arm.

"I don't think there is anything I can tell you," I told Michael as we walked, "that I haven't told you before. The audition is a tough test, but you're as well equipped as you can be."

"Yes, papa. I feel ready but... it's..."

"It's what? Go on."

"I'm scared papa."

I remembered my terror in front of Duke Adolf Friedrich when I was his age, and how not one single note would emerge from my lips. 'Go on, boy! Where's your manhood?' I felt for my son, but I knew he had it in him. Perhaps there *was* something more I could tell him.

"In my experience," I said, trying not to sound too much like an old fart, "when the time comes you will find yourself elsewhere, and your hands and ears will know what to do. It may not come naturally now, but in time it will drive you. Does that make any sense?"

"Yes, I think it does. Remember that day we played in the common room? The place was crowded, all eyes on us, but it... it didn't seem to matter somehow."

"That's it. Do that for Herr Steiner and all will be well."

"I'll try..."

We presented ourselves at the gate and the keeper didn't have us wait long—"I will send for Herr Steiner directly"—and a boy was sent running. Sometimes these little functionaries play with guests, using a special faculty they possess to determine the status of the visitor and, ergo, how long they can keep them waiting. Either we impressed him with our deportment or he didn't play those stupid games.

A man of my own age with a thatch of unruly straw-coloured hair appeared in a doorway at the end of a corridor. He came striding toward us with a huge smile on his face, and as he approached me with outstretched hand he began to laugh. I wondered very briefly why our visit should cause such merriment. But I knew him! Surely, I knew him.

"Yes, it really is you!" he cried as he took my hand. "Knew it was!"

"Me? What...?"

"It had to be you! How many trumpeting Jacob Hintzes are there in Mecklenburg? And just look at those fabulous cavalry whiskers!"

That tone of voice... Herr Steiner? Berthold? *Berthold Steiner*, by God's grace, my old friend Berthold! I was stunned, then I laughed, and then we were embracing and slapping backs while Michael looked on in bewilderment.

"Berthold!" I cried, holding him at arm's length. "You old bastard. This is wonderful. Incredible." Then I remembered poor Michael. "Berthold, this is my son Michael. Michael, Berthold, who I thought I had lost forever."

"I'm pleased to make your acquaintance, sir," he replied with schooled formality, sweeping off his hat and bowing low.

"Come in, come in!" Berthold swept us into the corridor, up some stairs and into a music room filled with instruments and papers, the two us babbling away all the while about old times, with Michael dutifully in the rear. "We'll talk later, you and me, but now," he rubbed his hands together, "your son! Sit, sit."

There followed a long interview where Berthold quizzed Michael on the details of violin art, the extent of his knowledge, and the tutoring he had already received. As this went on I sat aside watching Berthold, seeing the boy I knew wrapped about with the man he had become, appreciating how one had led to the other. I was lifted into a state of surprise and happiness, all the while bursting to know where he had been, what he had done, and who he now was.

The interview over, he stood and instructed Michael to get his instrument out and tune up.

"What are you used to? Here's our C," and he crossed to a harpsichord and sounded the note.

"Lower than I am accustomed to, sir," replied Michael as he eased his tuning pegs and gently plucked the strings, instrument to his ear. He rosined his bow and then he was ready.

"Just scales now, start very simple."

There was some nervousness in my son, but if he was scared, he covered it well. I was tolerably sure the raucous greeting between me and Berthold had eased the tension. As he played I could watch him relax, and as the demands increased so did his confidence. Soon he was instructed to play from sheets of music Herr Steiner assigned to him, prodigiously difficult to my ear. Then it was on to *scordatura*, where the strings needed to be retuned, and he even had Michael cross the two middle strings between the tailpiece and the bridge. This was now at the limit of my son's comprehension and development, and Berthold saw this and began to ease back.

"Funny, isn't it, *scordatura?* Invented here in Germany, but everything new has to have an Italian name! You can return the tuning to the standard now, Michael."[74] Suddenly there was a light in his eyes; he smiled over at me.

"Got your trumpet I see! Let's do it."

I laughed and pulled my trumpet from its bag, fumbling in my scrip for the mouthpiece and a bunch of extra tuning bits. "What have you got?"

He pulled out folders from a shelf and flapped some sheets onto three music stands. I tuned quickly to his pitch, played a few trial notes and nodded.

"You too, Herr Hintze der Jüngerer. Not done with you yet. This is some stuff from the boss, Herr Löwe and it's damned good. Take the second trumpet part on your violin. D-major. Easy. One, two…"

It was a most remarkable thing to be playing with a friend I thought I would never see again, and with my son who showed just how accomplished he had become. It was one of those occasions when, as it is actually happening, you are in a state of disbelief. We played through a few times, then I tried some fancy work, fluffed a note or two, and we all dissolved into laughter. Then Berthold become quite serious, motioned us to our chairs and interlaced his fingers.

"Herr Hintze der Jüngerer has passed my tests with no problems." We both smiled and relaxed a little. He raised both forefingers. "But, I must still present his case to Herr Löwe and seek his approval. In principle, he agrees because he consented to your travel here, but it is a formality we cannot avoid."

"I'm... no, we... are really happy," I started but Michael spoke for himself.

"I cannot thank you enough, Herr Steiner, for inviting me here and I am pleased that you find my playing acceptable."

"Does this mean," I asked, "that once this formality is passed, Michael will remain here and not return with me?"

"Yes indeed. As far as I am concerned, he may start right away. And now, gentlemen, it is the end of the day so let's go to my apartments where you will dine with my family."

Berthold had two children, both the boy and girl with unruly golden hair, and a wife, Magdalene, a gracious lady with an open and welcoming face. All this was new to me, and wonderful. After our meal we three sat with a flask of wine and, I must confess, bored Michael a little while we caught up.

"You can't imagine what I thought," he said, "when Löwe showed me your letter. I had been told you were dead; killed in the war. Couldn't bear it, quite honestly."

"Told I was dead? Who the hell?"

"When I was in Lübeck in fifty-four visiting Baltzar. He was there briefly."[75]

My God, fifty-four! I was being force-fed half the River Thames in a London basement, while he was playing the fiddle in Lübeck.

"Soldier from Schwerin I got talking to," he continued. "Said you had fallen at Breitenfeld fighting for the Swedes."

"Martin died there. Colleague of mine. He confused him with me."

"Well, when I saw your name on your letter I knew it wasn't true. Thanks be to God!"

"So, what happened when you left Schwerin in forty? God, how I missed you."

"I took off to London," he told me. "Got work there right away, thanks to my father's contacts. There was quite a lot of theatre work, some church music, but I was never really secure. And then with the Commonwealth, the damned Puritans, music was drying up everywhere. No theatres, nothing public at all, some private functions."

"So, when did you come back?"

"Fifty-four. I had run away from the war, but this is home. Once the Peace was signed..."

"Peace? Tell that to the Swedes!"

"Oh, right. And the Danes. Anyway, I'd met Magdalene by then. She was with her parents, some sort of diplomatic thing, and when she came back, so did I."

"You been playing here since then?" I asked.

"Oh, no. Kicked about quite a lot until I landed here. Perfect place; perfect appointment. Johann Löwe is great; tight musical discipline but expressive freedom. Ideal combination."

I looked over at him, sipping his wine, all self-assured in his world and realized how far we had both come. "Remember how we played duets in Frau Walther's common room?"

"Oh, yes..." His eyes went far away. "Remember Giselle?"

I glanced quickly over at Michael, but he didn't seem to be paying any attention. As I turned back to Berthold, I caught a look in my friend's eye that told me all I needed to know, and had wondered for years.

"Oh, vaguely," I replied, face flushing while he held himself back from laughing out loud. I glanced at Michael again; there would be Giselles aplenty in his world all too soon...

"Wonder what happened to Joachim? He wasn't killed, by any chance?"

Memories crowded in again and I felt the room shrinking about me. "No. No, I think he survived the war."

"Pity. There's one who should have been taken into Abraham's bosom and sorted out."

Oh, the times the opportunity had been presented to me! He was at large somewhere in the world, but it was God's task, not mine, to judge him. I shook off memories and we smiled and laughed again.

We shared the great divergent space in our lives, filled in details and bored my son exceedingly, although he handled it well. When I could, I involved him in the talk, describing our home life and prompting him to contribute. I was proud of my son and resolved to tell him so. We finished our glasses late in the evening, bade goodbye to Berthold and Magdelene, and made arrangements for the formal meeting of the next day.

We walked back to our hostel that night in fine form. Musical success, red wine memory, a warm breeze and half a moon smiling on us; and the magic of Berthold's appearance. We were comfortable with ourselves and at peace with the world.

"I'm proud of you, my son," I told Michael as I rolled into my blanket up in our room.

"And I'm proud of you, father," he replied.

I pinched out the candle, peace and darkness settling upon us.

"Papa?"

"What?"

"Who was Giselle?"

"Go to sleep."

Chapter Fifty-One

In which I sign apprenticeship papers, play some music and return
home to sickness

Kommt, wir wollen wieder zum Herrn; denn er hat uns zerrissen, er wird uns
auch heilen; er hat uns geschlagen, er wird uns auch verbinden
Come, and let us return unto the Lord: for he hath torn, and he
will heal us; he hath smitten, and he will bind us up
Hosea/Hosea 6:1

"So, I am told you enjoy my little *capriccios*," said *Hofkapellmeister*
Johann Jacob Löwe as he folded his considerable height into a chair
behind his desk. "Herr Steiner has told me of your impromptu trio."

I liked his sparkling eye and the wry mouth below the wide nose.
A man of my own age, filled with life experience and wisdom.

"Very fine pieces," I replied. "I had seen them before in Schwerin
and admired them then."

It was the next day and we were seated in Löwe's office, surrounded
by books and musical instruments. He had met us with Berthold at the
gate and ushered us upstairs, enquiring after our journey, making us
welcome and engaging in small talk.

"Now," he became all business, "Herr Steiner tells me that your
son Michael has passed scrutiny. Does he wish to be apprenticed
here?"

I glanced over at my son's face and saw a stoic calm that masked an
inner irritation. I so easily recalled my father and *Hoftrompeter* Breitkopf
discussing me as if I was elsewhere, and disposing of me as if I was a
chattel or an object of barter. I knew how he felt.

"That's for Michael to decide." A slight rise at the corner of his
lips told me he appreciated that.

"I would be profoundly happy if you were to consider employing
me in that capacity, sir."

The *Hofkapellmeister's* eyebrows raised and he smiled broadly.

"Then it is my role here merely to give approval. I will let you go
with Herr Steiner to deal with the papers." We were at the door when
he stopped us. "Herr Hintze, der Alte that is, you must meet our *Hof-*
trompeter before you leave. Play some more of those capriccios."

"It will be a pleasure, sir, and thank you."

The office of the scribe reminded me so much of Schlauklug's in
Schwerin; papers, books, writing equipment, folders and rolled parch-

ments, and one surface on a table to be swept clear prior to making signatures. I sat beside Michael, with Berthold and the scribe on the other side of the table, extracted the papers I would need and laid them out. The clerk swept his eyes over the birth certificate and my attestations as a landholder and property owner, and gave them back to me.

"All you need to do is sign the agreement to the boy's apprenticeship," he told me, "and pay the bond. It is two hundred *Reichsthaler* for the full two-year period of the apprenticeship." I looked over the paper quickly and dipped the quill; my signature was witnessed by him and sanded. I signed the duplicate copy as well, which I would take away with me, tangible proof that my son was setting sail.

"Room and board are provided for, but the boy will need spending money."

"And how will that be arranged?"

"An annual lump sum of twenty *Reichsthaler* deposited with me, apportioned on a weekly basis."

"It's not a great sum…"

"He will need very little. Room and board are taken care of, as I said, as are candles, beer and other necessities. Too much extra money might lead him into ill ways."

"Not on my watch he won't," put in Berthold, smiling wickedly at me. "Why, when your father and I were apprentices we kept our noses in our books, and our hands on our instruments. Did we not?"

Michael caught this—I could see that he did—but I just kept my expression neutral as I counted out coins from my purse and slid them across the board. The scribe wrote me a receipt and the deal was done.

"We'll do the rest," said Berthold. "I have to go over the details of the apprenticeship with Michael and then he must swear the oath. I don't think we need keep you any longer."

I stood as my son stood. I gripped him by the upper arms. I didn't have any words. He saw me to the door and then I flung my arms around him. "Go with God, my son."

Berthold rose and shook my hand. "He's mine now, but I'll keep him well. Write to me my old friend, and visit often."

I promised I would.

And I left.

Trumpet playing was in a wonderful state at Wolfenbüttel. Löwe had sent a message introducing me to Herr Kirnbauer, a short, stocky middle-aged *Hoftrompeter* with a barrel chest and a full beard. I spent a very healing afternoon talking music with him, comparing instruments and, of course, playing some of those lovely pieces of his master's. His best trumpet was by Michael Nagel—Nürnberg, naturally—very similar to my Birckholtz although not as decorative. We played some lovely pieces together and couldn't help reminiscing on how far our art had come in the hands of both composers and players. There is a close lockstep between the work of the composer, who knows what he wants to hear, the player who must carry out his wishes, and the instrument-maker who must satisfy both. We counted ourselves privileged and lucky to have seen in our lifetimes the trumpet in German music pass from an instrument of warfare and fanfare to one of subtlety and beauty in chapel and court.

The light was fading when we finally called a halt to our enjoyment, he to begin rehearsals in the chapel, I to my lonely little walk back to the inn. That night I wrote a long letter to Elisabeth giving her all the good news, telling her I would see her in less than two weeks. I asked my host to send the letter post haste.

Twelve days upon a horse passing through town and village and forest give a man a long time to think about life, to rejoice in health and contentment, and to praise God for the skills He has bestowed upon him. It was a gentle ride with no great urgency, stopping in villages to buy food, to drink and talk, or to attend holy service. It was in such a mellow mood that I approached Neu Heinde in the fading of a September day, keen now to sit with my people, tell all my news, and let the world unfold as it should.

It was quiet. I rode into Neu Heinde from the south, the sun slanting across my path and a cooling breeze springing up. Nobody was outside in the still warm air, no sound from door or window. I realized now that I had seen no one in the fields. I rode between houses in silence, hoofbeats clopping echoes, my fear rising as I went. Two houses I passed had white crosses chalked on their doors. This could mean only one thing. In a panic, I kicked the horse into a gallop and reined up at the door of the *Neuer Krug* at the far end of the village. It was quiet too. The shutters were down and there was no smoke from the kitchen chimney; there was *always* smoke from the kitchen chimney. The door opened quickly as soon as I had touched the hasp, and Elisabeth was in my arms, weeping.

"Oh, thank God you're back! The smallpox is here!"

"How long?"

"A week... more. Many in the village have been touched by it. Those who have not left are mostly dead." And tears burst from her as she clung to me.

A dark wing had swept over the region. Folk had dropped with fevers and aches, their skin turning foul with spreading blisters, breaking into pus-filled cavities. Contagion stalked from house to house, farm to farm, while from pulpits was roared the wickedness of the people, the wrath of God, and the overdue punishment for sin. In some houses the dead remained unburied as those still living lay in wracked suffering, bloating and rotting as their flesh opened into holes. The young and the old were taken first, the husbands and wives spared briefly to watch the death of their children and their parents, before succumbing even while they nursed them.

"And ours?" My heart stuttered as the images of our children sprang to my mind. "Not ours? Please, not ours!"

"No, no. But Clara has a fever and I fear for her."

"Let me see her," and I strode up the stairs through the silent house to the children's room with Elisabeth close behind me.

She lay there on her little mattress in a great sweat, rolling her eyes towards me as I entered, smiling weakly to see me returned. The other beds were bare and stripped.

"Where are the others? Where?"

"I have sent them away to Rostock. They are with the Schleefs."

"How can you be sure they haven't carried this thing with them?"

"I sent the four of them away with Anja as soon as the first illness was reported." Here she burst into more weeping and I held her closer in my arms. "I... I... kept Clara back for... for company. I couldn't shutter the place up... for fear of theft. I couldn't! I had your letter. I knew you'd come. So we stayed... waiting for you. I should never..." and the tears stopped her again. I kicked myself for my leisurely return, my self-indulgence.

I held her clasped for a long time while Clara looked on silently. The twilight deepened and shadows stole from the corners. Presently her weeping ceased and I was able to turn her face up to mine and kiss her softly, with my hand gentle under her chin. I sat down beside the bed.

"What form does it take?" I asked as I seized Clara's hot little hand.

"Herr Kraft says most people have the distinct, not the purples, thank God." Melchior Kraft was the apothecary from Belitz, the best we could muster, but neither physician nor surgeon.[76] "It takes the very old and the very young first."

"If she hasn't got the bleeding, stinking kind then there's hope."

"I... I thought if I kept us locked up here no harm could come but... it came anyway. And she was so terrified of leaving me behind!"

"We'll bring her through." I fumbled for flint and tinder. "But how are you? No signs?"

"None. Every moment I have prayed... I *have* to be here for her. I cannot be stricken!"

"What's Kraft prescribed?" I asked as I struck a light and lit the candle.

"He says to give her small beer and sweet white wine. And barley gruel with honey. I'm to keep her well wrapped up, but with air from the windows."

"All good, thank God." My parents had had a very practical way with illness and they passed on a lot of their common sense to their offspring. My father argued against the popular purgings and bleedings and blisterings of the book-read physicians, applying simple herbal remedies instead. Waves of illness would wash over our region, particularly during the war when pestilence was let loose and starvation became its helpmate, but by God's mercy little of it had come our way. I wondered often if our farm life made us hardier and more resistant to these ills.

"I'll sit with her. We both can. The fever has to peak."

We sat with Clara, one on each side of the bed, nodding in and out of sleep until morning light. The fever was still high, and the sun beaming in the window revealed a rash of red patches on her face and neck. She murmured nonsense words to herself as the fever carried her. As the day progressed the spots spread and coalesced until her whole body was rosy hued and covered with pustules.

The large, bearded and normally jolly Herr Kraft came to visit around midday, his face sombre.

"Why are you still here?" I asked him. "It's madness to work in the middle of contagion."

"I had the smallpox when I was child. You'd see my scars if it wasn't for the beard." He laughed but his heart was not in it. "How is the little one?"

"She has a rash of pustules spreading over her whole body," replied Elisabeth who had come downstairs when she heard the knock. "The fever is still gripping her."

He came up the stairs with us. "Yes, it looks like the distinct," he said. "Apply wet cloths, especially to her temples. And moisten her skin with an unguent of milk infused with rosemary, marsh mallow and lavender. Do you have these?"

"Rosemary and lavender I know I have."

"Start with those. I will bring marsh mallow later. Perhaps we could also give her a little of the poppy stirred into white wine."

Good as his word he returned towards evening and I greeted him in the front doorway. He handed me a bunch of herbs and a small fold of paper, then placed a hand on my arm. "Look, I have to be honest with you. You need to know that the chances are not good. I have just come from others for whom the fight is over."

"I know. Thank you..." That was all I was able say, but I think he understood.

For three awful time-stretched days the fever coursed through Clara's seven-year-old body, while the rash of spots wept yellow pus and her skin darkened to a rusty brown. Her face puffed up; her eyes were slits. The inside of her mouth and other parts became raw. We scarcely ate, we scarcely slept, we hardly ever left the room, praying for the shuddering, racking heat to break. The fever raged, the lesions crusted over and scabbed, and we ached for her. It was at the opening of dawn, into the fourth day, that Elisabeth reached over in the dim light to touch her daughter's skin and shrank back with a scream.

"She's cold! Cold! Oh, dear God, she's dead!"

With a rustle of blankets and straw, and a creak of bed slats, our child sat up. "I'm thirsty," she said.

We nursed her, rejoicing. She drank well, though cringing in pain, but it was a day before she could eat, a thin gruel at first but soon she could take solid food as her gums and the inside of her mouth healed. For near on a week we dressed her skin, we bathed away the scabs and dried matter, and swathed her in clean linen. As we washed away the dead, grey skin we found the scarring; it was disfiguring although nowhere near as much as we had feared.

All through Neu Heinde and across the region the contagion began to ease, people emerged from their homes or returned from exile, and again smoke drifted from the chimney of the *Neuer Krug*. Our family came home in the company of Anja and the elder Schleefs. There was much hugging and kissing at our door as friends and family rejoiced. We all attended holy service together, and the little church in Belitz rang with our thanksgiving… and with the grief of others.

Chapter Fifty-Two

In which life unfolds happily and I have a surprise visitor

Denn ich weiß wohl, was ich für Gedanken über euch habe, spricht der Herr:
Gedanken des Friedens und nicht des Leidens, daß ich euch gebe das Ende,
des ihr wartet
For I know the thoughts that I think toward you, saith the Lord,
thoughts of peace, and not of evil, to give you an expected end
Jeremia/Jeremiah 29:11

Being the landlord of a post inn meant I did a great deal less travelling, even though my trumpet still took me to other places in the region. On the other hand, working behind the counter of the inn, the world would come to me in the shape of voyagers from far places. I relished the role of landlord and would often spot a likely customer in the common room of an evening, idle my way over to his table and perhaps treat him to mug or a glass in exchange for conversation. I heard some wonderful tales from faraway places, and told a few tall tales myself, always keeping just this side of too much revelation. And truth, come to that. But there were private places in my recollection, I knew, that must never, ever be opened. Or so I thought then. When broadsheet news came to us of the death of Cromwell and the restoration of a king in England I held my peace, although inside where nobody would ever see I basked in the secret knowledge of my small role in it.

Sometimes, when I filled a mug and wandered over, I picked a dud, perhaps a smalltown functionary with nothing in his head but balance sheets, but more often I would enjoy a fine and expanding evening. News of the Great Fire of London came to us that way; a merchant from Hamburg told us the news before it was even published abroad. He had been there shortly after and saw the devastation close up. I kept the irony of this to myself—bad taste to smile at such misfortune —but I remembered my first impression of the city very clearly: how I thought the best thing would be to burn it all down and start again, beguiling though it certainly was. Experience had burned away any nostalgia I had for the place, but it had clearly been a terrible tragedy.

While I indulged myself with news of the outside world, the children and servants ran the inn. Elisabeth was the matriarch who saw that all ran smoothly, so in the evenings I could be mine host and play the role to the hilt. Mind you, I laboured mightily during the day. There were always things to attend to, particularly in the area of horseflesh, which was my specialty. As a part of my daily routine I would visit the stables every morning with our ostler Richard, checking the health of the mounts that had come in the previous day and reckoning their exchange value, along with the many other details of stable management. It was always a surprise to me how inferior some of the running gear was; you saw some pretty poor examples of tack even among the gentry, who dressed and equipped themselves well enough. There were visits to the blacksmith too, particularly for shoeings, which you saw a lot of with the state of our roads.

The only respite we all had from our work throughout the week was when the family went to holy service in Belitz of a Sunday morning. The inn was looked after by our staff, who took their service when we returned from ours. The place was never closed; couldn't be. So, all in all, I earned my evenings of good conversation.

I had always kept myself in very good physical shape, so when there was no hale and hearty son or servant to help, guess who lugged casks of wine and beer around? It wasn't just muscles; good lungs had always been my bread and dripping, both for trumpet playing, which I kept up with daily practice, and for swordplay, a skill I kept finely honed because you never knew. I always did my boffering with Hans, my strongest lad. He made us swords out of laths, nicely spokeshaved to shape and with the hilts bound around with cowhide. He was the strongest of my sons, very like his uncle Jürgen in strength—and brains too, I suppose—but I never let him best me. Never. Mind you, it cost me dearly to spar with a full-grown boy half my age. He would see me panting and puffing at the end of a bout, but I was certain he hadn't eased up on my account. Even if he did, I was damned if I would ask him if he had, and he'd never admit it anyway.

Although the sword had been my way of life, and its absence from my side was always unsettling, we also kept guns in the house. These were still troubled times, and people of my generation and older had vivid memories of violence and horror; enough to take precautions, even though the steel might rust and the powder go damp. Running an inn could be a hazardous business because you never knew who would grace your board, or what grudges they might carry with them, especially when the drink flowed. I had a harquebus and two pistols at hand in the hall armoire, and kept them ready. Just in case. I would sometimes speculate how different my life might have been if my parents had kept guns on the farm, and if they had used them. I was sure they wouldn't have, although old Jürgen would have led the defence, of course, blasting away to protect his kinfolk. If he had been there... Stupid, idle speculation. But we kept guns.

Speaking of Jürgen, our boy, his namesake, was now thirteen years old and proving to be the one with a head for education. He was destined for the Gymnasium so we enrolled him in the school in Güstrow as a residential student, although he came home more often than not at weekends. He rode well, but I wouldn't let him ride that far and on his own, so we packed him onto the coach, an easy day's stage on the road to Schwerin. He would be there for four years while they filled him with astronomy, logic and mathematics, the better to take over the books of this place or, who knows, find a post as a teacher or notary. He took after me; the idea of leaving home and travelling was very appealing and we knew that Güstrow and the Gymnasium were just a start. I often wondered where his wanderlust would take him, and how often we would see him once the education was done. I was pretty sure that totting up the books of the *Neuer Krug* wouldn't keep him content for long.

On one memorable occasion we had finished our supper in our private dining room and I had gone through to the common room. It was always a bedlam of conversation, woven through with tobacco smoke, beer fumes and the close aroma of packed people. I peered through the fug and spotted a man of about thirty or so sitting by himself, and when I caught his eye a shock of recognition passed between us. It was as if each of us had said "You?" at exactly the same moment. Even so, it took some moments before I could join the face to the name, and when I did I was astonished and surprised.

"Georg! Georg Speer!" I swung my mug into my left hand, and seized his right as he stood to greet me.

"Jacob Hintze! What're you doing here? On the way to Schwerin?"

I laughed. "I own this place. I live here."

He spread his arms with a huge smile. "Inn keeper? My God what a surprise!"

"And what about you? Here…"

"I work in Tübingen now; cantor at the *Stiftskirche*. I'm on my way back from a visit to Köbenhavn via Berlin."

"Cantor indeed. May I assume you have settled down?"

"Oh, yes. My wandering days are long done. Well… maybe."

"Maybe?" I asked with a swig of my ale. "You mean this jaunt to Köbenhavn?"

"No, that was business; musical business. Same as Berlin, then hurrying back to Tübingen. But there is position in Göppingen that *could* be mine. And then there's a young lady in Großbottwar who is of some interest…"

"Footloose as ever then, Georg?"

"Oh, no, not really. But I'm Daniel now, not Georg."

"Daniel then. When did that happen? And why?"

"Just after I left you... er... were you...?"

"In answer to your unasked question, no. I was not angry, upset, annoyed, whatever." I had been all of those things and more, but I wasn't about to tell him. "Continue."

"I did wonder if I had wasted your time." A slight shake of my head. "My brother..."

Even though we had been talking for a while, there was still an air of student deferring to master about him, but mine host wasn't having any of that. We were all the same when sitting at my tables.

"I told you before," I laughed. "If you mention your fucking brother one more time I'll throw your arse out of that door!"

We both fell about laughing, while other customers paused in their drinking and looked on curiously. I went to the cask still chuckling and brought back fill-ups. He was grinning widely when I plunked the mugs down, all hesitancy gone.

"My brother used my given name; *ergo*, from then on I would use my middle name." I nodded. I had figured this out. "So, Daniel Speer I now am."

"So, where did you go?"

"I travelled a lot. I did visit Constantinople you know, I did see Venezia, Egypt, all sorts of places. And I've written all about it. I'll show you some of the tales of my travels, and one of these days I might even find a publisher."

"So now, this position in Tübingen is to your liking."

"Fine. I am required to conduct the choir, play the organ of course, and compose cantatas for the feast days."

"What about Göppingen then?"

"Money's better. And maybe a bit more free time for my true love." He saw my renewed interest and grinned broadly. "The trombone, just in case you might have been wondering. But I love the trumpet too."

"Do you have your trumpet here?"

"What do you think this is, in front of your eyes?" he cried, pulling a trumpet out of a bag at his feet.

"Brother," I laughed, "you think you're a trumpeter, you cursèd whoreson!"[77]

"Well, you wanna find out?"

"Wait. Wait right here. I'll get my trumpet and we'll fight a duel."

It turned into an entertainment for our guests. We matched each other note for note, improvising as we went, with the whole room clapping and applauding. But who would have known, among about twenty guests in the place that night, there would be both a fifer and a fiddler? It's quite astonishing what fine and peculiar music you can make when four players bring their instruments and play together to the accompaniment of stamping and hand clapping. The other three were far more capable of playing together than me, so I let them go at it and threw in melodic bits whenever I could. Elisabeth and the kids were drawn in by the noise, and before you knew it we had a wonderful party in full swing, sawdust and rushes kicked up from the floor, lamp flames dancing and overall the smoke of pipe and fire.

It is occasions like this that make you praise God that He has let you live on this Earth, and has let you see the beauty and simplicity of His people when they are at play.

Daniel Speer went on his way the next day with promises to write and exchange music. As good as his word, he sent me some pieces he had composed and also some few pages of a romance he was writing. When he was married some years later I sent a flowery speech filled with praise and flattery, which I instructed should be read sonorously at their nuptials. I'm not sure if it ever was read out, but here's some of it:

> Be it known that Herr Speer had long lain with his first love ere this new and fair Euterpe claimed his hand. That he has succumbed to her charms can only mean that she is of such rare and captivating beauty that she alone can supplant his first love, who he still deftly plays with his lips and tongue while sliding in and out.

I was inspired.

Chapter Fifty-Three

In which sickness strikes again and my nemesis returns

*Unser Leben währet siebenzig Jahr, und wens hoch kömmt, so sinds achtzig
Jahr, und wenn es köstlich gewesen ist, so ist es Müh und Arbeit gewesen*
The days of our years are threescore years and ten; and if by reason
of strength they be fourscore years, yet is their strength is labour
and sorrow; for it is soon cut off, and we fly away
Psalmen Davids/Psalms 90:10

The smallpox of sixty-two was not the last time our lives would be
wrenched apart by pestilence, but this time it would be us playing the
hosts while our friends would be savagely attacked. A few peaceful
years along, we received a message from Chris Schleef in Rostock: the
black plague was there, brought, the city fathers suspected, aboard a
ship from overseas. Could we, he implored, keep the two youngest
Schleef children while he and Alena stayed back to maintain the business and the household? The older two were safe in Berlin being
schooled at the Gymnasium, while the younger two, he was sure, would
be in good hands with us if only we could take them. It was, of course,
impossible to refuse. The Schleefs had done us the same unthinking
service when Neu Heinde was besieged with smallpox.

He told me that he had begged Alena to travel with the children,
but she insisted she would stay with him.

The two children, Katerina and Barbara, ages ten and twelve, came
along with their maid and valises full of clothes and books, a day after
I had posted my reply. We settled them in a spare room on the first
floor and they were soon busily active with our Annamaria and Clara,
or in lessons with Elisabeth. They were as happy as we could make
them, but they missed their parents and were quite old enough to know
why they were absent, and to worry. The news we received from Chris
was not good; he told us that the contagion had spread widely enough
that the postal service would soon cease operations, and in view of the
complete lack of business and activity at the *Rathaus* he wondered why
he had decided to remain. He also wondered, poor man, why he had
not asserted his authority and sent Alena away while he could.

The news couldn't come by post.

A week of nothing, no word at all, then a lone rider reined up at
our door. He was a traveller fleeing the contagion, who Chris had
prevailed upon to carry a quickly written note to us before going on
his way. I was at the door when he swung down from his saddle, thrust

the note at me and went on his way, an unwanted and unhappy duty discharged as quickly as he could. That moment, as his hoofbeats faded and I unfolded the paper, is graven in my heart.

Alena Schleef was dead.

How in the world can you tell two children such a terrible thing? How can you take them aside, sit them down gently in some quiet place and break such news? It had to be done, and Elisabeth and I looked each other in the eye and knew we would do this together. In my prayers that night I asked God why I was so afflicted. I had seen my family under mounded earth, I had seen my comrades blown to pieces, I had seen my mentor dealt death and my first girl child waste away and die. Why, I asked Him, should I be further torn in my spirit as I had been that graven day, with the sun slanting through the window, the buzz of a fly on the pane, and the far twitter of some carefree bird.

On my knees, God told me about my selfishness. He showed me through the windows of my memory the wasted farms, the raped and slaughtered families, He showed me Frau Derbfuss (who did die of childbed fever), He showed me all those afflicted people torn apart by war, famine and pestilence, and He told me to rejoice in all the good things that my time on this Earth has given me, and the death I had been many times spared.

It was a message that should not have required prayer.

The peaceful and quiet time of my transition from soldier to innkeeper, the growing of my family and the increasing circle of my friends, was always underlain with an unease. Although I would forget for weeks at a time, I would be at some simple task or some word would be said, and suddenly there was the wraith of Joachim Wadegahte to tap me on the shoulder. He had tortured and damned nearly killed me in Osnabrück in forty-eight, and then he had nearly done for me again in fifty-four in England. He was out there somewhere and he would not rest. I had known years ago that he would spare nothing to kill me if he could, and I knew he could not be stopped. He would wish to hold me responsible for the vile life he had led, or had been forced to lead. The very first day we met he came at me with hatred. I was young, foolish and headstrong then, and undoubtedly made matters worse between us, but later did I not spare his life? He knew I had done this, yet that act of mercy clearly stoked his hatred instead of dampening it. I knew he had dedicated his life to my downfall, the sad, miserable creature. Given the choice, though, I don't think I would have treated him any differently; he was the victim of himself, and 'as ye sow, so shall ye reap'. So, when these reminders came to my mind, I would repeat to myself again that I must be vigilant and never let my guard down. But it is wearying upon the soul to have such vengeance hanging over you.

One summer evening my fifteen-year-old daughter Clara was sent to tell me there was someone out in the yard who wished to speak to me. I was close to the back of the house, so I peeped quickly through the window on my way through the hall to the back door, and there he stood: Joachim Wadegahte. I backed away from the window and stood stock still. It was as if no time had passed at all. As I realized who this shade from the past was, it was as if I had seen a rotten corpse with its flesh falling about it pushing its way out of the earth to confront me. The same tall arrogance, the same swagger, but with a seedy, furtive gloss that spoke of hard times, dirty dealings, and a life spent in hatred and unrequited vengeance.

He was back after all these years.

He stood there, feet astride, arms behind him as if standing down from parade. From my vantage point just to the side I could see that, behind his back he concealed a pistol in each hand. I would not be writing these words now if I had not taken that quick glance through the window before opening the door. All of a sudden, as I stood in the hall with clutched heart, it was if a hatch in mind closed, a door that led to my heart, my conscience, my belief in the value of life. The Dark Lord took hold of me and I was cold, mechanical and passionless. I would have to kill him. This could not go on. Twice I had spared him, but I dared not spare him again.

He would kill, so I would kill first.

I swept Clara aside, seized the pair of pistols from the armoire, checked their powder and pyrite, and wound their cocking keys. I shoved one into my belt and strode to the back door with the other in my hand. I flung back the door and fired immediately. It was a poor shot but it took him in the leg. As he fell in pain and surprise his first shot went wide, whanging off the bricks above the door, but the second gun was ready; readier than mine. He pointed it at my heart even as he fell to the gravel... and pulled the trigger.

Click! A puff of smoke, a flash in the pan, and no hot leaden death hurtling toward me. Now I had him! I pulled the second gun from my belt, walked over to him and pointed the barrel at his chest. He looked up at me, face writhing in pain, anger and fear...

I could not pull the trigger.

The hatch in my mind opened again, my madness fled on a flood, and my heart knew that Joachim Wadegahte would not die that day. I turned away, leaving him bleeding there in the dirt, and went up to my bedroom where I threw myself down in disgust and anguish.

Elisabeth came to me, startled by the gunfire and running feet, and threw her arms about me as I sat up to greet her. "They've taken him away. Who is he?"

We sat side by side on the bed in each other's arms, and talked long and hard. I had always kept my life in two quite separate places, the way we used to store our different grains on the farm. She knew the hardships I had faced in my duties to the Duke over the years of the war and the so-called peace, but never once had she probed and questioned. I never knew how much she guessed, and the subject was never raised between us, even in our most intimate moments. Only once had her resolution slipped, that day just before I left for London, but she had reined in and probed no further. Elisabeth had signed a bond in her mind back when we were still lovers, and she had never wavered from it. Now, the continuing threat to my life obliged me to unite all my grains in one bin. I told her the whole terrible story.

It was an immense release.

Chapter Fifty-Four

In which I bid you farewell

Herr, nun lässet du deinen Diener in Frieden fahren, wie du gesagt hast
Lord, now lettest thou thy servant depart in peace, according to thy
word

Lukas/Luke 2:29

I am relieved to have progressed thus far with this story of mine because my life is the hand of a clock, and my midnight is nearly here. Soon I shall meet my other family; those loved ones taken so cruelly from me all those years ago. I always hoped my brother Jürgen was alive somewhere, and I often thought I heard his tread upon the stair—he walked in a very particular way, you know—but it was never him. One day, I used to tell myself, that shadow in the doorway will be him, but it never was. The others... I had knelt beside their newly-turned earth, had visited it often, and knew that all I could do for them was to pray for their souls. Now I will meet them all in the hereafter, and I honestly cannot wait.

There are two reasons why I look forward to my passing. The pain that Michael saw when he started me writing this tale some months past has now become terrible. My father had this, and his father as well, and I am visited with the same curse. It beats in my side like a second and traitorous heart. I keep to my room a great deal now, and Elisabeth and my children come to sit with me when they can, and help me in my pain. The tincture of poppy is the best remedy Melchior Kraft can provide, but it does little good. I fret constantly that my Elisabeth will not be well provided for. Certainly, Jacob can manage the books, the orders, the bills, the servants; Hans will never stop working hard at anything he's put to; and Annamaria and Clara are wonderful with household organization. I know all this, but I still fret because it's not material comfort she would lack. She has told me how hard it will be without me here; not the living, not the *Neuer Krug*, but the absence I will leave. She speaks of a hole in her heart, and I know so well what she means. I have talked to Christophorus about this, as well; dear old Chris is lonely too amid plenty.

I saw my father waste away, but I now believe that particular fate will not be mine. That is the second reason to welcome my passing, and the merciful knowledge that it will be swift. It comes in the shape of my old enemy. I came down from my bed to the common room one day, as I still like to do when I am able, especially if there is lively company these summer evenings. One of our serving girls had been sent to tell me there was someone asking after me. There he was again: Joachim Wadegahte, sitting at a table in *my* inn. Three times his life had been in my hands; three times I had let him slip away.

He stood painfully. He locked eyes with me, and I forced myself to hold his gaze. Those eyes! Oh, how I remembered the eyes.

"I'm here for you!" A broken voice, ruined by drink and bitterness and hard living. He slapped the hilt of his sword. "Tomorrow at the last hour in the forest yonder. You and me. Like men. Be ready." And he turned and limped slowly through the door.

He has challenged me. He will cross swords with me. I am weak. Am I able even to wield my sword? I will lift it with my last strength; with every fibre of my being I will be again the fighting man I once was. But I cannot fight. He won't know I cannot—I will never let him know I cannot—and in his anger he will do me the greatest service any man can. He will speed me from this earthly, burning agony into the cool peace of everlasting salvation, where I am awaited.

Elisabeth will not hear of this; I must do this alone. I cannot let her love overrule my resolution.

But in placing myself on the point of his sword, am I encompassing my own death? Is it not a mortal sin to take your own life? In doing so are you not condemning your soul to eternal torment? But how is this different from galloping into possible oblivion in battle? No, I believe we all attain Heaven through God's grace. Only He can know our worthiness, and we attain His grace through faith alone. I believe I have served God well, and I believe I will receive just reward.

God will forgive me this last weakness.

If I am to be remembered at all, it will be first by my trumpet, and then by my sword.

Epilogue

Der Feind verfolget meine Seele und zerschlägt mein Leben zu Boden
For the enemy hath persecuted my soul; he hath smitten my life
down to the ground
Psalmen Davids/Psalm 143:3

Elisabeth Bauchen, widow of Jacob Hintze, had her beloved husband interred in the Lutheran church in Belitz on June 9, 1676. She paid twenty *Reichstaler* for a memorial plaque, which was hung on the south wall of the apse in 1677, the year she includes in the text. The inscription on the memorial plaque reads:

> I, Elisabeth Bauchen, have made this in loving memory of my blessed husband Jacob Hintze. In the 52nd year of his life, 1677.
> "For the enemy hath persecuted my soul; he hath smitten my life down to the ground."
> Psalm 143:3

On one side of the plaque the widow hung Hintze's sword, and on the other the trumpet by Wolfgang Birckholtz of Nürnberg. The sword is lost, but to this day a reproduction of the trumpet hangs beside the plaque, the original now being in safe keeping.[78]

The church register is written in Latin. Translated, the record of June 9 reads:

> Jacob Hintze, the New Krüger! He died of blows inflicted by Joachim Wadegahte, son of Heinrich, whom he had angered by hurling balls from an iron gun.[79]

In 1677 Elisabeth Bauchen married Christophorus Schleef, a wealthy notary of Rostock.

Jacob Hintze's grave was removed during renovations many years ago. It is not known where he now lies.

Historical Notes

All trumpeters in the German lands were soldiers at the time this story begins. Jacob Hintze was a staff trumpeter during the Thirty Years War, and therefore playing the instrument at the most intriguing time in its history. Trumpeters played ceremonial music at court, but increasingly during this period educated players performed with the court and church musicians as well. The Birckholtz trumpet that Michael Münkwitz found hanging on a church wall was no cavalry instrument; it is finely finished and decorated, and has silver-plated fittings and an elaborate cord binding. This is a musician's instrument. From this, it seems evident that Jacob Hintze would have played two opposing roles, and would have been obliged to reconcile them: he would be playing a musical instrument that was artistically idiomatic and expressive, but he would also be the cavalryman who sounded the signals of battle. Great advances in trumpet playing went hand-in-hand with a bitter struggle whose proponents showed no moral compass and scarcely a shred of chivalry. Fine musical art on one hand, and death, destruction and horror on the other, would have formed Hintze's two poles.

In creating a reasonable facsimile of a life for Jacob I have been aided by three very useful factors: firstly, as a staff trumpeter in the cavalry he did not enjoy high status and therefore remained a minor character at a time when so much of the historical record was laid waste. Secondly, the duchy of Mecklenburg-Schwerin did not figure very prominently in the history of the German-speaking region at this time; indeed, in his compendious history, *The Thirty Years War: Europe's Tragedy*, Peter Wilson cites Mecklenburg just a few times. Obscurity aided my devices. The third and most useful factor is that, because the spies' dealings and those of their masters had necessarily to be covert, an excellent pretext was provided for all sorts of confabulation, none of which can be scrutinized.

I have tried to take as few liberties as possible with the historical record as it relates to Jacob Hintze's story, and wherever possible I have tried to place his exploits into a realistic context. The major figures he meets are drawn from history, and the major events he witnesses unfolded as he describes in their correct time and place. The finer details of their interactions are, of course, the subject of creative story telling. All higher commanding officers, with the exception of those directly above Hintze, existed. *Hoftrompeter* Hartmund Breitkopf is fictional, but the more he developed as a character the more I wished that the young Jacob could have been guided by one such. Perhaps he was.

All the daily goings-on I detail at the ducal court of Mecklenburg-Schwerin are fictional. I have tried to paint a picture of what activity might have taken place on a daily basis, the better to fill in the context in which my story is embedded. Certainly, the departments of the court must have existed more or less as I describe in order to support the continuing function of a very large and complex organization.

Joachim Wadegahte was responsible for Hintze's death in a duel but I could find nothing more about him. He was angered at having balls shot at him from a gun, but that is all. I gave him courtly antecedents in order to establish his classic plot character; the nemesis who haunts our hero's career. Elisabeth Bauchen might have a more documented existence as a patrician and landholder. However, as the love interest plot device she fitted the role so perfectly that, like Wadegahte, I delved no further but created fictional lives to assist the development of my story.

I have taken the liberty of either stretching history or creating incidents from pure cloth in just a few places. The scene in Chapter Forty-five, where Jacob Hintze stands alone against the army of King Karl X Gustav of Sweden, has no basis in fact. But Karl Gustav had barged right through Mecklenburg with an army of ten thousand in times of 'peace' and, having read enough about this nasty character, I decided I wouldn't let him have things all his own way. I have taken the liberty of placing Johann Vierdank as *Kapellmeister* in Schwerin, although at this time he was organist in Stralsund. There is no evidence that a troop of cavalrymen from Schwerin ever took a trip to Paris to learn the art of equestrian ballet, but the knowledge had to spread in some fashion across Europe, so why not? Whether Eric Dahlberg really needed depth soundings of the bælts to aid in crossing on the ice is a moot point, and it is doubtful whether these would have been compiled in Schwerin. However, Dahlberg's earlier apprenticeship in Schwerin provided a fine hook upon which to hang a tale.

Where I have inserted these fabrications, I have been sure to refer the reader through a footnote to the known facts. Footnotes are not commonly associated with works of fiction, but they are there if the reader is interested, and it was a lot of fun putting them together.

For those who wish a flavour of the times, the two books of Speer and Von Grimmelshausen (see page 416) describing the adventures of their respective 'simple' characters are veritable gold mines of historical colour, while in *The Meeting at Telgte* Günter Grass adds strangely lovely local colour to the machinations of the Peace of Westphalia. Wilson's historical work cited above and C.V. Wedgewood's earlier compendium provide deep and disturbing details of the madness that was the Thirty Years War, a conflict spitted on the crossroads of manual and mechanized warfare. And Trevor Herbert's description of the trumpeter as musician and diplomat in an early period sets the stage for a good deal of speculation on the roles of those worthy and trusted gentlemen.

The fiction I have created follows what little we know and a great deal of what I would have liked to have happened. It may be that the life I have created for Jacob Hintze is more filled with adventure and challenge than was his own, but if so he is quite welcome to exchange this one for his. After all, it ends the same way.

Glossary

People and Institutions

Feldtrompeter	Field trumpeter
Gymnasium	High school
Hansa	The Hanseatic League
Hauptmann	Captain
Haushofmeister	Major domo
Hertzog	Duke
Hoftrompeter	High (chief) trumpeter
Kameradschaft	Trumpet-players' organization
Ratgeber	Town Councillor
Rittmeister	Riding master
Stabstrompeter	Staff trumpeter
Stadtpfeifer	Town piper – musical superintendent

Objects and Terms

Clarino I & II	Highest ranges of the trumpet
Flattergrob	Lowest note of the trumpet
Faul	Third note of the trumpet
Grob	Second lowest note of the trumpet
Hauk	Small coastal vessel
Hoey	Small, sloop-rigged sailing vessel
Kieselghur	Abrasive diatomaceous earth
Principal	Middle range of the trumpet
Kettledrums	Tympani
Pfennig	Smallest denomination of coin
Rathaus	Town hall
Reichsthaler	Common unit of currency
Schlachthof	Slaughterhouse
Shawm	Double reed wind instrument
Thaler	Common unit of currency

Place Names

Bælts	Channels between the Danish islands
Braunschweig	Brunswick
Brussel	Bruxelles
Donau	Danube
København	Copenhagen
München	Munich
Nordsee	The North Sea
Nürnberg	Nuremberg
Ostsee	The Baltic
Plsen	Pilsen
Praha	Prague
Venezia	Venice

A Selection of Readings

Altenburg, Johann Ernst (trans. Edward H. Tarr), *Trumpeters' and Kettledrummers' Art* (Bulle: The Brass Press, 1974)

De Pluvinel, Antoine, *L'Instruction du Roy en l'exercice de monter à cheval* (Paris: Menou de Charnizay, 1625)

Grass, Günter, *The Meeting at Telgte* (trans. Manheim, Ralph) (London: Harcourt Brace Jovanovich, 1981)

Herbert, Trevor, "'…men of great perfection in their science…': The Trumpeter as Musician and Diplomat in England in the Later Fifteenth and Sixteenth Centuries," *Historic Brass Society Journal*, vol. 23, 2011, pp. 1-23.

Heyde, Herbert, "A business correspondence from Johann Wilhelm Haas in the year 1719", *Historic Brass Society Journal*, vol. 4, 1992, pp. 45-56.

Moser, Hans Joachim, *Heinrich Schutz: A Short Account of his Life and Works* (London: Faber and Faber, 1967)

Smithers, Don, L., *The Music and History of the Baroque Trumpet Before 1721*, rev. ed. (Carbondale and Edwardsville, IL; Southern Illinois University Press, 1988)

Speer, Daniel (attrib.) *Ungarischer oder Dacianischer Simplicissimus* (Berlin: Rütten & Loening, 1978)

Von Grimmelshausen, Hans Jacob Christoph, *The Adventurous Simplicissimus*, translation Otto Schlapp (London: William Heinemann, 1912)

Watts de Peyster, J., *The History of the Life of Leonard Torstenson* (Poughkeepsie, NY: Platt and Schram, 1855)

Weaver, Andrew H., *Sacred Music as Public Image for Holy Roman Emperor Ferdinand III: Representing the Counter-Reformation Monarch at the End of the Thirty Years' War* (Farnham, UK: Ashgate, 2012)

Wedgewood, C.V., *The Thirty Years War* (London: Methuen, 1981)

Whitelocke, R.H., *Memoirs Biographical and Historical of Bulstrode Whitelocke* (London: Routledge, Warne, and Routledge, 1860)

Wilson, Peter H., *The Thirty Years War: Europe's Tragedy* (Cambridge, MA: Harvard University Press, 2011)

Yearsley, David, "Travel Music as Travel Writing: Froberger's Melancholic Journeys," *Keyboard Perspectives* (ed. A, Richards), (Cornell, NY: Westfield Center for Historical Keyboard Studies, 2016), pp. 87-112.

Notes

1 Adolf Friedrich, *Hertzog* of Mecklenburg-Schwerin (1588-1658) ruled from 1592 until 1628 and again from 1631 until his death. In this translation, the title Duke has been used throughout.

2 Thurn und Taxis was a noble German house with Italian roots that ran the postal service throughout the Holy Roman Empire, beginning in the 16th century.

3 This editor has no intention of being caught in the crossfire of the apostrophe wars. In this edition, the Thirty Years War does quite well without one.

4 The first floor was accessible by stairs or a ladder from the ground floor, which was often composed of rammed dirt sometimes skimmed over with tiles or cement.

5 This song first appears in the work of Swiss composer Ludwig Senfl (c.1486-1543) but it is likely to be older.

6 The *Gymnasium* was university preparation for wealthy children where they learned such subjects as astronomy, rhetoric, logic, mathematics, geometry and music.

7 Surprising though this may sound, Herr Pinklemann describes incidents that are known to have taken place.

8 Conrad Droschel (1596-1644) was one of the small cadre of brass instrument-makers in Nürnberg. A trumpet by him is preserved in the St Annen Museum of Lübeck, not all that far from Schwerin. Another was found in the wreck of the sailing ship *Batavia* off the west coast of Australia.

9 These pages were probably copied from the books of Danish court trumpeters Magnus Thomsen and Heinrich Lübeck, which date from the late 16th and early 17th centuries, and contain the earliest known notation for trumpets. How Pinklemann came across them is conjectural, but there were strong connections between the courts of Mecklenburg and Denmark at this time.

10 The Battle of Wittstock took place on October 4, 1636. Swedish allies under Johann Banér and Alexander Leslie decisively defeated a Saxon/Imperial army led by Melchior von Hatzfeldt and Johann Georg I, the Saxon Elector.

11 The *meile* was an extremely variable unit. Hintze's mile in Mecklenburg was average at that time; at about 1,700 yards it was a little shorter than ours.

12 Gerhart Evert Pilooth (c.1590-1629) began work in 1617. This was curtailed by war, and resumed again between 1635 and 1643.

13 Hintze's descriptions of the structure and practices of the *Kameradschaft* are typical of those from other regions of the German-speaking lands.

14 Johann Schop (ca. 1590-1667) was an accomplished violinist and composer living in Hamburg.

[15] Johann Vierdanck (1605-1646) is not known to have occupied the post of *Kapellmeister* in Schwerin while also being resident organist in Stralsund. He remained in the latter post for the rest of his life.

[16] Nicolaus Hasse (1617-1672) was organist at the *Marienkirche* in Rostock. The piece of music Bretikopf shows to Jacob can be heard on the CD recording described on page 424.

[17] Michael Praetorius (1571-1621) was a versatile and prolific composer who laid the groundwork for the Baroque style in German music.

[18] Heinrich Schütz (1585-1672) was the pre-eminent composer of his age. His numerous pupils, including Johann Vierdanck the Stralsund organist, carried his teachings throughout the German world.

[19] Cesare Bendinelli (1542-1617) was a trumpeter and diplomat. His work *Tutta l'arte della Trombetta*, which he presented in manuscript form in 1614, represents the refined state of trumpet-playing at that time. How these copies were acquired is conjectural, but this does point to a wider circulation than is perhaps credited.

[20] Girolamo Fantini (1600-1675) was highly renowned for his trumpet playing. His book *Modo per Imparare a Sonare di Tromba* (1638) was widely consulted throughout the 17th century.

[21] Thilemann Hoffmann (?-1628) was indeed waylaid and killed while on a diplomatic mission.

[22] The *Sprig of Rosemary* was one of several gathering places for dissenters, particularly Levellers, who were a strong political force.

[23] Mercury was applied to the open sores of syphilis with some apparent benefit. The reference to the two planetary gods Mercury and Venus accords with the alchemical and astrological world picture of the period.

[24] Robert Ramsay served Charles I until the break-up of the Court in 1642. He was taken on again after the Restoration and died in 1684.

[25] Oliver Cromwell (1599-1658) would be elected in 1640 to the Short Parliament as the member from Cambridge.

[26] William Brade (1560-1630) was an English violinist and an early exponent of the instrument. He is thought to have composed the earliest English works for it. He spent most of his working life in Northern Europe.

[27] *Buttasella* comes down to us as 'boots and saddles'.

[28] *Zapfenstreich* comes down to us simply as 'taps'.

[29] This is a fascinating glimpse of Ottavio Piccolomini (1599-1656), shorn of the usual sycophantic trappings of the official record.

[30] In 1633 Mathias Gallas was forced to abandon his artillery before a retreat through Saverne in snow because his soldiers had eaten the draft animals. He lost at least 12,000 men.

[31] Madlon's cavalry deserted the field. Leopold Wilhelm's punishment was vicious. The regiment's ensigns were publically shredded, and Madlon, together with his captains and lieutenants, was beheaded. The cavalry was decimated; ninety men, one in every ten drawn by lot, were hanged along the road to Rokycany, near Praha.

[32] Pietro Verdina (c.1600-1643) was ransomed but died soon after. The Emperor wrote a letter to his brother, Leopold Wilhelm, lamenting Verdina's loss and berating Leopold for taking him to war.

[33] This is a rather unflattering, but probably quite accurate, picture of Lennart Torstensson (1603-1651).

[34] This incident is a matter of record. Christian of Braunschweig (1599-1626), Duke of Brunswick-Lüneburg, Bishop of Halberstadt, was by all accounts a certifiable maniac. It was said that he once obliged the nuns from a convent he had sacked to serve wine to him and his officers while stripped naked.

[35] Christian IV (1588-1648) was an extremely popular king who built Denmark into a world power, and made his capital city Köbenhavn into a centre of culture and wealth.

[36] Gert Antonisson Rehnskiöld (1610-1658) was employed as accountant, surveyor and scribe. He had Erik Dahlbergh, the Swedish engineer, as an apprentice from 1641 to 1647.

[37] The song *Kong Christian stod ved højen mast* first appeared in a vaudeville play in 1778, but if Hintze knew of it, it must have already been in the popular repertoire.

[38] It is interesting to have an eye-witness description of Christian IV's behaviour that differs so widely from that of the official record. What is truth?

[39] This incident is reported by Watts de Peyster (see Further Reading).

[40] Alvise Contarini (1597-1651) diplomat and statesman is cited for his mediating role in the final document of the Peace of Westphalia. Hintze's later encounter with him shows him to have been a man of humanity and wisdom, rare at this period.

[41] This particular phraseology is the translator's privilege, *grace à* Dylan Thomas.

[42] Johann Erasmus Kindermann (1616-1655) was the pre-eminent organist and composer in Nürnberg.

[43] Johann Georg I, Elector of Saxony (1585-1656) has been described as 'harsh and unlovely' and a slave to drink and outdoor sports. He oversaw one of the most prestigious musical establishments of the period.

[44] Matthias Weckmann (1616–1674) was trained as a musician at the Dresden court by Heinrich Schütz, leaving with him for Denmark during the war. Hintze visited Dresden during Weckmann's later return as organist.

[45] Johann Jakob Froberger (1616-1667) was the preeminent keyboard composer and player of his age. He was starting four years of extensive musical travels between 1649 and 1653 when Hintze met him in Dresden.

[46] Froberger never did learn English, so when he arrived on Albion's shore beaten and penniless after a piratical incident at sea, he was unable to make himself understood and was taken for a vagabond. His *Plainte faite à Londres pour passer la mélancolie* tells the story, although we can never know how creative the retelling might be.

[47] It is unlikely that a Protestant reformer would have used this phrase as late as the mid-17th century, but by this time it had achieved common usage, so Hintze might well have picked it up in tavern conversation.

[48] This is Daniel Speer (1636-1709) before he dropped his first name. Little is known of his early life, so this reference adds much to our knowledge. The epigraph that Hintz has chosen for this chapter is eerily similar to a passage in Speer's *Ungarischer oder Dacianischer Simplissimus...* one of his 'autobiographical' novels, published much later.

[49] Georg Ehe (1595-1668) was from a brass instrument-making family that spanned the early 17th to the late 18th centuries.

[50] It is possible the Duke was reading Marcus Vulson, le Sieur de la Colombière's, *Le vrai Théâtre d'honneur et de chevalerie,* which had been published in 1638.

[51] It seems that Mozart was drawing upon an existing song of some antiquity when he wrote his canon with the same title.

[52] The original Academie was near what is now Place Pigalle. It is commemorated with a plaque above the entrance to the Hôtel Regina.

[53] The work of Antoine de Pluvinel (1552-1620), *Le maneige royal,* was published posthumously by J.D. Peyrol in 1623, but the 1625 edition by Menou de Charnizay, *L'Instruction du Roy en l'exercice de monter à cheval,* is far superior.

[54] Hintze's memory is probably faulty. It seems highly unlikely that Henry Le Bailly (158?-1637) would have written music for trumpets, even under compulsion.

[55] This is undoubtedly Prince Rupert of the Rhein (1619-1682). He fought valiantly for his uncle Charles I in the English Civil War, but was banished after a debacle at Oxford and took to a life of piracy and treasure hunting. He was a skilled linguist, scholar, scientist and natural philosopher, but above all he loved warfare. He eventually found favour with the Crown and returned to England on the Restoration of Charles II.

[56] It is interesting that Rupert of the Rhein left the pernicious exiled court of Charles II and his mother around this time, and was not heard of again until his reappearance in England six years later at the Restoration. Clearly, he was still very active in the Royalist cause.

[57] John Thurloe (1616-1668) was secretary to the English Council of State and spymaster for Oliver Cromwell.

[58] Edward Sexby (1616-1658) was a soldier of Cromwell's who turned against him and plotted an uprising of Royalists and Levellers for the spring of 1655. He was arrested in 1657 and died in the Tower the following year.

[59] John Gerard (1632-1654) was convicted with others in a plot to waylay and kill Oliver Cromwell. He died at the scaffold proclaiming his Royalist views but denying any complicity. It has been suggested that there was no plot, and that this was a ruse of Cromwell's to assert his authority. Hintze's story supports that theory.

[60] This phrase was first used by Robert Monro (1601-1680) in *Monro: His Expedition with the Worthy Scots Regiment Called Mac-Keys* (1637). For Hintze to have heard it, it must have been in fairly common use.

[61] Jacob Hintze would have smiled in irony at his work being published by one Loose Cannon Press.

[62] Hintze's description of Whitelocke's actions leading up to the grounding of the *President* are utterly at odds with what is recorded by his biographer. Perhaps Hintze's inexperience with things maritime, and his dislike of the sea, coloured his impressions of the great man? But would the captain have been so foolhardy as to set full sail in darkness without secure knowledge of his position, and would a gunner be so reckless as to fire a gun that was still lashed down?

[63] Samuel Morland (1625-1695) was a scientist, inventor, mathematician and linguist.

[64] This is probably John Wallis (1616-1703) a Cambridge mathematician employed by Thurloe as a cryptographer.

[65] Karl X Gustav (1622-1660) fought under Torstensson at Breitenfeld and Jankau, which gave him a taste for warfare that lasted as long as his short life.

[66] Carl Gustaf Wrangel (1613-1676) had a long career as a formidable commander throughout the Thirty Years War and beyond. He hardly features in this memoir, although Hintze mentions earlier spotting him before the Battle of Breitenfeld.

[67] Erik Jönsson Dahlbergh (1625-1703) was apprenticed to Gert Rehnskiöld for six years between 1641 and 1647, where he learned mapmaking, draughtsmanship and mathematics.

[68] Sweden had a colony in North America at this time.

[69] The church in Høje Taarstrup proudly celebrates this dismal phase in Denmark's history, and has a copy of the treaty on display.

[70] The manuscript has not survived. This is the only reference from this period to a *Musikalische Exequien* by Heinrich Schütz.

[71] It is frustrating that Hintze's description is so sketchy and incomplete. Could this have been a reworking of Johann Leon's text *Ich hab mein Sach Gott heimgestellt*, which Schütz had used in *Kleine Geistliche Konzerte* of 1636? We will probably never know.

[72] Joachim Tielke (1641-1719) went on to become one the greatest string instrument-makers of Europe.

[73] Johann Jacob Löwe (1629-1703) was a student of Heinrich Schütz's and had a long and productive career at Wolfenbüttel, Zeitz and Lübeck.

[74] The assertion that scordatura was 'invented' in Germany rests upon very slender evidence. Undoubtedly, there were folk traditions of tuning that predate its adoption by mainstream composers.

[75] Thomas Baltzar (1630-1663) was a famed German violinist who spent a great deal of his later career in England.

[76] There were several designations of smallpox among physicians at this time, 'distinct' or 'discrete' being the least harmful, comparatively, and 'the purples' or 'hæmorrhagic' being almost invariably deadly.

[77] Here is another passage from Speer's *Ungarischer oder Dacianischer Simplissimus...* where the hero encounters a trumpeter. Perhaps Speer sent the text to Hintze years before it was published, as he had promised on parting.

[78] The trumpet by Wolfgang Birckholtz is now in the collection of the Germanisches Nationalmuseum in Nürnberg, so after three and a half centuries it has returned to the city where it was made.

[79] The Latin reads: "Periit hic verberibus inflictis a Jochim Wadegahte, filio Hinrchß, quem irritaverat emishis globulis e sclopeto ferreo!"

The Music of Jacob Hintze's World

Brass instrument craftsman Michael Münkwitz made copies of Jacob Hintze's trumpet and organized a series of concerts in the Lutheran church where the original was found. This recording features the music of the locale and the era, played on those trumpets together with a range of other period instruments. You can hear the very cavalry calls that Jacob played, the massed trumpet music heard at court, and the fine art music of church and salon.

Raumklang 2009
RK 1805
Available from: trompetenmacher@gmail.com

𝕸aking a 𝕿rumpet in 𝕵acob 𝕳intze's 𝕯ay

This book describes a one-week workshop where participants make trumpets exactly like the one Jacob Hintze played. The workshop is offered three times per year in Europe and the U.S.A. Every stage of an essentially 17th century process is detailed in 52 colour photographs.

ISBN 978-0-9936881-1-9
Available from: www.loosecannonpress.com

Printed in the USA
CPSIA information can be obtained
at www.ICGtesting.com
LVHW041557010823
754076LV00008B/115

9 781988 657134